Praise for
Sloan Parker's Other Books

"Every once in a while I come across a book that knocks my socks off. *Breathe*, by Sloan Parker, is one of those books."
　　　　　　　　　—Dark Divas Reviews on BREATHE

"their chemistry leapt off the page"
　　　　　　　　　—three am on I SWEAR TO YOU

"suspenseful, dramatic, sexy, hot, loving and engaging"
　　　　　　　—Amazon Reviewer on MORE THAN MOST

"exciting, suspenseful and most importantly, romantic"
　　　　　　　—Literary Nook on HOW TO SAVE A LIFE

"a beautiful love story"
　　　　　　　　　—Book Lovers Inc. on BREATHE

"Sloan Parker strikes again with a suspenseful, sexy M/M read."
　　　　　　　—On Top Down Under on HOW TO SAVE A LIFE

"an emotional and sensual blockbuster"
　　　　　　　　　—Joyfully Reviewed on MORE

"Sloan Parker is an amazing writer. Her work is beautiful and touching and emotional. If you haven't read any of her books, I suggest you run out and do so!"
　　　　　　　　　—The Armchair Reader

OTHER TITLES BY SLOAN PARKER

MORE series
More (More Book 1)
More Than Most (More Book 2)

THE HAVEN series
How to Save a Life (The Haven Book 1)

Single Titles
Breathe
Take Me Home
More Than Just a Good Book
Something to Believe In
Friends and Lovers
The Break-In
Swept Away
A Lesson in Truth

How to Heal a Life (The Haven Book 2)

SLOAN PARKER

HOW TO HEAL A LIFE (The Haven Book 2)
Copyright © 2017 by Sloan Parker

ISBN-13: 978-1942517931
ISBN-10: 1942517939

Cover design by Sloan Parker © 2017

This is a work of fiction. The names, characters, and incidents are either the product of the author's imagination or have been used fictitiously. Any resemblance to actual persons or incidents are coincidental.

Published by
Sloan Parker Press
www.sloanparker.com
Version: 11.1.17

Author's Note

This book includes references to a character's past abduction and assault and his resulting post-traumatic stress disorder. Some content may emotionally trigger readers who have experienced a sexual or other violent assault or who suffer from PTSD.

How to Heal a Life

Prologue

Tortured, assaulted, caged like animals, six gay men in their twenties free after being held captive for weeks.

Raymond Vargas seized the newspaper off the hospital tray, balled it up, and thrust the entire thing into the bottom drawer of the cabinet beside him. No way was he leaving that lying around.

Fucking media. The headlines weren't holding back on the horrors.

As if he needed the reminder. As if he could ever forget. Every single one of those men had innocently walked inside his club, some paid for the privilege to do so, and found themselves in hell instead.

He refocused his attention on the monitor across the hospital bed. At four in the morning, his neck and back were aching like hell, but he made no move to get up. He just kept staring at those blinking green numbers.

Two whispering voices seeped in through the room's open doorway. Their words were indecipherable, but they still punctuated the quiet of the late hour. The heart rate on the monitor fluctuated. Vargas straightened in the chair, his total focus on the rising digits until they halted their climb. When it was clear the result wasn't enough to cause concern, he relaxed and bent forward in the chair again, returning to his earlier position with his elbows propped on his thighs.

He'd asked the nurses plenty of times what the various digits on the display meant, as well as their standard healthy ranges. He was getting good at scanning that screen for signs of trouble.

Another minute ticked by. Another.

An alarm went off.

No reason to panic. The IV fluids had simply run out.

Only, the nurse was taking too long this time, and the repetitious bleeping was far too loud. He clenched his hand into a fist to keep from pounding on the IV stand before the jarring sound could awaken the man in the bed.

With that thought, Vargas forced himself to look at the younger man's face, at the cut and bruised flesh, the purple and yellow battered skin around his eyes, the multitude of tubes and monitors he was hooked up to, recording his heart, lung, and kidney functions.

Seth Fisher's body was healing, but he almost looked worse than the first night. It took one hell of a beating to fuck a man up like that.

One of the regular nurses from the night shift entered through the curtain-covered doorway. Vargas shot her a quick glance but then went back to keeping vigil on the monitor's blinking numbers.

She was a tiny woman. At least a foot shorter than his six-foot-two frame. And maybe twenty-eight years old. Not that it mattered. When you were forty-three, everyone in their twenties was young.

She was also his favorite nurse. Sweet and pleasant. Full of the information he craved. She'd softly chat while she worked, giving him an update on Seth and his progress, on what the surgical and trauma doctors had noted during their previous visits with him. She never acted like she expected Vargas to contribute anything to the conversation, or get upset with him for not offering a word of thanks.

Right then, though, she didn't say anything as she stood at the foot of the bed.

Without looking away from the monitor, he said, "Don't make me leave."

She sighed heavily, a hint of humor in the sound. "Do I ever?" Stepping up to the IV stand on the other side of the bed, she began changing the bag of fluids. In a hushed whisper, she added, "He's really doing well. He should be moving to a regular room tomorrow."

Vargas let his eyes fall shut at her words. When the surge of relief had passed, he opened them again.

From across the bed, the nurse glanced over her shoulder. "Which also means I think you could take a night off and sleep in your own bed."

He gave her a half-hearted grin but otherwise stayed focused on Seth's heart rate.

"I don't know how you run a business on no sleep." She checked the IV where it was connected to Seth. "They said some of his friends came by to see him earlier today."

Vargas grunted an approving sound.

"He was in good spirits during their visit. Sat up for a while and ate some solid food." Finished with the IV, she returned to the foot of the bed where she lifted the blanket and examined the pneumatic compression stocking that helped to prevent blood clots on the leg without the cast. She readjusted the sock. Even without looking directly at what she was doing, there was no missing the severely bruised flesh of Seth's bare leg above that sock.

She settled the blanket over him again. "But he still won't talk to anyone."

Vargas squeezed his eyes shut once more and remained silent. She didn't deserve his anger. It was hardly her fault.

She moved to the head of the bed and eyed Seth's face, then tenderly brushed the dark hair off his forehead. "I think once he's home and he starts regular therapy, he'll be okay. He's a very strong young man."

He was.

Twenty-five years old, and he'd spent the past couple of weeks fighting for his life. Broken forearm and shinbone, fractured kneecap, ruptured spleen, collapsed lung, cracked ribs, and two herniated discs in his lower back. There were multiple, simultaneous operations. Screws and pins were put in place, his spleen removed. A team of doctors and surgeons from various departments were involved in his case: trauma, orthopedics, urology, plastics, respiratory, neurology.

The consensus was that his attacker had used some kind of hefty metal pipe, but the police never recovered anything of the sort.

Did it matter? The damage was done.

The trauma to his head and the resulting intracranial pressure, as well as the internal bleeding from the ruptured spleen, had concerned everyone. His condition had been rocky at first, but the swelling in his brain rapidly subsided, and there was no lasting damage. The surgeries to remove his spleen and fix his broken leg and kneecap had some complications too, but the repairs were successful, and Seth had awoken in no time.

To Vargas, all that meant one thing: Seth was a hell of a fighter.

Now came the long process of healing and rehabilitation. And not just for his body, but also the emotional trauma of being held captive for weeks by a sick, sadistic psychopath.

The nurse retrieved a wand from her mobile computer stand and returned to Seth. She carefully uncovered the arm without the cast. The bruises there were worse than on his legs. There were also numerous gouged and slashed areas all along that arm.

Vargas glanced down at himself. He had his white dress shirt rolled up to his elbows. His forearms were accented with several black tattoos. Various words and phrases. Some in cursive. Others in bold block letters. The newest one was on his left arm. The ink started at the crook of his elbow and continued down his forearm, stopping at his wrist.

The nurse scanned Seth's ID bracelet and then gingerly covered his arm again. She paused, her focus now on Vargas. "I need to wake him, so he can take his oral meds."

Vargas stood, removing his hand from the back of Seth's. With that move, the nurse threw him an exasperated look. He ignored her, rounded the bed, and kept on going.

"Why won't you let him see you? Why won't you talk to him?"

He stopped in the doorway. Despite the fact that he'd only ever had one brief conversation with Seth when he interviewed him for membership at the Haven, he was certain Seth would recognize him. He spoke without facing the room. "He doesn't need the reminder."

She scoffed. "You think after everything that happened to him, he can forget any of it? Forget that he was abducted from the club you own? Forget that someone left him there for dead?"

Vargas turned his head. She had a gentle, understanding expression in her eyes, and in that moment, he liked her even more. She said what no one else wanted to admit to him. That Seth Fisher would never be the same carefree young man he'd been before he walked into the Haven that last night.

She came forward. "Not one single family member comes to see him. Not his mother. Or his father. He has maybe three or four friends who show up. Seems to me he can use all the support he can get." She paused, her eyes scanning his. "He knows you're here every night. He might start talking if you spoke to him."

Vargas shot a quick glance at Seth. A healthy, vibrant young man before he'd been taken. Significantly shorter then Vargas with a slight build, but fit and toned. Lying in that bed, he looked frail, broken in more ways than just his visible physical injuries. No one should have to go through what he had, but someone that young, with his whole life ahead of him...

Vargas spun away again. "I'm sure he has nothing to say to me." Reluctantly he gave another look at the newest tattoo on his forearm. *You only fail when you stop trying.*

Breathing deep, he forced out the words, "Maybe tomorrow night." Without waiting for her response, he left.

Crossing the open area of the trauma ICU, he strode for the coffee cart situated in the far corner. Several nurses and ancillary staff members were seated at the main desk, and each smiled at him. He didn't have it in him to attempt a return of the polite gesture.

At the cart, he filled a paper cup with coffee and swallowed a gulp.

It was room temperature and tasted like ash, but he needed the caffeine to stay awake.

The first night he'd been there, he had nodded off. Until Seth started moaning in his sleep. Unwilling to sit by and do nothing, Vargas placed a hand on the back of Seth's, below where the cast ended, too afraid to touch his other hand where his fingers were purple and swollen like they'd been twisted in a vise.

With that simple contact, Seth awoke. He rolled his head to the side and just lay there, breathing heavily, staring at Vargas for several achingly long breaths, his eyes harboring a haunted expression Vargas almost couldn't bear. But no way was he going to look away. He ran the pad of his thumb over Seth's skin in a comforting stroke.

Eventually Seth lowered his eyelids and drifted off to sleep again.

The next night, the same thing.

After that, Vargas made a point of keeping contact with Seth throughout the night, touching the back of his hand or the lone patch of skin on his other forearm that had no bruises or cuts.

Since then, no more nightmares. Seth would sleep through the night. For whatever reason, knowing he wasn't alone, even subconsciously, was necessary for him.

That had settled it. From then on Vargas sat next to that hospital bed night after night, his hand on Seth's, his focus locked on those fluctuating numbers displaying Seth's heart rate and blood pressure.

Seeing him immobile in that bed, his body beaten and broken, the bruises and cuts covering his flesh too numerous to count was bad enough. Hearing those terrified murmurs as he became trapped in another nightmare... Vargas couldn't take that again.

If it helped having someone there while Seth slept, even the slightest bit, he was going to do it. Because there was no denying his part in what happened to Seth and the others.

It had been his club—a membership-only club at that—where they'd been targeted by that demented son of a bitch.

He ditched the cup on the coffee cart and jammed a hand into his pocket. He removed his cell and hit speed dial.

The man answered on the first ring. "Yeah?"

"Anything?"

"No. Lights have been off since midnight."

"He didn't meet with anyone earlier? Make any calls?"

"No, nothing."

"Dammit. Someone hired him, and I want to know who. Now."

"We'll find out. There has to be a paper trail somewhere. Just give Tucker time to figure it out."

Vargas sighed. "All right. Stay on him. You let me or Tucker know the minute you see something out of the ordinary."

"Will do."

He hung up and crammed his phone back into his pocket, feeling more agitated and frustrated than before the call. He needed to calm down. The team of investigators Tucker had put together was top-notch. They'd uncover who hired the attorney. And why.

A few minutes later the nurse exited Seth's room and came to Vargas. "He fell right back to sleep."

Vargas gave a nod and swallowed the last of the burnt coffee. He waited a bit longer and then returned to the room.

As soon as he was seated beside the bed, Seth's eyes flew open. His chest rose and fell with the rapid pants pouring out of him. He didn't blink, didn't make a sound. Something was different this time. He stared straight through Vargas as if he didn't see him and was lost to another time and the unspeakable things that happened to him there.

Vargas leaned forward and reached for Seth's hand. That time the gesture did nothing to calm him. Vargas had to do something to help. Anything.

"It's okay. You're safe now."

Seth blinked in rapid succession as if Vargas's voice had brought him out of the far-off place he'd gone. He searched Vargas's eyes. Maybe he saw the truth in them. Or felt it in the touch between them. His breathing slowed, and he nodded.

It was the first time Vargas had spoken to him.

He wanted to tell Seth how sorry he was for what had happened to him, how shitty he felt that he hadn't done more to keep him safe at the Haven. But it wasn't the time for any of that.

Instead he asked, "You remember me?"

Seth nodded again. Then his gaze darted around the room as if he couldn't shake the nightmare, or recall where he was.

"Hey, it's okay. You're in the hospital. You're safe here."

Another nod.

"You're going to be okay. I'm going to make sure of it."

Seth parted his lips. "Where—" He cut off and swallowed.

Vargas leaned in closer. "Yeah? What do you need?"

"Ch-Charlie?"

"He's doing fine. He's still with Walter and Kevin." Vargas knew Seth's friends had already told him about his dog and where he was staying. "They're taking good care of him." He hesitated, unsure if he should offer more. "I'd keep him with me, but I'm not home much right now." He didn't elaborate.

"He knows you're here every night."

"I stopped by to see him this morning." He pulled out his phone and clicked on the screen a few times. He held it out for Seth to see, swiping through the photos of the yellow Labrador. "They said he's eating good and getting lots of exercise."

Seth had met the two men who'd taken in his dog, but he hadn't talked to either yet, the same way he'd been with everyone who entered his hospital room, including all the nurses and doctors.

Except that wasn't true anymore. Seth was talking now.

To him.

Vargas didn't want to break the connection. "They said every night after they get home, he just sits and stares at the door, like he's waiting for you to pick him up. I told him it wouldn't be long and you'd be coming to get him."

Seth kept his gaze on the image of the dog that filled the phone's screen. "What—" He cleared his throat and tried again. "What happened to them?"

"Who?" Vargas lowered the phone. "Dylan and the others?" He didn't need to clarify. The others were the men who'd been kidnapped and held captive right alongside Seth.

Seth gave a slight shake of his head. "Dylan and Aaron came to see me." He licked his cracked lips.

"Here. Have some water." Vargas reached for the cup on the bedside tray. He held the straw to his lips.

Seth lifted his head and took two slow sips. "Thanks." He laid his head on the pillow again, closing his eyes. When he opened them he said, "I meant the one who took me. And the other one who..." He glanced down his body. "Did this."

Right.

The detectives on the case had been there to interview Seth multiple times. They'd asked him a slew of questions and waited in vain for him to fill them in on what had happened to him. When it became clear he wasn't going to talk anytime soon, they indicated they'd return when he felt better. Vargas assumed that before they left, they had offered Seth some details of their own. Seemed logical enough. What was it they said about assumptions?

"No one's told you?"

Seth shook his head.

"Maybe that's for the best. Until you're out of here." Until he was stronger.

"No." He rolled his head Vargas's way. "I need to know."

Those whispered words, the pleading look…

Vargas returned the cup to the tray. "All right."

Where to start?

Seth was asking about Prescott and Henderson. After Prescott had kidnapped the six men from Vargas's club—using a series of secret tunnels hidden under the Haven—he kept them locked in cages inside the basement of a nearby building. Then he tortured and assaulted them. Henderson, a corrupt cop and childhood friend of Prescott's, found the men there. Rather than rescuing them, he chose to frame someone else by taking Seth from his cage and beating him nearly to death.

"Henderson, the cop," Vargas began. For the next several minutes Seth stared at the far wall of the room, barely breathing, barely blinking, as Vargas explained how the cop and his father had originally hired Prescott to harass Vargas so he'd sell them the club. Only Prescott also decided to kidnap the men. Then Vargas told him about the search for the missing men and how Prescott had strangled Henderson in retaliation for Seth's beating.

Vargas ended with, "So there's no reason for you to worry about Henderson ever hurting you again. He's gone."

"And the other one? The one who—" Seth broke off. He was talking about Prescott. The one who'd started everything by gaining Seth's trust, drugging him, and locking him in a cage.

"He's in jail. Kevin and Walter found him in the basement next door to the club. He was shot, and the cops arrested him for the murder of Henderson, multiple counts of abduction, and a slew of other charges." Like rape and assault, but Seth didn't need to hear those words right then.

The psychologist Vargas had hired for Seth who specialized in the treatment of trauma and PTSD in victims of violence and sexual assault had told Vargas it was important to repeat words of comfort and reassurance.

"He's in jail, and he's going to stay there."

The doc had also told him that at some point there'd be many things Seth would need to talk about again and again. Repeated conversations about the ordeal he'd lived through could help minimize his post-traumatic stress. Vargas didn't want to think about how those conversations would go.

"Did he…" Seth's voice cracked with the words. He coughed. Vargas got him another sip of water. Then Seth spoke with more resolve. "Did he tell them what he did to me, to the others?"

Vargas opened his mouth, but he had no idea what to say. He desperately wished he'd thought to ask the psychologist what he should respond with to questions like this so early in Seth's recovery. He just hadn't even considered he'd be the first person Seth would choose to speak to.

Seth looked his way again. "I need—" He breathed deep like it was taking every last ounce of his energy to get the words out. "I need to know the truth."

"Okay." Vargas leaned forward, getting closer than he'd done up to that point. Then it hit him what he was doing: invading Seth's personal space. He drew up short. With all the examinations, the tests, the doctors and nurses and techs poking and prodding him at all hours—not to mention being held against his will in a cage by a depraved son of a bitch—Seth would need to feel like he had some control left, that he had some say in who got close to him.

So Vargas held still. How the hell was he supposed to say this?

He carefully watched Seth, hoping if he focused on him hard enough, he'd be able to tell when the time had come for him to shut the fuck up, that what he was saying was too much for Seth.

"Prescott's claiming he's innocent. He's likely going to plead not guilty. He said he was defending himself against Henderson, that he wasn't intending to strangle him. He said it was the cop who attacked him."

Seth seemed to be processing that. "What else?"

"Why don't we talk about this later?"

"No." There was determined strength in those wide brown eyes staring back at Vargas. "Please."

"Prescott said you went with him voluntarily. That all six of you did. That it was a BDSM thing. You agreed to stay with him in the cages and let him do whatever he wanted to you in exchange for room and board and... his attention, his affection."

Seth gaped at him. "Do they believe him?"

"No. No one does."

Seth was quiet for another minute. "What'll happen now?"

"It'll probably go to trial."

"Will I have to testify?"

"I don't know. I'm guessing that'll depend on what the prosecutor thinks they need to make their case." The lawyer working for Prescott was one of the best criminal defense attorneys in the country, but Vargas kept that thought to himself.

The panicked looked on Seth's face had Vargas taking a chance. He leaned forward and covered Seth's hand with his like he did when he slept. "The trial isn't anything that'll happen right away. And he might end up making a deal."

"Okay."

"Try not to think about it right now. Just focus on healing." Vargas silently winced. Nice choice of words. Was there any way someone could heal from what Seth had lived through?

And with that, Vargas knew…

He'd visit every day, repeat whatever words Seth needed to hear, and when Seth got out of the hospital, he'd take him to his PT appointments and fetch his groceries and whatever else he needed. He'd help him get strong and walk again.

No matter how long it took, he would help Seth Fisher move past this.

For a long moment, Seth just stared up at him as if he was trying to memorize Vargas's face or commit something else to memory. Then he lowered his eyelids.

"Try to get some rest."

Seth's eyes shot open. He clasped on to Vargas's hand. "Please don't leave."

Stunned, Vargas swallowed down the flood of emotion and held Seth's hand in return. "I'm not going anywhere."

* * * * *

Porter Logan Prescott III lay on his bunk in the jail cell, his eyes closed, his injured body hurting, and his heart aching for what he'd lost. He tried to drown out the frustrated voices of the criminals in the other cells around him, the flushing of toilets, and the squeak of the shoes the guards wore. He tried to ignore the scent of putrid body odor and mildew mixed with the harsh astringent of industrial strength cleaning products. He tried to pretend he was somewhere else.

With someone else.

Thinking about his boys in his life again was the only way he could tolerate the miserable loneliness and lack of control he now had to suffer through. The only thing that made the long days tolerable.

So he let himself float back to one night in particular.

* * * * *

He set his empty glass on the desk beside the bottle of scotch, stood, and opened the door. The room he entered had plenty of space for the cleaning area, his workbench, and the four-poster bed. The dank walls and floors were a nice touch. Gave the place a dungeon feel that went well with the leather, the tools, and the metal cages lining the back wall.

It had taken him three weeks to prepare the space, move his equipment there, and construct the cells. The cages were a necessity. He didn't want them trying to return to their old lives before they realized how much better their futures were going to be with him.

Truthfully, seeing his boys waiting for him in their cages gave him a thrill of power little else matched. He alone had taken control of what they needed.

He'd miss this room when they had to leave, but he knew better than to count on things. Tangible items could be destroyed, burned. The place and the toys he used were not his priority. The naked men inside the cages were.

He wouldn't abandon them.

He stepped to his workbench, peeled back the black case's covering, and ran the tips of his fingers along the neat row of steel, arranged by blade length and width. The smell of the leather case and the feel of the polished metal under his fingers urged him on.

As did the whimpers of anticipation behind him.

He picked up the gold key chain with the dog's picture. A yellow Lab. He actually felt bad about the dog, wished he could bring him here. But dogs made messes and barked. Too big of a risk when he'd be gone. Instead he'd give the boy the key chain to keep with him in his cage. He'd promised the boy if he was good during their next session, he'd let him have it.

He usually didn't like them to keep anything from their old lives. They needed to be cleansed of that filthy existence, but he never went back on a promise.

Never.

Another whimper came from behind him.

This one sure liked to make noise. Which was why he kept coming back to him more than the others. He sounded lovely, begging and crying out, letting Prescott hear everything he felt.

Now the boy was spread-eagle on the bed, wrists and ankles lashed to the four posts. His eyes were huge, watching him.

He liked when they watched.

He set the knife on the bed on one side of the boy, the key chain with the dog's photo on the other.

A voice rang out from behind him. "No matter what you do, we'll never be yours."

That was the newest one. Dylan. He talked a lot, even when inside his cage.

"Be quiet. It's not your turn."

"Someone will find us."

The boy on the bed shook now. Prescott leaned down to him. "Don't listen to him. He lies."

"Seth, don't listen to *him*. Listen to me. I'm Dylan, remember? We talked last night in the dark. We are going to get out of here. Just listen to my voice and hang on."

The boy on the bed glanced toward the voice and nodded. He looked innocent, lost.

His protector would find him. "I know what you need."

"Seth, listen to my voice. We're going to live. Do you hear me? Just hang on. Someone will find us."

The boy nodded again, tears streaming down his cheeks.

"We're going to go home. You just have to be strong until then. Just hang on. I promise we're going home."

No, they would never leave him.

Prescott kissed his boy's cheek and buried his nose in the skin of his neck. He smelled of sweat and fear. He smelled alive.

Seth shivered under his touch.

"That's it. I like that. Time for a treat." He showed him the knife, then released one of his boy's arms from the restraints and pinned it to the mattress alongside his body. Seth didn't fight him. "Such a good boy." Prescott placed the blade against the flesh of his upper arm. "Don't hold back. Let me hear you." He pressed down on the knife.

The beautiful screaming began.

* * * * *

Prescott sighed as he rolled onto his side. God, he missed that sound.

He missed Seth.

He missed all of them.

To keep the despair at bay, he pulled to memory the message his attorney had given to him at their first meeting: *"No matter what, you'll never spend your life in prison. He has a plan to get you out."*

Those simple words offered him the hope he needed to keep going. As did thoughts of what he'd do the minute he was free, where he'd go, and who he'd collect first.

He'd never leave without him.

Chapter One

He could do this.

Seth Fisher clutched the armrests of his wheelchair in both hands and pushed himself to a standing position. He shuffled his feet until they were firmly planted under him, and then he reached for the cane he'd propped against the wheelchair.

Not wanting to give himself time to rethink his plan, he didn't delay. Gripping the cane, he took a step toward the apartment door. Pain shot through his lower back and then his leg, and his thigh muscles burned with the added weight. The arm with the cane shook.

"Fuck."

Why was this so hard for him? It wasn't like he used the wheelchair all the time anymore. For the past few weeks he'd only been using it when he left the apartment, and only because he was too afraid he'd trip and pull something with just the cane. He didn't want to think about how helpless he'd feel if he fell in front of anyone. When he was at home for long stretches, he stored the wheelchair in his closet, but anytime he attempted walking toward the door like he was going out using only the cane, his body would betray him.

Just like today.

He held still, taking several deep breaths. He forced himself to get moving again. Two steps and he had to stop once more. At the rate he was going, he wouldn't even come close to completing this test before Dylan was done in the shower.

But he couldn't—*wouldn't*—turn back now.

He put another foot forward. Then another.

Finally he got close enough he could reach for the dead bolt lock. He got the door unlocked without any issue. Despite that success, his hand fell to his side. He took another deep breath, hoping that alone would calm the all-too-familiar fear.

The breathing wasn't helping. Panic welled in his chest. He tried to raise his arm, but he couldn't make a move. He stared at the closed door before him. The hope that he'd finally be able to do this on his own for the first time in two years began to slip away.

Then came that voice whispering in his ear, the feel of a heavy sweat-soaked body pressing down on him.

"You're mine. You'll always be mine. I will always be a part of you. Forever."

No. "Fuck you, asshole. You're not taking my entire life from me." Surging forward, Seth cranked the doorknob and tugged the door open wide.

The dim, narrow hallway loomed before him. Beads of sweat formed across his brow. He tried again to slow his breathing using the technique Dr. Arteaga had taught him. Deep breath in through his nose, down to his belly. Out through his mouth. In. Out. In. Out.

Leaning forward, he scanned the hall in both directions. He could see nearly all the way to the stairwell on the left, as well as to the right where the hall turned a corner and led to the elevator and another set of stairs. The entire hallway was empty.

He moved his cane forward and crossed the threshold. When his feet were planted on the hall carpet, he stopped and waited for more of the intense panic to grab hold of him. Oddly there was nothing that time.

He shot a look back into the apartment behind him. The sound of music floated out from Dylan's bedroom. With the thumping music on and the shower running, not to mention the low roll of thunder from the approaching storm outside, Dylan wouldn't hear him holler for help. Which was why now was the perfect time for this. It wouldn't be much of a test if Seth had too many opportunities to call in reinforcements.

Which was also why he'd left his cell phone behind. He had to see if he could do this on his own.

He shut the apartment door and locked it, an action both he and Dylan always insisted on. He pocketed his keys and took a single stride away, using the cane for assistance. He held still once more.

Was this too much?

Did he really need to do this right now?

"I know what you need. You need to cry, scream, let it all out. Let me hear you."

"Screw you."

He was doing this.

He *had* to do this.

He forced that menacing voice from his mind and started forward again. The earlier pain and panic had subsided. Nothing but determination surged through him.

It was time. He was ready for this.

He took another step, then another, the momentum building with each foot forward. He kept on going, gaining confidence the farther he made it and the more apartment doorways he passed by.

He paused again and glanced back in the direction of his place. He was halfway down the hall. Had he really gone that far?

A sharp crack of thunder tore through the hallway. Seth jumped. His heartbeat kicked up a notch, and sweat trickled down his temples.

Then came the faint, heavy thud of footsteps. From the direction of the elevator hidden around the corner at the end of the hall.

Seth sucked in a sharp breath and held it.

He was being stupid. He knew it. Other people lived in the building. Someone was usually always headed somewhere. He just couldn't stop the reaction.

All at once the chipped, painted surfaces of the hall walls began to ripple like they were flags blowing in the wind. They closed in around him. His heart felt like it was racing too hard and too fast. His throat tightened, and his legs shook. Then his field of vision shrank as the footfalls grew louder.

He couldn't move. Either forward or back. He clutched his cane tighter and laid his free hand against the closest wall to steady himself.

Goddammit.

He thought he was ready. Thought it had been long enough. Thought he could talk himself through the fear.

But now… he had to get back to the apartment before whoever was coming got any closer. Or before he passed out right there in the hallway.

Without taking his eyes off the far end of the hall, he backtracked a couple of steps. Just then a man rounded the corner.

Not just any man. Not a neighbor. Not a random visitor.

It was Prescott.

Seth froze.

Prescott didn't. His eyes locked with Seth's, and he started forward faster. "Stay right there. I'm coming."

That voice. Seth would never forget that vile, raspy sound. In none of his previous panic attacks had he ever heard that voice out loud.

This wasn't his imagination.

This time, it *was* Prescott.

Seth had been right all along. No sentencing, no prison, no lack of parole opportunities could ever keep that man from coming for him, from wanting to lock him away again.

Prescott picked up the pace. He held up a hand. "Don't move."

Don't move? Seth needed to run. He needed to do *something*. Anything. God, he couldn't just stand there and let this happen to him again.

Move, idiot!

"You're such a good boy. Stay right there. I'm coming. I'm not leaving you behind."

Fuck that.

Seth scrambled backward, tripping over the end of his cane. He landed on his hip with a thud, the cane sprawling out of his reach. Without more than a split-second hesitation, he shifted onto his hands and knees and lunged forward. Pain shot through his left knee. He got a hold of the cane and dragged it toward him. Using the cane for leverage, he pushed to his feet. As soon as he was standing, he rushed forward, heading toward his apartment door, limping but moving faster than he'd ever done in his physical therapy or at any other time since he'd last tried to get away from this man.

The footsteps drew closer, louder, more forceful.

Seth kept on going. He shoved a hand into his pocket for his keys and finagled the ring out as he traversed the last few steps.

When he reached the apartment door, he heard Prescott's heavy breathing behind him.

Then he felt it on the back of his neck.

He fumbled with the keys as he tried to get the door unlocked. A hand brushed across his right shoulder in a soft caress. Then the hand grabbed hold of him.

Seth swung the apartment door open and stumbled inside, whipping around to shove the door closed at the same time. Only...

There was no one there. The hall outside the apartment was empty.

A different voice called out for him.

"Seth, you okay?" His neighbor Ryder appeared in the doorway, out of breath and sporting a concerned expression. As soon as he caught sight of Seth, he held up a hand in a non-threatening gesture that signaled he wasn't a danger to him. "What happened?"

Seth braced himself on his cane with one hand and the doorjamb with the other. Ryder stepped back and gave him room as Seth leaned forward and glanced both ways down the hall.

No one was there.

He'd imagined the entire thing, maybe putting Prescott's face in place of Ryder's. He'd never done anything like that before.

He shook his head when he realized Ryder was intently studying him. "I'm okay. It was nothing."

"You sure? You look freaked as hell, man. Did you try leaving the apartment by yourself?"

"Yeah."

Alarm spread across Ryder's face.

"I only made it halfway down the hall. Don't tell anyone, okay?"

"Sure, if that's what you want. Next time you need to go somewhere just shoot me a text. I'll be right over."

"I will." Seth wanted to tell Ryder how much that meant, but he didn't want to embarrass him. Ryder was still a kid in many ways, albeit a massive kid. Whenever Seth went anywhere with him, it was clear that a lot of people passing them on the street mistook Ryder for stupid or slow, or a criminal or a gang member, but those assessments were ridiculous. Evidence that judgmental, racist assholes were alive and well throughout the world. Ryder didn't deserve that shit. He was nothing but honest and compassionate. A bighearted high schooler who loved video games, his grandma, and Seth's dog Charlie.

"Here." Ryder held out a covered casserole dish. "Grandma made extra last night."

She always did. Georgia and Ryder never failed to make Seth feel like he had a family. "Tell her I said thanks." He set the dish on the hall table beside the door.

"Sure. You need me to take Charlie out?"

"Nah. Dylan's here."

"Okay. Guess I gotta get going, then." Ryder took a step away from the door, then halted. "You let me know if you wanna try leaving alone again. If you really gotta do it by yourself, I can always wait inside the apartment. You can call me if you get stuck or something."

"That's a deal. Thanks, Ryder."

The kid shrugged, then gave another long assessing look at Seth.

Even without that examination, it was obvious Ryder worried about him. A lot. Especially once he'd found out that, without a spleen, Seth was more likely to get sick or develop serious infections. Seth hated that Ryder had any anxiety because of him.

"I'm okay. Really."

"All right, man. See you tomorrow." Ryder offered a nod in goodbye and then took off down the hall toward his place.

When he was out of earshot, Seth slammed the door shut and slapped his free hand against it. "Fuck." He couldn't ignore that he needed a teenager's help to walk down the damn hall of his apartment building.

The last time he'd attempted leaving the apartment alone, it had been bad, but nothing like what he just went through. How the hell had his mind played that kind of fucked-up trick on him? And why was his reaction to heading out alone even worse than months earlier? After all the talking with Dr. Arteaga, all the exposure therapy and anxiety management, why did he seem worse all of a sudden?

He spun around and sank back against the door, dropping his cane in the process. He swiped the moisture from his eyes with the back of his hand. He would not cry.

He wouldn't.

He banged his head on the wood surface behind him in frustration. Then he did it again for good measure.

Dylan's voice rang out. "Seth?"

Seth gave his eyes another swipe.

Dylan appeared at the end of the hall. "You okay?"

How many times would he have to answer that question before people no longer took one a look at him and felt compelled to ask?

He tried for another one of Dr. Arteaga's calming breaths, and then he carefully bent sideways and reached for the cane where it had landed propped against the hall table. The action sent a twinge shooting across his lower back. He did his best to ignore it. "Just dropped my cane." He held it up so Dylan could see he'd gotten hold of the cane again.

No way did he want anyone else knowing that he'd had another panic attack, not after all this time. And not just any attack. The worst one yet. If Dylan found that out, he'd never leave him alone that night.

And Seth needed him to.

Because no matter what had just happened in the hall, he was going to make it through one night alone in the apartment for the first time since he'd come home from the hospital.

He wouldn't fail again.

Chapter Two

Lightning struck overhead as Raymond Vargas grabbed the man by the lapel of his suit jacket and slammed him against the exterior brick wall of the courthouse, not caring if anyone saw them in that alley or if he hurt the son of a bitch and his precious three-thousand-dollar suit.

He gripped him by the throat. "Who hired you?"

The attorney clawed at Vargas's hands, sputtering like he couldn't get enough air to breathe, let alone work up an answer. The reaction was a complete exaggeration. This asshole was a trial lawyer. He knew how to put on a show.

Vargas gave him another solid slam. "Tell me."

"All right, all right. It was Prescott."

"Bullshit."

"He's my client."

"But he isn't the one paying you. He was all set to go with the public defender and consider a deal from the prosecutor in exchange for a confession until someone stepped in and hired you. I want to know who."

"No one *stepped* in." The lawyer continued trying to tear Vargas's hands away from him. After several more futile seconds, he quit his flailing and gave up on the struggle. "Look, I took Prescott on pro bono. It's a high-profile case. It's going to make my career if I get him off."

"Get him off?" It took everything Vargas had not to pummel the man for those words alone.

A crack of thunder tore through the air, but the rain that had been predicted that morning continued to hold off. Not that Vargas cared. Nothing would keep him from finally having this exchange.

He got farther in the man's face. "A jury already found Prescott guilty. He's in prison. He's never getting out. No matter how much paperwork you throw at the court." He gave the man another hard slam. That one felt damn good. "Besides, you hit it big decades ago."

Twenty years earlier, Glenn Lauber had been named one of the top criminal defense attorneys by *U.S. and Global News Today*. An accolade that landed him a run as a featured legal analyst for several cable news networks. There was hardly much further up for his career to go.

Vargas was sick and tired of this man's bullshit lies. He tightened his grasp on Lauber as if he were about to do more than slam him against the wall. "Tell me who hired you, tell me what Prescott meant in that courtroom, or I swear to God—"

Before he could finish the threat, someone grabbed him by the upper arms and tugged on him from behind. Vargas held his ground, as well as his grip on the lawyer. No way was he letting the bastard go now that he finally had a shot at getting the answers he'd been after for the past two years.

Too bad the fucker who had a hold of him was strong.

"Vargas." The name was grunted in his ear as the man wrapped an arm around his chest and yanked harder. It was Tucker. He continued trying to dislodge Vargas from the attorney. "Have you lost your goddamn mind?"

Lauber bobbed his head as he resumed struggling. "He has. He has. Get him off me!"

Vargas had lost his advantage. Reluctantly he let go and allowed Tucker to pull him away.

It didn't take long for Lauber to scramble for his briefcase where it had landed on the ground beside him minutes earlier. Clutching the case to his chest, he stumbled backward toward the courthouse parking lot. "I wouldn't think you'd have time to worry about me, Mr. Vargas. I know you're close to losing that club of yours. You think you'd be spending your time trying to save it, not harassing innocent people."

Vargas took a single step toward the attorney. Lauber spun around and made for the rear parking lot, scurrying away like the weasel he was.

Motherfucker.

Vargas whirled to Tucker. "Why the hell did you do that?"

"What? Save your ass?" Tucker pointed off after Lauber. "He could call the cops on you. File harassment charges. He still might."

"I don't care. He's the one who's protecting that son of a bitch."

"You'll care when you end up behind bars."

"Well, if I do, at least I can get at Prescott myself."

"Don't even joke about that."

He was right on that front. If Vargas got locked up, who'd Seth have to count on then? Still…

"I want to know what Prescott meant that day in the courthouse, and I want to know now!" He slammed the side of his fist against the brick wall. His skin split on contact. He ignored the blood and the pain. A crowd of people had started to gather at the end of the alley not long after he'd first had the attorney against the wall. A few were still gawking at them.

"Come on." Tucker tugged him toward the back lot and didn't let up until they were beside Vargas's SUV. "That lawyer's not going to voluntarily give up who really hired him or what Prescott meant when he offered up that message for Seth. Not after all this time."

"He will to me. We have to find out who's financing this appeal. We have to get them to convince Prescott to withdraw the case." He shook his head. "He can't get out. Not now. Not ever."

"I get that, but they've done a damn good job covering their tracks." Tucker's voice demonstrated his remorse. "You know, finding out who hired the attorney might not solve anything."

"We're out of options." Short of Vargas breaking into the prison and coming face-to-face with Prescott. What he fantasized doing to that man demonstrated why people who knew the victims couldn't serve on the jury.

Tucker was carefully studying him.

Vargas eased up on his anger. He shouldn't have lost his temper with a friend. He sagged back against the driver's-side door of his SUV, arms folded across his chest.

Tucker Nicodemus had been there for him in a lot of ways over the past two years. Their relationship began as a business arrangement not long after the night Vargas had learned that several of his members and employees had disappeared from the Haven, but it hadn't taken long for the two of them to become friends.

Tucker, and the rest of his private investigation and personal security firm, had gone above and beyond when it came to Vargas's requests. They had a stellar reputation, and Tucker knew his shit. He ran the PI firm with an old college buddy, and Vargas had liked both men since he first met them. Initially, he'd hired them to help with background checks on members and employees of the club. Now he had them handling a few extra security issues outside the Haven.

Security issues like Prescott's attorney.

Vargas had asked Tucker to find out who hired the lawyer after Prescott was first arrested. When they learned the jury had found

Prescott guilty, Vargas called off the investigation. It was time and money wasted on a man who'd be rotting in prison. As soon as he'd found out that Prescott's attorney was following through with an appeal of the conviction, Vargas had them resume the search and start tailing the lawyer 24-7.

Since then, they'd followed every lead, examined every public record, combed through Lauber's curbside trash, tracked his phone calls and movements, and reviewed all possible connections to the case, and still, they were nowhere.

That thought had the fury returning. Vargas kept his arms locked across his chest, his hands clamped down on his biceps.

Tucker continued eyeing him closely. "I'm not giving up on this. That's why I schedule myself for one shift every few days, so I can personally follow this scumbag and try to figure out who he's working for. I don't want Prescott out on the streets any more than you do."

"I know."

Tucker squinted at the hand Vargas had slammed against the brick wall. "You should get that looked at."

"It's fine." Without a glance at the damage or the blood, he swiped his hand across the side of his pants.

Tucker kept watching him with a focused stare. Even in the jeans and T-shirt Tucker had likely worn to blend in on the crowded sidewalks, he always looked like he was on some sort of high-priority mission for the secret service. Tall and lean but solidly-built, he had an intensity to him that spoke volumes about his past as a bodyguard, and also gave the impression he was ready to take a bullet for anyone, anywhere, anytime. Yet there was a softness to him underneath all that.

"Okay," Tucker finally said. "Then how about you tell me what's got you so worked up? All this time, and you personally go after Lauber now. Why?"

Vargas could barely get the words out through the clench of his jaw. "They moved him from the prison to a jail here in the city."

"Prescott?"

"He'll be staying there for the time being."

"Why?"

"So he can meet with his attorney about the appeal." Vargas shook his head. "I hate that he's this close." To Seth. He left those two words unsaid. "Is everything going okay with our other project?"

"Yeah. This week's reports show no signs of anything odd."

"Good. And the men we hired are keeping out of sight?"

"Just like you requested." Tucker paused. "You know it's usually—"

Vargas held up a hand. "I got it." Tucker had repeated the explanation enough times. What Vargas had them working on would probably be a lot more effective if it weren't a secret, but he wasn't ready to share that with anyone else yet.

He scrubbed a hand over the back of his neck. Earlier that day when he'd gotten the call from his friend in the DA's office about Prescott's recent move from the prison, he'd had his head buried in the club's finances and had developed a massive headache long before the call. The altercation with Lauber hadn't helped with the tension.

A droplet of rain landed on his forehead. The sky overhead was rapidly growing ominous.

"I'm gonna take off and let you get back to work." He shot a concerned look to Tucker. "You'll pick up his trail again?"

"Yeah, he's very predictable." Tucker pointed a finger at Vargas. "No more going off the rails, all right? You need to vent, you call me."

Vargas gave a nod. After another five seconds of that hard stare in warning from Tucker, the two shook hands in lieu of a verbal goodbye, and Tucker took off.

Ten minutes later, Vargas pulled into another parking lot. The rain was pouring by then, the heavy beads pounding the hood of his SUV like drums banging out a menacing beat that foretold some coming disaster. He got out and dashed for the brick building. At his private entrance, he slid his security card through the reader and opened the door. He took the stairs two at a time toward his apartment on the second floor.

Without stopping off to ditch his wet clothes or at least dry off, he bypassed the door to his place, made his way down the hall, past the security room and the second-floor reservation desk, then strode for the balcony overlooking the main floor below. Gripping the railing in both hands, he took in the view of the club he'd called home for years.

His haven.

It was still early in the day. The place was bare, except for the bartender restocking the bar near the front and housekeeping running a vacuum somewhere out of sight. Every light was on in the place, brightly illuminating the dance floor, the lounge, and the vast dining room. The result gave the entire first floor a completely different atmosphere from the heady, thrilling vibe it would have later that night when the lights were dimmed and the place was full of men, everyone eating, dancing, flirting, or heading upstairs to the private rooms for far more than flirting.

He'd surveyed the Haven that same way a thousand times before. Yet it was somehow different now.

He used to love taking in the sight of what he'd built, loved roaming the halls of the upper floors that were lined with guest rooms, many like those found in any upscale hotel.

When he initially bought the Haven's current location, he'd purposely kept the rundown exterior of the five-story brick building. In those less gay-friendly times, the abandoned look had been helpful to mask its intent. Nowadays the facade was more about setting a mood, giving the guys who walked into the club the feeling that they were doing something forbidden and salacious, even if the rest of their night would entail nothing more out of the ordinary than a plate of mushroom risotto with a glass of Pinot Noir, followed by a leisurely soak in a hot tub, then making love with their partner of twenty years on a bed draped with fresh linens.

Although there were members who preferred the darker side of the club, which was why he also had rooms that catered to the BDSM crowd, the glory hole set, and those who wanted an anonymous fuck in a back alley, all while they were safely tucked away inside the building.

The Haven offered any fantasy a gay man could want.

It had been more than two weeks since he'd been there when the club was open. He was starting to feel bad about that. Thank God for Carter Reed, the club's assistant manager and head security guard. Carter kept the place running smoothly and apprised him of the daily operations while he was otherwise preoccupied. As he'd been for months now.

Which just reinforced the idea that he needed to make a point of showing up when things were in full swing, let people know he was still on top of what went on there, maybe even mingle for a while, find someone to spend a few hours with in a private room upstairs. It had been far too long since he'd done anything of the sort. At the rate he was going, his dick was bound to think he'd given up on the damn thing ever getting any action with something other than his own hand.

If only it were as easy as showing up at the club at the right time on the right night. If only he deserved to feel that good.

Although that wasn't the whole story. Not even close. He simply had no desire for a meaningless hookup. Not after the dreams he'd been having.

Dreams of one man.

The same man who'd recently asked him the most complicated question of his life. A question he wasn't sure he could—or should—answer.

He pushed away from the railing and got moving for the main staircase that led to the public areas of the ground floor. He slowed his pace when he spotted Carter exiting the security surveillance room a few feet from the top of the staircase.

Now more than ever, Vargas liked how intimidating Carter appeared to most people, with his bald head, his somber expression that gave him the appearance of a slight scowl no matter his mood, and the serious muscle he was packing that had him looking like he'd stepped right off the set of an action flick.

Carter raised his brows as Vargas approached. "Fancy seeing you here."

"I do live here, you know."

"Thought maybe you were planning on moving out. You haven't been here much lately."

Vargas snorted. "I know I pay you to be observant, but that's overkill."

"Ah, but you forget, you now have guards on duty twenty-four hours a day. Which means I *always* know what's going on here." Carter laughed, the sound a deep rumble that fit the man's vast physique. His grin faded fast, though, as he asked, "Is he doing okay?"

"Yeah. That last surgery really seemed to do the trick."

"Glad to hear it." Carter gave him a thoughtful study. "Really hoping you don't fire my ass for getting so personal, but is something happening between you and him?"

"Why would you say that?"

Carter shot him a look of disbelief. "He's who you're spending all your time with, yeah?"

"It's not like that."

"It isn't?"

"No."

"Whatever you say, boss." The grin was back. Carter winked at him as he backed up toward the door to the security office.

Vargas ignored that. "Did you take care of that faulty lock on the kitchen entrance?"

"Yeah." Carter stopped again, his hand on the open door behind him. "We've got everything covered here." He tilted his head in the direction of the club's main door on the first floor. "So you can head on back to Seth's anytime."

Vargas gave him a look of warning, but they both knew the threat wasn't sincere. He wasn't the kind of boss to get pissy with his employees for a little razzing. He actually appreciated Carter's attention to detail. The man was loyal as hell, and Vargas trusted him to handle any issues.

He told Carter, "I'll be in my office returning calls. Let me know if you need me."

"You got it." Carter gave one last smirk, insinuating that he hadn't believed a word Vargas had said about Seth.

Vargas was left staring at the closed door of the security room, frustrated that Carter wasn't getting it. Things between him and Seth couldn't be like that. Not ever.

Seth Fisher was off limits. Period.

He pushed the thought aside, descended the stairs, and crossed the club, making his way to the staff-only doorway situated between the bar and the dining room. Once in his private office, he got settled behind his desk and went through the list of calls he needed to return. Most were from members wanting him to address their complaints. He steeled himself for what he'd have to deal with and started at the top of the list.

An hour into it, he slammed the phone down on his desk, cutting off the tirade of the latest asshole. "Fuck you too." He sat back heavily in his chair and glared at the phone. "Goddamn selfish motherfuckers."

He'd lost the will to talk to one more person. He didn't give a rat's ass what any of them had to say.

He didn't need to be dealing with this shit. He needed to stay focused on Prescott and devising a plan to keep him from ever getting free. Because if he got out, he would absolutely go after someone again.

During the investigation, the police found a journal that indicated Prescott had abducted other young men ten years earlier. The detectives were still trying to find evidence to charge him in that case and were also trying to learn if there were others before them as they suspected.

All that meant one thing to Vargas: Nothing except prison or death would ever stop him.

And worst of all, if he got free now, he might return for Seth and the others who'd been rescued from him.

Vargas was going to do whatever was necessary to ensure that never happened.

The phone on the desk buzzed. Carter's voice came over the

intercom. "Mr. Vargas, there's someone here to see you." The formality with which he spoke indicated this wasn't going to be good. "It's Edwin Morris. I tried to tell him your decision was final, but he's demanding to speak with you in person."

"Got it. Be right there." Vargas got up from his desk. If Morris wanted to talk, he couldn't have picked a more perfect moment.

The man in question was waiting near the club's main entrance. Carter stood beside him, and Neil, the guard on duty at the front door, was waiting directly behind them. Morris was dressed in a suit like he was on his way to work. Vargas had liked the man when he first met him at his membership interview three years earlier. He'd had a good feeling about him and never expected the guy to turn out to be such a total piece of worthless shit.

Time to show the man what happened to scum who walked through his front door.

Vargas approached the group of men. "Judge Morris."

"Mr. Vargas."

Vargas didn't take the offered hand the judge held out. He gave it a pointed look.

Morris dropped his arm in defeat but forged on anyway. "I wanted to explain in person."

"There's no need. You're done here." To make his point, Vargas signaled to Carter and Neil to escort the judge out. Both men moved in but then drew up short when Vargas held up a hand as Morris spoke again.

"If you'd just hear me out. That little shit found out I was married. He said I was an asshole for cheating and was going to tell my wife."

"I don't care."

"It was just one shove."

"You often shove someone with your fist in his face?"

"It wasn't like that. I only wanted to scare him, make sure he kept his mouth shut. This club's supposed to be discreet. He can't go around threatening to out me."

Vargas got in the judge's face. "I don't give a shit what your reason was. You are no longer a member of this club." He stepped back as if that was the end of it.

"This is unacceptable." The judge marched forward but quickly stopped when the guards moved in to flank him. Vargas gestured for Carter and Neil to hold still.

More calmly Morris asked, "Are you going to refund my dues?"

"No. You lied and violated the membership agreement."

"I most certainly did not."

"You got married after you applied for membership, and you didn't bother to update your records here at the club. That, and most importantly, hitting a member without his consent are violations of the club's policies that you agreed to when you enrolled. I don't owe you a thing."

The judge scoffed.

"You're going to leave now, and you are never stepping foot inside this club again." Vargas signaled once more to Carter and Neil. They converged on Morris. Each security guard grabbed the judge by an arm. They spun him around and encouraged him toward the door.

Morris shouted over his shoulder, "You're a fucking asshole, Vargas! You keep kicking people out and this place is going to become a joke. No one's going to stick around for your bullshit."

"If they're all like you, then good riddance." He waited until the judge was through the door. When it was closed behind him, Vargas took off for the bar and poured a glass of Glenlivet. He knocked it back in one try, then got another.

A minute later he heard someone approach.

"He's gone. Got in his car and left." Carter came to stand beside him at the bar. "I'll put the staff on alert to keep an eye out for him, just in case."

"Thanks."

"If it's any consolation, I liked the judge when I first met him. He didn't seem like the type to hurt anyone."

Vargas gave a nod in thanks. He appreciated Carter's comments, but it did little to make him feel better. After all, Vargas had liked Prescott when he first met him, and look what that got six of his members and employees.

Look what that got Seth.

Vargas couldn't help but recall how Prescott appeared in the courtroom months earlier, just moments before the verdict was set to come down. He seemed oddly unruffled and unconcerned about the outcome of his case.

After the guilty verdict was read, he'd simply, calmly turned to the spectators in the courtroom and scanned the crowd until he spotted Vargas. He looked him straight in the eye and said the words Vargas would never forget.

The eerie grin that lingered on Prescott's face was also burned into his memory. It was the smug smile of a man who knew something no one else did, a man who had a plan.

Vargas would do whatever he had to, to keep that warped monster from ever getting free again.

Chapter Three

"You're just going for the one night?" Vargas asked.

"Yeah," Dylan said from where he was leaning against the hall wall outside the apartment he shared with Seth. He continued repeatedly tapping the heel of his boot against the wall behind him. "I'll be back tomorrow. My cousin's accident wasn't bad. I just wanna see if he needs anything."

"Fair enough." Vargas focused on Toby. He had his long, lean frame propped against the opposite hall wall. "And you're still working nights?"

"For a little bit longer. I could use a vacation day, but Seth said he didn't want me taking any extra time off." He shrugged. "It seemed like he wanted to try staying by himself."

Which made sense. Seth had been mentioning more and more often that he couldn't stand inconveniencing people anymore.

Dylan and Seth had first moved in together when it became clear soon after Seth had left the hospital's inpatient rehab facility that he couldn't live alone. He and Dylan had decided on a larger two-bedroom apartment in Seth's same building. In most cases, the arrangement worked out well for both of them.

Except that Dylan had been gone a lot more lately.

Vargas looked to Seth's friends again, first one, then the other. They were waiting for his input.

When he'd arrived at the apartment a few minutes earlier, the door had flung open before he even had time to knock. Dylan and Toby rushed out, frantically closing the door behind them as if they were being chased. Turns out they'd just wanted to get his thoughts on Seth's plan.

"Well," Vargas said as they continued staring at him, "I think if he says he's ready, then we need to respect that."

"But what if—" Toby clamped his mouth shut as if he shouldn't have said anything. Which was bullshit. He had every right to speak up. He was Seth's oldest friend and had known him longer than anyone. Several years back, when they'd both been homeless teens struggling to survive, they had been each other's lone support system.

"What is it?" Vargas asked him.

Toby lifted his head. "I just worry about him."

"Me too. But he wants to move on, and only he knows what he needs and what he's ready for."

"Yeah," Dylan offered. "It's gotta be his call."

He got it. Of course he did.

Dylan hadn't known Seth before their ordeal, but he'd been stubborn about making himself a permanent presence in Seth's life. The two had become friends despite Seth's initial inability to speak to anyone but Vargas. It was a testament to Dylan's determination that he hadn't given up on Seth.

Vargas moved in to stand before the younger man. "How are *you* doing?"

Dylan laughed as he shook his head. "Man, you really need to get a new line. I'm fine. I'm not naked and locked in a metal cage, so it's a good day, yeah?" He laughed more.

"If you need anything—"

Dylan held up a hand. "Give you a call. I got it. It's your soundtrack." He glanced to Toby with an exaggerated eye roll. Studying Vargas's face again, Dylan shook his head and added, "Sorry. I don't mean to be an ass. I really don't. I appreciate the concern and everything you've done for all of us."

"It's okay. I'm a pushy bastard sometimes." Vargas turned to Toby and gestured to the apartment door with a tip of his head. "So all he said was that he's okay staying here alone overnight?"

"Yeah. He actually seems excited about it. But he did say something else weird to me when we were alone earlier. He asked if I was mad at him."

"For what?"

"Because he went to your club when I told him it was a bad idea, that it wasn't the place for him. I warned him something could happen."

That hit Vargas square in the chest as if the words had literally been delivered with a punch. Toby had never mentioned that before.

Toby shook his head. "I said that was ridiculous. That none of this was his fault because he went to some club."

"Why did he bring this up now?"

"I don't know."

"I do," Dylan said softly. "Last night he got a call from a reporter.

I got the same call. The guy wants to do a follow-up piece about us, show where we are now, how we've recovered." Dylan looked to the closed door of the apartment. "It's got Seth thinking about what happened, about where he's at in his life, about whether he's recovered at all."

"Dammit!" Vargas spun away from them. He didn't want to direct his anger their way.

Toby asked, "Why would a reporter contact you now?"

Vargas swung back around. "Because of Prescott's appeal."

"Yeah," Dylan agreed. "And..."

"What?"

"He told us about them moving Prescott to the jail here in the city."

Shit. So much for breaking the news gently.

Dylan continued. "Apparently the appeal's going to make what happened big news again."

Exactly what none of them needed. Definitely not Seth.

Two surgeries on his spine, months of physical therapy for his leg and knee, more for his back and to regain his strength after each surgery, week after week of visits to his psychologist, and now... he was so close to ditching the wheelchair for good, so close to being able to stay in the apartment by himself for more than two hours. So close to spending the night on his own. It wouldn't be long before he'd be able to leave the apartment alone.

Dylan said, "I told him to ignore any calls he didn't recognize."

"Good. Maybe if none of you talk to the press, they won't latch on to the story."

"That's what I'm banking on."

They were all quiet for a few breaths. Then Dylan pushed away from the wall. "Well, I've gotta get going."

"Me too," Toby said. "I'll walk out with you." To Vargas he added, "I can come back before work to check on him if you think I should."

"Nah. He'll be okay." Vargas wasn't about to consider the alternative.

"Okay." Toby held back while Dylan went to the apartment door and unlocked it for Vargas. Both men offered their goodbyes, but then Toby stopped Dylan with a hand on his arm. "Could you give us a minute?"

"Sure." Dylan headed down the hall and waited at the far end near the elevator.

Toby kept his voice low as he spoke to Vargas. "Promise me you'll be careful."

"Careful?"

Toby hesitated. He wouldn't make eye contact. Instead he raised a hand and ran the tips of his fingers along the scar on his cheek, the result of a childhood accident. His focus on the scar always seemed an unconscious move. Something he did whenever he felt nervous or insecure. Or maybe in this case, when he didn't know how to put into words what he wanted to say.

"Just say it, Toby. Whatever it is, it's okay."

"I've been worried about something for a while now. About you. I know things are different than before, but Seth was always getting a crush on every guy who was nice to him, everyone who paid him a little attention." He paused, pointedly staring Vargas down for the first time. "Especially older guys."

"Did he say something to you?"

"No. I just got to thinking that maybe…" He didn't finish.

Vargas tried to keep his reaction neutral, but he couldn't ignore the way his breath caught in his throat at the thought of Seth wanting something to happen between them.

"Toby, I'm just trying to be his friend."

"I get that, but…" Toby glanced toward the apartment door as if afraid he'd see Seth standing there, listening to them. "Just make sure *he* knows it."

"Okay. But I'm pretty sure he's still not in a place where he's ready for anything like that. He might not be for a while."

"I know, but that could change. Maybe before you even realize it, and then it'll be too late. His heart will get broken again, and maybe this time, with everything he's been through, it'll break *him*."

Vargas tipped his head back and drew in a deep breath. "Point taken." He met Toby's gaze. "I'll be careful."

"All right. Oh, and…" Toby grinned and nodded toward the open apartment door. "Don't get mad at him."

"Why?"

"He's working on a project."

"And I'm not going to like it?"

Toby laughed. Without adding more, he took off for where Dylan waited down the hall.

When the pair were out of sight, Vargas picked up the two bags he'd left sitting on the hall floor earlier. Drawing in another long inhale, he opened the door the rest of the way and headed into the apartment.

Metallic banging came pouring out from the kitchen. He had a hard time picturing what Seth was up to. He wasn't much of a cook. In fact, there hadn't been one thing Seth had ever made for him that hadn't been an effort to chew and swallow and offer a smile throughout.

Vargas dropped the bags by the door. The layout of the apartment was similar to Seth's old place with one large living room to the right, and to the left: a narrow kitchen with a single point of entry and a hallway that led to the apartment's two bedrooms and the lone bathroom. He went to the kitchen and stopped in the doorway.

Seth was lying on his back on the floor, his entire upper body inside the cabinet under the sink as he tinkered with something in there. He was talking to himself. No, repeating something over and over.

"Righty tighty, lefty loosey. Righty tighty, lefty loosey."

Vargas couldn't hold back the grin.

The tiny room looked like a storm had blown through it, leaving behind everything the wind had tossed about in its fury. Tools and other supplies were sprawled all over the floor. Screwdrivers, pliers, wrenches, plumber's tape. An iPad sat propped open, paused on what appeared to be a plumbing how-to video. Seth's cane was leaning against the stove. His wheelchair sat by the refrigerator, close enough he could access it without too much strain.

Seth was in his usual baggy gray sweatpants and a long-sleeve white T-shirt. The ensemble always left the fading scar above his right eye as the only visible evidence of the numerous cuts and wounds his body had sustained. He had one leg bent, the other leg with the previously broken shin and kneecap out straight. The brace he'd worn for months had been gone for a while now, but it was clear Seth still favored that leg whenever he got in and out of the wheelchair or when he walked with the cane.

Without moving from where he had his torso tucked inside the cabinet, Seth reached alongside his leg, groping for, and completely missing, the screwdriver lying beside him, all the while never letting up on the repetition of the same four words. "Righty tighty, lefty loosey."

Vargas approached, picked up the screwdriver, and held it inside the cabinet opening. "You looking for this?"

Seth sat up with a start, banging his head on the underside of the sink. "Shit." He immediately dropped to his back again.

Vargas winced. He should've announced himself. "You okay?"

"I'm fine." At that angle they couldn't see each other, but he could hear Seth furiously rubbing the top of his head. Then he froze. "Uh, Vargas, is that you?"

"It's me."

"Oh, good." An energetic laugh burst out of Seth.

Damn, that laugh sounded great. Vargas had been hearing it more and more lately, and the laughter never failed to brighten his day. That, and seeing Seth determined to do things for himself, had all Vargas's tension fading away in an instant.

He also couldn't help but picture the man lying before him as naked and vibrant and erotically-charged as he'd been in his recent dreams.

Vargas squeezed his eyes shut. *Fuck.* Toby was right. He had to be careful going forward. Very, very careful.

But not because of what Seth was feeling.

Chapter Four

Seth peeked out from where he had his head inside the cabinet under the kitchen sink and found Vargas staring down at him.

At the sight of that rare grin and the penetrating dark stare, Seth's heartbeat kicked up a notch and a swarm of butterflies hit his stomach with incredible force. A stupid, childish reaction, but there it was.

He'd seen Vargas almost every day for the past two years. There was no reason for him to feel like a nervous kid on a first date.

There was also no reason for him to think today was the day he'd get an answer to the question he'd posed a week ago. Still, he couldn't help but hope Vargas was about to agree to the idea.

The man in question was dressed in a black form-fitting T-shirt and jeans that perfectly hugged his muscular frame and left little to the imagination. The clothes were far more casual than his usual dress shirt and tie. The T-shirt also showcased the tats along the length of his solid arms. His dark hair was damp from the rain and was slicked back like he'd spent the drive over running his fingers through it.

Staring up the length of that vast physique from this new angle, Seth's breath came faster. His stomach muscles tightened as he forced out, "I was just working on something."

"I see that."

"You're uh... You're early."

Vargas's eyebrows rose. "Damn good thing too. How were you planning to get up?"

"Um..." Perhaps working on this right before Vargas was supposed to get there hadn't been such a great idea. Although Vargas didn't seem angry. Quite the opposite. The amused smile lingered on his face.

Again that nervous jolt shot through Seth. He tried to hold back the rush of excitement. "I got down here okay. I figured getting up couldn't be that much harder." He accepted the screwdriver Vargas held out for him. The side of Vargas's hand was scraped and bruised. "What happened to you?"

"Nothing. Just had a little run-in."

"With who?"

"Doesn't matter."

Despite the intense curiosity, Seth lay down inside the cabinet again and tightened the mounting screws. When he was done, he ditched the screwdriver and moved to sit up. With both hands, he gripped the top edge of the cabinet opening above him. Vargas wound a hand around his right upper arm, helping him slide forward.

Once all the way out of the cabinet, Seth sat up, moving with care so as not to strain or pull anything. He offered Vargas a smile in thanks, then faced the cabinet and finished the last few steps of the project. The entire time Vargas stood back and waited, giving him space to do this on his own.

When Seth was finished, he scooted sideways and leaned back against the closed cabinet door between the opening and the bucket he'd used to drain the water from the pipes. He just needed a minute to rest before he attempted anything more. It still took a lot out of him to do something like get off the floor and return to a standing position.

It had been several months since his last surgery to repair the second herniated disc. His doctor had initially hoped to treat it with pain medications and physical therapy, but the disc had gotten worse over time. It began putting pressure on the nerves in his lower back, causing him muscle spasms, weakness, numbness, and pain that radiated down his legs to his calves.

Since the surgery, he'd been healing well, and the throbbing ache in his lower back was less intense. But with all the muscle weakness and previous back pain he had, his leg and knee had never gotten the early rehabilitation they should have. Just another frustrating piece of the puzzle his life had become.

Vargas picked up the bucket of water, placed it on the counter, and sat on the floor next to him, casually resting his forearms on his bent knees. "What were you working on?"

"I installed a new garbage disposal."

Without a word Vargas glanced around the room at the supplies sprawled across the floor, then at the wheelchair near the refrigerator. Dylan had gotten the chair out of the closet for Seth earlier that morning so he'd be ready to go when Vargas picked him up.

Seth didn't want to think about climbing back in that damn chair. He gestured toward the open cabinet door over his shoulder. "The old disposal got all clogged up, and the motor overheated. The stupid building manager wouldn't do anything about it."

"Wasn't it heavy to lift into place?"

"I ordered a pretty small one, and I figured out a way to prop it up until I had it secure."

"I would've helped you."

"I know. I wanted to try and do it myself."

Vargas kept his gaze locked on Seth's. "I get that." He tilted his head toward the iPad. "You figured it out from a video?"

"It was pretty easy to follow."

"Score one for YouTube."

"I know, right? A lifesaver for guys with a loser dad."

Vargas's brows drew together in concern.

Seth shrugged. "I wasn't looking for sympathy. Just meant that watching videos online was how I learned a lot of stuff when I was a kid."

"Like what?"

"How to tie a tie, how to shave, how to put a condom on."

Vargas smirked and shook his head. "We didn't have YouTube when I was learning all that shit."

Seth couldn't help himself. "That's because you're really fucking old."

That got him a full-out laugh from Vargas. "Set myself up for that one."

"Yeah, you did."

They both laughed more, and the anxiety faded away for Seth. It was always like that with Vargas.

When their laughter died off, Vargas said in a more subdued tone, "Heard a reporter called you."

"Yeah." Seth sighed. "Guess I should've known Dylan would say something."

"You want to talk about it?"

"No. It was no big deal." He bit at his bottom lip. "It doesn't matter where they put him."

"Okay." Vargas didn't push about Prescott's move. "Were you able to get rid of the reporter?"

"As soon as he said he wanted to do an interview with me, I told him to fuck off and hung up on his ass. He didn't call back."

Another grin formed at the corners of Vargas's lips. "Good move." Then the amused smile faded again. "Sorry you had to deal with that."

"Wasn't the first time."

"If it keeps happening, we can get your number changed."

"I contacted my cell company this morning and got a new one."

With something like surprise, or maybe admiration, Vargas searched Seth's face. "I don't know why Toby and Dylan worry so much about you."

Vargas always had a way of making him feel strong and brave, even on his worst days. Sometimes it felt like Vargas was the only one who really saw him.

Neither said a word for several seconds. They just continued with the unflinching stare.

Vargas had also never been one to fill the quiet with meaningless chatter, which Seth hadn't minded in the least in the beginning. They'd sit together for hours, not saying much, just watching a movie or reading. Simply having Vargas there had Seth feeling less alone and afraid. He'd always appreciated that when Vargas spoke, it was intentional and deliberate.

Yet now Seth would give almost anything to hear more from him. He longed to know everything about Vargas that he hadn't learned yet. About his childhood. His family. His love life. Everything. He just never could bring himself to ask.

Like right then. He wanted to know what Vargas was thinking. Because lately, the silences between them had grown different, palpable. Like Vargas had more to say than ever, only he had no idea how to get started.

Or maybe he didn't want to.

Maybe it was something he knew Seth wouldn't want to hear.

Breaking the stare, Vargas tipped his head back to the cabinet door behind him. His eyes fell shut.

Seth settled on a change in topic. "How'd your meeting with Miyata go yesterday?"

Keeping his eyes closed, Vargas shrugged indifferently, but he wasn't fooling Seth. This bothered him. A lot.

"You still think he's keeping something from you?"

"Yeah. And my gut says it's about the club." He opened his eyes. "I hate thinking this shit about him."

"Makes sense. He's not just your accountant. He's your friend. It's normal to feel bad about it, but that doesn't mean you're wrong."

"Yeah. I think I just need to audit the books from the past couple of years, go over everything myself."

"I could help you."

"Doesn't sound like much fun for you."

"Actually it does." Seth sat taller. "A chance to get a look behind-the-scenes at the Haven? It'd be interesting to see how it all works."

Vargas snorted out a laugh. "Interesting? Most people think the financials are the least interesting part of running a sex club."

Seth laughed with him. "But I bet I could help you find out if he's up to something, if he's stealing from you."

"I bet you could."

"Have you been losing a lot of money lately? Losses he's been able to explain away a little too easily?"

Vargas hesitated like he didn't want to answer that. Seth silently cursed himself for bringing it up. Dylan had said he'd heard rumors that the club was in serious financial trouble, and Seth had been trying hard not to pry.

Eventually Vargas said, "The Haven's been losing money for a while now, and that has nothing to do with him. It was long before he began lying to me."

"Oh."

"It's not a big deal. I just—" He sighed and shook his head.

"If you think there's something wrong, if you think he's lying to you, you can't ignore that. Maybe because you've been losing money, he decided now was the perfect time to embezzle from you, and in the process, he's making everything worse."

"I guess. I just never thought he was that kind of person."

"But maybe he's changed. You should trust your instincts."

"You're right." He met Seth's gaze. "Thanks." But it wasn't gratitude visible in that look directed at Seth. Vargas was studying him like he was trying to read something in Seth's face. Or maybe was hoping to see it. Then he quickly looked away, focusing on Charlie's water bowl near the doorway across the room. "You sleep okay last night?"

"Yeah."

"Good."

Seth added, "They haven't come back."

"Okay." A pause followed. Then Vargas repeated the one word as though it had taken him a moment to fully accept what Seth had said. "Okay."

The nightmares that had plagued Seth's early days in the hospital had ceased not long after they'd started. When he'd been well enough to head home, the dreams had returned. So severely that Vargas had slept on Seth's couch every night, and it had helped immensely having someone else in the apartment for those first few weeks. Then Dylan had suggested moving in with him, and Vargas had gone back to his place.

Now, at least once a month, Vargas would ask whether or not the nightmares had returned.

If anyone else had done that—and with as much frequency as Vargas had—Seth would've gotten pissed. He hated how people's good intentions and concern made him seem weak and broken.

There was just something different about the way Vargas said the words, about the apprehension visible on his face and how he held his breath as he waited for Seth's reply, like the answer mattered to him even more than it did to Seth.

Guilt does strange things to a person. They either completely ignore the object of that guilt, or they obsess over it.

Seth didn't want to think about that too much. Not while he was waiting to hear Vargas's answer on the question he'd brought up the week before.

Instead he said, "So… I think I did it."

Vargas grinned. "The disposal?"

"Just need to give it a test."

"I'm impressed."

Seth elbowed him in the side. "What? You think basic plumbing is beyond me?"

"That's not what I meant." Vargas searched Seth's eyes, again looking like he was desperately trying to see something. Seth opened his mouth to tell him to say whatever was on his mind when the sound of scraping claws on linoleum cut him off.

Charlie was rushing toward them from the kitchen doorway. He went straight for Vargas, who harrumphed as the dog flopped onto his lap and set to licking his face.

"You finally wake up and figure out I was here?" Vargas loved on the dog for a minute, Charlie eating up the attention, his tail thumping repeatedly against the floor. He was always so dang excited to see Vargas.

Seth could relate.

Vargas gave Charlie another pat. Then he asked Seth, "You want to give the new disposal a quick try?"

"Sure. Can you plug it in? The outlet's under the cabinet."

"You got it." Vargas encouraged the dog to move off him so he could stand. He held out a hand and helped Seth up next, waiting there as he always did until Seth was steady on his feet.

Seth propped his hip against the counter. "I'm good."

Vargas crouched and bent inside the cabinet, then stood again. "All set."

Seth turned on the faucet and threw some food scraps into the disposal. Bracing on the edge of the sink with one hand, he pitched forward and reached for the switch on the back wall. The unit came on and ground up the food with no trouble.

Vargas smiled at him. "You did it."

"Yeah, I guess I did." Seth hit the switch again and got the faucet shut off. Without warning, his right hand slipped, and he fell sideways, his elbow knocking over the bucket of water in the process. The bucket went flying, and so did its contents. Some of the water landed on Seth, but the majority of it hit Vargas straight on.

The front of his shirt was soaked, his face and hair the same. Water dripped from his chin as the empty bucket clattered onto the linoleum floor.

Seth clasped a hand over his mouth. "Oh my God. I'm so sorry."

Vargas let out a boisterous laugh. Seth wasn't sure he'd ever heard him laugh like that. That got him going too.

They stood there in a fit of laughter for several breaths.

Vargas went for the towel hanging from the oven door handle. He gave a quick dab to his face, then returned to the sink and wiped the water from Seth's neck and face.

On the last swipe, the tips of his fingers brushed Seth's skin. Seth's breath hitched. He felt light-headed, and a rush of heat worked its way over every inch of his flesh. He hadn't had a response of instant arousal like that to such a simple, innocent exchange since he'd been a teenager.

And there was no way Vargas hadn't noticed. He stilled his hand, keeping the pads of his fingers in contact with Seth's bare skin. Then those fingers moved again, softly caressing the side of his neck. Seconds ticked by as neither looked away. Vargas leaned forward a fraction of an inch.

Then his eyes widened. He stopped, dropped his hand, and turned away. Burying his face in the towel, he scrubbed it dry, then swiped the sides of his neck. He attempted soaking up the water from his T-shirt next. The front of the shirt was drenched, whereas Seth's only had a few splotches of water.

Seth tried to appear casual before Vargas faced him again. He doubted he was succeeding.

Vargas gave up on the cleaning and ditched the towel on the counter. "This shirt's a lost cause." He reached for the hem and stripped it off over his head. Using the balled-up shirt, he wiped his damp chest.

Seth couldn't look away from the expanse of flesh and muscle before him, or the assortment of tattoos that covered those bare pecs and abs. He'd never seen Vargas without his shirt, much less gotten a full view of the numerous tattoos he sported on his upper body. Seth wanted to shove him to the floor, straddle him, and read every word written on that strong body, then kiss and lick each tattoo in turn.

His blood rushed south, and his cock began to fill.

He forced down a stiff swallow. "You can borrow one of my shirts." *Great idea.* Any shirt of his was going to be tighter than the one Vargas had shown up in.

"Thanks. Think I will."

Seth gestured toward his bedroom. "Help yourself."

Vargas headed down the hall, and Seth frantically set to wiping up the wet counter as a distraction, willing his body to quit betraying him.

All he could focus on was a single question: had Vargas been about to kiss him?

There was no way. He must've imagined that.

For weeks now Seth had been secretly hoping he'd one day find himself in bed with Vargas. It had been so long since he'd been with anyone. He wanted Vargas to be the person he could jump that hurdle with. Yet in all his thoughts on the subject, it hadn't occurred to him that Vargas would want to kiss him.

He'd pictured Vargas's erection between his lips, envisioned his own stiff cock in Vargas's large hands, and thought about what it would be like to be touched like that again, to touch someone else. But he hadn't let his imagination go beyond those details, hadn't even considered what Vargas would want, if anything.

Although lately, Vargas had been looking at Seth with an entirely new expression.

Desire.

There was no way to pretend it was anything else. Not that Seth wanted to, no matter the reason for Vargas's interest. After all, proximity and desperation could lead a man to wanting someone he might not normally go for. With Vargas's work and how much he'd been helping Seth and the others, he couldn't have had much time left for a social life.

Although…

Plenty of guys used to want Seth. They came on to him at the Haven and asked him to join them in the private rooms upstairs. He had that perfect twink look that some guys were into. A young face, slim build, and tight round ass that got him a lot of attention on the dance floor.

But all that was *before*.

That's how he always thought of it. Just… before.

If Vargas really did want to be with him, what specifically would he expect? A gradual, sensual buildup of kisses, of hands and lips exploring everywhere, bare body pressed against body? Would he want Seth to run his mouth over every inch of him? And vice versa?

A guy like Vargas, who owned the type of club he did, could have any lover he chose and any experience he craved. Would he be hugely disappointed by what Seth could offer him?

Vargas returned to the kitchen, and Seth halted the cleaning, completely stunned. Vargas was wearing a bright pink T-shirt with bold purple rhinestone-lettering printed diagonally across the front, spelling out the word *Tasty*. It was one of the shirts from the boxes stored in Seth's closet. Which meant Vargas had seen the clothes that Seth had hidden away when he moved into the new apartment.

Seth glanced down at his own attire: baggy sweatpants, plain long-sleeve T-shirt. No bright colors or logo or lettering. Nothing to draw attention to himself. For the first time since he'd packed away his old clothes, he wished he'd gone with something sexier.

A hand came to rest on his cheek. Vargas had stepped in closer and was eyeing him with concern. He traced the side of Seth's face with his fingertips. The same tender way he'd touched his neck earlier. "You look tired."

Plenty of people had touched Seth over the past two years—doctors, nurses, and physical therapists—but he felt like he hadn't been touched, really touched, in forever. Until it was Vargas's hand on him.

It took Seth a moment to find his voice. "I'm okay." He couldn't tear his focus away from Vargas's intense stare. That was until Vargas parted his lips, and then it was that mouth, those lips that Seth became obsessed with.

There was no denying it this time. Vargas was studying him with the same unspoken, burning longing that Seth felt, and Vargas was definitely leaning in.

But then, without warning, he was gone. He crossed the room and scooped up Charlie's water bowl. He dashed for the bathroom down the hall while Seth just stood there, leaning against the counter, gaping at the empty room before him.

What had just happened? What might've happened if Vargas hadn't walked away?

He'd been touching Seth more and more lately, offering little intimate gestures of support when they were out in public and he knew Seth was severely anxious, but this was the first time he'd done anything like those caresses when they were alone. Seth couldn't wrap his head around what that meant.

He licked his lips, unable to keep from picturing what it would be like. He could barely remember how it felt to be kissed, touched, wanted. Now the door was open to those thoughts, and there was no closing it.

When Vargas returned, he set Charlie's filled water bowl down and began picking up the tools and other supplies from the floor. Without a word on what had happened before he left, he said, "We've got a few minutes before we need to leave." He retrieved Seth's cane and handed it to him. "You want to go sit in the other room and wait or get going now?"

"Let's wait." Seth would rather be alone with Vargas instead of in a waiting room full of people.

Although the minute he started to move for the living room, he felt Vargas's stare on him, and he regretted that decision.

All week he'd been telling himself not to get his hopes up that Vargas would say yes to his idea. But now that Vargas had touched him like that, had looked at him like that, he couldn't avoid that hope. He wanted Vargas to agree to it more than anything.

Chapter Five

Only when Seth was out of the kitchen, did Vargas lean back against the counter and let out the uneven breath he'd been holding. He needed to knock it off with the touching. And not only because of Toby's warning. After everything Seth had been through, every violent, horrible violation that Prescott had put him through, it was insensitive to take such liberties. Any sort of intimate contact should be by Seth's direction. He needed to be the one to set the pace, decide when things turned physical in any relationship.

Which meant Vargas had been crossing a line he definitely shouldn't have. Seth deserved better.

Despite that knowledge, and despite what Vargas had been trying to tell himself about what Seth was ready for, keeping his distance went against every instinct screaming at him whenever they were together. Because it seemed like Seth wanted, even *needed*, those touches, that he was starving for the affection.

Heading for the living room, Vargas braced himself for what he'd face, including the conversation they needed to have at some point that day.

With one hand propped on the arm of the couch, Seth was easing down to a seated position. Once he got settled, he leaned the cane against the couch. As Vargas approached, Seth reached for the open book on the cushion beside him, moving it out of the way.

Vargas sat and gestured toward the bags he'd left near the apartment door. "I got you some more books."

"Thanks. But you don't have to keep—"

Vargas shot up and crossed the room to retrieve the bag. He didn't want to hear those words from Seth again.

Reading had been a big part of how Seth kept occupied during his long recovery in the hospital and the rehab center, along with watching documentaries on the internet. Those were the only TV shows or movies that seemed to interest him. He'd skip every comedy, drama, and police procedural, and instead went for a two-hour feature covering the history of space exploration.

And now, documentaries and books were still how Seth occupied himself much of the time.

Vargas grabbed one of his duffel bags and brought it to the couch. "I also ordered a couple dozen titles for your e-reader." He set the bag on the coffee table beside a stack of other books. "If you're done with these, I'll get them out of your way."

Seth didn't like to hang on to books once he'd already read them. He preferred to donate them to the library or a local charity so others could enjoy them the way he'd done when he'd been homeless and had no money.

Except for the book that had been lying on the couch. That one had been around for ages.

"Thanks," Seth said again as he took a look in the bag of new books, pulling out one after another, scanning the title of each as he set it on the table.

Vargas returned to sit beside him and indicated the older book still perched on Seth's lap. "That's a good one?"

"Yeah." Seth picked it up and placed the paperback on top of the others. "It's the fifth time I've read it."

"What's it about?"

"It's a fantasy." He didn't seem like he was going to offer more.

"Yeah?"

That one word did the trick. Seth continued, growing more animated the longer he talked. "It's about a guy who was orphaned as a kid when his mom died. He never knew his father. He inherited all these magical abilities that he has to keep hidden. Anyone possessing the powers of the Order of Serenity is immediately executed without question because the Order is known to be disloyal to the monarchy. The man rejects his heritage, and he ends up becoming one of the royal guards who's charged with protecting the king. After he gets the job, he finds out he's actually the son of a rebel from the Order who's been trying to overthrow the king. The son wants to marry the king's daughter, but the king will only give his blessing if the man finds his rebel father and kills him."

"Does he love the princess?"

"Yeah. But if he doesn't kill his dad, he knows he'll never have her in his life." Seth sat taller and turned toward Vargas, pushing up with both hands braced on the couch cushion. "When he meets his dad for the first time, he likes him and all the other people who are fighting for their freedom from the monarchy. He also finds out about the king's lies, about how he's been wrongfully imprisoning his own people, then trading them as slaves to neighboring rulers in exchange for more land."

"So what does the guy do? Does he take down the king?"

A slow smile formed. "You'll have to read it to find out."

Vargas grinned back at him. "I think I will."

Seth peered at the book's cover again. "I like how he had to work his way up to a position of respect, but he puts it all on the line when he's faced with making a choice he can't ignore. He has to..." He shrugged as if he couldn't find the right words.

"Do something incredibly brave?"

"Yeah, I guess." Seth changed his focus to the line of windows beside them that made up one wall of the living room, and stared at the construction going on in the building across the street.

Vargas asked, "So can I borrow it when you're done?"

Seth refocused on him. "You can take it now." He paused for a long beat. "They made it into a movie. Maybe after you read it, we could check out the movie together." It was clear by the way he'd spoken, there was far more meaning behind his words than that simple question.

"I'd like that." But then Vargas heard Toby's warning in his head, and he feared he'd gone too far. He folded his arms across his chest and sat back.

Suddenly Seth burst out laughing in an uncontrollable fit of giggles.

"What's so funny?"

That only had him laughing harder. He held his stomach and doubled over. When the laughter started to wane, he glanced at Vargas, and that got him going again. Tears formed at the corners of his eyes.

"Want to let me in on the joke?"

Seth emphatically shook his head. "No way."

"Come on."

"Okay." Seth straightened and drew in a deep breath. "But you can't get mad."

"At you? Not a chance."

"All right." When the last fits of laughter died off, he said, "I was so frustrated and nervous before my last surgery. I didn't want to be stuck in the chair anymore, and I just couldn't calm down. So while they kept me waiting in pre-op, I made up one of those drinking games. You know, where you take a shot every time a particular thing happens."

"You a heavy drinker?"

"No." Seth smiled again. "It just kept my mind preoccupied so I didn't worry as much." The grin grew.

"Why do I have a feeling I'm featured rather heavily in this drinking game?"

"Um… Because it's called the Raymond Vargas Drinking Game."

"Don't think I've ever been the subject of something like that before."

Seth let out another chuckle. "Yeah, sure."

Vargas threw him a questioning look.

"Don't you see how guys look at you at the club? You're an obsession for most of them. You could get any man you want there."

That might've been true years ago. But now? Not a chance. Not with the way he'd been tossing people out lately. Funny thing was, it had been a damn long time since he'd wanted any of them.

He nudged Seth in the side. "So what's this game entail?"

"The player takes one shot every time you do or say certain things."

"Like what?"

Seth tipped his head toward Vargas's torso. "Like when you fold your arms across your chest and get that way-too-serious expression on your face that means you're overthinking something."

Vargas glanced down at himself. He scoffed and uncrossed his arms.

"Or when you smile. That's worth two shots."

He snorted out another low sound. He had a crooked smile. It was the thing he liked least about himself, at least when it came to his physical appearance. "Any others?"

"When you silently read the tattoos on your arms."

He stared at Seth. "I didn't think anyone knew I did that."

Seth lowered his head, his thumb repeatedly rubbing the backs of his fingers on his other hand. "Another one is when you ask me if I slept okay."

"So you're saying that I'm boringly repetitive?"

"I don't mind. Especially when you ask about me."

If only Seth hadn't been chewing on his bottom lip as he fixated his gaze on Vargas's mouth. Because right then, all Vargas could think about was leaning in and tugging on that lip, freeing it with his own teeth, then nibbling on it until Seth parted his lips and let him slip his tongue inside.

Just like in his dreams.

He forced down a swallow and told his libido to calm the hell down before he made a mistake he could never undo. "You let me know if none of those new books sound interesting, and I'll get you some others."

Seth nodded, but the sigh that followed was loud and long. "You really don't have to keep—"

Vargas stood and gathered up the old books. "Yeah, I do." He shoved one book after another into the bag. "I don't leave my friends hanging. They need something, I'm there."

Seth eyed him for several breaths, then directed his stare toward the windows again.

When Vargas finished with the books, he rounded the couch and went to stand before one of the other windows so he wasn't blocking Seth's view. The renovations going on across the street were part of the extensive efforts to revitalize that area of the city. Entire floors had been gutted, new materials carried in. With the lights on in the other building and the overcast sky, they could see inside several of the windows. The crew was in the process of painting the walls and laying carpet.

"They're really making progress."

"Seems like it," Seth said. "I was watching them earlier. One guy kept staring at his phone while he was carrying rolls of carpet padding. He rammed the end of the pad into three walls and then ran face-first right into one of those portable work lights before he finally put the phone away."

Vargas laughed. "Well, cute cat videos on Facebook wait for no man."

"Is that what you watch?"

"Yeah, it's how I start every day." He had no desire to confess how he actually spent his mornings lately: lying in bed, jerking off to memories of the most erotic dreams he'd ever had.

They grew quiet for a couple of minutes as Vargas watched the crew go in and out of the building across the street. Most of the men and women seemed to be wandering around with no tangible goal or task to complete, just biding their time until the foreman said the job was wrapped up.

"Vargas?"

He turned to him. "Yeah?"

"I—" Seth stopped and breathed deep as if he changed his mind on what he was going to mention. Then he hurried to say the rest. "I didn't want to tell the other guys, but I'm really nervous about being here tonight without Dylan."

"That's understandable, Seth. Most people in your situation would feel the same."

Seth shook his head. "Not Dylan. He's not scared of anything."

"That's not true. Besides, you're different people, with different personalities and experiences."

"I guess. Have you ever been afraid of anything?"

Vargas swallowed down the instinct to evade that question. "Yeah, I have." He couldn't look away from those curious brown eyes directed at him, or hold back his next words. "Not too long ago I was very afraid. Terrified. So much so, I almost couldn't breathe." He stopped before he said more and gave away the moment in time he was referring to.

Maybe he didn't need to specifically say it. Seth nodded as if he understood, but then he said, "I can't picture you scared of anything."

Vargas returned his focus to the building across the street. He hated when Seth made him sound like some kind of goddamn hero, like a man who would never let anyone down.

He was no one's hero.

* * * * *

Vargas kept staring out the window, arms folded across his chest, his back to the room. Seth tried hard not to take the silence personally. Instead he quietly waited until Vargas spoke again, only not about what Seth wanted to hear.

"When are they supposed to finish up over there?"

"In a couple weeks. I guess they're having an open house soon to show off the new rental spaces. There's a brochure over there on my desk. It has pictures of what the main entrance and the apartments will look like."

Vargas glanced at where the brochure lay open beside Seth's laptop. "It's different." He crammed his hands into the front pockets of his jeans. The tension in his back and broad shoulders was undeniable, every defined muscle tight. God, he was a beautiful man. But now there was a sadness to him that he hadn't carried with him over two years ago, back when Seth used to spot him striding across the club.

"Different than what you expected?" Seth asked.

Were they really talking about the renovations of a building neither one of them were going to live in? Seth chewed at his bottom lip. He really needed to quit doing that. It was a habit he'd never had *before*.

"No," Vargas finally said. "Just different. I wish I'd seen it the way it used to be. Wish I could've done something to..." He trailed off.

There was no way he was talking about the building that time.

He faced Seth. "We should get going or we'll be late."

"Okay."

Even though it was close enough, Vargas went to retrieve the cane and handed it to him.

Seth got off the couch without incident, then made his way to where they'd left the wheelchair in the kitchen. He lowered into the seat, laid the cane across his lap, and undid the brake on the chair. Once he was back in the living room, he turned the chair toward the door, but then he halted with his back to the room. "Vargas?"

He heard Vargas approach behind him. "Yeah?"

"What you said earlier about being there for your friends." The next words got caught in his throat. He tried again. "Are we friends?"

Vargas was around him in two strides. "Of course we are." The expression on his face was strikingly different from any way he'd ever looked at him. Seth scanned those serious eyes, desperately trying to understand what he wasn't saying.

But then Vargas abruptly spun away. "I'm going to hit the bathroom before we head out." As he moved, he ran a shaking hand through his hair.

All at once Seth got it. What Vargas had been talking about as he stared at the renovation project across the street.

All this time, all the hours they'd spent together, all the months where Vargas was the only one Seth could talk to—hell, the only one he still felt comfortable talking to most days—and the guilt hadn't dissipated for Vargas.

Seth had assured him countless times that he didn't blame him or the club for what happened, and yet Vargas was still holding on to that guilt as much as he ever had. Seth stared off down the empty hall, his mouth gaping in disbelief. Of course, he'd always known how bad Vargas felt, how much he'd initially blamed himself because he granted Prescott access to the club, but now Seth got it. None of that had faded for him.

For the first time in a long while, Seth considered what he could give to someone else. There wasn't anything he or anyone else could do to change the past, but after everything Vargas had done for him—making his apartment accessible for the wheelchair, driving him to his appointments, picking up his groceries, cooking him dinner, and keeping him company when he didn't want to be alone—the least

Seth could do was help Vargas forgive himself and move beyond that guilt.

Even if that meant that someday Seth would have to watch him walk out of his life for good.

Because it didn't matter if Seth got rid of the wheelchair, or the cane, or if he was ever able to leave the apartment alone without a full-blown panic attack. His mere existence would always serve as a reminder to Vargas of what had happened inside his club.

There was no way Seth could continue to put him through that.

"Need me to get anything else for you?"

The words brought Seth out of his thoughts. "No, I'm ready." He called Charlie to him and held the dog's face in his hands. "I'll be back in a few hours." He gave Charlie a kiss on the snout and turned for the door.

Once they were out of the apartment and in the hall, Vargas went for the handgrips at the back of Seth's chair and got them moving for the elevator.

A few minutes later they reached the white Ford Transit parked at the curb in front of Seth's building. Since he could now get in and out of the van with little or no help, they were no longer using the vehicle's lift, but it was nice to know it was there, that if his doctor reversed the prognosis and said he needed another surgery, he'd have a way to get around.

It didn't hurt that the van with the lift also came with Vargas.

Although Seth needed to stop thinking along those lines. He needed to start accepting that Vargas would, at some point, no longer be a part of his everyday life.

Vargas came around the wheelchair and shifted the foot rests aside. Then he placed a hand on Seth's right arm below his elbow. With that extra help, Seth lifted up out of the chair and stepped into the van.

Once he was situated in the passenger seat, Vargas asked, "All set?"

"Yeah."

But he didn't let go of Seth's arm. He didn't glance away either. It was the same intense stare as earlier in the apartment. "You know I'd never hurt you, right?"

Seth nodded. "Of course."

"Good." Vargas remained locked in that pose for another moment as if he were going to say something else. Then he drew back and closed the passenger door. He proceeded around to the rear of the van to load the wheelchair in the back.

Seth reached for his seatbelt and couldn't help but wonder what that look and those words had really meant.

A minute later Vargas got in behind the wheel. He had a hard edge to his expression that hadn't been there before. Without a glance at Seth, he started the van and pulled out onto the street.

After several blocks he said, "I've been thinking about what you asked me last week."

Here goes. Seth forced down a swallow around the lump that was forming in the back of his throat. "Yeah?"

"Are you sure this is what you want?"

"I'm sure."

"You think you're ready?"

"I know I am."

Vargas briefly peered his way, then concentrated on the street ahead once more. "Okay. If Dr. Arteaga still thinks it's a good idea, then how about this weekend?"

Slowly Seth let out the breath he'd been holding. "That sounds good."

"All right." Vargas turned the van at the next intersection. They were only a block away from their destination. "This weekend, then."

"Thank you."

Vargas pulled the van into the parking garage, found a spot, and cut the engine. He undid his seat belt and turned to Seth. "You never have to thank me. Never. If there's something you need, and I can help you with it, you'll get it."

"Okay." But Seth couldn't stop the flood of doubt. Was what they'd be doing that weekend really what he needed? Or was he trying to force himself into something he wasn't ready for? Would this hurt him instead of help?

He pushed those thoughts aside. No way was he going to change course now that Vargas had given the go-ahead.

It was time for him to move past his fears.

Chapter Six

"Have you remembered anything new?"

Seth shook his head. "I don't think I will. Not after all this time."

Dr. Arteaga gave a nod from where she sat facing him in the middle of the open area of her office. He could tell she didn't believe his words. Even though he'd been drugged on and off during his captivity, she thought he would one day remember everything and that his mental blocks were about his mind trying to protect himself.

If that last part were true, he wasn't sure he ever wanted to remember the missing pieces. What he already recalled was bad enough.

She crossed her legs and leaned sideways to rest her elbow on the armrest of her upholstered chair. "Have you given any more thought to what we discussed last time?"

"I told Vargas about it, and he said he'd help." He left off the part where Vargas had agreed to it for that weekend.

"I'm glad. Maybe for our next meeting we can arrange a time and give it a try."

"Sure." He didn't want to lie to her, not after everything she'd helped him through, but he'd already come up with a plan. And it didn't involve her.

When he'd first met with Dr. Arteaga, he'd still been in the hospital and wasn't talking to anyone other than Vargas, and yet she continued visiting with him. Time and time again she'd sit quietly beside his bed on the off chance he wanted to share something. She told him he was suffering from PTSD and that he'd likely continue to be for a while. Everything she described about the condition sounded exactly how he felt. The nightmares, guilt, anger, shame, anxiety, and powerlessness. She wanted to help him, and she hoped that one day he'd feel comfortable enough to talk with her.

He had. Thanks to her incredible patience.

He just couldn't imagine ever talking to her, or feeling as

comfortable with her, the way he did with Vargas. It had been that way since he'd first awoken in the hospital and saw Vargas sitting beside his bed.

Since then, no matter what he wanted to talk about, no matter when, Vargas made the time to listen. Always.

The one thing Seth had never been able to bring up with him in any detail was the specifics of what Prescott had done to him. And not just because of the gaps in his memory. What he'd gone through during his captivity whenever Prescott hauled him out of the cage was the hardest part for him to say aloud. As a function of his therapy, he'd gone over it with Dr. Arteaga again and again, but he'd only ever mentioned those details of his captivity once in front of Vargas and that had been at the trial.

Dr. Arteaga offered an attentive stare combined with the slightest smile that didn't quite meet her eyes. Her signature expression whenever there was a pause in the conversation. Most likely it was a method she'd learned in her training. Look supportive but never too happy. The expression just made her look like she'd painted on a creepy clown face.

She asked, "How's the drawing going?"

"Good. Thanks for suggesting it."

"Sometimes it's hard to find the right words to describe how you're feeling. Drawing can help with that."

"Yeah."

"Is there anything you've created recently that you'd like to talk about?"

His cheeks flushed. He shook his head.

She'd always told him that the sketches would only be for him, that he didn't need to talk about them or show them to anyone, not even her, unless he wanted to.

True to her word, she didn't push the issue. "Have you had any more panic attacks?"

He should've shown her the drawings. "One."

"Were you trying to leave the apartment alone?"

He nodded.

"How far did you get?"

"Halfway to the elevator."

"That's great. That's the farthest yet."

"I guess." He should tell her about who he'd seen during the panic attack, but he didn't want to talk about what that meant in relation to his progress.

"Have you stayed the night in your apartment alone?"

"Not yet."

She was quiet for a minute. Then she asked, "Has anything else been on your mind lately?"

He almost scoffed out loud at her uncanny guess, but he held the reaction at bay. Maybe she was picking up on the enormity of what he'd been thinking about. She clasped her hands together and continued to intently study him.

He liked her. He really did. After talking with her at least once a week, he was more at ease around her than most others, but sometimes she made him feel like someone who needed coddling, like a child. Although he guessed she was trying to do the exact opposite.

As if to prove his point, she added, "I think there's something you want to say."

"I guess."

"You're safe here. You know you can talk with me about anything. No matter how personal."

"I know." They'd already discussed a shitload of private stuff, including specific details about his emotional and physical reactions once he'd started masturbating again. It didn't get much more personal than that. "I think I'm ready."

"Ready for what?"

"For..." If he couldn't even say the word, how was he going to do it? But what if he was wrong? He kept telling himself he was ready, but what if he couldn't even kiss someone? What if he never felt secure enough to take it further? He blurted out, "For sex."

She nodded, then clicked the end of her pen and jotted a note down on her yellow legal pad. "And why do you feel that you're ready for sex?"

He shrugged. "Why not? I'm single. I'm in my twenties. Aren't I supposed to be having lots of sex?"

She gave him that standard eyebrow lift and creepy clown face.

He swiped an arm through the air. "Dylan's been—"

In a rare move, Dr. Arteaga leaned forward to interrupt him. "Seth."

He dropped his arm. It landed loudly on the armrest of his wheelchair.

She clicked off her pen and set it on the pad resting on her lap. "We've talked about this. You cannot compare yourself with anyone else. Even those who've gone through something similar to you. Dylan has his own issues to work through. Let's stay focused on you." She shifted back in her seat again. "Do you have someone in mind that you'd like to have sex with? Have you met someone special?"

He picked at the edge of the padding that covered the arm of his wheelchair. "Why does it have to be someone special?"

There was that look from her again.

"It's someone I trust."

She smiled at him. More sweetly than usual. "That's wonderful."

He rolled his eyes. "It sounds stupid."

"No, it doesn't. Many people need to know and trust the person they have sex with. It's very common. And for you, feeling safe and comfortable are going to be important elements of any sexual activity. You will likely never be able to have casual sex with someone you just met. We can't erase what you've been through, but you can heal from it. We can lessen or even eliminate your PTSD symptoms, and you can have healthy intimate relationships again."

Her favorite word. Heal.

He gave up on plucking at the armrest and met her stare. "That's what I mean. I *am* healed. At least about that part of it." And maybe he was as healed as he was ever going to get about all of it, but he kept that to himself. Most days he felt good about where he was, about how far he'd come. He wasn't so sure she considered his progress the same as he did.

As perceptive as she always was, she said, "You are doing great. Many men who've been assaulted live in denial for years. You have opened up and talked to me. You've been dealing with what happened to you head-on, and that's an incredibly brave thing to do."

She picked up her pen and clicked it on again but stopped short of writing on the notepad. "But I think there's more we need to discuss, more you need to work through. We've talked about how you might always want to have these appointments, to know you have someone to talk to, someone impartial, and that's not a bad thing. What you've been through has changed you. We can't pretend it hasn't. You're not going to be the same person you were before, and that's okay. The things we live through, good and bad, shape us, impact who we are, and it's important for you to accept that. But that doesn't mean you'll always see yourself as broken or damaged. You will rebuild yourself around what you've been through, and you will learn to live fully again."

He didn't want to think about that too hard. He glanced sideways toward her glossy mahogany desk. She never sat behind it during their appointments. Did she ever? The desk appeared too kempt and unblemished to be a surface used in everyday life. Nothing was that flawless. Maybe that's why so many people were unhappy in the world. They expected complete perfection.

He didn't. His goals were more along the lines of not freaking out the minute he left his apartment.

The blinds behind the desk were drawn closed. She'd started doing that not long after his first appointment in that room, when it was clear that he was going to spend the entire time watching the world go by rather than talk to her. Why did she still have to close them for every appointment? He wasn't that same scared, traumatized victim he'd been in the beginning.

Was he?

According to her he'd changed, but into what?

"Seth." She paused as if waiting for him to look her way. He kept his focus on the dark blinds.

She continued. "You will likely need those first physical steps with a man to go slowly. So you can explore touch again and develop intimacy with someone who will be patient and understanding if any triggers arise."

Triggers. Another one of her favorite words.

"And beyond that, the man you have sex with may *always* need to be someone you love."

That time he did look back at her. Love? This wasn't about that, no matter what he'd been feeling about Vargas lately, or what he'd been secretly fantasizing. This was about sex. Simple, uncomplicated sex.

He just wanted to have an orgasm or two with someone. What was the big deal? He already knew where he wanted it to happen, and how. He could manage to keep his head in the man's lap long enough to get him off without putting too much stress on his lower back. All he had to figure out was the when. And also hope to hell he didn't make a fool of himself in the process.

Or freak out.

Avoiding eye contact with her, he focused on the framed painting adorning the wall over her shoulder. The print depicted a mother and father holding their newborn child. The parents each had one arm under the baby and the other around their partner. They were looking into each other's eyes, their faces alight with utter amazement and affection, clearly in love and devoted to each other. Usually the picture made him sad, reminded him of his broken relationship with his mom and dad. Today he identified with what it felt like to care for someone so deeply you wanted to share every significant moment with them, to spend every day with them, to give them the world, to never stop loving—

He drew in a sharp breath as the truth slammed into him with incredible force. For the first time since he'd come up with the idea he'd proposed to Vargas, he got why it was so important to him.

He *was* in love. It was that simple.

He'd been in love with Raymond Vargas for a long time. He'd just been desperately trying to ignore it. Because deep down he knew, his heart couldn't take being with Vargas—*really* with him—and then losing him.

"Seth, rate your fear."

Her voice jostled him out of the startling thoughts. "What?"

Dr. Arteaga propped her elbow on her notepad and rested her chin on the back of her hand. "From the last time you were alone in your apartment." When he said nothing, she asked, "You were alone this morning?"

He nodded. "For a few minutes."

"What was your level of fear? One to ten."

"Why do I always have to do this?"

"Because fear, especially when you're alone, is one of the things that is debilitating for you. Avoiding specific feelings or situations is only going to keep you from recovering. We want to get you to the point where you can go out into the world by yourself, where you aren't afraid he'll come after you, where your rational thoughts can stamp out that fear."

Easy for her to say. Although most people, Dr. Arteaga included, had been incredibly understanding with him about his limitations. If it hadn't been for his supervisor at Dr. Kistler's office letting him work from home, he wasn't sure what he would've done.

She added, "I know with all you've been through, being afraid of him feels logical to you, but he's in prison. He can't—"

Seth slapped both palms on the arms of his chair. "Nine. My fear was at a nine."

She jotted a note onto her pad, taking more time than necessary to write down a single word. How hard was it to remember one fucking number? Every time he was alone, every time he was afraid, his fear level was *always* a nine.

Although seeing Prescott in the hallway outside his apartment earlier was the closest he'd come to a ten.

As if sensing his change in mood, she shifted forward in her chair, her hands clasped before her. "Seth, you really are doing great, and I'm glad you feel ready to move on to a new level of intimacy with someone. Next time I'd like to hear more about this man you're interested in."

"Sure." But he didn't want to think for another second about what he'd realized regarding his feelings for Vargas.

She straightened. "Okay. Our time is up for today."

Without a word, he started to spin his chair around but paused when she spoke again.

"I'm also glad you want to try my idea. Whenever you're ready, we can set up a time, and we'll have our session at the Haven. I'm sure Mr. Vargas will let us in when they're closed in the morning."

Seth nodded. Vargas would agree to anything she thought would be good for him.

He really should tell her he'd come up with a better way to confront the place where he'd been abducted—and where he'd been left for dead—but he didn't want to hear anyone tell him it was a mistake to be at the Haven for more than an hour.

Especially now that Vargas had agreed to let him stay with him in his apartment at the club.

Before the guilt of not telling her the whole truth could change his mind, Seth rolled his chair for the door.

"Seth."

He came to a halt once more.

"For our next appointment, I'd like to see you walk in here with the cane."

He sighed and faced her. "I use it at home. The chair goes in the closet most of the time."

"I know. But your doctor has cleared you for walking full time now. I worry that you're hiding in that chair."

He shook his head, but... Was he doing that? Using his wheelchair to hide? From who? The world? Himself? Or someone else in particular?

He tried to picture leaving his building without the wheelchair, even with someone right there beside him. He couldn't see it, despite how badly he wanted that very thing.

He said, "I'll think about it." He started for the door again. He didn't want to see her attempt to cover the disappointment with that creepy clown face.

More than anything, he wanted to be free of the wheelchair. He wanted to be able to go outside alone. He wanted to feel whole, alive, at peace. He wanted to be himself again.

Was that last part even possible?

According to her, no.

Then who was he going to become? And would that man ever stop being afraid?

Chapter Seven

Seth exited Dr. Arteaga's office and found Vargas leaning against the far wall in the waiting room, his arms folded across his chest, the black tattoos on his forearms standing out predominantly against the taut pink T-shirt. He had his head down, his total focus on the floor before him. His expression was set in a hard glare of frustration.

The second he spotted Seth crossing the room, he straightened, that harsh look dissipating instantly. "All set?"

And just like that, Seth couldn't find his voice. How could he have been so stupid? How could he not have seen it? Felt it? *Known* it? Because it was most definitely there inside him. It had been almost from the beginning.

You're in love with him.

He swallowed and forced out, "Yeah."

"It go okay?"

"Sure."

"Good." Vargas reached for the back of the wheelchair and got them moving out of the waiting area. In the elevator, he stood silently beside Seth, and they watched the numbers light up over the door as they descended.

Passing the sixth floor, something unfurled inside Seth. He blurted out, "She said I'm never going to be the same person I used to be."

The elevator stopped on the next floor, and the doors opened. A man and woman came forward to enter.

Vargas got in their way. "Take the next one." He hit the CLOSE button on the elevator control panel. As soon as the car started up again, he smacked the EMERGENCY STOP button with the side of his fist. Facing Seth, he leaned against the side wall as if they had all the time in the world. "You didn't like hearing that?"

Seth pointed to the closed elevator doors. "I don't think you're supposed to do that."

"Don't worry about it. How did you feel about what Dr. Arteaga said?"

"It pissed me off. I know I'm not the same. I know my life right now is not what it would've been without what happened to me. It's just that—" He clamped his mouth shut in frustration, unsure exactly what he felt or how to explain it.

"Hey."

He looked to Vargas.

"It's just what?"

He shook his head. "I don't know. It's nothing. We should go before someone comes to see what's wrong."

"It's not nothing." Vargas remained still. But when Seth didn't—couldn't—say more, Vargas pushed away from the wall and pressed the EMERGENCY STOP button again. When the elevator began its descent, he hit another button. That time for the second floor.

"Where are we going?"

"Someplace I've been meaning to show you. I stumbled across it a while back."

Seth decided not to ask why Vargas had felt the need to wander the halls of the Parkview Medical Office Building. Or how often he'd done that.

The elevator came to a stop on the second floor. A minute later they were through the skywalk that connected Dr. Arteaga's office building with Parkview Hospital. The same hospital, with its inpatient rehab facility, where Seth had spent weeks of his life.

Once inside the hospital's main building, Vargas directed them through a series of winding turns until they reached the surgical wing. He halted before a nondescript closed door. Seth didn't have time to search for a sign indicating what the room contained before Vargas opened the door and signaled for him to enter.

Seth rolled inside, then abruptly came to a stop.

Glancing around the expansive windowless space, he couldn't believe they were still in the hospital. The room had blue walls, gleaming hardwood floors, delicate lighting, and dozens of potted tropical-style plants in vibrant yellows and reds and greens. Rows of padded folding chairs were positioned in a horseshoe pattern in the center of the room, all facing a waterfall that made up a large portion of one wall, the water literally cascading down the surface of the stone wall. Piled rocks sat at the base of the waterfall and were flanked by more vivid foliage. The place was absolutely gorgeous.

Seth inched forward down the center aisle of the chairs toward the water, then stopped in the middle of the room in complete awe. He wished he had his sketchpad. He could spend hours there drawing the intricate plants alone, not to mention the interesting effect of the waterfall.

"What is this place?"

"It's a meditation room."

"It's huge."

"Yeah." Vargas passed by him to stand before the waterfall.

Seth couldn't take his eyes off the other man as he moved, cursing himself now for not having his sketchpad for an entirely different reason. There was just something striking and utterly masculine about the way Vargas always carried himself.

A minute of silence passed with only the sound of water flowing over the stone wall. Then Vargas pointed toward the door where they'd entered. "The plaque over there says the room was donated in memory of a surgeon who spent his career here at the hospital. He had an undiagnosed brain aneurysm that ruptured while he was on duty. He died in the operating room right beside his unconscious patient."

"That's awful."

"Yeah."

"And not very good advertising for this hospital's services."

A laugh escaped Vargas. "Good point." His eyes held that amused expression that Seth was becoming intimately familiar with.

Yet something about that look seemed more intense than ever before.

Seth was suddenly overwhelmed with the need to feel Vargas's hand pressed to his cheek like earlier in his kitchen. Only he had no idea how to get them to that place again. Or if he should. "I like all the plants. It's like being outside."

Without a word, Vargas came to sit in a chair at the end of an aisle so he was directly beside Seth's wheelchair. "You like it here, then?"

"I do. Thanks for bringing me."

"Been meaning to for a while." Vargas fell quiet as he watched the water. Like he'd wait there all day if he had to. Like he just knew Seth was on the verge of sharing more. His patience never failed to amaze Seth.

Another minute of silence, and Seth sighed. "I don't feel as bad as she makes it seem. I mean, I feel stronger, more in charge of my life than I did six months ago. I'm working full time again. I'm living. I'm happy to be alive."

"That's all great, yeah?"

"She just makes it sound like there's so much more I have to do. Just because I can't leave my apartment without—" He cut off. He clenched his right hand into a fist and slammed it down on the arm of his chair. "Goddammit. She's right. I'm still royally screwed up."

"You are not."

"What kind of grown man can't even walk outside alone?"

"You're doing great. And if Dr. Arteaga isn't getting that, then maybe it's time to see someone else."

"No. She said the same thing today. She's done a lot to help me, and I like talking to her most of the time."

"Okay. But I don't like hearing you doubt yourself."

"I want to get past this." He pounded both fists on the arms of the wheelchair. "I want to get out of this fucking chair for good."

Vargas shot to his feet and crouched down before him. "You will. You're going to be okay, Seth. I've seen how strong you are. Every step of the way. You can handle anything."

"I want to believe that."

Reaching for Seth's clasped fists, Vargas tenderly wrapped his hands around them. "Believe it."

Seth lowered his eyes. He unclenched his hands, turned them over, and gripped Vargas's in return. The same way he remembered doing two years earlier in the hospital. Only this time, there was a current of excitement zipping through his body with the touch. He swept his fingertips over Vargas's wrists, then farther up his forearms, running the pads of his fingers over the warm flesh.

In the next lock of their eyes, he saw far more than friendship and support directed back at him.

The air in the meditation room grew hot and heavy. Seth's breathing picked up speed. He became very aware of their proximity, of the way Vargas's inhales also grew more rapid. Then Vargas's lips parted, and his tongue swept out to moisten them. Seth wanted to feel those lips against his own, that tongue on his. God, he wanted to know what kissing him would be like, how it would feel being touched by him in far more intimate ways, and how it'd feel touching him in return.

The enormous room seemed to shrink in size around them, creating a private haven as they held the stare between them.

Seth dropped his gaze to those lips he wanted to kiss so badly. And just like that, Vargas leaned forward. Seth did the same. Easy. Right. Like breathing.

Their lips only inches apart, Vargas jerked back. "I'm sorry. I shouldn't have—"

"It's okay. We don't have to—" Seth shrugged. "I mean, I get it."

Vargas studied him. "Do you?"

"Yeah, sure."

"I meant what I said earlier." He gripped Seth's hands again and caressed the backs of them with his thumbs. "I will never hurt you." He reached up and cupped his cheek. "Never."

"I know."

He watched Seth for another moment, then stood, his focus back on the steady stream of water cascading down the stone wall.

Seth silently waited. Should he say something? Tell him it was okay to touch him, to kiss him? That he wanted it? He just wasn't sure he could actually say the words, and he had no idea why.

When Vargas came back around, he said, "We should get going."

"Okay."

Without making eye contact, Vargas moved in behind the wheelchair. Less than fifteen minutes later, Seth was getting situated in the passenger seat of the van while Vargas loaded the wheelchair in the back. Neither had said a word on their return journey through the hospital and into the parking garage.

Once in the driver's seat, Vargas got the van started. As he pulled out of the garage, he said, "I was thinking..." He paused as he turned onto another street. When he began talking again, his words were measured, cautious. "I'd like to get rid of the van."

Seth whirled his head in Vargas's direction. "What?"

Embarrassed by the reaction, he faced the front windshield again, trying not to let the disappointment show. Vargas had been the one to pay for the van. If he wanted to sell it, then he should. The time had come for Seth to start taking the bus to his appointments. He couldn't expect Vargas to put his life on hold forever. In fact, Seth didn't want him to. He wanted Vargas to let go of the guilt and live a normal life again.

Despite that, panic gripped Seth's chest as he pictured riding the bus with a slew of strangers, not to mention actually making his way out onto the crowded sidewalk to get to the bus stop.

Well, too bad. He'd just have to figure something out. No way was he going to make Vargas feel bad about his decision.

"That sounds good. I'll ask Dylan to get me the bus schedule."

Vargas frowned. He let up on the gas, then steered the van into a shopping center and directed them to a parking spot near a 7-Eleven. After cranking the gear shift into park, he faced Seth. "I meant since we're not using the lift anymore, I'd trade the van in for something smaller, something that's easier for you to get in and out of. I figured my SUV would be just as tough for you as the van."

"Oh."

The alarm on Vargas's face faded as he exhaled. "I'm not going anywhere, Seth. You get to say when you're ready to try things on your own. Okay?"

"Okay."

Vargas lowered his eyelids for a few seconds. Then without another word, he turned back to the wheel and got them moving again.

They were quiet as they drove toward Seth's next appointment. Eventually Vargas asked, "You still want to go ahead with this weekend?"

"Yeah, I'd like to." Although a part of Seth was rethinking the entire thing. Especially after what he'd realized about Vargas's guilt.

"Then it's a go. I'll get a room ready for you."

The same intense anxiety Seth had felt while they'd been discussing nixing the van landed in his chest. "A room in the club?"

Vargas's brows drew together. "No. One of the guest rooms in my apartment. Or did you want to stay in the Haven?"

"I want to stay with you. I mean, at your place."

The slightest smile hit Vargas's lips. Seth would've missed it had he not been staring directly at him.

"Then it's settled. We'll get you set up in my apartment."

A moment later they turned into the parking lot for the Midwest Orthopedic Surgery and Rehabilitation Center. When Vargas had the van parked, he focused on Seth again. "How about I come by the day after tomorrow before the club opens to pick you and Charlie up?"

"Charlie too?"

"Absolutely. We're not leaving him behind."

"Okay, thanks. We'll be ready."

"Good." Vargas gave him a long, focused stare.

Seth couldn't understand what he saw in those dark eyes. It was a different look than earlier. Regret, maybe.

Then the look was gone and so was Vargas.

He got out of the van and retrieved Seth's wheelchair and his cane from the back. As Seth was getting into position to slide off the front seat, Vargas set the brake on the chair, but he didn't step back and give Seth room to maneuver as usual. He came around to stand between him and the wheelchair. "You and Charlie can stay at my place as long as you need, all right?"

Seth gave a nod. He had to tell Vargas the entire truth about Dr. Arteaga's suggestion, that she wanted to be there with him when he faced the club for the first time.

Later. After his PT appointment when they were alone in his apartment again.

Once inside the rehab facility, Vargas took a seat in the waiting room while Seth rolled up to the desk to sign in. When he turned to go wait with Vargas, the man working the desk whispered to a woman sitting at a computer beside him.

"God, I hate when that guy shows up. He's always so rude."

They weren't talking about him.

Seth spun around. "He's not rude. He just gets frustrated coming here. Because of what happened to me. Because he feels partly responsible, even though it's not his fault at all. So how about keeping your damn opinions to yourself when you have no idea what you're talking about?"

The two mumbled their apologies, then went back to work, their heads down.

Assholes.

Vargas didn't deserve that kind of shit.

Seth whirled his chair away from the desk and found the man in question standing before him, an intense look of admiration in his eyes.

With that expression locked on him, Seth was beyond relieved that Vargas wanted him to stay at the club. Because going to the Haven was about more than moving beyond what happened to him there.

Much more.

And if there was even the slimmest chance something would happen between them, he wanted to go for it.

No matter what they'd be to each other in the end.

Chapter Eight

Vargas flipped through the cooking magazine and found nothing he'd ever want to attempt making. Irritated, he ditched the magazine onto the table beside him. He was the only one left in the waiting room, and the empty space didn't afford him the necessary distractions he needed whenever Seth was in his PT.

He hated waiting there, hated this part of his week.

When Seth had first started his physical therapy at the hospital's inpatient rehab center, Vargas had made the mistake of watching the workout. The pain etched on Seth's face as the therapist pushed him to strengthen his injured and unused muscles was excruciating to witness. Vargas almost lost his lunch five minutes in.

Plus Seth had seemed embarrassed that first day. Better to let him have those moments of torture and triumph alone with the therapist.

Seth insisted the PT was better now, difficult but nothing compared to those first few months. Still, Vargas hated to think of the pain he might be going through in there three times a week.

He sighed and tipped his head back. The pale beige ceiling was even less distracting than the magazine.

One thing he did miss about the previous rehab facility at the hospital was the waiting area. From there he couldn't hear anything going on in the workout room nearby. At this specialized rehab center where Seth now did his PT, he and his therapist typically used the space directly around the corner from the waiting room. Vargas was forever trying to tune out the sounds of Seth's straining grunts. It didn't always work.

Although today, Seth had barely made a sound or said a word to the therapist. Why? Was he upset? Was it what they'd discussed in the van about him staying at the Haven? Or something else?

Early on Dr. Arteaga had encouraged Vargas to let Seth talk about whatever he chose to, whenever he wanted. She said he might only share details of what happened to him in spurts, whenever he felt comfortable enough or had something particular on his mind. She told Vargas not to pressure Seth into saying more than he was ready for, that it might take years before he could open up to the people in his life about the days he'd been held captive.

Vargas did his best not to push, but it nearly killed him to see Seth wanting to talk and not being able to.

"You're doing great. Just one more." That was his therapist.

There was a pause, then Seth grunted out, "*Five* more."

Vargas grinned at those words. Seth pushed himself harder than anyone he'd ever met.

The smile quickly faded, though, as he considered that more carefully. Was now the right time for Seth to visit the Haven? Or was it going to do more damage than good? Vargas hated the idea of questioning Dr. Arteaga and her approach to Seth's treatment, but he couldn't stand the thought that going to the club would in any way hurt Seth or impede his progress.

Only, Vargas had already made the promise, and he wouldn't back out. He had to trust that, after months of therapy to combat his PTSD, Seth knew what he could handle and what he couldn't.

The image of the last time Vargas had seen Seth traverse the club's first floor, looking so carefree and happy only minutes before Prescott had overpowered him, was burned into his memory. He'd do almost anything to see him like that again.

Yet he also couldn't deny that he wanted Seth in his apartment for other reasons. Reasons he shouldn't have even been considering.

What had happened in the kitchen that morning and again in the hospital's meditation room had definitely come too close to what he'd been telling himself wasn't an option when it came to Seth.

Easier said than done. Especially with the way Seth had offered that wide-eyed, unblinking stare that spoke volumes about what he was hoping would happen between them.

Vargas closed his eyes, and for the briefest unbridled moment, he let his mind wander to exactly what he did want: Seth in his bed. Naked. Groaning, not from pain but pleasure. His eyes alight with lust and affection and…

Gratitude.

That one word summed up why it might not be such a bad idea to consider stepping over that line with Seth. To help him be intimate with someone again, help him move beyond that barrier. As a friend.

But then what?

He'd have to give Seth up, that's what. Let him move on, move past what happened to him. Meet someone. Fall in love.

Vargas shot out of the chair and paced the length of the empty waiting room, needing to move, to cut off the thoughts spinning around in his head.

He heard the familiar squeak of Seth's wheelchair. A second later, Seth rounded the corner and came to a standstill before him. He lifted his chin and peered up at him, and Vargas found himself staring into those lust-filled brown eyes.

He took the cane Seth had draped across his lap. "You ready?"

"Yep." Seth held the stare for another beat, then headed for the door.

Vargas forced himself to be more clinical about how he helped Seth into the van that time, and the drive home passed by without conversation. When they reached Seth's apartment, Vargas took the keys from him and opened the door, then flipped on the overhead light and moved aside for Seth to enter.

Once a few feet inside, Seth stopped short. It was like he was unsure what to do next, which was odd. He usually couldn't wait to ditch the chair and get settled on the couch.

Charlie came barreling out of the living room, running right for them. As Vargas had done countless times before, he lunged for the dog and held him back with an arm around him and a hand on his sparkly pink collar before Charlie could attack Seth in his excitement. He was still afraid the dog would get a paw run over or knock Seth down as he tried to stand. Even after all this time, Charlie was a spastic mess whenever Seth got home, like the relief of seeing his owner was as real for the dog as it had been that day Seth had first entered the apartment after being released from the hospital.

That moment was another memory that would never fade for Vargas. The minute Seth had wheeled inside, Charlie pounced. Vargas did his best to keep the dog from climbing all over Seth, who was still seriously hurting at the time. But that was tough when Charlie sounded like he was literally crying, yelping and whimpering as he tried to get closer.

Seth had cried too. The first time for that.

For ten minutes Seth had simply loved on Charlie, and in return the dog crawled his front half onto Seth's lap. Eventually Charlie had settled down, and Seth leaned his forehead against the dog's. The two stayed locked in that pose for several breaths, Seth stroking Charlie along his sides as he said, "I won't go away again. I promise."

Witnessing the pair reunite had gotten Vargas choked up too. The closest he'd come to serious tears since he'd been a kid and stood before his father's casket.

Even now, it was pretty damn hard to watch them together after Seth first came in the door.

"It's okay," Seth said. "Come here, boy."

Vargas let go of Charlie, and the dog ran for Seth, his tail wagging a mile a minute. He got his front paws on Seth's lap and set to nuzzling his face all over.

Seth petted him, then gave Charlie a kiss on the top of the head and encouraged him to get down. Without moving farther into the apartment, or even attempting to get out of the chair, Seth asked Vargas, "You have to take off right away?"

"I'm not in a hurry."

Only then did Seth set the lock on his chair so he could stand. He braced his hands on the armrests and pushed his weight up. When he was steady on his feet, he took the cane Vargas handed over. "Thanks."

Was that for the cane or because he told him he'd stay?

It wasn't that Seth couldn't be there alone at all, but he definitely preferred it when someone was with him when it was going to be more than a couple of hours.

When he and Dylan had first moved in together, Dylan had made a point of spending as much time at home as he could. They would just hang out together, watch movies, play video games, or simply read in the same space. Dylan had also made an effort to include Aaron, one of Prescott's other victims, in their movie nights more often than not. If Blake, Foster, and Ollie, the other three men who'd also been abducted, had stayed in the city, Vargas was certain Dylan would've invited them to join in with the group activities.

It said a lot about a man when he didn't run from the people who'd seen him in the worst experience of his life.

With the help of his cane, Seth made his way toward the living room, favoring his left side the way he always did. He stopped halfway to the couch, held still for several seconds, then changed directions and went into the kitchen instead. He returned with Charlie's leash. Moving with agitation, he passed Vargas and hurried for the door, Charlie tagging along once he spotted the leash.

"Come on, Charlie. Time to go out."

"Seth..."

"Don't. I'm taking my dog for a walk. Alone." Despite his words, he halted at the door. His back to Vargas, he made no attempt to open the door or turn around.

"Seth, you don't have to do this." Vargas carefully approached, stopping a few steps short of him. "I'll go with you."

"No! I'm doing this on my own." But he still didn't move.

"You don't have to prove anything to anyone."

"Yeah, I do. I have to prove it to myself."

"Seth…"

"I can do this."

Cautiously Vargas closed the distance. "But it doesn't have to be today."

"You don't think I can do it?"

"I know you will. When you're ready."

Charlie pressed his snout to the back of Seth's hand that was clutching the leash. As if the dog sensed what was going on and wanted to offer his own brand of support, he licked Seth's hand and then took off for the living room, giving up on the idea of a walk. On his way, he scooped up one of his toys, a short length of knotted rope. He hopped up onto the couch, spun around in a tight circle, then sat. He had the rope dangling from both sides of his mouth, his eyes locked on Seth's back where he still stood in the entranceway.

Seth remained motionless for another minute, his breaths shallow and rapid, his fist clasped around the leash so hard his knuckles had lost all color. It took everything Vargas had to wait him out, to give him the space and power to make his own decision on this.

Eventually Seth turned to him. "I will do it."

"You will."

"When I'm ready."

"Exactly."

Seth must've spotted Charlie waiting for him. He laughed with his next breath. "I'm coming." He eased by Vargas and headed for the sofa, ditching the dog leash on the coffee table on his way by. By the time he was seated, sweat had broken out across his forehead, and he was out of breath. That wasn't typical.

Vargas advanced on instinct but then stopped at the edge of the room. "Was the PT tough today?"

"It wasn't bad." Seth reached for the rope in Charlie's mouth and tugged on one end. The dog scrambled to a standing position on the couch, and the two played tug of war, Charlie obviously taking it easy. When Seth let go of the rope, Charlie tossed it in the air, caught it, then hurled the toy up again, content to play with himself for a stretch. On the next toss, the rope flew sideways and landed on the floor beside the couch. Charlie made no move to retrieve it. He looked to Seth.

Seth pitched forward over the arm of the couch and reached for the rope, but it was out of his range. Vargas was itching to step up and help, but right then wasn't the time to offer assistance unless Seth asked for it.

Seth lifted his ass off the cushion. Bracing his other hand against the couch, he extended the stretch. That time his fingers came into contact with the rope, but he still couldn't get a hold of it.

Vargas sighed. "Seth..."

"I can do it myself." He stretched his arm out more. All at once he winced and jerked back, his ass landing on the couch cushion. "Shit."

That did it. Vargas got moving.

Seth held up a hand. "Don't. Please."

Vargas forced himself to stop. "You okay?"

"Yeah. It wasn't bad. I just need a minute."

"All right." As much as Vargas longed to keep Seth from getting hurt, he also wanted to respect his need to do things for himself. He waited, but he couldn't stand still a second longer. He went for Seth's wheelchair and wheeled it down the hall toward the bedroom closet where Seth stored the chair between uses.

As he opened the accordion doors, he braced himself for what he saw every time he did this: the colorful pillows stacked on the floor, the sparkly beads hanging from the ceiling at the back of the closet, the lamp with a pink and orange glass shade positioned on top of a small plastic table, and the open area beside that for the wheelchair. Seth had asked Dylan to help him create the space not long after he'd gotten home from the hospital. Dylan said Seth often sat in his chair in the closet, a pillow behind his head, a book in his hands, and the closet doors shut.

Vargas figured being in such tight quarters would've been an impossible move for him after the way Prescott had kept him captive in what amounted to an oversize dog crate. But Seth seemed to like the enclosed space of the closet, liked being surrounded by the remnants of his old life. Maybe he felt too exposed, too vulnerable in open areas.

All because of what that asshole did to him.

Vargas closed his eyes until the frustration passed. He gave one last look at the pillows on the floor and then shut the closet doors. He returned to the living room to find Charlie lying on the couch, half of him on Seth's lap, the other half sprawled on the couch cushion as Seth rubbed him behind the ears. The abandoned toy rope now lay on the couch beside them.

Vargas moved the toy and sat. He petted Charlie along his back. "Why don't I take him out?"

"You have time?"

"You bet." He offered the dog a few more rubs along his side. Charlie sat up and shifted around to lie across his lap.

"He sure likes you."

"The feeling's mutual." He gave Charlie some more love, then let up on the scratching. "You ready to take a walk?"

Charlie immediately shot up and scrambled off the couch.

Seth laughed. "I guess so."

Vargas hesitated. He'd taken Charlie out loads of times after Seth's therapy when Dylan was gone or had plans to stay out late, and each time it took incredible resolve for Vargas to walk out the door with Charlie, knowing Seth would be there alone after he'd just had a session with Dr. Arteaga. How the hell was he going to leave him there for the entire night?

"I won't be long." He rose, picking up Charlie's leash from the coffee table. He waited until Seth offered a smile before he got Charlie ready and headed out with him.

He made quick work of their walk, anxious to get back. Once inside the apartment again, he let Charlie off the leash. The dog went for a drink in the kitchen, and Vargas returned to the living room.

Seth was standing before the bookshelf opposite the couch, the cane at his side. One shelf served as an entertainment center with a TV and Xbox. Most of the other shelves were filled with random items like cords for cell phones and other electronic devices, pairs of sunglasses, and several framed photos.

Vargas approached, ensuring he made enough noise he wouldn't startle Seth like he had earlier in the kitchen.

Seth's focus was on the shelf that was eye level with him. It contained a collection of unicorn figurines, all in varying sizes and colors. He seemed to be focused on the largest and most elaborate one, which had stripes of purple running through its thick, flared mane and matching swirls of color circling its horn. Its front legs were in the air as if in the middle of some epic battle. Was he thinking back to when he'd acquired the statuette? Or about something else entirely? Maybe about the framed picture of the little girl that sat amid the unicorns. They'd never talked about her. Vargas had never brought her up, not knowing if the topic was a good idea or not.

He still didn't.

So instead he asked, "You hungry?"

"Nah. Dylan made us a big lunch earlier. I think he felt bad about not coming back tonight." Seth gestured over his shoulder toward the kitchen. "You can make something for yourself if you want."

"I'm good."

Seth moved back to the couch, proceeding much more rapidly than before. Lately he'd been coming home from therapy more and more despondent, yet also agitated.

Or maybe today it was about something other than the therapy.

Either way, Vargas did what he'd done each time before when Seth had been in a similar mood. He sat beside him and waited.

Charlie returned to the couch, and Seth set to petting him again. A minute passed. Then another.

His hand stilled on the dog. "Who did you fight with this morning?"

"It wasn't a fight. Someone just pissed me off, and I took out my frustration on a brick wall."

"Who pissed you off?"

"A lawyer."

"Prescott's?"

"Yeah."

"They're going ahead with the appeal, aren't they?"

"Yes."

"And you still don't know who hired him, who pushed Prescott to plead not guilty?"

"No. But I'm going to figure it out."

"Does it matter anymore?"

"It might."

The dog jumped off the couch and went to curl up on his bed in the corner of the room. Seth turned to Vargas. "I have an idea. You said Tucker located some of the attorney's financial records. I could take a look at them. Maybe there's a way to track the payments he's receiving. Or maybe he's hiding the money somewhere. I might be able to figure it out."

Vargas shook his head. "You don't need to. Tucker has his best people working the money angle."

"But I want to help. I need to do something." The look of desperation about broke Vargas's resolve.

"What if you helped me with the club's finances?"

"Find out what your accountant is keeping from you?"

"Yeah. The whole thing's driving me nuts."

Seth seemed to be considering that. "I know what you're doing."

"Yeah?"

"You're distracting me so I won't go near Prescott's case."

"Is it working?"

He said nothing at first, then, "Maybe." But his expression remained impassive.

Vargas folded his arms across his chest and sat back. He would not relent on this. Despite all his efforts to help Seth in feeling empowered, keeping him safe was goal one. Seth could help review the club's finances, but no way was he getting anywhere near Prescott's attorney.

Just then a smile spread across Seth's lips.

"What?"

"I was thinking about that drinking game." He gestured to Vargas's folded arms.

"I'm glad I can amuse you."

"The game was just something I could think about that made me feel good." He paused, his focus locked on his hands as he flicked the end of one thumbnail with the other. "*You* always make me feel good."

Despite everything Vargas had been admonishing himself for earlier, he cupped Seth's chin in his hand and lifted his head until they were eye to eye. Then he swept his palm over Seth's cheek. "I'm glad."

Seth's eyes fell shut, and he leaned into the touch. With that reaction, Vargas couldn't stop the contact, even if he'd wanted to. He ran the pad of his thumb across Seth's lower lip.

Instantly Seth parted his lips and sucked in a sharp breath like he relished that touch, like he wanted more of it. A hell of a lot more. So Vargas kept it going, tracing that gorgeous mouth with his thumb again and again. He took in the sight of Seth's face. He'd looked at him hundreds of times while he slept in the hospital. He'd memorized every curve, every line, the shape of his mouth, the fullness of his lower lip, the long eyelashes that seem darker when his eyes were closed.

"No one will touch me." Seth opened his eyes. "It's like everyone's so afraid that I'll break. Or I'll lose it or something."

"I'm not afraid." Although that wasn't the entire truth. He wanted to touch Seth, more than anything, but he was also scared as hell he'd hurt him.

Seth bit his bottom lip. Without taking his eyes off Vargas, he reached up. The tips of his fingers brushed Vargas's lower lip as if he were in awe of its existence. Then with his index finger, Seth traced his mouth like Vargas had done to him. Their breathing fell in sync.

Seth leaned in and only removed his fingers from Vargas's lips a second before he pressed their mouths together.

That was all it took. Vargas had no desire—no will—to stop him.

Seth's lips were warm, his touch tentative. But at the same time, it felt like every molecule of his being was focused on that one point connecting them, like experiencing that simple kiss was surging something back to life for him and he might explode if he didn't keep it going. It was heady, having all that bottled-up desire directed at him in a single, chaste kiss.

What the hell would more than that kiss be like?

Everything in Vargas screamed at him to grab hold of Seth and haul him forward until they were plastered together, until Seth was in his arms where he longed to feel him.

But then abruptly, Seth jerked back. "I'm sorry." He shook his head and scrambled backward on the couch. "I'm so sorry."

"It's okay." Vargas held out a hand, signaling that everything was all right. "Don't be sorry. I'm sure as hell not."

"You're not?"

"Not at all." He slid closer. He wanted to wrap his arms around Seth and hold him until that look of uncertainty vanished. Then do far more than hold him. He reached out and gave Seth's cheek a caress with the backs of his fingers. "It was lovely."

Seth nodded, those brown eyes staring back at Vargas with complete trust. "It was." Seth turned to sit with his back against the couch. A smile emerged. "It was."

Afraid the silence that had descended would make Seth uncomfortable with what he'd just done, Vargas asked, "You want to watch a movie together?"

"You don't have to go to work?"

"Not tonight. I thought I'd stay until Dylan gets back tomorrow, if that's okay with you."

"Spend the night here?" The relief in Seth's expression said it all. He wasn't ready to go it alone. "Will you think less of me?"

"Absolutely not. I brought a bag, just in case. It's over by the door, but it's your call. Whatever you want."

"You sure you don't have to get back to the club?"

"I'm sure."

"Then... could you stay?"

Vargas nodded. "It's a done deal. So how about a movie first, then dinner later?" Something they'd done dozens of times before, but it didn't matter. This time was different. No pretending otherwise.

They picked out an action flick to rent online, one of the *Fast & Furious* movies. It seemed a safe bet. Nothing too dramatic or serious. Just crazy stunts with cars.

Vargas got the movie cued up. "You ready?"

Seth nodded.

Ten minutes into it, Seth scooted closer and laid his head against Vargas's shoulder. "Is this okay?"

Vargas didn't hesitate. He pressed his lips to the top of Seth's head. "It's more than okay."

Chapter Nine

Vargas lay back on the pillow and let out a guttural moan as wet, slippery heat swirled around the tip of his cock again and again. Then that remarkable tongue swiped across his slit, sending a shiver of pleasure throughout his body.

They should not be doing this.

He needed to get up and put a stop to it. He'd only come into Seth's room to make sure he'd fallen asleep okay. Not for this.

But then a sleepy, cuddly, warm Seth had reached out for him.

And now... damn, Vargas didn't want the delicious friction sliding over the crown of his dick to end. Nothing had felt this good in far too long.

Yet it was more than that. He wanted to make Seth feel good in return, to let him take control of the moment and find pleasure in touching, in being touched again. But only if that was what Seth truly wanted.

Vargas lifted his head to say something, to make certain Seth was okay with this, that it was his choice to keep it going. But words escaped him as he took in the sight before him: Seth kneeling over him, wearing only a pair of skin-tight briefs. His eyes were closed, his hair stuck up all over. His mouth was wrapped around Vargas's shaft, creating that incredible suction. God, he looked amazing.

He did that swirl thing again. Vargas fisted the bedsheet in both hands. He threw his head back and groaned, a long gruff noise that didn't sound like him. He was never that vocal during a blowjob. It was just all too much. The sensations, the knowledge that it was Seth touching him, Seth's mouth on him.

He heard the familiar rapid sound of flesh beating flesh. He lifted his head again. Seth's hand was flying over his own cock, the movement hidden underneath his underwear.

Then with sudden urgency, Seth sat up. He yanked his own underwear off, then straddled him, settling his bare ass on Vargas's thighs. He reached beside them and retrieved a bottle of lube. After he squirted some in his hand, he tossed the bottle aside. Staring down at Vargas, he bit his bottom lip in that incredibly sexy way of his.

Vargas waited for him to take his shaft in hand and slather the lube on him, prepare them for the inevitable.

Instead Seth lifted up onto his knees and reached behind himself. His lips parted, and he sucked in a rush of air. Vargas couldn't see him touching his own ass, but that look of utter pleasure on his face was intoxicating.

There was no denying it. Seth wanted this. He was ready for it.

Seth shifted farther up the bed. With an arm behind his back, he closed his fingers around Vargas's cock and lowered himself down. As the tip breached the tight ring of muscle, Seth dropped forward onto his hands. "Vargas?"

"Yeah?"

"Don't hold back. Fuck me. Please."

"Are you—" Vargas gulped air. "Goddamn, Seth, I want this, but I don't want to hurt you."

"You won't. I want to feel it, feel how much you've got to have me right now, that you can't stop yourself from plowing into me and—"

Vargas thrust up off the bed and sank into Seth, bringing them together completely that time. Seth moaned in sheer pleasure.

When Vargas had his shaft buried fully inside him, Seth met his stare and said, "God, I love you."

That did it. Vargas gripped Seth's hips and rolled them over as one, never breaking that intimate contact between them. He drove forward, sliding deeper inside Seth, letting go, giving Seth everything he had to offer in that move, in the pure ecstasy of their bodies coming together.

Seth lifted his legs higher, opening up more, offering himself in such an erotic, exquisite move, it nearly did Vargas in. Then Seth grasped his own cock in one hand, and with the other, he reached out for Vargas. He held him by the back of the neck as he stroked himself. "Yes. God, yes!"

Vargas snapped his hips faster, thrusting into Seth over and over. He was close. Seth was too. So Vargas did what Seth had begged for. He fucked him with everything he had. Again. And again. And again.

He was almost there.

Something wet and cold poked him in the ear. Then came a sloppy lick up the side of his cheek.

What the—

He threw his eyes open. He lay alone on the couch in Seth's living room, a raging hard-on pushing against the seam of his jeans.

A dream.

Another goddamn dream.

He turned his head and found Charlie's snout three inches from his face. The dog whimpered, and then backpedaled two steps as he let out a high-pitched bark.

Vargas threw off the blanket and sat up, swinging his legs off the couch at the same time. Elbows propped on his knees, he held his head in his hands. His heart was racing, and he was hot as hell, sweat pouring off him, blinding desire still thundering through him. He wore only his jeans and a white T-shirt. His feet were bare. Breathing deep, he tried to shake off the erotic images: Seth moving above him, underneath him, his own cock encased by the heat of Seth's ass.

Charlie nudged the back of his hand.

"What's the matter, boy?"

As if the dog had been waiting for that question alone, he spun around and took off, running past the kitchen and down the hall. That's when Vargas heard it. Low moans coming from Seth's room. Then, "No. No. Stop. Please stop!"

Vargas shot to his feet and sprinted down the hall. Charlie stood waiting for him outside Seth's room. The door was ajar, and as soon as the dog spotted Vargas coming toward him, he slipped inside. Vargas shoved open the door the rest of the way and followed Charlie in, crossing the room at a quick clip.

Seth was in the bed, curled up in a ball on his side.

Charlie rounded the bed and jumped onto the far side. He headbutted Seth in the upper back as if he was trying to wake him. Seth remained asleep, trapped in the nightmare. He was letting out little whimpers, his hands clutching the blankets before him in tight fists.

Vargas sat on the edge of the mattress and placed a hand on Seth's forearm. "Seth, wake up."

Seth moaned again. He started writhing back and forth, thrashing his head from side to side as if he was trying to get away from someone.

"Seth."

His eyes shot open wide. "What?"

"You were dreaming."

He scrambled to a sitting position, retreating from Vargas, his face contorted in pain, either from the dream or the physical agony of moving that quickly. Maybe both.

"Take it easy." Vargas got up and held his hands up, palms out, signaling to Seth that he wasn't a threat, that he wouldn't hurt him or touch him.

Seth halted. Then, more carefully, he slid up the bed the rest of the way until he had his back against the headboard. "I'm okay." After several beats, he nodded. "I'm okay."

As Vargas had always done, he went with his instincts. He moved to sit beside him, lifting one knee onto the bed. "Just take a couple deep breaths."

Seth complied, inhaling deeply several times before he spoke. "It wasn't a memory. Just a nightmare."

"Thought they were over."

"They were." He pulled the sheet up over his lower half. "I don't know why…" He shrugged.

"The reporter. The appeal." And Prescott being so goddamn close.

"I guess."

"You want to talk about it?"

He shook his head.

"You need a pain pill?"

"No. It's not too bad."

"Okay." They were quiet for a few breaths. "Think you can go back to sleep?"

"I don't know. Probably not."

"All right." Another minute passed, Vargas waiting in case Seth changed his mind and began talking, but he offered nothing. "You want to watch another movie? I've got my iPad with me. We could sit right here and watch until you feel like nodding off again."

"I don't want to keep you up."

"I'm not tired."

Charlie, who'd been standing on the mattress watching them, circled twice, then lay down alongside Seth's thigh on his other side. Seth laid a hand on the dog's head. "I guess a movie sounds good."

"Great. I'll be right back." Vargas stood and strode for the living room. When he returned with the iPad, he went to sit again but stopped short. He gestured to the empty spot beside Seth. "Is this okay?"

"Yeah." Seth scooted sideways to give him extra room.

Vargas got settled on the bed and handed Seth the device. "I downloaded a couple of new movies yesterday. See if there's anything that sounds good to you. If not, we'll rent something else."

Seth browsed the collection. But then his focus shifted to the forearms Vargas had crossed over his chest. His next words were whispered so low Vargas had to strain to hear him.

"Do you think the scars are gross?" Seth didn't pause long enough for Vargas to answer. "They're bad. Especially this one." He set the device on his lap and laid a hand over his upper right arm. The long-sleeve T-shirt he'd worn to bed covered where he indicated. He held his hand there for a beat, then pushed his shirtsleeve up as far as he could.

There were minor scars along his forearm, but the one on his upper arm was the worst. The word *MINE* had been carved into his flesh. Vargas had seen that scar at the hospital, but maybe Seth needed to show it to him on his own terms. He'd never once mentioned any of the scars before.

Seth pulled down his shirtsleeve. "Every time he got me out of the cage, every time he did stuff to me, he'd cut me."

Vargas forced down the blind rage coursing through him, the need to do something, anything to punish the man who'd hurt Seth. "I'm sorry you have to see them all the time. You shouldn't have to relive it like that."

Seth shrugged. "I would've anyway, at least in the beginning. I just hate the thought of people knowing about it, being able to see what he did to me. It's like I can't get away from it. Even after all this time."

"You have nothing to be ashamed of or embarrassed about. Nothing. You were the target of a horrible crime. People may feel sorry for you, Seth, but the ones who matter are never going to think badly about you because of it."

"That's just it. I don't want people to feel sorry for me." He tilted his head back to the headboard and stared at the ceiling. "I wish..." He squeezed his eyes shut and didn't say anything further.

"You wish what?"

"I wish the scars weren't so ugly." He turned his head toward Vargas. "What do you think when you see them?"

"That—" Vargas cut off. He'd started talking without thinking. Seth didn't need to hear all the excruciating ways in which he wanted to torture Prescott and make him suffer unspeakable pain.

"What? You think they're ugly? You feel sorry for me too?"

"Seth, I look at you, and I think you're amazing. You fought hard in the hospital and during all the rehab, and you're pushing through everything—the pain, the powerlessness, the fear—to take back your life. I think you're the strongest, bravest person I've ever known, and I admire the hell out of you."

Seth sucked in an audible breath. "Some days I don't think I'll ever stop being afraid."

"You will. It's just gonna take time. Try not to be so hard on yourself."

"It's already been so long."

"Not that long. Not for something like this."

"I just keep…" He exhaled another ragged breath and shook his head. "Nothing."

"What? Tell me."

"Dr. Arteaga thinks I need to confront my fear."

"That's why she wants you to go to the Haven?"

"But I think it's about more than the club."

When he offered nothing else, Vargas took a chance and asked, "What are you afraid of?"

Seth shrugged. "Stupid stuff."

"Nothing you think or feel is stupid."

Seth watched as Charlie jumped from the bed and trotted into the hall. The faint sound of lapping water from the kitchen soon followed. Seth remained silent for another minute. Then he asked, "Why did he pick me?"

Vargas wasn't certain if he meant Prescott, the one who'd kidnapped and tortured him, or Henderson, the cop who'd beaten him so severely. But he had a hunch it was still Prescott he was talking about.

"Was it because he didn't think I'd fight back?"

"Seth…" Vargas turned so he was facing him. He hesitated, more afraid than anything he'd say something wrong. He opened his mouth to speak, but Seth beat him to it.

"I tried to get away from him in that room in the club. I really did."

"Of course you did. Did you mention all this to Dr. Arteaga?" Not that Vargas didn't want Seth to share. Quite the opposite. He just had no idea what to say, how to help him, and he didn't want to fail him.

"Yeah. But it's… it's easier talking to you." Seth ran his thumb over and around the main button on the iPad, but he didn't turn the device on. "What made me different from the others?"

"How do you mean?"

"I was his favorite. He said he couldn't resist me."

Yet again Vargas swallowed down the fury. He kept quiet, kept still, holding back the urge to pummel the hell out of something, or to say shit Seth didn't need to hear right then. He needed to feel safe, to express himself in his own words, in his own way.

Seth spoke again. "I keep trying to figure out why, but you know what? It's not healthy for me to sit here and try to understand why he did anything. Because that's impossible. He was a sick fuck. They both were. I will never be able to understand their motives."

"You're right. And none of it was your fault. It wasn't what you wore or how you carried yourself or anything you did or didn't do."

Seth stared at the dark screen of the tablet sitting on his lap. "You saw the boxes of my old clothes in the closet?"

"I did."

Seth scoffed. "Kinda stupid, huh? To think I could hide after the fact?"

"I understand the instinct."

"But I can't hide from him."

"You don't have to. He's never getting near you again. That's what 'life in prison with no chance of parole' means."

No matter what Prescott had said in the courtroom, no matter how strong the case for the appeal, Vargas had to believe the original sentence meant something.

Seth nodded. It seemed like he was done talking and would, at any moment, turn on the iPad and select a movie. But then he said, "I saw him. Prescott."

"What? When?"

"This morning. I tried to leave the apartment by myself, and I had another panic attack. I thought I saw him in the hallway, but it was just Ryder. It seemed so real. Like he was really coming for me. Just like he promised."

Vargas closed his eyes. "I never should've told you he said something that day in the courtroom."

Seth jerked his head in Vargas's direction. "God, don't say that. You're the only one who's never lied to me." There was desperation in his eyes.

"The others meant well."

"I know they did. I know they just didn't want me to be worried and afraid, but I needed to know. Just like I need to know you'll always be the one who's truthful with me. You have no idea how much I count on that. How much I count on—" He broke off, but he didn't need to say the rest. How much he counted on their friendship.

Vargas leaned forward until Seth looked his way again. "You got it. Always."

"I just… What if he…" He shook his head, rubbing the back of one hand with the thumb of the other, like there was a dirty spot he had to scrub clean.

It was probably best for Seth to say it aloud, but Vargas couldn't take the silence that lingered. "He's never getting near you again."

Tears welled in Seth's eyes. He nodded.

"He's in prison."

Seth bit his bottom lip and nodded again, his stare now focused on the far wall of the bedroom. "I try to tell myself that all the time, but if he wins this appeal—" His voice caught. "What if he comes for me, takes me away again, and no one ever finds me?"

Again Vargas moved on instinct. He wrapped his arms around Seth and pulled him close. "He's not going to win. He's not going to get out. Ever."

Seth slid an arm around Vargas's middle and laid his head against his chest. "He's never going to forget me. Never. If he has the chance, he'll come for me. Just like he said."

Prescott's words from the courtroom filled Vargas's head. The same way they had every day since then.

"Tell Seth not to worry. This is only temporary. I'll come for him soon, and then we'll be together again. Forever this time. I promise."

Vargas rested his chin on the top of Seth's head and rubbed his back in comforting circles. "I won't let him near you. No matter what."

Seth's breath hitched once more. He held on to Vargas tighter.

"I won't let him anywhere near you."

Chapter Ten

Vargas held still and continued softly running his hand up and down Seth's back. A minute passed. Then another.

Eventually Seth's body relaxed against him. "He's in prison."

Vargas offered another gentle caress. "He is."

"He won't get out."

"He won't."

"Okay."

Vargas waited for any sign that Seth needed space, that he needed him to back off, but this was the first time he'd ever held him like that, and he didn't want to let go.

Not then.

Not ever.

The realization hit him with such intensity that he had to force the thought from his mind. Seth needed him right then.

Seth drew in a long breath and sat up. "I'm okay now." He reached for the tablet on his lap like he was going to pick out a movie. Instead he said, "I was thinking. When I'm done with my PT, maybe I should take a self-defense class."

"That sounds like a great idea." Vargas hesitated. "But it wasn't your fault that he took you. You didn't do anything wrong."

"Yeah." Seth looked to him. "I know." He picked up the iPad and silently examined the selection of movies. Vargas wasn't sure Seth was paying attention to what was on the screen until he snickered. "You've got the entire first season of *Queer as Folk* on here."

"I may have watched it a few times."

"Oh man, I bought the DVDs when I was in high school. Every week when my parents were at bible study, I'd put it on and watch until the minute they got back. I had the sex scenes memorized."

Vargas shook his head. "You and I had very different teenage years."

Seth returned the tablet to his lap. "Why do you say that?"

"I never even saw two men kiss until I was nineteen."

"Really? Who was the first guy you were with?"

He hesitated, unsure if this conversation was a good idea right then.

Seth nudged him in the side. "Please just talk to me like a normal person. You've always done that."

Vargas gave a nod. "It was my mom's next-door neighbor."

"Really?"

"Yeah. He was a real estate agent. I was home for the summer from college, and he paid me to clean his pool. One day when he came home early from work, he changed out of his suit into swim trunks and sat in a lounge chair by the pool, watching me work. I knew right away what he wanted with me, and it was a hell of a rush knowing a guy was into me like that. I'd never experienced anything like it before. It wasn't long and he had his hand down his shorts, touching himself, staring me down as I kept on cleaning the pool. Less than an hour later, I was on that chair with him, his dick in my mouth."

Seth grinned at him. "That sounds like the setup to some cheesy porn."

Vargas laughed. "Yeah, it does."

Seth intently watched him, waiting for him to go on.

"Shitty thing, though, the guy was married. He's still married to her. He's got three kids, several grandkids now. He still lives in the same house next to my mom." Vargas paused and considered that. "I see him sometimes when I visit her. Man, he always looks miserable. He'll spot me across the lawn and just stare at me with this dismal longing. I feel bad for him, but mostly all I can think is... that could've been me. If I hadn't wanted to accept who I was, if I'd ended up married to a woman, my life would be completely different, and I probably would've hurt a lot of innocent people along the way."

"Is that why you opened the Haven?"

He didn't want to talk about the club like that. Not with Seth. He gestured to the iPad. "Let's watch something."

"Okay." Seth picked up the device and browsed the collection. Several swipes across the screen later, he said, "Can I ask you another question?"

"Sure."

"Do you have any brothers and sisters?"

"I did. A couple of years after my mom had me, she delivered twins. Both boys. But they were born too early. They didn't live long."

"God, I'm sorry. That's awful."

"Yeah. Especially for my mom. I think losing those babies broke a part of her that—" He stopped. What the hell was he thinking?

"That would never heal?" Seth offered.

"Maybe heal isn't the right word."

"Maybe it is."

Before Vargas could say anything to that, Seth asked, "Do you remember your brothers?"

"No. I was only two at the time."

Seth nodded. "My little sister died when we were kids. She had a heart defect. They couldn't fix it."

"I'm sorry. She's the one in the picture in the living room?"

"Yeah."

"She liked unicorns?"

He bobbed his head again and gave Vargas an appreciative glance. "They were hers. After she died, I hid them in a box in the attic. A few years ago, I snuck in when my parents were gone so I could get them. I knew they'd never let me have the unicorns if I told them why I was there."

"That completely sucks you had to do it that way."

He shrugged as if it didn't matter, but that was a lie to lessen the pain. Vargas feared that Seth was getting skilled at that act.

"She was so sweet. Back then, she was the only one I could really be myself around. We played together all the time. I had a train set, and we'd sit her dolls on top of the cars and pretend they were on parade floats. Sometimes we'd put them in gowns and walk them along the banister on the second floor like they were on a runway. She never made me feel like I was a freak for what I liked or how I acted. She was the one person in my life that I knew without a doubt loved me just the way I was. After she died, my parents hated me even more."

He snorted as if that were funny. "That was long before I ever told them I was gay. I guess they knew before I did, and they thought they'd get proactive with their homophobia. I thought after I was gone for a while they'd miss me and see how wrong they were. I've tried to go visit them a couple of times, tried to say and do what I thought would please my dad, but it's always a disaster."

And he'd ended up living on the streets because of those pricks. Vargas wanted to track them down and give them a piece of his mind for everything they'd done to Seth, everything they'd made him go through on his own.

"You deserved better. A hell of a lot better."

"I always figured if those were the parents I had to have to get my sister, then it was worth it. Besides, I found a better family than them. When I first met Toby, he and I just clicked. We were both trying to stay clean and get off the streets. I don't know what I would've done without him. Or Ryder and Georgia. Once I moved in next to them, I felt like I had a real family."

Vargas wanted to tell Seth that he'd never be alone again. He wanted to hold him and make promises that he wasn't sure he could even find the words for.

Just then Charlie returned and got on the bed to lie beside Seth again. Seth stroked his fur. "My sister used to beg our parents for a dog. Constantly. For one of her birthdays, they got her a stuffed dog instead. They didn't get how much that would disappoint her. She cried all that night. But starting the next morning, she dragged that little dog everywhere with her. One day when I was really missing her, I went to the animal shelter and got Charlie. He was just a puppy, this excited ball of energy, and I knew she would've loved him."

"Her stuffed dog was named Charlie?"

Seth turned his head in surprise. "It was."

"What was her name?"

"Victoria."

"That's pretty."

"I used to think if I ever had a daughter, I'd name her that."

"You want kids?"

He shrugged. "I used to think about it sometimes. About the ways I'd be different than them with my kids."

"What changed?"

He said nothing for a moment, then, "Everything."

"Seth, you're going to make a great father. Don't let anyone take that away from you. Don't give them that power."

"Yeah. I know." He refocused on the iPad. "How about this one?" He handed over the device and pointed to a movie. A comedy.

"Sounds good." Reluctantly Vargas clicked to start the film.

Five minutes in, Seth spoke again. "Vargas?"

"Yeah?"

"Was it okay that I kissed you?"

Vargas tapped the screen to pause the movie. "It was more than okay. It was perfect."

That got him a smile. Seth settled into the pillows and pointed at the iPad. "Press play."

Vargas started the movie again. A few minutes later, he got up the courage and asked, "Seth, would it be okay if I held your hand?"

Seth turned to look up at him and nodded. He held out his hand, and Vargas laced their fingers together.

Halfway through the movie, Seth's head landed on Vargas's shoulder, and a slight huff of air blew across his chest with each exhale. Despite the stiff shoulders and knot in his lower back, Vargas stayed perfectly still as he let the movie play to the end. When it was over, he shut the iPad off and remained motionless. He really should've been headed back to the couch, but he couldn't bring himself to move.

Seth still had his hand in his, and during the last half of the movie, Seth had turned his entire body inward so the side of his face was pressed along Vargas's upper arm. His lips were parted, a relaxed, contented expression on his face. Vargas's chest grew tight with each detail he took in.

There was no denying it any longer. This wasn't just about a kiss. Or anything more. This wasn't even about being what Seth needed or helping him get over any fears of intimacy.

This wasn't merely about friendship either.

It hadn't been for some time. Vargas had been fooling himself to think otherwise.

The way he wanted to be there for Seth, to protect him, comfort him, to touch him and be with him like in his dreams, it was all more than what he felt for the other men who'd been kidnapped from his club. He'd do anything he could to help the others, but with Seth, it was different.

God help him. It was completely different.

He was in love with Seth.

Vargas dropped his head back to the headboard behind him and whispered to the ceiling. "Fuck."

Chapter Eleven

When Seth awoke the next morning, the sun's rays were streaming in through the bedroom window, creating a narrow band of warmth across the foot of the bed. He'd slept late, probably because of the dreams. First the nightmare, then the dream of him and Vargas in his bed. The two of them were lying together, their limbs mingled, the bare flesh of their bodies pressed close as they kissed again and again.

The day before on the couch seemed a hazy fog that he couldn't distinguish from the dream. Had they really kissed? It was such a short press of their lips. So different from the erotic kisses of that dream.

Just then he felt the weight of an arm around his waist. A hand was pressed flat to his stomach. He peeled back the blanket and found the arm underneath was covered in black tattoos. With the sight of those inked words, Seth knew he still had to be dreaming.

He didn't want to wake up. He slid a hand over the one lying against his abs.

Immediately he knew. This was no dream. Raymond Vargas had stayed the night in his bed.

Carefully, without dislodging the arm from his waist, Seth rolled to face him. Vargas was asleep, his head on Seth's other pillow. The arm he didn't have around Seth was tucked up close, his hand lying on the pillow below his chin, fingers curled inward. His facial features held a tranquil softness that wasn't normally there during waking hours. The vulnerability of that pose had Seth wishing he had his sketchpad within reach, but he also didn't want to move and disrupt the moment.

He listened to the man's deep, even breaths until he couldn't stand merely observing any longer. He didn't give it too much thought, just leaned in and pressed his lips to the side of Vargas's warm neck. He inhaled the faint scent of his fresh, woodsy cologne. It always had the aroma of what Seth imagined lying outside on the grass in the open countryside and gazing up at the stars would smell like. From this new perspective, that scent was even more intoxicating.

Vargas made an appreciative groan. He snuggled in closer to Seth, held him tighter with a hand splayed across Seth's lower back. Was he still asleep?

Apparently not. He raised that hand and cupped the back of Seth's head, then tilted his own head back, encouraging Seth without words.

Seth slid his lips along Vargas's rough unshaven flesh toward his jawline, then back down to the spot where neck and shoulder met. He followed the path up again, wishing he had the nerve to let his tongue do the exploring. Then he gave one last soft press of his lips to the man's bare skin. As he pulled back, he felt his cheeks flush at what he'd done, at the boldness of it.

He'd expected to feel more tentative and nervous doing something like that, but there was no doubt or fear or uncertainty. He wanted this. He wanted Vargas.

Vargas opened his eyes and grinned at him, a lazy, blissful smile. "Morning. You get some sleep?"

"Yeah. Thanks for last night."

"Anytime." He still had his hand cupping the back of Seth's head. He slid in closer. "Come here." That time it was Vargas who offered a slow, sweet kiss. Then he rested his forehead against Seth's. "That was one hell of a way to wake up."

The heat was back in Seth's cheeks. He remained frozen in place for several breaths, just taking in the closeness of the man before him. Until it dawned on him he had no idea how long they'd slept. He checked the clock over Vargas's shoulder. "Oh wow. It's really late. You don't have to wait for Dylan if you have to go."

"I've got nowhere else I need to be." Vargas rolled onto his back and stretched his arms overhead. Charlie lifted his head off the bed where he lay beside Seth's feet. As soon as he spotted that they were awake, he got up and jumped down, then trotted out of the room, likely heading for the kitchen.

Vargas sat up. "I'll go take him out for a walk and get him some food, then fix us something." He drew back the covers and stood. He still wore his jeans and T-shirt. He'd been on top of the blankets when Seth had fallen asleep during the movie. Which meant Vargas hadn't simply drifted off to sleep where he sat. He'd consciously made the decision to stay and had gotten under the blankets with Seth. Was it just to make sure he didn't have another nightmare? Or was there more to it?

Vargas rolled his shoulders and stretched his back again. "If you don't mind, I think I'll grab a shower while I'm at it."

It took Seth a moment to find his voice. "Sure. Thanks for taking Charlie out."

"No problem."

After Vargas left the room, Seth stared at the empty pillow beside him. The surface held a depression that offered visible evidence of Vargas's choice of sleeping arrangements.

That gave Seth an idea.

He retrieved his sketchpad from the dresser across the room and crawled back into the bed. With his good knee up, he balanced the sketchbook on his thigh and began drawing. When he finished some time later, he lowered his leg and took in the completed sketch. A rushed job, but it wasn't too bad. The drawing—and what had happened that morning—did make something clear for him, though.

I have to tell him.

He just didn't think he could take hearing what he suspected Vargas would say in response.

Did that make him a coward for not even trying?

Well, he was done feeling like one. He closed the sketchbook and set it on the nightstand, then slid down to lie on the bed again. That time, he wrapped his arms around the pillow Vargas had slept on, dragged it to him, and buried his face in the fabric. It smelled of the woodsy cologne. He breathed deep.

He wasn't sure how long he'd lain there before he drifted off to sleep again. He awoke to the sound of footfalls heading toward him down the hall.

Vargas came to a standstill in the bedroom doorway. "Sorry. Were you sleeping?"

"Just dozing." Seth moved to sit up and at the same time slid Vargas's pillow back to its original position.

Vargas's hair was damp, and he now wore black slacks and a black dress shirt. The top two buttons of the shirt were undone, and a tie hung open around his neck. He came to the bed and sat facing Seth the way he'd been the night before when he'd awoken him from the nightmare. "Bathroom's all yours. I'll go get started on breakfast. Got a preference?"

"Whatever's fine, thanks."

Neither made a move to get up.

Vargas spotted the sketchbook on the nightstand. The previous week he'd mentioned that he'd love to see the drawings if Seth ever wanted to share. Seth had been considering it ever since. Right then, though, Vargas didn't say a word. He never pressured him. About anything.

Showing the drawings to anyone was a hugely personal thing for Seth. Like cracking open his head and letting someone browse around, allowing them to see his thoughts and desires, his hopes and fears.

But this was Vargas. Maybe showing him the drawings was a good way to begin the conversation Seth couldn't seem to get started. He reached for the book and handed it over.

"You sure?"

"I want you to see them. Just you."

Vargas eyed him for a long moment. "I'm honored."

Seth held his breath as Vargas opened the sketchbook.

* * * * *

Vargas remained where he sat on the bed and reveled in the meaning behind Seth's decision to show him the drawings. It meant a great deal to him that Seth was trusting him with this.

He turned to the first drawing. It was done in pencil, outlined with blunt black lines and shaded in with sharp, thick strokes. It depicted a figure who was half man, half rabid beast. A vicious creature with a deformed forehead and serrated claws in place of hands. He was snarling, saliva dripping from his razor-sharp teeth.

It had to be Prescott. He towered over a smaller representation of Seth, a metal cage visible behind them.

The next several drawings showed the same monster clutching various items: lengths of rope, chains, knives, and the paw-print key chain Seth had been holding when Vargas found him in the club. Then Prescott was taping a series of photos to a wall, each photo contained a close-up of someone in restraints: his bound wrists, his tied ankles, his gagged mouth. The next image was of Seth standing in the middle of the same room. Behind him was a crowd of people holding drinks and mingling as if they were at a party. Seth's mouth was open wide in mid-scream. Not a single person in the room seemed to hear him or even know he was there.

In the next drawing, the same figures from the first were repeated, this time with Seth now the larger of the two. The drawing after that depicted Prescott slumped on the floor, in full human form now. The next showed him locked inside a metal cage.

As Vargas continued flipping pages in the sketchbook, the pencil marks and shadings of the drawings became softer, less severe. He paused at one that featured Seth running in an open field of grass and dandelions, Charlie at his side. They were heading for a pond, Seth laughing, his wheelchair and cane nowhere in sight.

After that illustration, there were occasional blunt, angry drawings of Seth walking down the hallway outside his apartment, but the rest of the pages were filled with landscapes, mountains, streams, and rolling wheat fields, running horses and unicorns. Each drawing included striking details. Attention had been paid to the individual petals of a flower, the ripples around a stick floating in the water, the hooves of a horse smacking the earth beneath it. These sketches were drawn with a lighter touch, but they were also contrasted by select areas of shading that really brought the images to life.

"These are fantastic, Seth. It seems like sketching was a good way to process what you were feeling."

"It really helped. A lot at first. But even now, it's helped me to realize something. Something that I really want."

Curious, Vargas kept turning pages. There were additional sketches of unicorns and other animals, as well as open prairies and wilderness areas. Nothing in the city, no people, and not one thing made of concrete or metal.

"God, these are beautiful."

Seth laughed. "Don't sound so surprised."

"I've just never known someone who was as into numbers and math as you are that could also do something artistic like this."

"I always loved drawing as a kid, and I was pretty good at it back then. When Dr. Arteaga suggested it, I realized how sad I was that I hadn't kept up with it."

"Well, you didn't lose your talent, that's for sure. Every single one of these is incredible." Vargas went through more pages, then stopped halfway through the book, unable to look away from the image before him. "When did you do this one?"

Without seeing which sketch it was, Seth said, "The other night. We were watching that show about Mount St. Helens and you fell asleep."

"This is… This is amazing."

Seth ducked his head. "Thanks."

Vargas couldn't take his eyes off the drawing of himself. He was lying on his back, his head propped on the arm of Seth's couch, his lips parted in sleep and his arms folded across his chest. The sleeves of the dress shirt he wore were pushed up to his elbows, allowing an unobstructed view of the tattoos on his forearms. In contrast to those stark inked words, there was a tranquil, gentleness to the expression on his face as he slept. Was that how Seth saw him?

"There's more."

"Of me?" Vargas turned to the next page. He was on the couch again with his arms across his chest, but that time he had his shirt off. In the drawing after that, he was in Seth's bed, completely naked, his cock rock-hard. The drawing was eerily close to what he looked like nude, sans the tattoos on his torso and groin.

"When I did those I hadn't seen you with your shirt off yet."

Or with his dick out.

Vargas could not stop staring at the picture. He couldn't believe how accurately Seth had drawn his erection without ever having seen it. Although he wasn't quite that big. "You were far too generous."

Seth let out a shaky laugh. "Not from what I can tell."

Vargas glanced over the top of the sketchbook. Seth was staring at the mattress near his feet.

"You're incredibly talented, Seth."

"You're not mad, then?"

"Why would I be?"

Seth shrugged. "The last one... the one with me. It was from a dream I had last night. After the nightmare."

Vargas turned to the last drawing in the book. It was the two of them together in bed, both naked, Seth straddling him, their cocks smashed together, Vargas's hand wrapped around both of their shafts. "You dreamed about this?"

Seth shifted on the bed. There was no missing the evidence of arousal forming a heavy bulge at the front of his sweatpants. That, combined with his parted lips and those wide eyes, had him looking incredibly sexy.

Without giving it too much thought, Vargas returned the book to the nightstand. "Seth..." He practically breathed the name. He didn't allow a moment's hesitation to dwell on what he was doing or give himself time to put a stop to it. He cupped the back of Seth's neck and slid forward.

There was nothing chaste about the kiss that time. The minute their mouths connected, Seth parted his lips and brushed the tip of his tongue along Vargas's lower lip. Then their tongues met, and Seth immediately let out a guttural moan like that one contact was more than he ever hoped he'd get. He opened his mouth wider, wound his arms around Vargas's shoulders.

With that touch, they inched in closer, kissed deeper.

Vargas massaged Seth's nape as the kiss went on and on, as Seth poured what felt like months of longing and need into the embrace.

Vargas matched that intensity with his own, and it was better than every single one of his recent dreams.

When they needed air, they broke the kiss, each breathing heavily against the other's lips. Neither moved away or let go. Vargas wanted to somehow get even closer.

He kept a hand on the back of Seth's neck and wrapped the other arm around his waist. As if Seth could read his mind, he shifted onto his knees and slid in so there was barely any space separating them.

"Easy. Watch your knee."

Seth held Vargas's face in both hands. "I'm okay. I can be on it for a little while." He dived back in for more without delay. Only this time he ended the kiss by trailing his lips down the side of Vargas's neck, humming and moaning as his tongue swept out and took a taste again and again, nothing light or tentative in his touch.

The wet, warm contact sent goosebumps racing down Vargas's spine, a familiar swell of need building in his lap. His breath came in heavy pants he hardly recognized from himself.

He swept his hand through Seth's hair as he tossed his own head back and closed his eyes, relishing the feel of Seth's warm lips traveling along his flesh. Those lips moved lower and lower. Seth parted the top of his shirt.

Vargas dropped his head forward. "Wait. Is this what you want?"

Seth nodded and sucked his bottom lip between his teeth. "I've wanted this for so long."

Vargas searched his eyes, taking in every detail of the passion he saw in those brown depths. "Seth, I..." He hesitated. Was now the time for this? Was saying anything the right call at all?

But he'd always been honest with him. It was that simple.

"I need you to know something. Something I realized last night. I..." He trailed off again, desperately trying to find the right words. He kept his attention locked on Seth's face. He didn't want to let in any thoughts on how this might be the wrong move. He didn't want to stop touching Seth, stop holding him in his arms, stop feeling him so full of life and passion.

Suddenly Seth looked terrified. Like he didn't want to hear whatever it was Vargas was going to say. Or maybe he didn't want anything to derail the moment. He shook his head. "Can you just kiss me again? Please."

Vargas would give him whatever he asked for. "Come here."

Seth leaned in. Using the pads of his thumbs, he traced Vargas's bottom lip. "I love kissing you." He didn't wait for Vargas to offer his own assessment on what it felt like to finally feel Seth's mouth on his.

Their lips met once more, and that did it. Every other thought, every last denial, every fear and concern that this was a bad idea flew out the window, and Vargas gave himself over to the moment. He let the kiss consume him, let the uncontrollable fire build.

Seth kissed him again and again, keeping it going as he reached for the tie Vargas had hanging loose and slid it off. Then he went for the base of his dress shirt. "I want to touch you." Without undoing another button, he had the shirt up and over Vargas's head in one motion. The shirt momentarily got stuck at the buttoned cuffs, but Seth didn't relent, and he got it the rest of the way off in no time.

Their lips met again, and Vargas wound his arms tighter around Seth. He gently drew him even closer, opening his mouth wider, their warm, wet tongues connecting over and over.

God, he wanted more.

He deepened the kiss, and he couldn't help himself. He groaned. Seth followed with a whimper, rocking his body and repeatedly brushing up against him. Vargas relished in that unbridled, erotic movement.

Just like in his dreams.

Then everything stopped with the sound of the apartment door opening. Dylan's voice floated down the hall and in through the bedroom doorway.

"No way, Aaron. That's not true."

A reply followed in the quieter voice of Aaron. "It is. I saw them do it in a video."

Dylan snorted out a laugh. "Yeah, and no one fakes shit like that."

Vargas held Seth's stare and didn't let go of him. No way was he going to make it seem like Seth should in any way feel bad about what they'd been doing, or be embarrassed. There was no avoiding the disappointment in Seth's eyes as Dylan's footsteps drew closer.

With clear reluctance, Seth moved away and flattened his back to the headboard. Vargas shifted around to sit beside him so he was between Seth and the door. He reached down beside the bed and swiped his dress shirt off the floor. He tossed it at Seth's lap to cover the erection tenting the front of his sweatpants.

As soon as the shirt made contact, Seth sucked in a sharp breath. Vargas was dying to know if the reaction was because of the fabric pressing against his aching dick or the mere fact that it was the shirt Vargas had been wearing now sitting in Seth's lap that was getting to him.

Dylan either had the world's worst timing.

Or the best.

Chapter Twelve

As soon as Dylan appeared in the doorway of Seth's bedroom, he came to an abrupt stop. His jaw dropped.

Vargas glanced to Seth but couldn't read the look on his face. He wasn't sure if there was anything about the moment that would upset him. All he knew for sure was that Seth wasn't making eye contact with him, and he hated that.

Dylan lifted his chin in greeting. "Hey."

Seth didn't respond. His breathing was as labored as a minute ago.

Vargas offered a reply to Dylan. "How's it going?"

"Good." Dylan pointedly looked his way with raised brows. "You?"

"We're good."

"I see that."

"How's your cousin?"

"Fine. His car's totaled, but he wasn't hurt bad." He directed his next words to Seth. "Figured I'd head home early and see how you were doing. Aaron and Toby are here too. Thought we could play some Quelldon Quest."

Seth still didn't speak, just nodded. It was reminiscent of his interactions—or lack thereof—months earlier.

Dylan tilted his head, indicating down the hall. "Looks like Charlie got sick in the kitchen. Thought maybe he ate something he shouldn't have."

That got a reaction. Seth slid his legs off the bed and reached for his cane where it was perched against the nightstand. "I'll go check on him." He stood, then turned back to the bed and held out Vargas's dress shirt. He still wouldn't meet his stare.

Vargas grabbed the other end of the shirt and gave a tug before Seth let go. "Hey."

Seth lifted his gaze. There was panic and fear in those brown eyes.

Vargas threw him a smile, feeling like a dope, but what did he care? No way was he going to stand by and let Seth feel bad about this, or think he should regret anything that happened. "We'll finish our talk later, okay?"

"Okay." Seth searched Vargas's eyes for a moment, then returned the grin and said again, "Okay." He let go of the shirt and headed for the door, slipping past Dylan on the way out.

As Vargas got off the bed and donned his dress shirt and tie, Dylan folded his arms across his chest and leaned against the doorjamb, the confusion and surprise evident on his face. To his credit, he didn't ask anything or offer an opinion.

Neither said a word as they made their way to the living room. Vargas greeted Toby and Aaron and then sat on the couch, waiting for Toby to say something about what they might've walked in on. But he also offered nothing as he sat in a chair facing the couch. Aaron remained standing at the edge of the room.

A couple of years ago, when Vargas had first interviewed Aaron for membership at the club, he thought the young man was too shy and reserved for the Haven. He liked his younger patrons to be a little more outgoing and flirty. That made the regulars happy, but there'd just been something about Aaron's sweetness that he'd been unable to turn away.

So in the end, Aaron had been a member when Prescott targeted him the same as he did with Seth and Dylan. Just another layer of guilt that Vargas couldn't evade when it came to what Prescott had done in his club.

Seth entered the room, Charlie nowhere in sight.

Vargas asked, "He okay?"

"He seems fine. I'll keep an eye on him. I put him in my room for now." That was for Toby's benefit. He'd been attacked by a dog when he was a kid. An incident that left him completely uncomfortable around Charlie or any dog.

Seth moved to the couch and sat beside Vargas, lying his hands awkwardly over his thighs.

Dylan dropped to sit at Seth's other side. "How was your night?"

"Good." Seth pointed at Vargas. "I didn't stay by myself."

"I'm glad."

Just then Vargas's phone vibrated on the coffee table, signaling a text message. He'd left the phone there the night before and had forgotten all about it.

Toby pointed to the cell. "It's been going off like that since we got here."

Vargas checked the display. He'd missed two calls and several text messages. He scanned the latter. "I need to return these calls and check in at the club."

"Okay." Seth indicated the other guys. "We're going to hang out and play video games anyway."

"Sounds good. I'll be by to pick you and Charlie up tomorrow." He stood and gave a nod in goodbye to the others.

Dylan got up like he planned to walk him out.

Seth's total focus was locked on his own knees. Vargas hated the thought of leaving him like this. What if he wanted—*needed*—to talk about what had happened in his bedroom and what he felt about it?

Vargas wanted to stay right there on the couch with him, wanted to protect him from any further pain or heartache.

He placed a hand under Seth's chin. With the slightest pressure, he silently asked him to look his way. "You okay?"

"Yeah." Seth must've seen something he liked in Vargas's face. His entire body relaxed, and he smiled up at him. "I'm great." There was a lightness visible in his eyes that hadn't been there before.

Vargas swept the pad of his thumb across Seth's lower lip. "Me too." He repeated the action with his thumb. "Call me if you need anything. Even if it's just to talk."

"I will."

"Anytime at all."

Seth nodded. "I promise." He gave Vargas the same look he'd given him when he traced his mouth between kisses. Then Seth licked his lower lip, and that about did Vargas in. He had to force himself to drop his hand and step away.

Dylan's gaze narrowed as Vargas passed by him, but he made no move to follow him to the door.

Once Vargas was out in the hall, he braced himself against the wall beside the door and dropped his head back to the plastered surface. Seth was just starting to really open up to him about what he'd lived through when he'd been abducted. More than anything, Vargas didn't want to wreck that. He didn't want to take advantage or hurt him in any way.

But there was no doubt about it now. Vargas may not have ever experienced it before with anyone else in his life, but he finally understood what he felt for Seth.

And more importantly, he now knew without a doubt what Seth felt for him. It was evident in every line of those sketches, every way Seth looked at him, every touch.

How could he walk away from that?

* * * * *

That afternoon Vargas stepped into the headquarters of Simon Security Systems. He'd called ahead so the receptionist led him right in. He entered the office and offered a nod in hello. "Simon."

From behind the executive desk, Walter Simon took one look at his friend, got up, and rounded the desk. "What the hell's wrong with you?"

"Nothing. Just wanted to check on how our project's going."

Walter gave him a skeptical glare, then pointed to an empty chair. "Sit." He didn't wait for Vargas to move before returning to his own seat. With his arms folded across his chest, he leveled another silent, steady gaze on him. That, combined with the charcoal suit and dark tie Walter wore, gave the moment an interrogation feel Vargas was completely uncomfortable with. Walter was still a detective, no matter how long ago he'd left the force.

Vargas took a seat.

Despite the suit, Walter appeared frazzled and disheveled, like he'd been missing a few night's sleep. His dark hair, with the hint of gray, didn't have its usual sleek appearance, and there were dark patches under his eyes.

In spite of all that, Walter continued with that focused, scrutinizing stare. He was good at this game. Which meant there was no way Vargas was getting out of talking about what was really on his mind.

Time to distract. "How's Kevin?"

"Good." Walter shot a sideways glance to the cell phone perched on his desk. He and Kevin had been living together for nearly two years and were in a perpetual state of bliss. Vargas couldn't imagine anything had changed between them.

"So why the anxiety?"

Walter sat back and rolled his eyes. "I hate when you do that."

"You should talk. So what's up?"

"I'll tell you mine, if you tell me yours."

Vargas snorted out a laugh. "Are we really going to resort to that?"

"I'm thinking it's the only way to get you to spill."

"All right, fine. You first. What's wrong with Kevin?"

"Nothing's wrong. Not yet anyway."

"Sounds ominous."

"He's just working on a new story that's got me a little nervous. Several people have died in home fires recently. The fire investigator ruled them as accidents, but Kevin has a source who says the fires were arson and there's a conspiracy to cover that up. He's out digging into it today."

"And you're worried the wrong person will find out he's looking into it."

"Something like that."

"Then you know what you have to do."

Walter's brows rose. "Oh yeah?"

"Get out of this office, out of that suit, and go help him. You know you miss investigating shit. Even if he's not a cop, Kevin's a damn good reporter, and the two of you make a great team."

Walter eyed him for another moment, then shifted his focus to the phone again. A grin formed. "You're right. On all counts."

"Of course I am." Vargas held his arms out wide. "I don't know why the hell you don't come to me and ask me what to do. I should be making all your decisions for you."

"Sure. Because you're so good with your own life."

Vargas ignored that and changed the conversation once more. "So have your sources come up with anything?"

"Nice try. But I won't forget you haven't shared yet." Walter grew serious as he leaned forward and propped his elbows on the desk. "Here's what I know so far. Ever since Prescott got to the jail, he's been held in a cell alone. He eats, shits, and sleeps there. He gets time outside with the other inmates, but he's cordoned off from them and under heavy guard. He showers alone. Doesn't talk to anyone. The only visitor he's had is his lawyer. No mail. No trips to the infirmary. If he's planning some kind of escape, he has to have someone helping him from the outside, and it was likely prearranged before he went in."

"Could it be a guard?"

"That's a possibility. But my source in the jail says most of the ones who've had contact with him have worked there for years. They're trustworthy. The newer guards start off covering the front desk and the cameras."

"Anyone can be bought."

"True. I'll stay at it. I've got a couple of guards I trust keeping an eye out for anything abnormal."

"Thanks."

"I don't want that son of a bitch out any more than you do."

Of course he didn't. Not after the way Prescott had targeted Kevin.

Walter added, "If I had to guess, I think he's placing all his bets on this appeal working out in his favor. From what the guards have been hearing, he talks like it's a done deal and he'll be released soon. I think that's what he was going on about in the courtroom that day."

"That's why we need to know who's pushing for the appeal, who's financing the attorney. They might be able to put an end to the case before it's too late. And they might know if Prescott is planning something else."

"You still got people on his parents?"

Vargas nodded. "Yeah."

"But you don't think they're the ones paying for the lawyer?"

"No. They didn't seem like they were interested in helping him. They cut him off financially years ago. I got the impression they want everyone, especially their rich friends and business associates, to forget he was ever their son."

"Seems like a waste of money to focus on them, then."

"Maybe. Or maybe they're clever at hiding what they're really up to. Because I can't figure out who else it could be. Who else would want to help that bastard?"

"You're investing a lot of cash on a big-ass maybe." Walter leaned back in his chair. "I know a couple of years ago the club was doing well, but from what I've been hearing—"

Cutting him off, Vargas stood and marched to the far corner of the room. A round conference table held a single flat-screen monitor. He couldn't ignore the frustration and anxiety etched on his reflection in the blank screen.

A minute later Walter spoke again, his voice taking on a more thoughtful tone. "Here's what I know for certain."

Vargas faced him.

"It's long past time you stop blaming—"

"Don't." He turned away again.

"You've got to let yourself off the hook. Just because those men were taken from your club does not mean you're responsible."

Vargas spun back around. "The fuck it doesn't. That asshole snuck inside my club and busted holes in the walls so he could hide there, attack men, and abduct them, all while I slept peacefully in my apartment on the second floor not hearing a goddamn thing. I could've stopped him before he'd taken anyone if I'd just been more observant." He ran an unsteady hand through his hair. "Fuck that. I met with that son of a bitch. I *liked* him and fast-tracked his approval. I gave him access to every one of those men. How am I not responsible?" He whirled away and returned his focus to the monitor. Only he didn't see the blank screen or his reflection.

He saw Seth lying on a table in the club's dining room, his lifeless body covered in blood, the gold key chain with Charlie's picture clutched in his hand.

"Vargas." Walter's voice startled him. He hadn't heard him leave his chair or move in closer. "That man was in your club because he was trying to fuck with your business, trying to get you to sell the place. He was putting on a show for you. There was a lot riding on him getting you to believe he was trustworthy. If anyone's to blame for his access to the club, it's that cop Henderson. He was the one who hired Prescott to fool you and get inside."

He was right about that. Henderson, and the man's father, wanted to strong-arm Vargas into selling the club so their business associates could use the building—and the tunnels underneath—to traffic illegal goods. At the time, they had to be putting enormous pressure on Prescott to make that deal happen or else face the consequences of some rather unscrupulous people.

Walter didn't wait for Vargas to respond. "What's going on with you? If anything, you've gotten worse lately, and I'm thinking it's about more than those six men and what happened to them."

Vargas shook his head, but the words left him uncensored and unbridled, his voice trembling as much as his hands. "I'm seriously fucking things up."

"How?"

"I think..." He hesitated, then made his way back across the room to where he'd been seated earlier. He sank into the chair with a heavy sigh. "I might've made a huge mistake."

Walter came to stand facing him. "With Seth?"

"Tell me I'm doing the right thing."

"In what way?"

"Having him come stay with me."

"Oh." Walter settled back against the edge of the desk and waited a beat before speaking again. "I don't think this is about him coming to the Haven. This is about your feelings for him."

Vargas gaped at him in surprise. "How did you know?"

"I've got eyes. I've seen you two together."

"It's that obvious?"

"To anyone who's looking at you? Yeah."

Vargas let out another exaggerated exhale. For some bizarre reason, he could never keep his reactions from Walter. "I didn't mean for this to happen."

"No one usually does."

"Did you try to fight it with Kevin?"

"Hell, yeah. The age difference bothered me. A lot. But the

alternative, giving him up..." He shook his head. "That wasn't even an option. Not in the end."

"Yeah." Vargas let his eyes fall shut, and he was right back to their kiss in the bedroom that morning. He could feel Seth's arms tightening around him, Seth's body brushing against him.

But it wasn't just the physical stuff. He couldn't even imagine what it would be like if he didn't have Seth in his everyday life, if he couldn't listen to him, talk to him, laugh with him.

"You know, the age difference isn't what bothers me. He just doesn't need someone like me."

"What? A good guy?"

"The Haven, the fact that I live there... I'd be a constant reminder of what happened to him. I just want to help him heal, so he can really live again, so he can learn to let someone else in." That hurt like hell just to say.

"Seems to me he is living. He's come a long way in the last two years. Hell, the last year. He was still barely talking to anyone then. Only you."

Vargas got up again and paced the room behind the chair. "He's been through so much." He stopped before a bookcase filled with high-tech equipment. The lack of books on the shelves only reminded him of the ones Seth was always reading. "His own fucking parents didn't even come see him in the hospital. Did you know that? His dad is some big shot back in their hometown, owns a slew of factories and businesses. The townspeople treat him like he's a fucking king." He scoffed. "He's a disgusting shit who let his own son become homeless rather than accept who he was. I called their house after I found Seth in the club. I thought, considering what had happened to him, that he'd almost died, that maybe—" He swallowed down the anger and disgust.

"But after I finished telling his dad about the kidnapping and the beating, all he wanted to know was if his son was still a fag. I said he was gay, and his dad hung up on me. Can you imagine turning your back on your kid like that? When he needs you the most?" He faced Walter. "He deserves to be happy."

"Why can't he be that with you? What if the two of you together makes him happy for the rest of his life?"

God, that sounded good. Vargas sighed again and returned to the chair.

Walter leaned forward and placed a hand on his shoulder. "If you came here hoping I'd tell you that you'd be making a mistake if you pursued things with Seth, then you're talking to the wrong man. I learned with Kevin that there's no fighting something that intense, something that right." His hand slid from Vargas's shoulder, and he sat back. "Or maybe that's exactly why you came to see me. Because you knew I'd tell you what you really want to hear."

"Which is?"

"That if you love him, really love him, don't for a second think of letting him go. Because you might just be the best thing that has ever come into his life. And he might be the same for you."

He already knew Seth was that for him. If he walked away from that, what kind of a shithead did that make him? "I don't want to fuck up his life."

"The monster who abducted him already did that. Seems to me you're the one who's helping him get past it, helping him have a future."

"That's why I can't just do whatever I want. Not when it comes to him."

Walter didn't say anything more.

"God." Vargas sank back and scrubbed both hands over his face. "I'm in over my head here." He dropped his arms and stared at his palms. "I feel like I've got his entire future in my hands, and if I make one wrong move, I could mess everything up for him."

"He's a grown man. He can make his own decisions. You need to trust that he knows when he's ready to be with someone again. I've seen how he is with you. He's beyond infatuated. He's halfway in love with you."

Vargas let his eyes fall shut, and he was right back to that morning in Seth's bed. "He's already all the way there. I'm just not sure he wants to admit it to himself yet. Or to me."

"Well, there you go. And if you walk away from that, then you're a damn fool."

Vargas stared his friend down. "You're right." He *was* a fool. An idiot. He would never hurt Seth. Not intentionally. He loved him. He did. And if Seth was feeling anything close to the same, then they could figure everything else out together.

He wanted Seth to know he'd never be alone again. No matter what he had left to deal with and work through, Vargas would be there for it all. He'd be the worst kind of asshole for keeping that truth from Seth any longer. For not showing Seth exactly what he meant to him.

"Shit, you're right about everything."

A grin hit Walter's lips. "If you could just remember that fact, these conversations of ours would be a lot easier and go a lot faster."

He stood. "Now, when you realize I'm also right about the fact that everything—the bad days, shitty days, good days, the sex, *everything*—is better when you get to be with the person you love, you can bring me a bottle of scotch to say thanks."

Vargas laughed, letting some of the tension fade. He was done fighting this.

Because if Walter's words were true, then Seth deserved to have all that, to be with the person he loved.

Chapter Thirteen

Prescott sat on the concrete floor in the corner of an otherwise empty jail cell, his elbows resting on his bent knees, his thick forearms folded over each other. He had his total focus on the iron bars that were keeping him locked away from what he wanted most. His shoulder ached, a reminder of the bullet wound he'd sustained two years earlier. The doc who'd worked on him had reassured him after everything healed there'd be no residual pain, so he attributed the occasional twinge to his subconscious desire to never forget his past.

As he had countless times before, he lowered his head until his forehead was resting on his arms, then brought to mind images of his boys. He focused on each one in turn until he got to the last one: Seth Fisher. The sounds of chains clanking and soft whimpers filled his head.

He had no reason to worry about a cellmate gawking at him as he recalled those beautiful memories of being with his boy. Since he'd been transferred from the state penitentiary back to the county jail, they'd put him in a cell alone, one that usually accommodated up to ten men. The guards at the jail didn't trust the other inmates, not with so many of them wanting to take down the newest arrival who'd been prominently featured on the news for the past two years. The "pervert" who most thought needed far more than an ass kicking.

He'd once been a decorated firefighter who'd rescued twin girls from a burning building. Now he was a criminal. Tried and convicted in court, and in the media long before that.

His attorney, Lauber, said they had an excellent chance with the appeal of his case after the combined trial of all the charges brought against him. Especially with the way the cops had blundered everything about the investigation, starting with not knowing the lead detective in the disappearances, Conrad Henderson, had been Prescott's childhood friend who'd been covering for him for years.

During the trial, the judge did the unthinkable and admitted evidence that Henderson had been in charge of, evidence that never should've been allowed in the courtroom. Or so Prescott's attorney had assured him.

All Prescott thought about whenever he heard his former friend's name was that he was glad the son of a bitch was dead. Henderson betrayed him in the worst possible way by trying to kill one of his boys. And this after Prescott had once saved Henderson's life when they'd been kids. For that act alone, he deserved better.

He should've strangled Henderson years earlier.

At least now, Conrad Henderson's mistakes were helping with the appeal. Although from what Prescott's attorney had promised since the beginning, the appeal wasn't his only hope.

"No matter what, you'll never spend your life in prison."

Which meant Prescott couldn't care less what people thought of him or which cell they stuck him in. He would one day get to be with the ones he wanted to hold, to care for, to love. He just had to be patient.

"Psst. Prescott." A soft voice interrupted his thoughts and pulled him back to the present.

After all this time, he still hated that name, hated how it made him feel, but he could never refer to himself as the Protector again. Not after he let his boys get taken from him, after he failed them.

"Prescott." The name was said with more force, but it still came from a timid voice.

Prescott gave in and raised his head. The old man with the books was back. He stood outside the cell, wearing the same orange jumpsuit as Prescott. Although the old man looked so frail there was a good chance his jailhouse ensemble would slide right off his body at any moment. He had a bony, wrinkled hand resting on the handle of a metal cart that was loaded with boxes of books. The cart seemed to be the only thing keeping him standing.

"Would you like a new book to read?"

Prescott got off the floor and went to the bars. The old man watched him move with wide eyes, but to his credit, he didn't so much as flinch as Prescott's massive frame came in close. He never had.

"I'll take one."

"Got a preference?"

"Fiction. Nothing light or funny."

"Hmmmm." The old man searched his cart. "How about... Ah, yes." He slid out a tattered paperback and grinned up at Prescott, reverently clutching the book in his hands as if it were his "get out of jail" papers. He was missing two front teeth. One on the top and one on the bottom. The two black holes and the surrounding chipped, yellow teeth created a checkerboard effect. "How about a mystery?"

"Perfect."

The old man went to hand Prescott the book but stopped short when an inmate in the crowded cell across the aisle groaned in annoyance.

"Hurry it up, old man."

Prescott swore under his breath at the interference. He hated impatient people, hated the arrogance and entitlement. Everyone in today's world was unbearably selfish and downright rude. Apparently that phenomenon didn't bypass inmates in the county jail.

"Come on, you old fart." The shithead across the aisle gripped the cell's iron bars in both hands. His hair was slicked back with his own body's grease, and his oily face needed a serious scrub. He was likely one of the men whose stench had permeated into Prescott's cell.

The grotesque man's complaints grew louder. "Hurry it up or I'll make you suck my dick for keeping me waiting." He laughed. His cohorts in the same cell followed suit.

That did it. Prescott jabbed a finger through the bars in his direction. "You. Leave him alone."

"Or what? You gonna kill me with your finger from all the way over there?"

"You know why I'm here?"

"Yeah. Cop killer." The man scoffed. "Sick pervert faggot too, I hear. Kidnapped guys. Raped and tortured 'em. Fucked 'em up good. You are one messed up son of a bitch, that's for sure."

Prescott kept on staring him down. "If I have no qualms killing a cop who happened to be a friend of mine, what the hell do you think I'll do to a guy like you?"

The man glared back at him but kept his mouth shut. He knew the score. He was far from close to Prescott's size.

Prescott gestured to the old man with the books. "You so much as touch one hair on his head or even speak to him again, and you're going to personally find out how sick I am."

The inmate held still. Then he waved his hand through the air as if neither of them were worth the trouble. He backed away from the bars into the darkness of the cell.

The old man held out the mystery he'd selected. "Chapter thirty-three's my favorite. That's when the bad guy almost gets away."

Prescott took the book. "Let me know if that asshole, or anyone else, gives you any more shit."

The man smiled at him, then shuffled off down the aisle, pushing the cart before him.

When he was gone, Prescott turned away and crossed the cell, dropping the book on the thin mattress as he passed by. With his back to the far wall, he eased his large frame down and returned to sit on the floor.

They could put him in jail with trash, send him to prison for the rest of his life, take away everything—everyone—he cared about, but they could never take away who he was.

A protector.

He tipped his head back, closed his eyes, and let the images of his boy slide into view once more. He pictured Seth in his cage. Naked, quivering, waiting. Gorgeous. No one had ever been as responsive, as attentive to Prescott's every move.

Prescott dropped his head and rested his forehead on his folded arms as he'd done earlier. This time he imagined them together, not as he remembered, but how they'd be one day. In a little cabin he'd build, nestled inside a dense forest, far away from civilization, nothing but the sound of crickets and the occasional hoot of an owl.

And of course, the sound of Seth. Those little whimpers and cries he always let out.

God, he wanted him back.

Rolling his head to the side, Prescott reached for the book the old man had given him. He flipped to chapter thirty-three. A folded piece of paper lay between the pages. He opened it.

Yesterday Seth Fisher walked out of his apartment alone. He hasn't made it out of the building yet, but he's getting closer.

Prescott sighed with tangible relief. After months of surgeries, infections, setbacks, more surgeries, complications, and countless hours of hounding by the cops, his boy was going to be okay.

He let that thought wash over him and ease his anxiety.

Then he studied the final words of the note.

Someone will approach you with an offer. Take it. Hang in there. You'll see him soon.

There were times when he'd doubted it, times when he couldn't allow himself even a glimmer of hope, moments when he knew for certain he'd never be happy again, never be at peace. But now...

A smile spread across his lips as he imagined all the things he'd once again get to do with his boy.

Soon.

He'd be with him again soon.

* * * * *

Sitting behind his grand executive desk, the man tightened his grip on the printed financial reports until the pages were crumpling along the edges, but it wasn't the figures defining the recent struggles and failures of his various businesses that held his attention. Instead he was focused on only one thing.

A memory.

A day he'd spent with his son when the child was ten years old. They'd gone on a trip to Cedar Lake, rented a cabin in the woods, and spent a week there as a family. They swam, rowed out onto the lake in a canoe, built a fire, and told ghost stories. Taking such an extended stretch off from his work was a rarity for him, but it had become necessary. His son was losing his way.

That was before their rift, before his son had taken off, leaving him and his mother brokenhearted and alone.

Giving in to the memories, the man ditched the reports, picked up his phone, and opened the photos app. The picture of his son had been taken at the lake that week. At such a young age, it had been hard to tell if his boy was going to match his father's six-foot-three frame and muscular build, or if he'd be slight like his mother. In the picture, the boy was seated in the canoe. He held an oar in both hands, ready to take off on their next adventure, a dopey grin on his face. He'd smiled like that the entire trip. Which had only confirmed for the man what he needed to do: toughen the kid up, make him into more of a man.

And yet, somewhere along the way he'd failed.

Well, no longer. He was not letting his son down now.

A knock reverberated on his office door.

"Enter." The man's own fractured voice startled him. He swallowed down the emotion and repeated the word with more force.

The door was gradually pushed open. A young man dressed in a business suit too sizable for his lean figure stepped into the office. "Sorry for the interruption, sir, but would you have a minute?"

Sighing in frustration, the man behind the desk sank back in his chair. "We've talked about this, Jarrett." He paused for emphasis. "Never apologize to anyone. Ever. Not even me."

"I know. But it feels wrong, sir. It wasn't how I was brought up."

"Why don't you give it a try? Just once."

"All right. Next time?"

The man studied Jarrett Gates. It had been two years since the younger man had signed on as his newest assistant. Yet Jarrett still couldn't get this one rule down, despite that he'd done everything else asked of him. The man knew it was, at least in part, due to his own standing as head of the corporation. He intimidated people without trying. He'd be considered old to someone of Jarrett's age, but he didn't look it or carry himself that way. He'd been fit and toned his entire life, classically handsome with a square jaw and broad shoulders.

As he strode through the office on a day-to-day basis, he watched his underlings whisper and scurry from his approach. Not Jarrett. Despite his obvious nervousness and low self-confidence, he'd walked right up and introduced himself, his hand out. At the time, Jarrett was just past thirty, working in the corporation's mail room. That day was one of the reasons the man had selected Jarrett for the coveted position as his special-assignment assistant.

Jarrett didn't sit at a desk outside the man's office, greet visitors, or answer the phones. He completed confidential and personal tasks that had nothing to do with the man's businesses.

The man liked Jarrett. He was smart and loyal as sin, and his determination reminded the man of himself when he'd been younger. Only Jarrett was more of a nervous sort, a people pleaser. The man blamed that on Jarrett's father. He'd probably spoiled Jarrett instead of giving him the tools he needed to foster positive self-esteem, to gain the discipline and confidence to succeed at anything in life.

So the man took it upon himself to mentor Jarrett, offer him the authoritarian influence he hadn't received as a kid, give him what the man had tried so hard to provide to his own child.

He'd always hoped that one day his boy would give up on the alternative path he'd chosen in life and would return to his side to learn about the business. But that was never going to happen. His wife had been trying to tell him that for years. They'd lost their son when he was a teenager. There'd been glimmers of hope when his boy had met with him on several occasions, even taking an interest in the business and in pleasing him. But then, they lost him again.

Now all the man had was the plan he'd so painstakingly put together.

He flipped to another photo on his phone. This one more recent. He'd gotten a copy from a detective friend who accessed the case file and took a snapshot of the picture for him.

It was his son. Lying on a gurney. Bruised, damaged, broken. His child, his flesh and blood that he'd never stopped loving, no matter how disappointed he'd always been in him.

Which brought him back to the other reason he'd moved Jarrett into the coveted position as his assistant.

Jarrett was a member of the Haven, had been for a couple of years.

The man set the phone on his desk and refocused his attention on Jarrett. "Now would be best."

"All right." Jarrett stood straighter, his confidence building. This time he skipped the apology for interrupting. "I have a message for you."

That had the man smiling. "See? That wasn't so bad, was it?" He pointed at Jarrett. "Now, what have you learned?"

"Everything's in place. The men you hired said they've got what they need and are ready to go at a moment's notice."

"Perfect." He held the smile for a moment, then gave Jarrett a hard look. "I want you to stay on top of every detail. Nothing can fuck this up. Got it?"

"Yes, sir. I'm on it." Jarrett turned and scurried off.

The man picked up his phone and returned to the picture of his boy. He wouldn't fail him again.

Chapter Fourteen

"You and Vargas?" Dylan slapped a hand to his chest and gaped across the living room at Seth. "Wow."

Seth took another bite of his pizza and shrugged. What was the big deal? "It's just sex."

"It is so not just going to be sex between you two. The way that man looks at you... Holy shit, it's going to be intense. Am I right?" Dylan glanced between Aaron and Toby who were situated on the couch on either side of Seth. Neither had taken another bite of their slices of pizza.

Toby gulped down a swallow. "Yeah."

Aaron nodded his agreement, his eyes wide.

Seth tried to play that off as an exaggeration as he took another bite of his pizza, but what had happened with Vargas earlier in his bedroom had been insanely intense. The most passionate, erotically-charged moment of his life and all they'd done was kiss.

Dylan tossed his half-eaten slice of pizza into the box on the end table beside him. "Do you think he has feelings for you?"

"It's not like that. He cares about me, but I think he mostly feels bad—even guilty—about what happened to us, what happened to me and how I'm all messed up now."

"Hey." Dylan's expression had hardened. "There's nothing wrong with you. We survived. We deserve to be happy. All of us."

Without a word, Aaron nodded again. He swiped several strands of blond hair off his forehead as he looked down at the piece of pizza he held in his other hand.

Seth knew they were right about what they deserved. He just couldn't get his hopes up where Vargas was concerned. He couldn't allow himself to imagine he'd have more than one night with him.

As if a thought occurred to Dylan, he sat up with a start. "Seth, if you're not emotionally ready—"

"He's just my friend."

"He's my friend too, but he doesn't want to fuck me."

That had Toby and Aaron laughing.

Then Toby grew serious. Lifting a leg onto the couch, he turned to face Seth. "We just want you to be careful. I don't want to see you hurt any more than what's already happened to you." It was a rare moment when Toby mentioned what Prescott had done to them. He wasn't trying to be mean or heartless by not bringing it up. Quite the opposite. He'd been the one to warn Seth against going to the Haven in the first place. But Seth hadn't listened then. Maybe he should now.

Maybe taking things any further with Vargas was the wrong move. He didn't believe what they were implying about Vargas having feelings for him. Not like that.

Or did he?

The way Vargas had touched him, had clasped on to him and dragged him close had felt like more than passion and need. It was like nothing Seth had ever experienced before. Was it merely an uncontrollable, carnal surge of lust? Or was it more? He'd never been in love, never had anyone love him. How did he know what it felt like?

Was he avoiding seeing what was right in front of him? And if so, why?

Because deep down, no matter what he said to his friends, if for one second he let himself believe that Vargas might be falling for him, and then he found out that wasn't true, that would... devastate him. He couldn't take that blow on top of everything else.

Vargas was attracted to him, sure. But that was it.

It had to be.

"So..." Dylan was grinning at him again. "He's coming back tomorrow?"

"He said I could stay with him."

"What?" It was the first time Aaron had addressed the group since they'd sat down and started in on the pizza. "You're going to stay at the Haven?"

"Yeah, I am."

Dylan scrutinized him. "For how long?"

"He said for as long as I need." When no one replied with their thoughts on that, Seth added, "I want to move past this."

That time Aaron spoke to his knees. "We all do."

Seth hated how sad Aaron sounded. How broken and miserable. He hadn't known him before their abduction, but he had to wonder what he'd been like. Was he as quiet and shy as he was now? Or did he feel as different as Seth?

Toby leaned forward until Seth looked his way. "Come on, talk to us."

"God, I feel like all I do is talk. I want to *do* something for once." Which had him thinking about what he was hoping would happen at Vargas's. He wanted more of that kissing, more of Vargas's hands on him, wanted to feel the man's naked flesh pressed against his own.

Toby asked, "You think going to the Haven will help you?"

"I don't know, but I want to try. I have to try something."

"You could get hurt."

"How? It's just a building."

"You're wrong," Dylan said in a curt tone. "It's not just a building. Going to the Haven..." He shook his head. "That's just fucked up."

Seth's jaw dropped. "You're there all the time."

"And it hurts like hell. Every time I walk in the front door." Dylan gave him a steady look that seemed to say more than Seth could read. "Don't kid yourself that it'll be easy. Because it won't be."

He wanted to ask Dylan why he went to the club if it was so horrible being there, but he thought better of it. Dylan was trying to heal in his own way. They all were.

Seth took in the continued concern on the faces of his friends. Was he making a huge mistake? He still hadn't told Vargas what Dr. Arteaga had suggested about having a session there. Even if talking to Vargas alone always made him feel better than his therapy appointments, it was wrong to keep the truth from him. He felt awful about that. But every time he considered mentioning it, one thought stopped him: there was no way Vargas would let him stay at his apartment inside the club if he heard about Dr. Arteaga's plan.

Seth had told his friends the truth when he said he had to try something. And soon. He needed to start facing the world on his own.

There was only one person who made him feel brave, who made him feel like he was whole again. Who made him feel wanted and desired.

He didn't want to lose that. Not yet.

He wanted to hold on to it—and Vargas—for as long as he could.

* * * * *

Vargas left the security office on the second floor of the Haven and paused at the balcony overlooking the main floor. A slew of men filled the bar and dining room below. After months of dealing with irate, frustrated members, it should've had him feeling good to see the club so full of life.

Instead it annoyed the hell out of him. There were too many

people in the crowd. He had one purpose for scanning the first floor: to spot someone who shouldn't be there, someone he couldn't trust.

Finding no one who stood out, he eased up on the search.

"Vargas."

At the sound of his name, Vargas spotted Tucker traversing the last of the steps leading to the second floor. He was dressed casually in jeans and a blazer with a button-down blue shirt underneath. He wasn't a member of the Haven, but all the security guards knew him, and he had a free pass to enter the club at any time. Vargas had few people in his life right then he trusted that implicitly.

He held out a hand as Tucker approached. "I didn't know you'd be by tonight."

They shook hands, and Tucker tilted his head toward the hall leading to Vargas's apartment. "I wanted to see how that company did finishing up inside your place."

"Was just about to check that out myself. I didn't have a chance to take a look since I got in. Been following up on the other additions we talked about. I need to have everything in place by tomorrow afternoon."

"That soon?"

"I didn't want to make Seth wait any longer."

Tucker rested his hands on the banister and surveyed the first floor of the club the same as Vargas had been doing a minute earlier. "Is the place always this busy?"

"That's right. You've never been here when the doors are open." Vargas joined him in eyeing the crowd. "Actually this is busier than it's been in some time."

Tucker's gaze continued to sweep over the crowd of men. He paused on a couple at the bar. One was seated on a stool facing the other man. They were embracing, their mouths locked, lips parted in a deep kiss, each clasping on to the other.

There was something odd about the way Tucker was taking in the sight of them. Like he'd never seen two men kiss or touch like that. Which made sense. Even though he once mentioned he had a gay friend he'd been close to since college, the way the men in the bar were clinging to each other wasn't what most people did in the company of others, not outside a place like the Haven.

Vargas studied Tucker. If he hadn't known better, he would've thought his friend was checking out that couple with more than mere curiosity.

Much more.

"You've never seen two men together?"

That got Tucker's attention. "What? Oh, sure. Just not like that. It's so…" He refocused on the couple. "Passionate. Sensual."

"Did you think it was all slam, bam, now get the fuck out of my bed?"

He laughed. "Maybe." He shook his head, his gaze locked on the two men in the bar. "I don't know what I thought."

Vargas almost added, *maybe you're not as straight as you thought you were.* He mentally shrugged off the thought. Tucker didn't deserve that kind of teasing, which could infuriate plenty of straight men, even the more liberal ones.

Walter had once mentioned that Tucker hadn't dated anyone since his only child's death to leukemia and the resulting deterioration of his marriage. Vargas would have to see if he could think of any single women he could set Tucker up with.

With that plan tucked away for later, he gestured toward the hallway that led to his apartment. "Why don't we have a look?"

"Sure." With what seemed oddly like regret, Tucker eased away from the balcony.

He'd been inside the apartment before, so there was no need to give him a tour. They were quiet as they made their way into the larger of the two guest bedrooms down the hall.

Vargas crossed the room and gave the new computer panel a once-over. "Looks like it's activated." He turned to Tucker. "They said someone will be here tomorrow to go over everything with me, but just in case, you're up on this model?"

"I reviewed the materials."

"If I need help explaining it, would you—"

Tucker held up a hand. "Just give me a call." He moved in closer and got a better view. "Are you sure this won't upset him?"

"No, I think it might actually be a big help." Or so Vargas desperately hoped. It was the only thing easing his apprehension about Seth coming to stay with him.

Screw that. Who was he kidding? He was still nervous as hell, worried Seth being there—and what Vargas had to tell him about what he was feeling for him—was going to be too much for Seth. But at least he now had a plan. He needed to take things slowly, wait until Seth had been at the club for a while, help him work through the reasons he'd come there, and then when Seth was emotionally ready, Vargas would—

"Man," Tucker said in a long, drawn-out tone. "Are you on something?"

"What?"

"Don't think I've ever seen that expression from you before. You look high."

Vargas laughed. But he couldn't deny that, despite all his concerns and anxiety, he did have a rush of excitement surging through him. He was so damn eager to have Seth there in his apartment with him.

It was getting harder and harder to walk away and leave him at the end of the day.

* * * * *

The next day when Vargas arrived at Seth's, the apartment door swung open wide without haste. Dylan stood there, a stern look on his face. He didn't say a word, just stared Vargas down.

Vargas had never seen the young man looking so steadfast, so still and quiet.

"Something wrong, Dylan?"

"You bet it is." Dylan stepped into the hall and tugged the door shut behind him. He got in Vargas's face and jabbed a finger at him. "Don't you dare fucking hurt him."

"What? That's the last thing in the world I want to do."

Dylan harrumphed. "I like you, Vargas, and I appreciate all you've done for me, for all of us, but I swear—"

Vargas held up a hand. "Listen, I know you care about him. I care about him too." He paused for emphasis. He had no desire to explain the specifics of how he felt to anyone else, not until he could talk to Seth about it, and that would be when Seth was ready to hear it and not a minute before then. But Vargas also hated the idea that Dylan was worried. "I care for him more than anyone does, and in a way that means I will protect him, even from me, with my last breath."

Dylan's eyes widened. A grin spread across his face. "Oh man. I knew it!" He spared a quick glance at the closed door behind him. "He has no idea."

So much for not sharing too much. Vargas shook his head. "Don't say anything to him."

"I won't. But why?"

"Taking him to the Haven is about helping him heal. Not about what I'm feeling for him, and I'm definitely not going to rush him into something he's not ready for." No matter how great it felt to have him in his arms the other day. "I will always be there for him, and I want him to know that, but I have to do this the right way."

"Okay." Dylan hesitated as if he had more to say. But then, without a word, he offered a grin, went to open the apartment door, and stepped inside. Vargas followed him in.

Seth was coming down the hall from the bedrooms, a smile on his face, the cane at his side. He moved cautiously but with more assuredness than usual. Or maybe it only seemed that way since typically when Vargas came to pick him up, Seth was already in his wheelchair.

There was something else different about him. His hair wasn't spiked like he wore it to the club two years earlier, but it looked a little fuller, like he had product in it. The gray hoodie was unzipped halfway, and visible underneath was a pink T-shirt. The same shirt with the word *Tasty* across the front that Vargas had on the day before.

Vargas returned his smile. "You ready?"

"Yeah."

Dylan went to Seth. "You text me if you need anything."

"I will. You'll be okay here by yourself?"

"You know it." Dylan offered him a playful jab in the arm and then took off down the hall toward his bedroom.

When Seth turned to him, Vargas asked, "You sure you want to do this?"

"I am."

"Okay." He noted the packed suitcase and duffel bag sitting by the door. "This everything?"

Seth nodded. "You sure I don't need anything for Charlie?"

"I got it covered." Vargas had texted Seth earlier to let him know he'd picked up two bowls, a bed, extra toys, and Charlie's food from the store. That way Seth didn't have to worry about any of that. "Got what you need for work?"

"Just my laptop. It's in that bag."

"Okay. I'll go get your chair." Vargas started down the hall.

"No."

He stopped.

"I'm not gonna take it with me."

Emotion welled in Vargas's chest. There was only one word to describe it. Pride. He returned to Seth. "You sure?"

"Yeah. I don't need it. I'm okay with the cane." Seth smiled at him again, looking so light and carefree, almost a replica of the man he'd been on the club's video feed the night he disappeared. It was hard to believe they were headed to the place where his life had so drastically changed.

Seth moved to the kitchen doorway, using the cane to support his weight with every other step. He grabbed the leash and harness from the hook inside the kitchen and called out for Charlie. The dog came barreling down the hall, a stuffed pink bunny rabbit with long, floppy ears hanging from his mouth, his tail wagging like crazy as soon as he spotted Vargas. He dropped the toy and ran to him.

Vargas loved on the dog until he bounded to Seth. While Seth got Charlie situated, Vargas collected the dog's toy and picked up Seth's bags. He waited by the door.

When Seth and Charlie stopped beside him, he said, "If this is too much, you tell me. I can bring you back anytime. Even if it's the middle of the night."

"Okay. Thanks."

Vargas hesitated. "Before we get there, do you want to go in the front door or the back way that leads right up to my apartment?"

Seth seemed to be giving that some thought. "The club won't be open yet, right?"

"It won't be opening up at all tonight."

"Because of me?"

"Because I didn't want a crowd of people there. Not your first night."

Seth grew quiet for a moment. "The front door, then."

Chapter Fifteen

"Wow." Seth couldn't believe everything he'd just heard. He stared across the front of the van at Vargas. "That sounds like a lot."

"It should've been that way from the beginning."

"Why? It's the *Haven*. Not the White House."

Vargas snorted out a laugh as he turned the van at the next intersection. That smile on him was good to see after the past fifteen minutes of his intense explanations regarding the new security protocols at the club.

As soon as they'd begun their drive across town to the Haven, Vargas started going over the details of the changes that were in place, including the manual check of photo IDs at the club's entrance, the guards he now had positioned on most of the exterior doors, the on-site person monitoring the video feeds around the clock, the new guard posted outside his apartment, and the fact that all the security personnel were now armed with stun guns.

Vargas continued with his explanation. "I've got cameras everywhere except the private rooms upstairs for obvious reasons."

"Sure. Although I doubt some guys would care if they were being watched."

Vargas chuckled again. "That's for sure. None of the employees blinked an eye when I told them about the camera going up in the employee locker room."

Seth laughed too, but it was a half-hearted gesture. "It all sounds expensive."

Vargas's brows drew together. He returned his focus to the street ahead. "I just wanted you to know that you don't have to worry about someone getting in when you're staying there, whether the club is open or closed."

"Okay." Seth wanted to add that he wasn't worried, but he didn't want to lie to Vargas. Since they'd left his place, he'd been a hot mess. It felt like his body was shaking apart from the inside out, the same uncontrollable shivering that comes from standing in the open wind of a winter storm. Only he wasn't cold. For some odd reason, that thought had a tense laugh bursting out of him.

Vargas grinned at him from the driver's seat. "What's so funny?"

"Nothing."

"Tell me."

"It's just... I'm just nervous, I guess."

"I'll be there with you the whole time."

"Thanks." Seth breathed deep. As he'd done all morning to distract himself, he thought back on the day before in his bedroom and what might've happened had Dylan not shown up. Would he have been able to go through with what they'd been headed toward? Would Vargas? Or would he have stopped them?

"Vargas, are you seeing anyone?" Seth almost smacked himself on the forehead. He could not believe he'd blurted that out. "I mean, I know you're not serious with anyone, but..." What was he thinking? Did he really want to know how many people Vargas had slept with in the past two years?

"But what?"

He shook his head. "Nothing." He so needed to shut up. Where was the sexy, confident flirt he'd once been? What did it matter if Vargas had been—or was—having sex with someone else? It wasn't like Seth believed what Dylan had implied about what Vargas was feeling for him.

It was just sex.

Yet no matter what, Vargas wouldn't want to take advantage of him, or the situation, which meant Seth was going to have to give him a clue that he wanted more to happen between them.

Hell, he'd probably have to give him a lot more than one clue. He might have to jump him and beg Vargas to fuck him.

Just thinking those words had a flush creeping over Seth's face and neck, heat pooling in his lap. That was one way to stop shivering.

It had been so long since he'd felt that rush of being suddenly turned on. After he'd gotten home from the hospital, months had gone by before he even felt like jerking off. Now those private sessions with his hand had been coming more and more often lately, Vargas the star of every one of his fantasy-filled handjobs.

As if Seth's life was some cosmic joke that existed to give the universe a laugh, the van pulled up in front of the Haven.

Vargas cranked the engine off. He reached into the back seat and unhooked Charlie's harness from the seat belt, then attached his leash and encouraged the dog to get down so he was standing in between the front seats. "After we get inside, I'll have someone move the van around back and get your bags."

"Okay." Seth sat motionless for a moment. Then he went for the passenger door handle. As soon as he had the door open, Vargas shot out of the van on his side, taking Charlie with him. He rounded the front end and stood beside Seth's open door.

Seth slid off the seat, Vargas holding on to his arm until he had his cane in hand and was steady on his legs. He took Charlie's leash from Vargas. "I'm ready."

Vargas shut the door to the van, but Seth held still again. The street and sidewalks around them were empty. Not a car or pedestrian in sight. Had Vargas paid someone to close off the street in front of the club? Seth nearly let out another burst of laughter. Not that Vargas wouldn't pay to give him that, but who would think of such a thing? He doubted even Vargas would go that far.

The exterior of the club appeared the same as it had the last time Seth had been there. Everything he'd been feeling and thinking that night came back to him in a flash, including how he'd spent that entire day hoping things would go well with the guy he agreed to meet in a room upstairs. He'd been so flipping excited about the date.

A soft voice from beside him, like a warm caress to his skin, brought Seth out of the memories.

"I'm right here. You take as long as you need."

Seth nodded, but he started for the front door anyway. Holding on to Charlie's leash with his free hand and the cane with his other, he raced forward as hastily as he could manage, wanting to get this part over with, needing to be inside the building more than he imagined he'd feel.

At the entrance, Vargas was right there, sliding his access card through the reader. He opened the door and signaled to the guard on duty. The guard gave a nod and stepped back. Vargas held the door open wide for Seth and Charlie.

No avoiding it now.

Seth made his way inside, going slower than he'd been traversing the sidewalk, but once he passed the threshold, he sped up again and didn't stop, just kept navigating his way farther into the club. He went past the lounge and the bar and then right into the dining room.

Behind him he heard Vargas speaking low with the guard, asking him to move his post outside until further notice.

The first floor of the club was lit brighter than Seth had ever seen it. Was that how it always was when the place was closed? He decided not to ask. He wasn't sure he could form words right then anyway.

Other than the lighting, the club looked similar to every other time he'd been there, minus the crowd of men. He was grateful for the absence of people. Although he didn't want to avoid that situation forever. He needed to step foot inside the place when it was filled with men, the lights low, the music in the bar thumping away. He had to face all that.

And he would soon.

He also had to confront the private room upstairs where he last remembered being inside the club, where he'd gone willingly to meet Prescott. He had no memories of Henderson severely beating him and leaving him on a table in the dining room, but he did recall the instant Prescott had overpowered him and drugged him in the room upstairs.

Vargas came to stand beside him. He took Charlie's leash from him and gave the dog more leeway so he could sniff around a bit. "If you're not ready, we can—"

"No. It's okay." Seth scanned the vast open space around them. The tables in the dining room were cleared of the usual dinnerware and linen tablecloths. A sea of bare wooden surfaces. The starkness seemed strangely comforting. "You don't have to worry so much. Really, I'm okay."

His fear had considerably diminished once he'd stepped inside. He felt oddly calm and detached. His last memories of the Haven's first floor weren't horrible ones.

He gestured at the array of tables. "Which one was it?"

Vargas pointed to an open area between two tables. "There. I found you lying right there."

"On a table?"

"Yes." Vargas kept his focus on the patch of empty carpet, like he was taking in what he'd seen there on another night. "After the cops took what they needed for evidence, I had the table removed."

"You should put a new one there. It looks off-balance like this."

"It's fine the way it is." Vargas whirled around and took a couple of steps away. He came to an abrupt halt as if he realized he still held the end of Charlie's leash and the dog wasn't following him. He kept his back to Seth.

All Seth's planning and worrying, all his hopes that he was doing the right thing for himself, and he hadn't once thought about how hard this would be on Vargas just having him there.

Vargas had been the one to find him, beaten and bloody. He'd been the one to call for the ambulance, and then wait with him for the long minutes it took the EMTs to arrive. He had to talk to the police and describe what he'd found.

And now Seth was making him relive that night.

He wouldn't put Vargas through that for another second. He spun away from the open space where that table had been and headed for the main staircase, stopping at the base of the stairs. "Can I see your apartment?"

Vargas didn't respond. He turned once more to that empty carpeted area between the tables. He had his jaw clenched, his hand tightly clasped around the leash.

"Vargas?"

He snapped his head up. "Yeah. Absolutely." He came forward, leading Charlie. "But let's head up this way." He pointed toward the elevator to the right of the stairs, and together they walked that way.

Vargas stopped before the elevator doors. He didn't say anything right away, didn't make a move to push the call button, just stared at the closed doors as if they'd automatically open at any moment. Maybe he'd installed some sort of motion detector or invisible retina scanner.

Seth leaned on his cane and tipped forward so he could get a good look at Vargas's face. "Is everything okay?"

"I thought the elevator would be better, so you didn't have to traipse up all those stairs, but—"

"What?"

"That's how he took you out of here. In the elevator shaft."

"Oh. It's okay. I don't remember that. Or the tunnels. I woke up in the room where he kept us." An odd wave of relief rushed through Seth at saying the words. He hadn't gone over the specifics of that night with anyone in a while.

"And Henderson?" Vargas asked, his focus locked on the elevator doors.

"I still don't remember any of that. Just him injecting something into my arm before he took me out of the cage. I don't remember him leaving me here."

Vargas looked his way. "You sure about this?"

"I am."

"Okay." He pressed the button on the elevator.

They got off on the second floor and made their way past the main security room. When Seth had first joined the club, he'd heard that Vargas had an apartment there, but no one ever said they'd seen the private rooms or even mentioned they knew where they were located.

As Vargas had explained earlier, a security guard stood in the hall outside the apartment. Two men waited behind him. Vargas pointed to the first man. "Seth, this is Carter. He's the head of my security force here at the club and helps manage the place. If you need anything and I'm not around, you talk to him."

Seth shook Carter's hand. "It's nice to meet you."

"You too." Carter leaned down and let Charlie sniff his hand, then gave him a pat. "And you too, Charlie." Carter was a big guy, tall and broad, with a kind smile that seemed in direct contrast to the serious scowl he'd sported when they first approached.

Vargas said, "Carter will be on duty outside the apartment tonight, then after that it'll be either him or two others. At least for right now." Vargas signaled to the other men, and they came forward. "This is Ian and Neil." Both were similar in height and build to Vargas, but Neil was younger, closer to Seth's age. He smiled at Seth, and the two men offered him a "hello" in greeting.

Vargas gestured to the closed door of the apartment. "Only you and I can enter without showing a photo ID. Everyone else must have their ID and they must be on an approved list. Even if they are with one of us, they have to be on that list ahead of time. So if you want Toby or Dylan or anyone else to be able to visit, let me know, and I'll get them added." He motioned to Carter, and the man opened the apartment door, silently closing it behind them after they stepped inside.

Seth proceeded through the apartment's entranceway and into the living room, scanning the furnishings as he crossed to the center of the room. The place was neat and modern but with a quiet, homey feel to it. The walls were adorned in a collection of framed prints, a mix of old sailing vessels and depictions of early 1900s baseball games. On the coffee table were several cooking magazines, model car catalogs, and a copy of *The Count of Monte Cristo*. A pair of glasses sat perched beside the reading materials. Seth had never seen Vargas wear the glasses.

There was so much he still didn't know about him.

Vargas waited at the threshold between the entranceway and the living room, Charlie at his side. He unhooked the dog's leash, and Charlie barreled into the room, sniffing around like mad, jumping up onto the couch, circling once, twice, then hitting the floor again to inspect more. He rounded Seth again and again.

"Easy does it, Charlie. You're gonna bust up the place."

"He's just excited. No worries." Vargas remained where he was as he added, "Right now it's just the three guards, you, me, Walter, and Tucker on the list for the apartment. No one else can get in here."

Seth wanted to say that was overkill, but instead he said, "I like that."

"Me too." Vargas grew quiet as he studied him. "You doing okay?"

"Yeah. I feel... fine, comfortable."

"Good." There was a pause. Then Vargas drew in a heavy breath like he'd barely been taking in enough oxygen since they'd gotten out of the van.

Seth glanced around the room again. "I like your place."

"I'm glad." A hint of the look Vargas had given Seth right before they'd kissed the previous morning flashed across his face.

Seth wanted nothing more than to forget everything else, walk over there, wrap his arms around Vargas, and pick up where they'd left off. He could still feel the press of Vargas's lips against his, the way Vargas had held on to him, like he never wanted to let go.

If only Seth could make himself take a step forward.

Vargas kept his stare fixed on him. "Seth, what you asked me earlier... I'm not seeing anyone."

"Oh."

"I haven't for a while."

"Okay."

"I haven't been with anyone for the past two years. Not even a one-night stand."

Seth wanted to ask why, but instead he nodded. "Okay."

Vargas held his gaze for another moment, then indicated an open doorway to the right. "The kitchen and dining room are through there." He motioned toward a hallway. "This way are the bedrooms. I'll show you where you'll be staying." He started down the hall, proceeding quickly as if he needed to get away from what he'd admitted in the living room.

Seth followed.

"At the far end are the master bedroom and bath. Across the hall from that is my office. And this is your room." Vargas held the door open with an outstretched arm.

Seth entered the guest bedroom but then abruptly stopped. "Wow." He wasn't sure what he expected, but it wasn't this. The walls were painted a brilliant, beautiful shade of blue, and there were several plants situated around the perimeter like those in the hospital's meditation room. Golden sunlight was filtering in through sheer drapes over the windows. Decorative pillows accented the bed, and an upholstered recliner sat in the corner of the room beside a bookcase. The space was comfortable. Serene. Everything plush and inviting.

Except for one thing.

On the side of the room opposite the bed was a flat steel door built into the wall, a harsh contradiction to the rest of the room's decor. It had a three-prong spindle-style handle on the front. Like some kind of vault. "What's that?"

"That's for you. I had it installed this week." Vargas moved to an access panel on the wall directly beside the steel door. He pulled down the panel's cover, revealing a touch screen interface. He placed his thumb on the device, and it scanned his fingerprint. Then he kept talking as he hit several buttons on the screen. "It runs the length of this room and is six feet deep. I had this outer plaster wall added so the entire wall wouldn't be steel and ruin the aesthetics of the room. This guest room used to be quite a bit bigger."

He punched in a last command. A red light on the panel changed to green, and a series of metallic thumps followed. When they came to a halt, he reached for the handle and rotated until it quit spinning. He yanked. There was a low hissing sound as the door unsealed.

When he had the door all the way open, he spoke again. "The walls, the ceiling, and the floors are all made of reinforced steel, and the entire thing is encased in a bulletproof lining. There's a concealed hinge on the door and an automatic battery backup. It has a dual bolt-locking system, separate ventilation, and it's been stocked with emergency supplies." He turned to face Seth and gestured to the open doorway beside him. "You don't have to use it if you don't want to, but I wanted you to have the option."

Seth gaped at him until his mouth went dry. He blinked and swallowed. "It's a safe room?"

"Yeah."

"You added this for me?"

Vargas looked into the open doorway, then back at Seth. "Yeah. I wanted you to feel safe here."

Chapter Sixteen

Vargas installed a safe room for him. Talk about intense.

Seth couldn't wrap his head around what that implied about Vargas's motives—or his feelings for him—and he wasn't sure he wanted to give either of those questions thought right then.

"You don't like it?" Vargas was studying him with concern.

"No, that's not—" Seth stopped and tried again. "It must've cost a fortune."

"It wasn't bad." Vargas gestured into the opening. "Take a look if you want."

Seth approached the doorway and peeked inside. From what Vargas had said, the entire interior space was made of steel, but the floor of the narrow room was carpeted and the walls had been covered in drywall and painted like any normal room. Two of the walls featured upholstered bench-style seats that connected in one corner to form an L-shaped seating area. Each bench was lined with plush cushions, blankets, and colorful throw pillows. Seth pictured himself curled up there with a book for a couple of hours.

On the interior wall closest to the bedroom stood a bookcase filled with books. He moved into the safe room and got a better view of the titles on the shelves.

Vargas waited in the doorway and gestured to a second computer panel that hung on the inside wall near the open door. "I can show you how these work. I'll input your thumbprint and give you the access code. Only the two of us and Carter will ever be able to open this door." Then he motioned to a storage cabinet positioned along the wall beside the bookcase. "In there are the emergency supplies." He hesitated as if he didn't know what else to say. His next words poured out in a rush. "You can come in here anytime. Leave the door open or shut. Use it for any reason. Even if you just want some time to yourself to read or whatever." He indicated the bookcase. "I got ones by authors I know you like."

"It's…" Seth took another look around the room. "This is…"

"What?" There was a nervous hitch in that one word.

Seth turned back to him. "It's perfect."

"The books or—"

"All of it. Thank you."

The tense expression on Vargas's face eased. "You're welcome." He held Seth's gaze for another few seconds, then went to stand at the foot of the bed, his back to the safe room door. "If there's anything else you need, you let me know."

"I will." Seth stepped into the bedroom. "Can I see the rest of the place?"

"Sure." Vargas led him down the hall, pointing out a second smaller guest room and then the master bedroom. Vargas's room was similar to the others but was far less plush and colorful. Tidy. Stark. No extra pillows on the bed, no plants, no trinkets on the dresser or the nightstands. A simple room with a hardwood floor, a black and white bedspread, and a similarly colorless abstract print hanging over the bed.

On one of the nightstands was another pair of reading glasses. They sat perched on a paperback copy of *Under the Dome* by Stephen King. Seth hadn't read that one, but he knew it had to do with an entire town being trapped inside an inescapable, invisible dome. The paperback was tattered like it had been read many times over.

"I'm not in here much," Vargas said softly from behind him as if offering an explanation for something.

Seth pictured sitting on the bed beside Vargas, both of them leaning back against the headboard like they'd done the other night at his place. Then he imagined them doing far more than they had that night, everything he'd been dreaming about. The kissing, the touching, the intimate whispered words, the groans and pleading whimpers pouring out of him that he hadn't let anyone hear in such a long time. Their clothes off, Vargas's hands and lips and tongue all over him, fingers stroking up the inside of his thighs, brushing over the flesh of his ass, dipping in between his ass cheeks. His breath caught on that last vision as if he'd actually felt the touch.

Vargas approached behind him. "You okay?"

Seth cleared his throat. "Sure."

Vargas didn't press, but he gave Seth a minute, then continued the tour. The last room was his private office.

A wooden desk sat in the middle of the room, covered in a mass of papers and file folders, and beside it was a rolling cart stacked with several boxes containing additional files. A couch was pushed up against one wall. It held a blanket and pillow, both haphazardly tossed in the corner. Did he crash here some nights?

The wall perpendicular to the desk featured a window with curtains on each side that were pulled back. Seth moved in closer and found himself looking out over the first floor of the empty club. From this angle the space appeared smaller, unintimidating, like an architectural model of the building's interior. He was uncomfortable with that assessment and wasn't sure why.

He turned back to the rest of the office. The wall opposite the desk was covered floor to ceiling in a series of wall-mounted shelves, each shelf lined with numerous model cars, boats, and planes. Everything from steam-powered vessels to modern sports cars. There were commercial airplanes, sailboats, clipper ships, destroyers, U-boats, helicopters, tanks, and luxury cars. At least a dozen models were on display on each shelf.

"Did you make all these?"

"Yep." Vargas went to stand before the shelves. He repositioned a replica of a Ford Model T, moving it a fraction of an inch to the right. His fingers lingered on the front fender of the car as if in reverence. "My mom and I started working on them together when I was a kid."

Seth felt like he was getting insight into Vargas's personal life in a way he never had before. This office was Vargas's private refuge, where he told Seth he now worked most days—and maybe where he slept. Where he spent time thinking, planning, and regretting.

Seth spotted an unassembled racing yacht in its sealed box on the bottom shelf near the corner of the room. Was that his next project? How long had it been sitting there waiting for him?

"It's so neat that you made all these."

"My dad was really into working on model boats before he died. I think that's why Mom started the first one with me. As sort of a tribute to him. We had a good time with it, so we kept building them. I still do. I work on maybe half a dozen a year." He pointed to a car at the far end of the shelf near the window. It was a red and white 1967 Mustang Shelby GT500. "That's the last one I did."

Something about the way he said the word *last* bothered Seth. "When did you finish it?"

"I don't know. Two years ago, I guess."

Just as Seth had feared. He was about to press for more when Vargas spoke again.

"It's remote controlled."

"It actually works?"

"Yeah, it's the only one that's like that. It's electric, runs off batteries. The motor came with the kit." Vargas lifted the car, turned on a switch at the bottom, and set the vehicle on the floor. He retrieved a handheld controller from the shelf and turned that on too. Then he pulled the trigger on the remote, and the car lurched forward.

"That's so cool."

"You wanna try it?"

"You sure?"

He handed over the controller. "Go for it."

Seth drew back the trigger the way he'd seen Vargas do it, and the car took off. Using the steering wheel on the remote, he got a feel for the maneuverability before taking it any faster. Then he raced the car around the room, spinning it in circles. He nearly crashed it half a dozen times, laughing with each near miss.

"I suck at this, but man, it's awesome." He had no idea driving something that small, that fast could be such a rush.

"You never had anything like this as a kid?"

Seth shook his head as he jerked the controller's wheel left, then right. "The train set I had barely moved compared to this." He sped the Mustang up, circling it around one wooden leg of the desk, then the next. On the last turn, the car hit the desk and tipped onto two wheels for a second, then slammed back onto all four. "Sorry." He eased up.

"It's fine." Vargas flipped a hand through the air. "Go to town."

Seth laughed more as he hit the accelerator again. Out of the corner of his eye, he saw Vargas lean back against the edge of the desk, arms folded, a grin on his lips, his complete focus on Seth, not the remote-controlled car.

Seth slowed the vehicle, worrying his bottom lip as he watched the car return to him. How childish and stupid did he look right then? And here he'd been trying to figure out how to make himself seem sexier.

Once the car came to a complete stop, he switched it off and returned the controller and the car to the shelf. He kept his back to Vargas for a few seconds more before he turned around.

Maybe it didn't matter how big of a dork he was. What with the way Vargas was taking in the sight of him. The grin was gone, replaced by a penetrating look that could only be described as pure longing.

Seth stared him down in return, mentally scrambling for what to do next, how to make a move, how to get them back to where they'd been headed the morning before when Dylan had interrupted them.

But something inside Seth wouldn't let him speak. Not about that.

He didn't want to examine why. He gestured to the window and moved in closer. "It's so neat that you can see into the club from here." The first floor was still brightly lit with no one around. "So, do you sit up here and check out which guys are hooking up?"

Vargas snorted out a brief laugh. "Sometimes." He was still leaning with his ass against the desk. Then he got up and moved in behind him. "Let me close those curtains."

"No, it's okay." Seth studied the empty dining room and the bar. All at once he was back to the first night he'd ever come to the club. He'd felt so free and alive. God, he wished he could walk down there the next time the place was open, and be that man again. "I used to like it when I came here and people would stare at me. I liked the attention. When I was growing up, I was always the freak kid in school. All that time, and then later when I was living on the streets, I just tried to blend in, tried not to stand out. Then when I got my membership here, it felt so liberating, like I could finally be myself. I could finally..." He wasn't sure what word he was looking for.

"Shine."

He turned to look up at Vargas. "I hate that I can't stop being afraid of someone noticing me now. I never thought I'd feel that way again. Never thought I'd be so scared—" He shook his head. He hated those words, hated that he still felt that way after all this time, hated that he'd admitted it aloud. He searched the room for anything else he could focus on.

He settled on a baseball bat that hung prominently behind the desk. "Did you used to play?"

Vargas glanced over his shoulder at the bat. "In college."

"Really?"

"Find that hard to believe?"

"No. When I first met you, I wondered if you played sports."

"What else did you wonder about me?"

"Nothing I'm going to tell you."

"Oh, really?" The grin was back. "I'm sure I could get you to spill."

Yeah, he could. Vargas had no idea the power he had over him. An odd nervousness Seth never had around Vargas overcame him. He crossed the room and explored more of the collection of ships and vehicles.

Vargas moved in alongside him. "This one is my favorite." He indicated a long cargo-hauling ship. "It's a lake freighter. The SS *Edmund Fitzgerald*. She's a plain ship—or boat as these freighters are called—but she has an interesting story. You ever heard it?"

"I don't think so."

"She sank during a storm on Lake Superior in 1975. The entire crew was lost. They found her submerged below 530 feet of water, only seventeen miles from safe harbor. The hull was broke completely in half. They never recovered a single body."

"That's awful."

"Everyone always talks about the horrendous stories of men trapped on the USS *Arizona*. Or the *Titanic*, such a grand ship going down on her maiden voyage and the massive loss of life, but we know why those sank. With the *Fitzgerald*, there are all these theories on why she went down, but no one knows for sure what happened. There were no witnesses."

"Maybe there's no reason, no explanation."

"There usually is one. Something or someone to blame."

"But the why doesn't always matter, does it? The horrible thing already happened."

"Maybe. Or maybe if we knew why, we could keep it from ever happening again." Vargas kept his focus on the replica of the massive boat, and the silence stretched on between them.

There was so much Seth wanted to say. He longed to make things better for Vargas but had no idea what would work, what would get him to stop blaming himself.

Vargas suddenly rotated to face him as if he desperately needed to get a look at Seth, like that was all that would keep the dark thoughts at bay. Or maybe would keep them from fading away. Then he moved, crossing the room in a quick stride.

Seth let it go. For now.

Vargas had stopped near the cart overflowing with cardboard file boxes.

Seth approached. "What's all this?"

"The club's financial records. I've gone back through a couple of months, but so far everything's checked out. I just can't figure it out, can't understand what he's not telling me." He sighed. "I don't know. Maybe I'm losing my mind."

"You're not. Now that I'm here, I can take a look."

"You really don't have to."

"I want to. Let me do something for you for a change."

Vargas seemed to be considering that. "All right." He pointed a finger at Seth. "But you get your own work done first before you start on any of this."

"Deal." Seth moved around the desk, propped his cane against it, and took a seat in the office chair. "Is this everything? Are there electronic files on your computer I can access? An accounting program?"

"Yeah. Here's the log-in info." Vargas grabbed a pen and jotted down the information on a notepad.

Seth opened the top file folder on the closest stack.

"You don't have to do this now."

"Why not? I have my work done for today." He grinned up at him and then reached for a receipt in the folder.

Vargas laid a hand on Seth's. "Not on your first night, all right? Why don't we have some dinner?"

"Sure." He returned the folder and got up.

Vargas didn't move from where he blocked Seth's path around the desk. He gave him a long look. "Seth, I know it's hard for you to imagine right now, but you're going to feel less afraid. You're going to feel safe again. And…" He caught Seth's chin in his hand and tipped his head back so they were eye to eye. "You still shine. You may not feel it. You may think you're hiding it beneath those baggy clothes and the wheelchair, but it's still there." He ran the pad of his thumb over Seth's cheek. "I see it in your eyes every time I look at you."

Seth drew in a sharp breath. He wanted to grab hold of Vargas and lay the best damn kiss on him he could manage.

Before he could make a move, or even decide for sure that he should try, Vargas dropped his hand and rounded the desk. With his back to Seth, he stood stiff and straight, like he battled some inner war. He threaded an unsteady hand through his hair. "I'm going to have security bring up your bags so you can get settled in while I fix us something to eat." He snatched the phone off his desk and made a call to the security room. After he hung up, he offered Seth a tentative smile. "How about one of your favorites for dinner? Tacos?"

"Sure."

"We'll talk more while we eat, all right?" The way Vargas said the words, it was like there was something particular on his mind. Or maybe something he hoped Seth would bring up.

Then with haste, Vargas rushed out into the hall.

Seth gaped after him, trying to figure out why Vargas was working so hard to avoid a repeat of their kiss. Was he afraid he'd hurt Seth? Either emotionally or physically? Was he afraid Seth would get too attached?

Or maybe…

Was Vargas scared that whatever would happen between them

would lead to heartache for himself? Had Dylan been right? Was this about more than sex for Vargas?

Hope welled inside Seth with such force that, for the first time since he'd had the idea to stay with Vargas, he realized he hadn't come close to understanding how much he could get hurt.

* * * * *

Vargas had the majority of the food ready and was finishing chopping the tomatoes and other vegetables by the time he heard Seth coming down the hall.

At the kitchen doorway, Seth hung back, leaning his weight on his cane.

Vargas asked, "All unpacked?"

"Yeah."

"Dinner will be ready in just a few minutes."

Seth came forward. "I'll set the table."

While Seth quietly moved around the room, Vargas finished the meal prep, pointing Seth to the cabinets that held the plates and glasses, then the drawer with the silverware. Seth's unsteady stop and start movements seemed less pronounced the longer he was in the apartment. He also favored his left side far less.

The relative silence lingered as they ate, each offering a few words here and there, but for the first time in two years, the quiet between them felt awkward and uncomfortable.

And Vargas hated that.

As Seth set his napkin beside his cleared plate, Vargas fished out the key card from his wallet. He slid it across the table. "This is for you. It opens all the doors in the Haven and the ones here at the apartment. The hallway outside leads to a set of stairs. At the base is a door that goes out into the back parking lot, so you never have to walk through the club if you don't want to."

Seth nodded.

"You got your phone with you?"

He pulled his phone from his pocket and handed it over.

"This is the number for the main security office." When Vargas had the number saved, he gave the phone back and added, "Like I said before, if you need anything and I'm not here, you talk to Carter."

"Okay, thanks." Seth slipped the key card into his back pocket. "Does your accountant ever come to the club?"

It took Vargas a second to adjust to the shift in conversation. "He usually stops in a few times a week. He's got an office downstairs.

Not that he needs to be here that much, but it gives him a reason to come by sometimes, check out who's here."

"He's gay?"

"Yeah."

"Is everyone who works here?"

Vargas laughed. Then he sat back and considered that for a minute. "Pretty much. Tucker doesn't actually work here, but he's straight."

Seth seemed to be thinking that over. "When did you know for sure?"

"About Tucker?"

"About yourself. That you were gay."

"That day by the pool with my mom's neighbor."

Seth leaned forward and planted his elbows on the table, propping his chin in one hand. "Did you have a hunch before then?"

"I guess I kept trying to tell myself all the thoughts I'd been having about men were just normal guy stuff. That noticing another guy was just me wanting to be like him, admiring his body and his life, that it wasn't about attraction. But once I had a taste, once I made that guy come with my mouth, there was no going back."

Seth grinned. "It's kind of powerful."

"Was it like that for you?"

"Yeah."

"Who was he?"

"A guy who lived down the street from me during my freshman year of high school. One day after school, we both missed the bus home and had to wait until someone could come get us. We ended up hanging out in this alcove at the back of the building near the band room. We talked shit for a while, shared a cigarette. My first one. My first experience in a lot of ways, I guess. He was two years older and started going on about how much it sucked to be hard up all the time and not have a girlfriend."

Vargas snorted out a laugh. "Smooth."

"Yeah. It was his idea to jerk off at the same time. He was also the one who touched me first, but I was the one who turned it into a blowjob."

"Did it freak you out how much you liked it?"

Seth met his stare. "No." His gaze shifted to the arm Vargas had draped across the empty chair beside him. "It did him, though. He wouldn't talk to me, wouldn't even look my way on the bus. I made myself a promise after that day. I'd never date a guy who thought he was straight or wasn't out."

Vargas wondered if that was the reason Seth had joined the club? Especially with his limited financial means. Walter had said once that it had something to do with Seth feeling safe there. The shittiest irony of all ironies.

The silence between them was back.

Vargas cleared the plates and silverware from the table and began loading the dishwasher. He heard Seth approach behind him.

"Vargas... I'm sorry if this is weird."

"If what is weird?"

"Having me here in your space."

Vargas closed the dishwasher door. He snatched a towel off the counter and turned to Seth. "It's not weird at all."

Seth was intently watching him work the towel between his hands as he asked, "Have you ever lived with someone?"

"No." Vargas returned the towel to the counter. "Came close once, but it ended before we got that far."

"Did he end it, or did you?"

"It was me."

"Why?"

"I didn't love him. I cared about him, but I knew that wasn't enough."

"Have you ever been in love?"

He hesitated. "Real love? Only once."

"Do you still think about him?"

"All the time."

Seth nodded as if that confirmed something for him. "Do you still see him?"

"Yeah. A lot."

"Then maybe you guys could try again someday. Maybe you could work it out."

Vargas took a step forward, and they spoke at the same time.

"Seth—"

"Could you—"

He gestured for Seth to go ahead.

"Could you show me how the control panel for the safe room works?"

At first Vargas couldn't find his voice. He didn't want to push too hard, didn't want to scare Seth. He had to trust his gut when it came to him. Like he'd always done. He replied simply with, "Sure."

A minute later they stood at the exterior panel situated on the wall of the guest room, Vargas explaining the various functions on the screen. Seth concentrated on each word as if he'd be tested on it later. Or maybe that serious expression was about something else.

Seth gave a try at opening and shutting the door, then locking it, and when he finished, he moved to sit on the foot of the bed, looking tired and worn out.

"You hurting?"

"No. Which is weird. All the walking with the cane... I thought I'd need a pain pill by now, but I feel pretty good. Just tired."

"Want to turn in early?"

"I might just read for a bit."

"All right. I'll leave you to it." Vargas started for the door.

"Vargas?"

He halted in the doorway.

"Thanks for letting me stay here, for the safe room, for everything. I couldn't have faced this without you."

"You're welcome. I'll always be here for you. Always. Anything you need." He almost left, but he stopped short again, his hand on the doorjamb, practically squeezing the wood trim into splinters to keep from marching over there and climbing into the bed with Seth. Not to start something physical, but just to be near him. "I'm glad you're here, Seth. And not just because I want to help you." He looked to him again. "But because I want you here with me. I want to be with you."

Seth's eyes widened. His lips parted. It took him a moment to respond. "I'm really glad I came."

Chapter Seventeen

Seth hit the save button on the patient file he'd been editing and stretched his arms overhead. Working on his laptop at Vargas's kitchen table for the past two hours, his back was beginning to protest. He'd been scheduled for a light day of paperwork, but it had taken him longer than he expected to finish entering the billing forms and complete the insurance claims he needed to get done. Same thing as the day before.

Actually, same thing as every day that week.

He'd just been so unfocused since the night a week ago when he'd begun staying with Vargas. His mind kept wandering, reliving that morning in his bed at his apartment when they'd kissed, trying to figure out how to bring it up with Vargas, what to say, what to do. They hadn't talked about it since, or about what Vargas had said Seth's first night there about wanting to be with him, and Seth was terrified of hoping for anything more.

Throughout the week, they'd gotten into a comfortable routine. Vargas would work on club business in his office, and Seth would spend the day on his laptop in the living room or the kitchen or even on the couch in the office with Vargas. They took breaks for lunch and an afternoon snack and then later to drive to Seth's PT appointment. Seth had made a point of not scheduling any sessions with Dr. Arteaga for the week. He hadn't wanted to lie to her about where he was staying or what was going on in his life right then. He'd simply told her it wouldn't work out with his schedule.

Each night, after he and Vargas ate dinner together, they'd sit on the couch and watch TV. They were in the process of working their way through the first season of *Queer as Folk*. That had been Seth's brilliant idea, hoping the erotically-charged show would set the mood for something to happen between them. But once they began the first episode, he realized what a shitty idea that had been. He sat there hard as hell the entire time while Vargas's attention was locked on the TV screen.

Just thinking about it had Seth shifting in the kitchen chair for reasons other than the ache in his back.

He glanced at the clock on his laptop. Four-thirty in the afternoon. He had time before he'd need to figure out what to make himself for dinner.

Earlier that morning, Vargas had said he had several deliveries to oversee and other club-related tasks he personally needed to take care of, so for the first time that week he spent the day in his other office downstairs in the club. Before he'd left, though, he repeatedly asked Seth if he would be okay alone in the apartment. Seth had to insist multiple times that he felt comfortable enough to stay there on his own for a few hours. Then after each of the deliveries, Vargas had returned to check in with him and take Charlie out for a walk, once staying long enough to fix them grilled sandwiches and bowls of tomato and basil soup for lunch. How he made such a simple dish taste so amazing was beyond Seth. As they had their lunch, Vargas said he had several meetings he couldn't miss and would be gone until later in the evening.

Plenty of time for Seth to get started with what he'd been dying to dig into: reviewing the club's financial records. He gripped his cane and headed down the hall toward Vargas's office.

Planning to sit at the desk to work, he gathered the laptop and a few of the files from the cart, and stacked everything on the desk. He stepped around to sit in the office chair but drew up short. The curtains were closed on the window that overlooked the club. Same as they'd been all week, except for that first day.

Without giving too much thought to the fact that he was about to face the Haven by himself for the first time, he went to the window. He leaned his cane against the wall. Raising both arms, he threw back the curtains. As was typical for most weekdays, the club hadn't opened yet, but there were several servers and bartenders preparing for the dinner hour. It felt different seeing the club with some people in it. More tangible, more real.

But he wasn't panicking. He felt calm and unaffected by it.

He kept watching as a young man with blond hair who reminded him of Aaron came into view. The guy had an unassuming way about him as he moved around the dining room, positioning napkins and silverware at each place setting. Yet as Seth watched the man smile at a coworker strolling by, he saw there was a flirtatious spark hidden underneath that meek veneer. Was that what Aaron was like before?

The thought saddened him. Not just for Aaron, but for himself. He was definitely different. He couldn't even attempt another kiss with Vargas, let alone more.

He snatched his cane and spun away from the window. He went to sit at the desk and got started on the files. A half hour into it, the doorbell rang.

With the cane at his side, he made his way through the apartment and opened the door. Ian, the guard on duty, stood there blocking the entrance.

Ian gave a nod to Seth. "Good evening, Mr. Fisher. You have a visitor." The top of a head popped up over Ian's shoulder as Dylan got on his toes for a peek. "He's on the list and has already been cleared."

"Thanks." Seth stepped back from the door, but Ian didn't move to let Dylan enter.

"I'd like to hear you say verbally that it's okay for him to come inside."

"Oh. Yeah, sure, he can come in."

Ian still didn't move. "You don't have to say that just because he's standing right here. You tell me you don't want to see someone, and I'll keep them out. No questions asked."

"I appreciate that, but it's okay. I want to see Dylan."

"All right." Ian moved aside. His thoughtfulness had Seth feeling bad about his initial response to the man and his duties.

At first having a guard outside the door all day had weirded Seth out, and he wasn't sure if that was because it was a new experience for him or if it was something else. If he had to guess, it was Ian and Neil that bothered him. They were always nice to him, but there was something about both men that put Seth on edge. He found the contradiction jarring. He thought about mentioning it to Vargas, but he didn't want to make a big deal out of a reaction that wasn't based on anything real.

Vargas trusted them. Which meant Seth could do the same. He had to learn how to trust people again.

Dylan rounded Ian to enter the apartment. As soon as Seth had the door closed, Dylan's jaw dropped. "Wow. I thought I was going to have to give that guy a blood sample to get in here."

Seth laughed it off. "It's not that bad. Vargas just likes to be thorough."

"That's because he's one paranoid man." Dylan meandered farther into the apartment and surveyed the living room. "So, this is where he lives?"

"Yep." Seth sat on the couch, leaning his cane against the cushion beside him.

Dylan gave the space a last scrutiny. "Very tidy. And sparse." He came to the couch and plopped down. "Doesn't he ever let loose? Get a little crazy?"

Seth laughed again, but he couldn't keep the mental images of their kisses at bay, couldn't refrain from recalling the way Vargas had tugged him closer, his hands wandering all over him like there wasn't a part of Seth he didn't want to touch, his body shifting against him with both incredible power and remarkable restraint.

Dylan leaned forward and snapped his fingers in front of Seth's face. "Helloooo."

"What?"

"Where'd you go?"

"Nowhere."

"Sure." Dylan grinned at him. "So what's it been like staying here?"

"It's nice."

"Nice?" He sat back and scrutinized Seth. "So the sex with Vargas is... nice?"

"We haven't..." Seth glanced away and shook his head.

"Not yet, huh?"

"I'm not sure he wants—"

"You can't tell me you don't see it, Seth. He wants you."

"Wants me? Yeah, I guess."

Dylan studied him again. Without Seth offering more, it was clear Dylan got what he really wanted with Vargas, what Seth could barely admit to himself, and how scared he was that it wouldn't work out.

"Okay." Dylan patted Seth's thigh. "We don't have to talk about it." He got off the couch and wandered around the living room. "Where are you sleeping?"

"One of the guest rooms."

"Can I see it?"

"Sure." Seth got up and led Dylan down the hall to his room.

Dylan stepped inside. "Pretty cool digs." He went to stand before the steel door of the safe room. He pointed at it. "Is this what I think it is?"

"Yeah."

"A panic room?"

"It's called a safe room."

"I take it that's new?"

Seth went to sit at the foot of the bed facing the safe room door. "It is."

"Because of you staying here?"

He nodded. "It's really neat, actually. Fancier inside than you'd think. He stocked it with books and other stuff and there's a bench with pillows. Oh, and I guess it's bulletproof."

Dylan moved closer to the metal door. He gave the surface a rap with his knuckles as if he had to touch it to see if it was really made of steel. "You're so wrong, man." He looked back at Seth. "It'll never be just about sex for him."

"He just wants me to feel safe."

"He wants all of us to feel safe, but he's not spending a shit-ton of money to buy the rest of us expensive-ass, steel-encased, bulletproof safe rooms."

Seth said nothing to that.

Dylan came forward and sat beside him. "I know I'm right. He has serious feelings for you. But I also think you're the one who's going to need to make the first move. I don't think he'll do it. Not now. Not here. You should ask him what he's feeling. And you need to tell him what you're feeling. Or else you're always going to wonder what could've happened between you two."

"I don't know if I can do that."

"You can do anything, Seth."

He scoffed. That description fit Dylan far more than him. He'd seen Dylan do the unimaginable. The thing was, though, he used to feel that way about himself.

Dylan sighed in frustration, but he dropped the conversation anyway. They chatted for the next half hour about what Dylan had been up to and the recent movie-night marathon he'd had with Toby, Aaron, and Ryder.

After they said goodbye and Dylan was gone, Seth returned to the office and got back to work, needing to do anything other than think about what Dylan had said. He went through the file folders, comparing the figures on each bill to what had been entered into the software, marking each receipt when he finished reviewing it.

Halfway through the last pile of folders on the desk, his pen ran out. He searched the desktop for another but found nothing to write with. He opened the top desk drawer. There were loads of sticky notes but no pens. He moved on to the right-hand side of the desk. In the tall bottom drawer sat a stack of books and loose-leaf printed pages. He went to close the drawer, but then the title of the top book caught his eye. *When the Person You Love is a Survivor of Rape.*

He read the title several more times, staring at each word in turn until all he saw was the word *love*.

He reached for the stack and pulled everything out. There were half a dozen books and more printed articles from websites covering topics like PTSD, anxiety, victims of kidnapping and abduction, rape survivors, male victims of sexual assault, and various therapies for treatment. He leafed through them, reading each title. Several stood out:

When Your Significant Other Has PTSD.
How to Support Your Loved One During Therapy.
How Sexual Assault Affects Relationships and Sex.
Rebuilding Intimacy with a Sexual Assault Survivor.
How to Help Your Partner Heal.

Seth opened one of the books. Vargas had dog-eared numerous pages, each page marked with highlighted text and handwritten notes in the margin. Most of the marked sections were about how to listen when the victim wanted to talk, what to do when they didn't, how to offer other types of support, and why it was important not to push too hard. Each of the suggestions could've been describing Vargas and his actions and reactions over the past two years.

Seth continued flipping through pages until he arrived at a section specifically about physical interactions. He read the passages Vargas had highlighted. They mentioned how someone suffering from PTSD after a physical assault may feel on guard or anxious or worried much of the time, and that they may not be able to completely relax or feel at ease enough to be intimate with anyone.

He moved on to another section Vargas had marked.

This one addressed how the victim may feel fine for a long time, years even. Then without warning, when they are touched, it might trigger a fight-or-flight response or cause them to completely freeze up. The article gave suggestions on being patient and not taking the victim's actions, decisions, or reactions personally. The partner should instead learn how to be gentle, how to avoid the triggers and create a safe and loving environment.

Another passage talked about how the survivor may have difficulty lying under their partner. It suggested being accommodating to the positions that allow them to feel safe, helping them find ways to be intimate that won't trigger memories of the abuse, and giving them lots of chances to say that something doesn't feel good. The article went on to point out that all those actions would allow the survivor to see that their partner is concerned and wants to know how to be with them in ways that allow them to relax and enjoy the experience.

Seth quit reading and sat back. How long ago had Vargas read those books and articles? How long had he been hoping they'd be together like that one day?

Did he still want him? Did he love him?

Seth bit at his thumbnail. Did he really need to ask those questions? Hadn't Vargas already told him with the way he cared about him, the way he'd always been there to listen, the way he touched him and kissed him? The way he'd been avoiding taking it any further because he most likely didn't think Seth was ready?

Dylan's words came back to him.

"He has serious feelings for you."

Chapter Eighteen

"I don't get it. Why'd you come here?" Tyrell Brooks practically whispered the words, but they still echoed off the walls of the empty concrete room in a way that clearly made the man uncomfortable. He didn't want anyone to overhear what they were discussing.

Vargas sat back in the metal folding chair and breathed deep, summoning the last of his patience.

Seated at a table in the cafeteria-style dining area of Fire Station 14, the two men stared each other down. The scent of cornbread baking and the faint aroma of simmering chili filled the air. Dinner would be up soon, and the dining room would become packed with the rest of the firefighters on duty. They didn't have long to finish their conversation in private.

Did it matter? Vargas could already tell this was going to be another lost cause.

He didn't need to be an ass about it, though. It wasn't this guy's fault he didn't have the right answers.

Brooks spoke again. "Like I told you last time we talked, I didn't know him well."

"You were his friend. He didn't have many of those."

"Jesus!" Brooks shot a look at the open doorway leading into the hall. "We were *not* friends. We worked together, man. That's it. I was just the one he shot the shit with the most."

"Okay. But at some point, he must've told you a story or an anecdote, something about a friend, a family member, someone he cared for."

"No." Brooks nervously glanced again at the doorway as several of his colleagues passed by. "It wasn't like that."

When the fire chief had first mentioned that Brooks and Prescott had been friends, Vargas thought Brooks might be the one helping Prescott with the attorney, but after initially meeting the man, he'd ruled that out. It was clear what Prescott had done disgusted Brooks.

Vargas sat forward, propping his elbows on the table. "Listen, I'm not judging you in any way. He was talented at hiding who he really was. I get that. But I need to know who might be helping him."

Brooks fidgeted in his seat for several breaths, then stilled. "I want to help you out. I really do. I just don't know anything. He did his job well, never complained about the overtime or the pay or any of that shit. He was a quiet guy, kept to himself a lot."

The same thing everyone said about Prescott.

Vargas had talked to his parents, his extended family, childhood friends—although there weren't many of those, despite his fancy boarding-school upbringing—and several others who'd worked with him over the years. He'd searched for friends from Prescott's adult life but hadn't found a single one other than the man sitting across from him.

Brooks added, "I'm telling you, I don't know anything. If I did, I'd say something. I would."

"I believe you."

Brook's eyebrows drew together in doubt. He scrutinized Vargas for a long breath, then leaned forward and gestured at him. "Let me ask you this. After everything he did, what makes you think anyone in the world would actually help that man?"

"Someone is."

"Are they? Really?"

Vargas stood. "Yes." He had to believe there was someone responsible and that whoever that was could be stopped. He thanked Tyrell Brooks for his time, but as he walked to his SUV, Vargas couldn't keep from wondering if there was something to what Brooks had said.

Maybe he'd never find someone who'd be willing to put themselves on the line for Prescott because that person didn't exist.

Maybe this wasn't about anyone *helping* Prescott at all.

Maybe it was about something else entirely.

Well, no matter what, he was going to figure it out. He was going to keep Seth and the others safe. Even if it cost him his last dime.

Even if it cost him the club.

* * * * *

It was nearly midnight by the time Vargas entered the apartment. The place was dark and quiet, and he mentally cursed himself for being gone so long. He'd had a number of issues to deal with in the club after his meeting with Brooks, and in the process, he ended up leaving Seth alone far longer than he'd intended.

Maybe that was a good thing. Maybe it gave Seth time to think and feel whatever he needed to go through. Wasn't that the reason he'd come to stay with him?

Down the dark hallway, Vargas found the guest room door shut. Every night of the previous week Seth had fallen asleep by eleven, sometimes while they were on the couch watching TV, so he'd likely gone to bed already.

Still, Vargas couldn't help but check in on him. He started to give a soft knock but broke off when he spotted light pouring out from his partially open office door at the end of the hall. He approached and pushed the door in the rest of the way.

Seth sat on the floor in front of the desk. He wore flannel pajama pants and a long-sleeve white T-shirt. File folders and papers were stacked in piles on the hardwood floor all around him, and Vargas's laptop computer sat perched on his lap. Seth's total focus was on the screen of the laptop. He looked determined and completely engrossed in whatever he was reading. He hadn't heard Vargas approach.

Vargas undid his tie and the top two buttons on his shirt as he leaned against the doorjamb. "Hey."

Seth glanced up and grinned at him. "Hey." There was something different about the look on his face. Something much more relaxed and serene and... hopeful.

"What are you working on?"

"Figuring stuff out." He gestured for Vargas to come closer.

Vargas traversed the room, weaving in and out of the stacks of papers with each step. He ditched his tie on the desk and crouched next to Seth. "Isn't your back hurting sitting on the floor like this?"

"It actually feels much better this way." He flipped a hand over his shoulder at the desk behind him. "It was really aching sitting in your fancy desk chair." He then gestured at the papers all around them. "I also needed more space." He smiled again, excitement radiating off him.

Vargas couldn't help but grin back. He stretched his legs out and sat on the floor beside him. "You're understanding this mess?"

"Oh, yeah. The accounting is pretty straight forward. I haven't found any discrepancies yet, but I'm really just getting started organizing everything."

"You're enjoying yourself?"

"I am. It's like a puzzle. I know the answer's here. I just have to find it. Plus it's interesting seeing how the financial side of the club works."

"Yeah?"

"I never really thought about all the business stuff you have to take care of. The supplies, the inventory, the insurance, the vendors you work with. I just wish I could figure out what I'm missing."

"It's late." Vargas tilted his head toward the hallway. "Maybe if you get some sleep, the problem will jump out at you tomorrow."

"Maybe," Seth said, but he didn't make a move to get up. Instead he refocused on the computer screen before him. "I did learn a few helpful things so far. About some of your expenses. It explains why you're not making the money you used to."

Fuck. Vargas knew exactly what expenses Seth was referring to. He should've considered that when he'd given him carte blanche access to his records. Seth had just been so interested and excited to help. There'd been no way Vargas could tell him no.

Seth hesitated. "You're spending way more than you ever did on security. You have too many guards on duty, especially when the club is closed. Then there's Tucker's men following Lauber." He paused. "And these other security expenses through an outside firm."

Vargas jerked his head up. "Those have to stay."

"What are you paying them for?"

"It's just an extra layer of security that I didn't want to use my regular staff for."

"You already have this placed locked down like it's a bank. It's overkill."

Vargas tipped his head back to the desk behind him and sighed. "You shouldn't be up so late working on this."

Seth didn't respond with anything right away, and Vargas couldn't bring himself to look at him until Seth eventually spoke. "I guess I was too excited to sleep."

"About what? Going over my financial records?"

"Not just that." Seth focused his attention on the open doorway across the room. "I've been here for a week already, and I haven't fallen apart." A smile spread across his lips. "I'm doing okay."

"Yeah, you are." Vargas took in the look of pride on Seth's face. He cupped his chin and turned his head so they were eye to eye. "You're doing great."

Seth studied him as if he were hoping to find the answer to a question he hadn't asked yet. Then his gaze dropped to Vargas's mouth while he sucked his own bottom lip in between his teeth. The two of them were close, mere inches from what they'd done the week before at Seth's apartment.

And damn, Vargas wanted it again. He wanted Seth, plain and simple.

He wanted the sweet, passionate lovemaking of two people emotionally connected. He wanted to kiss and stroke and love on him and remind Seth of all the beautiful ways one man could touch another.

But he couldn't fool himself. He also wanted to fuck Seth, a primal pounding of sweaty male bodies, grinding and thrusting until they both collapsed in that blissful release.

A reminder that he had to think this through with his mind, not with any other part of him.

Seth broke the silence, his voice wavering at first, then growing stronger. "I meant what I said the other night. I'm glad I came to stay here."

"Me too."

"Then can I ask you a question?"

"Sure."

"You'll tell me the truth?"

"Absolutely."

Seth didn't speak again right away, just looked over his shoulder to the desk behind him. When his head came back around, he said, "The other day, in my bedroom, did you really want to kiss me?"

"I did."

He nodded slowly as if he was processing that. "Do you want to kiss me right now?"

"Yeah, I do." Vargas tried to keep from saying more, but that was a lost cause the minute those wide, hopeful brown eyes lifted and stared back at him. "I want a hell of a lot more than just to kiss you."

There went that bottom lip between Seth's teeth again. "Then what's stopping you?"

"You."

"But… I'm ready."

"Ready for what? Sex?" Vargas lowered his eyelids and held them closed. He forced down a swallow and looked to Seth again. "Because that's not the only thing I want."

"What do you want?"

"Everything." Sometimes a man just had to take a leap and trust that honesty would never be the wrong course. He reached for Seth's hand and held it between both of his. "I love you, Seth Fisher. I have for some time."

Seth searched his eyes. "You love…" He pointed at himself. "Me?"

Vargas nodded. "With everything I am." He shifted around so his entire body was facing Seth. "I don't want to pressure you or scare you, but I'm pretty sure I know what you're feeling for me too." He smiled at Seth, who was still gaping at him, eyes wide.

"You love me?"

"Yes." His heart was aching with wanting to take Seth in his arms and hold him, show him how much he loved him, but Seth needed space to figure out how he felt and what he wanted, to make his own decision on this, to control his own life and future.

Vargas dropped a kiss on the back of Seth's hand. "I can give you some time alone if you need to think."

"No." Seth emphatically shook his head. He reached for Vargas and tugged him close. The minute their lips connected, Vargas had the confirmation he needed. He kissed Seth back, once again feeling that explosive power in the simple joining of their mouths. How had he ever thought he could walk away from this man?

Seth parted his lips and deepened the kiss, whimpering when their tongues brushed in greeting. He grabbed at Vargas, pulling him even closer, then kept the contact going as he held Vargas's face in both hands, stroking his cheeks with his thumbs like he couldn't quite believe this was happening again, that it was Vargas he was touching.

In one quick move, Seth sat up. Swinging his legs around, he straddled Vargas's thighs.

"Careful." Vargas helped ease him down onto his lap. "Don't hurt yourself."

Seth didn't say anything to that, just wrapped his arms around Vargas and kissed him again, something deep and primal pouring out of him. Vargas offered everything he had in return, all the while gliding his hands up and down Seth's back, wanting to touch every inch of him.

Then all at once Seth pulled back. He ran the pads of his thumbs over Vargas's bottom lip. "I don't need time to think. I want you."

"I want you too." With his hands splayed across Seth's back, Vargas brought him in for another kiss. Now that Seth had verified he was on board with this level of physical contact, Vargas couldn't get enough of him.

As if Seth heard his thoughts, he spread his legs wider, sliding farther up his lap so his thighs bracketed Vargas's hips and their bodies made complete contact. Such a beautiful, sensual move.

The embrace went on and on, their mouths molded together. They clutched at each other's clothes, let their hands explore as far as they could reach, the sweet slide of their tongues making contact again and again.

Vargas could feel Seth's flannel-covered erection against him. His own cock responded, coming to life in a rush he hadn't felt in years. He shifted his hips into the touch, and a raw groan tore from him that he had no hope of containing. He slipped his hands under the hem of Seth's shirt, wanting to touch his skin so badly. When his fingers met flesh, it hit him what he was doing. He stopped. "Is this okay?"

"Uh-huh." Without hesitation, Seth lifted his shirt off and tossed it onto the floor. Vargas wanted to take a minute and admire the sight before him, but he didn't want Seth to feel overly scrutinized in any way. It was the first time he'd gone without a shirt in front of him. The fact that Seth felt comfortable enough with him to quit hiding the scars on his upper body meant the world to Vargas.

He swept his palms up Seth's bare back, stroking the warm skin from the top of his ass to his nape and back down again, exploring the body he'd been dying to feel for months now.

Seth looked him in the eye, a level of confidence visible that Vargas had never seen in those brown eyes. "Touch me? With your mouth?"

"Oh yeah." Vargas didn't hesitate. He ducked his head and pressed his lips to the center of Seth's chest. One kiss after another, he took his time, rubbing his cheek along the bare flesh, breathing in Seth's scent, trailing kisses all over his torso until he had him squirming in his arms. He ran his lips along Seth's collarbone, then higher, up the soft skin of his neck, his own breath coming in harsh rapid pants.

Seth had his head tipped back. He looked so open, so unfettered. Then he dropped his head forward, grabbed on to Vargas, and kissed him again. All the while he kept moving against him, begging for more without words.

And God, did Vargas want to give him more. He wanted to make Seth squirm and writhe and shudder with release. He wanted to do every salacious thing he could think of to make Seth feel so unbelievably good. He wanted to somehow get Seth closer, to get them naked and move against him, reveling in the feel of Seth's bare body pressed against his own. He cupped Seth's tight ass in his hands and drew him forward.

Seth broke the kiss and winced.

"Shit." Vargas jerked back, giving Seth some space but still holding on to him for support. "I'm sorry."

Seth gripped Vargas by the shoulders. "It was just a spasm. Guess I did sit on the floor too long." Despite that he was clearly still hurting, he focused on Vargas again and smiled. "Wanna move this to the bed?"

Vargas let out a tension-filled laugh, but it did little to ease his concern. "Here. Try to get up." He held on to Seth's waist and helped him stand. Then Seth propped a hand on the desk as Vargas scrambled off the floor.

"What do you need?"

"Maybe to take some pain meds and lie down."

"Okay." He retrieved Seth's shirt from the floor and his cane from where it was leaning against the side of the desk.

Once Seth had his shirt on and was lying in the guest room bed, Vargas went for the pain medicine and a glass of water.

Seth took the pills and lay back down. When they'd first entered the room, Charlie had been asleep on the bed. Now he moved in to curl up against Seth's right leg. The pain that had been etched on Seth's face in the office was no longer as prominent.

"It already feels better." Despite that, he sounded winded.

"You sure?"

"Yeah. I think I just need to lie here for a bit. Maybe try to sleep some. That usually helps."

"All right. You get some rest." Vargas turned off the lamp. He stepped away from the bed but came to a stop in the middle of the room. He didn't want to go, didn't want to leave him for another goddamn night.

From the dark behind him came Seth's soft voice. "I saw the books and articles in your desk drawer."

Vargas faced the bed. With the help of the brilliant moonlight filtering in through the curtains, he could see Seth lying there, watching him, waiting.

"I wanted to know how to help you. And I wanted to be sure I never hurt you."

When Seth spoke again, his voice was louder, more certain. "I trust you, Vargas. I'm ready for more. It doesn't have to mean anything. Not unless you want it to."

Vargas returned to him and sat on the edge of the mattress beside Charlie. "Seth, it would mean everything to me." He leaned in and dropped a kiss on his lips. "You didn't believe what I said to you?"

"I…" Seth lowered his eyes and kept them closed. "I know you care about me."

"It's more than that."

When Seth opened his eyes, Vargas laid a hand in the middle of the man's chest and came forward again until their lips were almost touching. "I've fallen in love with you."

"Are you sure? Maybe you're just confused because you feel so guilty. Maybe you just—"

Vargas pressed a finger to Seth's lips. "I love you." He stood and rounded the bed. Without a pause, he kicked his shoes off, folded back the blankets, and climbed in. Then he held his arms out. "Your back okay to come here?"

Seth stared at him for several shocked seconds, then nodded and slid into the embrace. He laid his head on Vargas's chest. Right where he was meant to be.

Where he'd always belonged.

Vargas wrapped his arms around him and closed his eyes, relishing in how wonderful holding him felt, how perfect all of it was: having Seth there in his apartment all week, eating every meal together, hanging out on his couch at night, joking around about some lame commercial on TV, hearing every one of Seth's laughs, and seeing his smiles.

"How I feel is because of you. Of who you are. Nothing else."

Seth's breath hitched. "Okay."

Vargas dropped a kiss on the top of his head. "Now get some rest."

"Okay." But then Seth added, "I think I'm too freaked out to sleep."

"Freaked out in a bad way?"

"No."

"Good." He glided a hand down Seth's back. "I like the way you feel in my arms."

"Me too." Several minutes of silence passed. Seth's breathing shifted, became slow and even like he was drifting off. Then a moment later came, "Vargas?"

"Yeah."

"Would you take your shirt off?"

"Sure."

Seth shifted out of the way, and Vargas got his dress shirt peeled off and on the floor. He moved to lie back down, then thought of one better. He stripped off his dress slacks and socks. He got back in the bed, folding the sheet and blanket over his lower half. He grinned at the stunned expression on Seth's face.

With no encouragement needed that time, Seth slid in close. He leaned over him and surveyed the assortment of tattoos, clearly taking the time to silently read each one as he ran his fingers over the words covering Vargas's torso.

When he was finished, his cheek made contact with Vargas's bare chest, and he let out a long exhale like he'd been waiting months for that contact alone. He swept the pads of his fingers over the words tattooed directly over Vargas's heart. *In the dark, a fire can light the way.* Vargas wasn't sure if Seth knew the poem the words came from, but he guessed he did. Two other lines from the same poem were tattooed elsewhere on his body. One was still hidden beneath his underwear.

On Seth's second pass over the tattoo, he followed his fingers with a soft kiss to each word.

"You really need to quit that and go to sleep."

Seth lifted his head. "Why?"

"Because you're poking a bear who doesn't want to hurt your back any more tonight."

"Okay." He settled his head on Vargas again, lying a warm palm over his pectoral muscles. "But you're not a bear. You're more like a... salmon."

"The fish?"

"Uh-huh. They're very persistent, determined animals. They travel thousands of miles across the ocean to get to a specific river, and then they swim upstream, jumping waterfalls and rapids to reach the place where they were born. They're so worn out from the journey, they can't return to the ocean to feed, and they die there."

"Let me guess. You caught a documentary on salmon?"

"Yep."

"There really is one?"

"Uh-huh. Fifty minutes all about salmon. It was really interesting, actually. There are several theories, but no one knows for certain how they find their way back to the exact river where they started their lives." He paused and more softly added, "But most of them do. They struggle against all odds to make their way back."

Vargas slid his arms around him farther and held on tighter. "You will too, Seth. I promise, you'll feel less afraid and stronger soon."

Seth turned his head and gave another kiss to Vargas's skin.

They grew quiet again, locked in that embrace.

Then a thought hit Vargas. He lifted his head off the pillow. "Hey. I thought salmon swam upstream so they could mate, not to see the sights where they were born."

Seth laughed. "Yeah. They lay their eggs in the same river where they were hatched."

"And then they die. Very uplifting story."

"Hey." Seth tickled Vargas along his sides. "Stop teasing me."

"Okay. Okay." He squirmed to get away from the tickles, but then he forced himself to lie still so he wouldn't hurt Seth's back. They settled into the calm embrace once more, Vargas combing his fingers through the back of Seth's hair. "Get some rest."

"You're staying?"

Vargas dipped his head and pressed his lips to Seth's forehead. "I'm staying. If that's okay with you."

"I'd really like that. Just one more thing."

"Yeah?"

"I love you too."

Vargas let his eyes fall shut as the whispered words washed over him.

Seth breathed deep. "I've been in love with you for such a long time. I was just trying to pretend it didn't exist because I was so scared you didn't feel the same way. That you never would."

"I should've told you as soon as I realized. I just didn't want to push too hard."

"Because I'm broken."

Vargas kept one hand in Seth's hair and slid the other down his back. "You're not broken. You've been through a horrible experience. But you're healing, you're working hard to deal with everything, and you're going to be okay. Try to be patient with yourself, let yourself feel whatever you need to. There's no reason for us to rush anything. What I want most is to be close with you, just like this. The rest of it? The reason I haven't been with anyone else in two years is because you're the only one I want. I may not have consciously known it at first, but I've been waiting for you, Seth, and I'll keep waiting. For as long as you need. Because that's what I want to do. Okay?"

Seth kissed Vargas's chest once more. "Okay."

Chapter Nineteen

Seth awoke in the early morning hours expecting to feel worn out as he always did after he had to take his pain meds, but all he felt was amazing. He stretched and waited for a back spasm to hit or the usual ache in his knee to surface. There was nothing.

He should probably try to fall back asleep. It was far too early and still pitch-black outside.

Instead he reached for the bedside lamp and turned it on to the lowest setting. He rolled over the other way, propping himself on one elbow to take in the sight of the man asleep next to him.

Vargas lay on his side, one hand tucked under his cheek. His lips were slightly parted, his closed eyes fluttering from side to side like he was dreaming. Not a nightmare, though. More peaceful than that. Seth reached out and followed the path of those beautiful lips with the tip of his finger, remembering what they felt like pressed against his own, wanting more of that contact, more of everything.

Most of all, though, he longed to hear Vargas again say those three incredible words he'd uttered the night before.

God, Seth loved him, and it was the biggest relief allowing himself to really feel that, and *knowing* Vargas felt the same in return.

Without opening his eyes, Vargas grumbled at the disturbance. He rolled onto his stomach, wrapped his arms around the pillow, and buried his face in the fabric, snuggling into it. It was an adorable move. Then his eyes shot open as if he just remembered he hadn't gone to bed alone.

He spotted Seth and visibly relaxed. "Hey. How's your back?"

"Better."

Vargas lifted his head to glance at the clock on the nightstand. "Couldn't you sleep?"

"I was just thinking." Seth leaned in and offered a soft, lingering kiss. "I don't want to wait. I don't *need* to wait any longer. I want to be with you."

There was a subtle panic in Vargas's eyes as he scanned Seth's face. "I couldn't take it if I hurt you."

"I know. I wouldn't put you—or me—through that if I thought I might not be ready. I don't think I knew for sure until last night, but I know now."

Vargas didn't respond.

"I promise, I'll tell you if anything's too much."

"You sure?"

"Yes. Be with me?"

They moved in at the same time.

Vargas cradled Seth's face in his hands. "I love you." Then he kissed him, taking the gentlest, sweetest taste of his lips before turning the kiss into something silky and wet and damn perfect. Seth wrapped his arms around Vargas and slid closer, marveling again at how absolutely wonderful it felt to kiss this man.

With each passing moment, there was an unfurling of something electric, a passionate need inside Seth, as if a part of him that had lain dormant for so long was just now waking up, stirring back to life. Somewhere inside him wires were uncrossing, batteries recharging.

He rocked into Vargas's weight, relished in the press of that strong body against his, felt the rush of heat land in his lap. His erection grew as Vargas's hands traveled down his body and palmed his ass. Seth moaned into the kiss.

When he pulled back, he saw the same desperate hunger replicated in Vargas's eyes. That unblinking stare again stirred something inside Seth he unconsciously feared might've died that day he almost did. It was like he was being reunited with his body. He wanted to be naked with Vargas, wanted to feel the man's skin connecting with his own. He wanted Vargas's mouth and hands and lips everywhere on him at once. He almost couldn't bear waiting another second.

He lay back on the bed. "Please touch me. Everywhere."

There was a hint of a smile as Vargas came forward and kissed him again, sliding a hand under Seth's shirt and lifting it several inches. He kissed his way down the side of Seth's neck and at the same time ran his palm over the exposed flesh of his stomach. The touch was electrifying, and it drove Seth's desire higher with each swipe of fingers to flesh. He closed his eyes, reveling in every stroke, every brush of breath along his skin, as well as the knowledge that it was Vargas touching him, driving him crazy with need.

Vargas raised the shirt higher and planted an openmouthed kiss on Seth's belly, circling his tongue around his navel. It tickled. Seth laughed and squirmed, and Vargas let up.

"No." Seth gripped him by the back of the head. "Don't stop."

Vargas swept his lips over Seth's skin again as if intent on learning every inch of his body with only his mouth. There was a kiss below his belly button. One lower still, above the waistband of his pajama pants. A swipe of Vargas's palm up his side pushed the shirt farther out of the way. Seth reached for the bottom edge of the shirt, dragged it over his head, and tossed it aside. He lay down again and buried his fingers in Vargas's hair.

All the while Vargas never stopped with the caresses or the kisses. He was loving on him, and Seth finally understood everything Vargas felt for him. It was evident in each touch, in the deliberate, gentle way he explored his body. Seth ran his hands through Vargas's hair, trying to communicate that understanding and his utter love and desire for him in return.

Vargas proceeded upward. He offered a chaste kiss below Seth's right nipple.

Beside it.

Above it.

Without lifting his head Vargas asked, "You okay?"

Through an exhale, Seth breathed out the word, "Yeah."

"You tell me if you need me to stop."

"I will."

Then Vargas parted his lips and wrapped them around that nipple. He flicked it with the tip of his tongue, sending a spike of pleasure throughout Seth's body.

Seth arched up under him. He was painfully hard now, aching. He wanted—*craved*—release in a way he hadn't in so long.

Vargas raised his head. "God, you're gorgeous." Without taking his eyes off him, he slipped a hand into Seth's flannel pajama pants and cupped the bulge hidden beneath the underwear. He smiled when Seth parted his lips and sucked in a gulp of air. Then Vargas ducked his head again and focused his attention on Seth's other nipple, all the while cupping and massaging his cock and balls through his briefs.

Uninhibited in a way Seth hadn't been in ages, he shifted his hips forward and back. When Vargas tugged on his pajama bottoms, Seth lifted up, and Vargas lowered the pants over his erection and down Seth's thighs. The low-rise briefs he wore were tight and black. They barely covered the hair above his cock and left little to the imagination when it came to what was hidden underneath.

Vargas ran the tip of one finger over the fabric, tracing the outline of Seth's heavy bulge. "You always wear this kind?"

"Yeah. I just... I like how they look. They make me feel..." He couldn't find the words. Every ounce of him was focused on one thing. He sucked in another ragged breath as Vargas used a thumb to explore the head of his cock.

"What? Sexy as hell? Because that's how you look right now." And maybe that's why Vargas sounded so out of breath.

"Yeah?" Seth worked his bottom lip between his teeth. Nearly every time he'd pictured being naked with Vargas, he wondered if he'd be mortified at exposing the scars covering his body. But he felt none of that. "You like me in them?"

"That's an understatement." Vargas rose up and guided the flannel pants the rest of the way off. On hands and knees, he kissed his way back up Seth's body, one kiss after another, starting at Seth's inner thighs. Crouched over him like that, Vargas looked delicious in only his underwear, all taught muscle and tattooed flesh. He paused long enough to nuzzle Seth's erection, then mouthed it, running his moist tongue over and around the head of Seth's fabric-covered cock.

Oh fucking hell.

Seth couldn't believe it. Raymond Vargas had his mouth on him.

Seth gave up watching and dropped his head back, grateful Vargas found his underwear sexy but also wishing to hell they weren't in the way.

Then Vargas continued on, traveling up Seth again, sweeping those lips and that beautiful, talented tongue along his flesh until they were kissing, their tongues brushing in a wet, ravenous dance of increasing arousal. Vargas kept on touching him, running his hands everywhere, all over him, except where Seth desperately wanted them.

As if sensing his need, Vargas slid down the bed once more until his head was at Seth's groin. Rubbing his thumb over Seth's underwear-covered cock again, he said, "I want to taste you. Would you like that?"

"Yes. Please."

Apparently that was all Vargas needed to hear. He peeled Seth's underwear over his erection, then down and off his legs in one fluid motion. Vargas didn't hesitate. Repositioning his head over him, he drew Seth's cock between his lips and kept going until he was swallowing all of him. Then he held there, keeping the entire shaft cradled in the heat of his mouth for several seconds before slowly, sensually pulling his lips to the tip.

"Oh God." Seth groaned as unbelievable pleasure zipped through him.

Vargas gave a lengthy suck to the head, swirled that skilled tongue over and around it, laving the ridge and slit over and over again, driving Seth crazy with sensations. Knowing it was Vargas's mouth on him, made the moment even more intense, and the most erotic thing Seth had ever seen or felt. Until…

Vargas pulled to the tip again. With his mouth open wide, he let his tongue linger on the head for several seconds as he stared up at Seth, like he was overcome by the feel of that intimate contact between them and urgently needed to get a look at Seth's face. His tattooed arms flexed as he held himself up over him, one hand wrapped around the base of Seth's shaft.

"This okay?" he asked, his warm exhales sweeping across the head of Seth's cock.

"Uh-huh. More."

Vargas smiled at him. He closed his eyes and lowered his mouth over Seth's length again, that time taking it faster, his head repeatedly bobbing up and down, his mouth working with fierce tenacity, his hand racing up the length to follow the movement of his lips. A few more of those rapid tugs and he eased up, alternating the faster, electric pace with deliberate, sensual strokes, his moist tongue swirling and tasting, never letting Seth become too accustomed to any one sensation before moving on to another rhythm.

It was all driving Seth crazy. In the most delicious way.

Then, after another long upward caress, Vargas switched to stroking Seth's shaft with just his hand while he kissed and mouthed his balls. Seth spread his legs, and Vargas took the cue. He climbed between them to lie on the bed. The sight of Vargas with his head flanked by Seth's thighs was sexy as hell. Seth grasped the fitted sheet in both fists and raised his knees as high as he could. His left leg wouldn't bend as far as his right, and he didn't want to strain his back, but the move was enough to give Vargas room if he wanted to go lower.

He did.

He licked along Seth's taint, gliding his way back and forth between balls and ass. After several rounds, he swept his mouth up Seth's shaft again until he was repeatedly sucking on the head of his cock. He reiterated the move from cock to balls to ass and back up over and over, his hand stroking Seth's length whenever his mouth went lower. The varying sounds of his slick mouth and the swift slap of a hand working over flesh surrounded them.

Seth had never had such a drawn-out, sensual blowjob. No one had ever spent so much time, used their mouth on every part of him like that.

It left him dizzy with need, had him dying for release. He whimpered, shifting his hips. He tried his best not to gag Vargas or wrench his own back, but he couldn't keep still. That movement seemed to urge Vargas into higher gear. He worked Seth's cock with more vigor, the drag of his lips offering no respite.

Seth's legs shook. He was close.

With sudden urgency, Vargas raised up and spun around so he sat with his back against the headboard. "Come here. I want to see your face the first time." He gestured for Seth to straddle him the way he had earlier. "Go easy."

Seth carefully moved to him, but it was torture taking his time. From this new angle, there was no missing the bulge of Vargas's substantial erection hidden beneath his underwear.

When Seth was settled on Vargas's lap, Vargas kissed him, and Seth could taste his own precum on the man's tongue, adding to the intensity of need rushing through him.

Then Vargas raised a hand and licked the entire length of his palm. He grasped Seth's shaft, the spit from the blowjob and his hand creating a sleek stroke. "Come for me."

That penetrating stare as Vargas watched him would've been enough to send Seth over the edge. Add in the remarkable, sure strokes of that large hand, and Seth was a goner. He jerked his hips. His stomach muscles tightened, and he groaned as everything in him tensed. He shot so hard, a stream of cum hit Vargas's lower lip. Vargas didn't hesitate. He licked his lip, capturing the beads of Seth's release. That had Seth shooting more.

"Oh God. Yes!" His entire body felt like it was humming, alive with sensation. He jerked again, more release landing on Vargas's hand and abs. Only then did Vargas slow his hand over him, squeezing out the last of his cum.

When Seth's shuddering eased, he collapsed forward, rapid pants pouring out of him, his forehead resting against the headboard over Vargas's shoulder.

Vargas ran a hand down his back. "You okay?"

"Uh-huh." Seth turned and kissed the side of his neck. "Shit. That was… Wow." Another kiss. "Thank you."

"You're welcome." Seth heard the grin wrapped around the words.

He nuzzled into Vargas's neck and planted another kiss on him. When he could move more, he pulled back and met Vargas's stare. He wanted to say something, meaningful words that would convey the enormity of what that intimacy between them had meant for him, but nothing seemed like enough.

Vargas nodded. "Yeah. Me too."

Those words meant everything to Seth. He leaned in and brought their lips together, savoring the knowledge that he wasn't alone in this moment or what he felt about it.

This kiss was more languid, like they had all the time in the world to show each other what they felt.

Only Vargas hadn't come yet.

Seth wanted to be the one to give him that pleasure. Without breaking the kiss, he shifted backward, snaked one hand between them, and slipped it inside Vargas's underwear. The hefty cock felt even larger in his hand than it had looked trapped inside the snug boxer briefs. Seth wanted to see it, wanted to learn every inch with his fingers and lips and tongue.

He slid his hand along the length and released Vargas's entire erection from the underwear. That's when he saw it. A tattoo. An inch from the hair above his cock. Seth scooted backward to make room between them so he could read the words. *Don't let the fire of your life go out. Stoke it, fuel it, feel it, bring it to life.* It was from a famous poem titled "Life: all its pain and glory," the same poem as the phrase tattooed over his chest.

Seth couldn't have come up with a more fitting line. The fire inside him had awoken, brought to life by Vargas's touch.

Seth traced the letters of the tattoo. The muscles of Vargas's abs quivered with the contact. His breathing sped up. Seth reached for him again and met his stare as he stroked Vargas's shaft, taking his time, using both hands, learning the feel of him, the path of each vein, the girth and weight of his length, the shape of the flared head, and the texture of his scrotum. He could not believe he was touching Vargas like this. Just that thought had his own cock raring to go again before long. A fact that Vargas didn't miss.

"Come closer," he said. "Like in your drawing."

"Yeah. Yeah." Seth let go of him.

Vargas drew him in with both hands on his ass until they were lined up perfectly, thanks to the ample size of Vargas's erection. He grasped their shafts in one hand.

Seth thought feeling Vargas's mouth on his dick had been erotically intimate. Their bare cocks pressed together, both gaining pleasure from the slide of Vargas's hand and the touch of the other man's shaft, took that intimacy to an entirely new level.

Vargas started off slow, but it wasn't long and his palm was racing along their lengths. His breath hitched, and the rhythm of his movements became erratic as he picked up speed. He splayed his other hand across Seth's lower back and held on as he bucked up under him again and again.

Vargas groaned. "Ready?"

"Yes. Please."

Vargas gave another powerful thrust up into the touch. He groaned again, louder, longer, his hand really flying over them. Grunting out a litany of profanities, he came. The warmth of his release exploded over his palm and down the length of Seth's cock.

That nearly did it for Seth. He was close. Again. Vargas didn't relent. He kept his tight hold on Seth, kept his hand moving over them, and it wasn't long before Seth followed him into that unrestrained release. He gripped the top of the headboard over Vargas's shoulders in both hands. Jerking his hips forward, he came for the second time that night, his body moving against Vargas until it had given everything over to the moment.

They stayed pressed together for several minutes.

Eventually Seth eased up on his death grip on the headboard, and Vargas let go of their softening shafts.

When Seth pulled back, Vargas smiled at him, a look of pure contentment in those dark eyes. "Seeing you like that… God, that was beautiful. *You're* beautiful." Then those eyes closed for several seconds. When they opened again, there was an alarmed expression on his face.

"What?" Seth asked. "Did I do something wrong?"

Vargas's eyes widened. "Not at all." He traced Seth's lips with his thumb. "You were wonderful. I just… I shouldn't tell you what to do. Not like that."

Seth gave him a questioning look.

"When I had you sit on my lap." ·

"Oh. I liked that." He glanced away.

Vargas placed a hand beneath Seth's chin and, with the slightest pressure, he brought his head around. "There's nothing you can't tell me."

"I liked it because I want to know what you want, what will make you feel good. And if I can, if it doesn't hurt me, I want to give that to you. Does that sound wrong coming from me?"

"No. I get it. I want to do the same for you." Vargas cupped Seth's cheek and kissed him. "More than you know." He shifted them down the bed so they were lying together, Vargas on his back, Seth draped over him, their limbs entwined.

Seth couldn't keep the smile from his lips. "We did it."

"We did."

"I feel incredible."

"Yeah?" Vargas tightened his hold and let out a contented sigh. "Same here. I want to stay just like this forever."

"Me too." Seth slid a hand across the back of Vargas's nape and dropped one kiss after another along the side of his neck, not wanting to give up the touching, loving the feel and scent of the man in his arms. He couldn't believe they were here in this moment together. He shifted down and settled his head on Vargas's chest. "Guess we have to move eventually, though. You have an early meeting downstairs."

Vargas groaned. "I'm canceling it."

"Don't." Seth thought about what he really meant by that and what Vargas may have been saying as well. "I'll be okay. What we did... it was perfect. I'm not going to freak out or anything."

Vargas was quiet for a long breath. "You sure?"

"I'm sure."

"Okay." Vargas raised a shoulder, encouraging Seth to lift up and look at him. "But if there's ever anything that upsets you or that you want to tell me, you need to say it. Even if you think it'll worry me or hurt my feelings, I want to hear it. It would hurt more if you held back."

"All right." Seth returned his head to Vargas's chest. "I want to take Charlie out. By myself." Before Vargas could say anything, Seth added, "I'll go down the back steps. I won't take him for a walk, not yet. I'll just let him out on the leash to get some air and go to the bathroom. Is that grass area along the back of the building still there?"

"It is."

"Good. I want to try it." For himself, but he also wanted to show Vargas how much being there at the club and in his apartment had helped, that he was ready to explore more in other areas of his life. And to show him that what they'd done had been everything he'd been dreaming of, and that it was okay for them to take it further, that Vargas didn't have to be so afraid he'd hurt him. "I think I can do it."

Vargas kissed him on the top of the head. "I know you can."

Chapter Twenty

"All right, Prescott," whispered the guard standing on the other side of the bars. He was the one with the lazy eye who'd shoved Prescott around on his first day in the jail. "We got a deal?"

Prescott considered the offer. Whether he wanted to admit it or not, this might be the only chance he was going to get. He had to take it. Even if he was sure he was putting his life in jeopardy by doing so.

When he'd been housed at the state penitentiary, there was no way one guard could've slipped him out, but now that he was in the county jail, that might be different. Someone working the inside would surely know if he could manage to get him out unnoticed or not. Besides, this guard said he'd been the one who'd come up with the idea to move Prescott to a new cell earlier that day, capitalizing on fears that Prescott's mere presence around the other inmates was a disturbance the guards didn't need to deal with. So now Prescott was in a dilapidated, unused section of the jail, where the cells on either side of him and across the way were all empty. So long as the guard took care of the video feed like he said he would, there'd be no one to see when Prescott made his escape.

Lazy Eye shifted on his feet, hiking up the polyester pants before they slid completely off his thin frame. It was like he was wearing his big brother's uniform. Apparently the county jail couldn't afford to appropriately clothe their officers.

The guard said, "Everything you need will be waiting where we discussed."

"And I won't owe you a fucking cent once it's done?"

"No. All you have to do is deliver that message for me. Make sure the guy believes that you'll kill him if he doesn't forgive my debt."

"And if this bookie doesn't do what you ask, I don't really have to kill him?"

"No, you never have to see him again. One look at you, and he'll do exactly what you say."

"Good." Prescott had no taste for killing. Although he'd done it when he had to. He could do just about anything when necessary. "Well, how can I refuse such a fair offer?"

"Exactly." The guard came in closer and pointed at Prescott. "But if you don't make good on your end of the deal, I will get someone to pay a visit to your folks' house and you will not be pleased with that outcome."

Prescott feigned concern as he held back a laugh. He had no intention of making any threats on this man's behalf. Lazy Eye would never go through with having someone killed. No matter how macho he tried to appear, his bravado was all for show. That's why a guy like him would always need someone else to do his dirty work.

Not that it mattered in this case. The last reason Prescott would never do as he promised was because this guard's offer—and his story about a bookie—was complete and utter bullshit.

An act. All to sell the believability of the escape plan.

How stupid did the old man think he was?

Prescott had known since the beginning who his anonymous benefactor was, who'd hired the attorney, and what the man ultimately had planned for him.

That didn't mean Prescott would ignore the opportunity. He was going to use the situation to his advantage.

Once he was free, he'd only have a short window of time to get away. Which meant that he wouldn't be able to collect all his boys. He'd have to pick just one. That about broke his heart and almost had him reaching through the bars and clasping the guard's throat in his hands just to have something to do with all his anger and frustration.

Instead he focused on what he'd do when he was out. His benefactor and the police would assume he'd go for someone who was fit and mobile, someone he could get away with quickly. Maybe even one of his boys who'd moved out of the city. Or the last one he'd been fixated on when he was shot and arrested, the reporter Kevin Price.

They'd never imagine he'd go for the one he had in mind, the one he wanted the most, the one who *needed* him the most.

The one he'd never run away without.

Seth.

Prescott grinned at the guard waiting for a definitive answer. "We have a deal."

"Good. Be ready to go at a moment's notice." The guard hiked up his pants again and sauntered away from the cell as if nothing untoward had gone on between them.

Prescott backed away from the bars and returned to lie on his bed, listening to the squeak of the guard's shoes fading in the distance. In the silence that remained, he kept the smile going, thinking through what it would be like to see his boy again. What he'd say to him. Where he'd take him.

And of course, the first thing they'd do together when they were finally alone.

* * * * *

A knock sounded on the man's office door. He told whoever it was to enter, and Jarrett Gates crept into the room. He came to a stop several feet away, nervously glancing up and down between the surface of the desk and the man's face.

The man sat back and folded his hands over his taut stomach. "Spit it out."

"He's no longer staying at his apartment."

"Where is he?"

"The Haven. That club where—"

"Yes." The man waved a hand through the air. Of course he knew the name of that place. "You're sure?"

"He's moved in with the owner. It might be a temporary situation, but he took several bags with him."

The man shot forward and jammed a finger in the air toward Jarrett. "How did you not know this was going to happen? If we can't get to him at the right time, then this is all for nothing. We might as well call the whole fucking thing off."

"I..." Jarrett started.

"What?"

"Well, I have an idea. I've found someone who works there who's not above taking a bribe. He'll get you into that club. For the right price."

The right price? There was no cost too high for what he had planned. The man eased back in his chair and pretended to give the new information more thought. The Haven had always been one possible location where everything could go down. He figured it'd be best for it to seem like Jarrett's idea to get him into that club when the time was right. Of course he'd probably have to push Jarrett into actually going through with it, make him do something he'd normally never have the balls to do.

"Yes," the man said. "This will work out quite nicely. Everything's all set with Prescott?"

"Yes."

"And he still believes his anonymous benefactor is trying to help him?"

"It appears so."

The man shook his head. "Life in prison with no chance of parole, and the dumb son of a bitch still thinks someone is trying to save him. Fucking moron."

"After he's out, we'll have someone on him 24-7 in case he tries to leave the state right away."

That had the man laughing. "He won't leave. Not until he collects what he thinks is his. Which is going to play right into my hand." The man rose and went to the wall of windows behind his desk. He stared in the direction of his latest acquisition. He recalled telling his son about the possibility of that deal the last time they'd been in contact. The boy had no interest in hearing the details. That had hurt. He was man enough to admit that.

He spoke to Jarrett again. "I heard what Prescott said in the courtroom. I know what he's planning, and I'm going to stop him. Then I'm going to end him. It'll be perfect. I can take care of everything in one moment."

"Very well, sir. I'll oversee the final preparations."

The man faced Jarrett. "And double check with the guard at the jail. Make certain everything is *exactly* as we discussed." He didn't want anything to block Prescott from getting out. He needed him in a position where he could access him without interference.

The man spoke again, but he wasn't talking to Jarrett that time. "He's going to pay for hurting my son."

Even though the Haven had too much security, an alarm system, and guards on duty at all hours, it was going to be the ideal place to finish things with Prescott. An enclosed space. Nowhere to run. No one there who'd give a shit about saving him.

Yes, the man thought, *the perfect place for revenge.*

For himself.

For his son.

Chapter Twenty-One

Seth stood at the Haven's back door, Charlie's leash in one hand, his cane in the other. Using his body to keep the door propped open, he watched Charlie at the end of the leash. The dog was sniffing around the narrow strip of grass along the back of the building. They'd already been there for a while, but Seth wanted to give him a few extra minutes outdoors. Besides, even if Seth was technically standing in the doorway and no one else was around, and he'd also been texting back and forth with Vargas, he'd made it outside by himself for the first time since being hospitalized two years earlier. He wanted to savor the victory a little longer.

He tilted his head back and let the sun's gentle rays warm his face. His thoughts wandered back to earlier that morning, and he couldn't contain the resulting grin.

He'd had sex.

With Vargas.

And he hadn't panicked or flipped out or felt anything except intense desire and pleasure. A man could get lost in that kind of ecstasy.

Charlie let out a bark. It was his signature "come closer and give me some attention" bark. Someone was nearby.

Seth scanned the back of the club and then the parking lot. He spotted a man making his way to the building from a row of parked cars. Seth couldn't tell who it was. He expected to become rattled at just the sight of someone heading their way. He waited for the typical reaction, but there was nothing. All he felt was calm and steady. And that felt amazing.

The man came in closer. "Hey, Seth." It was Neil, one of the guards assigned to watch Vargas's apartment. He approached and offered a smile. The man had a great smile. It lit up his eyes. "Everything all right?" he asked.

"Sure."

As always, Neil seemed nice enough, but as he advanced, that familiar panic suddenly hit Seth. His breath came in rapid pants, the sound of his own gasps overwhelming his ears and drowning out nearly everything else.

"Hey, take it easy." Neil's expression had turned to one of alarm. He placed a hand on Seth's shoulder. "Just take a deep breath."

Seth tried to slow his breathing. "It's okay. I'm all right."

"Okay," Neil said slowly as he lowered his arm. He continued studying Seth with concern. "Why don't I wait here with you until you're finished, and then we'll head back in together?"

"No, it's okay. I'm fine, really." Seth tried again to get his breathing under control. There was just something about Neil—or the situation—that was unsettling. Only he couldn't put what that was into words. Maybe it was the pity-filled look on Neil's face or how he'd touched Seth's arm. Both innocent gestures to most people, but to Seth they felt invasive and triggered that mix of fear and anxiety zipping through him.

Neil took a step back but kept a careful eye on him. "It's no big deal. I mean, Vargas said you can't be outside alone, right? It's okay to need help."

"No! I need to do this on my own."

Neil shook his head. "That was really rude of me to say. I'm sorry."

"No. I shouldn't have snapped at you. I appreciate the concern."

Charlie let out another bark. Neil offered the dog a scratch behind his ear, and without glancing up he asked, "You sure you'll be okay?"

"Sure."

Neil gave Charlie a final pat and a last encouraging smile to Seth, then started for the employee entrance.

Alone once more, Seth tried to push aside the disappointment that maybe nothing had changed for him since he'd come to the club.

Although he'd made it outside. That was something.

He turned to Charlie. "You ready?"

Without more than that, Charlie raced forward and slipped inside the open doorway. Together they headed up the back stairs to Vargas's apartment. Once inside, Seth returned to the office, anxious to complete his own work and get back to his review of Vargas's financial records.

By seven that night, he was down to the last two stacks of the club's paperwork. Throughout the afternoon and early evening, he and Vargas had texted a dozen more messages back and forth, and Seth had taken Charlie out two more times without any further incident or anxiety. For Vargas, there'd been one crisis after another in the club, and he hadn't been able to return as often or as early as he'd originally told Seth.

Which worked out okay since it gave Seth time to get through a considerable amount of the club's records. He'd been hoping to locate something significant before Vargas's meeting with the accountant that night, but he couldn't find any discrepancies. He trusted that Vargas's instincts were right about something being off with his friend. Which meant, maybe whatever was going on had nothing to do with the club's finances.

Seth set aside his notes and leaned back in the office chair. He stretched his arms overhead, moving with care, testing out his body's reactions, waiting for his back to spasm, but there was nothing. While he'd been reviewing everything, he got up every so often to gather additional files off the cart, but still, he couldn't believe he'd been sitting there for hours without taking a pain pill. He had to wonder how much of his issues lately had been mental and not physical.

He reached for his cane and stood. He went to the window beside the desk. The club was open and full of people. The overhead lights were dim, and the glow of golden light that flowed from the sconces on the walls and the votive candles on the tables gave the atmosphere a classy feel that wasn't what anyone would expect from a sex club. It was early enough in the evening that most of the activity was centered in the dining room, with couples, and even some threesomes, drinking wine and enjoying their meals. The beat of music from the bar was subdued, not the striking thud of dance music that would emerge later.

Seth spotted Vargas stepping out of the door that led to the staff offices. He was followed by a man that had to be his accountant, Ken Miyata. The man was half a foot shorter than Vargas and stockier. He had a kind face and moved with a gentle gracefulness rarely seen in a man with his build.

The two shook hands, and Vargas headed back toward his office.

Miyata remained in the club. He ordered a drink in the bar and meandered around the dining room, stopping to talk to a few people. He seemed friendly enough, which gave Seth an idea. He wanted to meet the man, see if he could read anything about him that Vargas might be too close to see. But...

Could Seth trust his own instincts when it came to reading people? He'd been horribly wrong about Prescott when he first met him. And look how he'd reacted to Ian and Neil, Vargas's trusted employees.

How could he expect to judge a man he'd never met before when

Vargas couldn't figure out what might be going on after the two had been friends for years?

As Seth kept his focus on the dining room, he watched the accountant talk to a younger man Seth didn't recognize. They whispered with their heads together, and then the two strolled toward the main staircase. They started up.

In the background, Seth spotted another man on the second-floor balcony. This guy had his back to Seth, his arms held awkwardly at his sides. In one hand was a cell phone. He quickly raised his arm. Seth couldn't tell if he was snapping a picture of the first floor below or reading a message on the screen. He dropped his arm just as rapidly.

Fifteen seconds later, the man repeated the action, again letting his arm fall to his side in what appeared to be an attempt to hide his actions. Which made sense if he was doing what it looked like. Taking photos inside the Haven was prohibited. In fact, according to the club's membership policy, cell phones were to be kept out of sight at all times so no one could secretly video or photograph other members without their consent. Not that everyone kept to that rule, but most did.

The man in question took another snapshot, if that's what he was doing, then spun around, facing Seth for the first time. It was Neil.

He slipped the phone into his pocket and got moving down the stairs. Was he taking pictures for Vargas? Maybe that's why he was in plain clothes. Maybe it was a function of his security role to blend in and record the night's activities. But why take pictures? There were video cameras covering the entire first floor.

Something wasn't right.

When Neil reached the bottom of the stairs, he drew up short and surveyed the crowd. He seemed nervous, like he was afraid of getting caught or was trying to find a man he was meeting. He stilled his gaze as if he spotted someone across the club. Then he took off in the opposite direction, hauling ass for a hallway off the dining room.

Seth scanned the crowd for who Neil could've seen. Carter was moving through the dining room with determination, heading in the direction Neil had gone. He paused at the end of the hallway, quickly scanned the crowd behind him, and then followed Neil down the corridor.

Unable to curb his curiosity, Seth got moving. Before he could change his mind, he left Vargas's office and hurried down the hall to the apartment door. He flung it open.

Ian turned to face him. "Good evening, Seth."

When Seth didn't move or speak right away, Ian added, "Can I help you with anything?"

"Um, yeah. There's a hallway downstairs that's marked with an Employees-Only sign. Just off the dining room. Where does that go?"

"To the employee locker room."

"Thanks. I'm going down into the club."

Ian eyed him with concern. "Would you like me to get someone to go with you?"

"No, thanks. I'll be okay."

He searched Seth's eyes.

"Really. I'm okay."

"All right. If you need anything, let one of the guards know."

Seth gave a nod and got going, moving as swiftly as he could with the cane. He wanted to see why Carter had followed Neil into the locker room, and what Neil had been up to with his phone. But what was he going to do? Confront them? Question them? Maybe he could overhear what they were saying.

He passed by the security room and was at the club's main staircase in no time. He hit the first step and came to a halt.

Everything in the club was harsher than it had appeared through the window in Vargas's office. The music was louder, the lights brighter. The chatter of voices was deafening. The crowd of men milling about seemed impenetrable.

He couldn't go down there, couldn't walk through that mass of people.

His heart raced. There was no slowing the gasps pouring out of him. He gripped the banister beside him in one hand and the cane in his other.

Walking down into the Haven should've been easier than standing at the door outside. There were security guards everywhere in the club, and he was in plain view. He was safe there.

If only the logical part of his brain could get the rest of his body to believe that.

He couldn't move. He was frozen in place by the sights and sounds before him, by the sea of men, all with their own desires and agendas.

No. He wasn't giving up this easily.

He forced himself to plant his foot on the second step. Mission accomplished. He tried for the next one. Done.

Okay. He could do this.

Another step.

Another.

The breath came easier. His head felt clearer and calmer.

Then two men he'd never seen before appeared at the base of the staircase. They started up without a single hesitation, the first one taking the stairs two at a time, obviously anxious to get on to the rest of their night's activities.

The first man lifted his head and looked right at him. Seth froze.

It wasn't the man heading toward him that he saw. It was Conrad Henderson, the cop who'd beaten him nearly to death.

Henderson stood over him, grasping a metal pipe in his fist. Seth was lying on his back. He knew he was on a table in the club's dining room. Two of the Haven's overhead lamps were visible behind Henderson, casting his face in shadows, but Seth could still see the rage in his eyes. Weren't cops supposed to help people in trouble?

Helping was most definitely not what this guy was doing.

Seth could taste the blood in his mouth. His right eye was swollen shut, and his side and leg were throbbing like hell. He was clutching his paw-print key chain, the one with Charlie's picture. He kept thinking if he just held on to that key chain, kept it from slipping from his grip, then maybe he'd be okay. He wanted to close his eyes and fall into the darkness, drift away from the pain, but he was too afraid to go there, afraid he'd never wake up.

Henderson raised the pipe, and with one swift move, he struck.

Seth stumbled backward on the steps as if he'd just taken the blow like he had that day. He blinked, and the vision of Henderson standing over him disappeared, replaced by the two men ascending the steps.

Seth spun around and rushed back up the stairs, then down the hall toward the apartment.

Ian stepped forward as he approached. "What is it? What's wrong?"

Seth shook his head. "Nothing." He dashed inside, stopping only long enough to make sure the door was closed and locked behind him. Once in the safety of Vargas's office, he hurled that door shut as well and collapsed back against it. Nearly hyperventilating, he tried for a couple of deep breaths, but he couldn't calm down. He paced the wall lined with model boats and cars.

Then he went to the window overlooking the club. The multitude of men were still there, talking, dancing, flirting, not crying and running away like a scared little kid. For them, nothing significant had just happened.

"Fuck!" Seth slapped the wall beside the window with an open hand, then curled the hand into a fist and threw a punch at the painted surface. He expected his knuckles to burn and sting. He felt nothing.

He punched the wall again.

Nothing.

He clutched the cane in his other hand and went to pace the room again. The end of the cane caught on a leg of the desk. He stumbled forward. "Goddammit." He raised the cane. "You stupid fucking thing. I hate you." He clutched it in both hands and smacked the end against the leg of the desk. That felt good. Damn good.

He struck the cane on the seat of the office chair next, then the back of the chair. He kept on going, hitting the wall beside the desk, then the wall with the window. He wildly swung the cane again and again. He heard a crash, but he didn't let up. He couldn't.

"I hate you! I hate you! I hate you!"

Arms folded around his waist from behind. Then came Vargas's soft voice. "Seth. Stop. You're gonna hurt yourself." He got hold of Seth's wrists. "Let go."

Seth clutched the cane tighter. "No! I hate him! I hate him! I hate him!"

"I know. I know. It's okay."

"No, it's not. It's never going to be."

"It will. Let go, Seth. Just let go."

Seth opened his hands and dropped the cane to the floor.

Vargas kept talking in that low, comforting tone. "You're okay. You're safe here."

Seth whirled to face him and wrapped his arms around Vargas's middle. "I'm sorry. I just—" He shook his head. Without his consent, his legs gave out. Vargas held on, and together they slid to the floor.

"It's okay." Vargas pulled him onto his lap and held him. Seth buried his face in Vargas's neck.

Vargas said again, "It's okay. You're safe. I've got you."

Tears streamed down Seth's cheeks, uninvited and unrestrained. His body was shaking without his consent.

Vargas stroked his hair. "Just breathe with me. You're safe. I've got you."

Seth squeezed his eyes shut and listened to that caring, steady voice repeat those words over and over.

"It's okay. You're not alone. I'm here with you. You're safe."

Eventually the tears subsided. Vargas kept hold of him, and the tension and anger drained away with each passing second in those strong arms.

"It's okay. You're safe now."

Yeah, he was. Vargas was there with him.

Seth opened his eyes. One of the model boats from the shelves lay on the floor on its side. The reality of where he was and how he'd reacted came back to him in a flash.

"Oh God." The boat had a crack along the hull, and several pieces of the pilothouse were scattered across the floor. He must've hit the model when he'd been swinging his cane around like a nut. He read the words on the busted hull: *Edmund Fitzgerald.*

His favorite.

"Oh my God." He crawled to it. "I'm so sorry."

"It's okay." Vargas came to kneel beside him. He laid a warm hand at Seth's nape. "It's just a silly model."

"No. I fucked it up. I fucked it all up."

"You did not."

Seth reached for the battered model. "I need to fix it." He frantically gathered the various pieces off the floor. "I need to fix it."

Vargas stopped him. He held Seth's face in both hands, lifting his head up until he looked at him. "Don't worry about it. These models mean nothing to me compared to you."

"I have to fix it. I have to."

Vargas searched his face. "All right. We'll fix it together. Okay?"

"Okay."

Vargas took the broken pieces and placed everything on the shelf. Then he encouraged Seth off the floor and into the office chair. He leaned the cane nearby and sat on the edge of the desk facing him, clasping one of Seth's hands in both of his. "What upset you so much? Before the boat."

"I tried to go downstairs."

"Into the club?"

Seth nodded. "I only made it down a couple of steps." He gestured to the window beside the desk. "I was watching you and Miyata. Then I saw something I thought was suspicious, and I wanted to check it out, but..." He shrugged. No need to say more. Vargas had seen the aftermath of that attempt.

Vargas shook his head. "Now my paranoia has made you paranoid."

Seth snorted out a laugh. "I have PTSD. I was already paranoid."

"Don't make light of what you feel."

"Why? It's my life. I should be able to laugh at myself if I want." He wiped the last of the tears from his eyes. "I think I was just looking for any excuse to try going into the club. And then..."

He didn't want to share what he'd remembered about Henderson. He didn't want Vargas to regret bringing him there.

But no matter what, he didn't want to hold back with Vargas. He'd always been truthful with him. "I remembered Henderson hitting me."

"When you went downstairs?"

"Yeah. I can remember lying on the table. He'd already been beating me, and it hurt so bad. I couldn't move, but he wasn't done. The look on his face... He was enjoying it. I thought that was how I was going to die. Naked, bleeding, crying, weak. I remember thinking how glad I was to be out of the cage. That it was nice to die somewhere that I liked, somewhere special, inside the Haven."

Vargas squeezed his hand. "I can't imagine how horrible that was for you. I'm sorry you had to relive it like that. But maybe it's a positive thing that you're remembering."

"I just feel like I take one step forward and then five back. I can't win."

"You're doing great. Every day."

Seth drew in a steadying breath. "I feel like I'm missing out on so much of my life."

"Maybe we should go back to your place. Maybe being here isn't the right call."

Seth pulled his hand from Vargas's and sat back. "No. I'm okay now. I think you're right. It's better that I remember." He got up, grabbed his cane, and went to stand before the window, feeling none of the panic from earlier when he'd tried to go down there. He watched two men seated at the bar. They chatted and snickered over their beers, one man casually batting at the arm of the other as if he'd just heard the funniest thing in the world. "Why did you decide to live here in the club?"

Vargas didn't say anything right away. When he did, his tone held less concern. Maybe he sensed Seth's need to change the subject.

"When I bought this place, I wanted to live close by. I figured it was better to spend a little more and add the apartment rather than go further into debt renting someplace else. Then later when my earnings had increased, I realized I liked mixing my personal and professional lives, so I expanded the apartment and renovated it. I'd poured my heart and soul into this place, and I didn't want to leave."

There was a long pause. Then Seth felt his presence behind him right before Vargas spoke again, this time in a whisper. "Can I hold you?"

Seth nodded.

Vargas slipped an arm around Seth's waist and settled a hand over his stomach. Without letting go, he lifted Seth's left hand. Bruises were forming on the knuckles from where he'd punched the wall.

"We should get this looked at."

"It's okay. It doesn't really hurt."

Vargas tenderly kissed each knuckle before lowering Seth's hand. He wrapped both arms around his waist and continued to hold him.

Seth settled back into the embrace. "Why did you first open the club?"

"I wanted to get laid."

Seth turned in his arms.

Vargas had a slight grin on his face. "Seriously. It was that simple. There was no place to go back then that didn't feel seedy and dangerous. Which can be exciting, don't get me wrong, but I wanted something more. I started hosting private parties with friends and acquaintances, and it grew from there." He glanced out over the club, pride visible on his face. "When I purchased this building, I wanted to create a safe haven where gay men could meet, whether they wanted to drink, dance, talk, fuck, or whatever, without worrying about getting their asses kicked or for some cop to arrest them in a public bathroom. It took a long time and a lot of work before the club started to look like it does today." He shook his head. "I was so young then. If you had told me that one day I'd have all this, I never would've believed it."

"But you wouldn't have done it differently?"

Vargas laughed. "I guess not." The smile rapidly vanished from his face, though. "There's one or two things I would've done differently." He held still, that stern expression locked on his face. Then he let go of Seth and gestured at the files covering his desk. "I've been thinking about all this. You don't need to go through the finances anymore."

"Why not?"

"I've made a decision." He went to the desk and sat in the chair. "I'm done with it. I'm going to close the club and sell the building."

"What? No." Seth hurried forward until he stood between Vargas and the desk. "You can't do that."

"The Haven doesn't mean to me what it used to. I can see that now."

"Only because you're letting it. You love this place."

"I did."

"You still do. You just don't want to admit it to yourself." Seth propped his cane against the edge of the desk and leaned back. "My dad used to say that the worst thing a man could do was lie to himself."

"Your dad's an asshole."

"He is, but he was right about that. You're letting all your guilt and your anxiety, your need for all this unnecessary security run your life."

"I want to be with you, Seth, and I can't do that here. I can't have this place in my life every day."

"No, that's not—" Seth sighed, not wanting to let anger and frustration take hold of him anymore that night. "Please don't sell the Haven because of me. Someday you'll regret it, and I don't want to be responsible for that."

"I won't regret it. And you have nothing to feel bad about. This is my decision."

"You're making the wrong one. Please don't do this."

Vargas got up, and without saying more, he went across the hall. Seth gathered his cane and followed. In the master bedroom, Vargas was already undressing for bed. Seth kept quiet and simply watched him, not knowing what to say or do to get the most stubborn man he'd ever met to listen to him.

When Vargas was down to his underwear, he sat on the edge of the bed as if all the energy had been zapped from him in an instant. Seth moved to stand before him, getting an even better view of that amazing body than he had the night before. He wanted to climb onto the bed with him and forget that he'd ever heard anything about selling the Haven, but he couldn't do that. He wouldn't let Vargas ruin his life for him.

The silence was heavy between them. Vargas exhaled a long breath. He dipped a finger into the waistband of Seth's pants and tugged him closer until Seth stood between his spread thighs. "I have to do what feels right. For me."

"I know. But what happened to me isn't about the club or this building. I'm going to be able to walk downstairs someday and not freak out. I'm going to be able to go outside by myself. I know it. I just had a setback tonight."

"That's all it was, Seth. You will be able to do everything you want."

"I will. So please don't give up. This place is your dream."

Without hesitation, Vargas shook his head. "Nope. Not even close." He got up and slid his arms around Seth. "You're my dream."

The words washed over Seth. Two weeks ago, he hadn't imagined he'd ever hear such things from Vargas. He held him in return. "Just please don't decide anything right now. Don't do anything you can't take back. Think it over a little more? For me?"

Vargas hesitated. "All right. I'll give it some more thought."

"Thank you."

"But right now…" Vargas tipped his head toward the bed behind him. "Come to bed with me?"

Seth nodded.

Without a word, Vargas undressed him until Seth stood there in only his underwear. They slipped under the covers, and Vargas slid in close behind him, spooning him along his length, an arm around his waist.

Seth heard the distinct padding of Charlie's paws on the floor as he came into the room. The dog jumped onto the bed and curled up alongside them, his back butted up against the front of Seth's calves.

"Charlie, get down. This is Vargas's bed."

"No." Vargas held Seth tighter and kissed the back of his head. "He's perfect right where he is."

* * * * *

Vargas kept hold of Seth until he heard him drift off to sleep. Only then did he roll onto his back and think about what had happened.

Walking into his office that night and seeing Seth so distraught and out of control had broken his heart. He'd read enough about PTSD to know that the outburst was a common response. He'd just never seen Seth go through something like that, and witnessing it had nearly paralyzed him. He hadn't been sure what to do, if trying to stop Seth and comfort him had been the right call, but he had to do something. He didn't give a fuck about his office or his models, but he'd been terrified Seth would hurt himself.

Which also helped him make another decision.

He couldn't hold off any longer. He had a theory, and he had to know if he was right. There wasn't anything in the world he wouldn't do to keep Seth safe, to keep him from ever having to live through another nightmare.

Which meant Vargas had to do the one thing he never thought he'd do: talk to the man who could finally give him answers.

Chapter Twenty-Two

Vargas folded his arms over his chest and glared across the table at the man he despised with every fiber of his being. "I wanted you to know I figured it out."

Prescott scoffed and sat back in his seat. The cuffs securing his wrists and the chains locking them to a ring on the table scraped across the surface.

They were seated inside the visitation room of the county jail. Two guards stood nearby, their complete focus on Prescott. The rest of the room was empty of all other visitors and inmates, cleared out before Prescott had been brought in.

It had taken a call to Prescott's attorney to arrange the visit. Lauber had seemed skeptical that his client would agree to the meeting, but curiosity must've done a number on Prescott. He said he'd meet with Vargas that same day.

As the silence stretched on, Prescott's scowl became more prominent. He seemed thinner than at the trial, but he was still a well-built man, far stronger than most. The orange jumpsuit he wore was open at the top, allowing an unobstructed view of the scar on his neck from where Dylan had stabbed him with a screwdriver. The slow smile that formed on his lips was smug. Vargas wanted to pummel it right off the son of a bitch's face.

Instead Vargas kept his expression neutral, hoping like hell Prescott wouldn't pick up on the lie.

Prescott finally asked, "Figured what out?"

"Who hired your attorney."

He shrugged. "I've always known."

Vargas had expected that. Whether it was the truth or not was another story. "I'm guessing he had no intention of you finding that out."

"Good guess."

"Do you know why he wants you out of prison?"

"Of course."

When Vargas didn't respond or alter his determined stare, Prescott spoke again, his hard glare unflinching.

"So he can try to kill me."

That, Vargas hadn't expected. Not exactly. He remained impassive, burying his surprise. Brooks had been right. All this time, and Vargas had been looking for someone with the wrong motive.

There was a man out there who wanted to kill Prescott, and he was willing to put Seth and Dylan and the others at risk in the process.

The list of people who'd want Prescott dead was long, Vargas's name right at the top, along with the other family and friends of Prescott's victims. Prescott hadn't corrected him when he'd called the person who'd hired the attorney a man, so Vargas went with his hunch.

"Because of what you did to his son."

At first Prescott didn't react. He just kept glaring at him. Then he simply grinned again, a disturbing, spine-chilling smile that confirmed Vargas's words.

Fuck. Vargas mentally ran through the list of who it could be. He settled on the two most likely. Not that it mattered which one. Seth finding out either man was helping to get Prescott out of prison would be traumatic, even if it was motivated by a desire to end the man.

"Why not hire someone to kill you in prison?"

"He wants to do it himself." Prescott sat forward. "But does the why matter? I'm going to get out of here."

"No. This appeal isn't going anywhere."

"If you really believed that, you wouldn't be here." He leaned farther forward and rested his forearms on the table, the chains clanking along the metal surface once again, the sound harsh and grating, as were his words. "And when I get out, you know who I'm coming for."

It took every ounce of Vargas's restraint not to lunge and attack the man. "You're not getting anywhere near him."

Rage immediately replaced Prescott's grin. "He's not yours."

"You're right. I don't own him like he's something I paid for. But I will protect him from you no matter what I have to do."

"Go ahead and try. It'll make it more fun."

"You can delude yourself all you want, but you're never getting free. Your attorney can write all the briefs in the world, but no judge is ever going to let you out."

"You know as well as I do there was evidence that judge never should've allowed. The cops and prosecutors wanted someone to blame, wanted someone they could offer on a platter to the press. So they twisted my relationship with my boys into something—"

Vargas shot forward, slapping both hands down on the table. "You'll *never* get out. Because I did far more than learn who hired Lauber for you." He stood and kicked his chair back, the metal legs scuffing the concrete floor. "I figured out how to make him stop trying to get you out. You'll have no one helping you any longer."

Prescott's eyes widened for a brief second. Then that glare was back.

Vargas was done. He had what he came for. He turned his back on the son of a bitch and headed for the door. He just hoped he'd said enough, hoped being in the presence of that disgusting, depraved monster—and being unable to beat the hell out of him—had been worth it.

An hour later, he sat waiting in the lobby of an office building after relieving Tucker's man who'd been following Lauber. Despite Prescott's jailhouse locale, it wouldn't take long for him, or whoever might be helping on the inside, to get a call through.

Sure enough, Vargas spotted Lauber stepping off the elevator. The man made a mad dash for the front entrance and got in a cab. Vargas followed in a second cab in an attempt to blend in, telling the driver to keep some distance, but no way was he losing this chance.

Lauber took the cab four blocks to another office building and scurried inside. Vargas stayed on him through the lobby until Lauber ducked into a crowded elevator going up. Vargas held back. He couldn't risk being spotted.

The lighted numbers above the elevator door indicated that the car made stops at multiple floors. No way to know which floor Lauber got off on. Vargas marched over to the information kiosk and scanned the directory. One name leaped out. The owner of the entire building and CEO of the corporation whose offices filled the top floor.

"Son of a bitch."

* * * * *

Jarrett Gates waited silently off to the side in his boss's office, trying his best to keep his nerves at bay and avoid fidgeting. The attorney had been there and gone thirty minutes earlier. One of their contacts in the jail had gotten in touch with the lawyer to let them know that Raymond Vargas had visited with Prescott in the jail, and that Vargas had said he knew who hired his attorney, although he didn't offer a name. Vargas also told him he had a way to get Prescott's benefactor to back off.

But the worst part was that, during the conversation, Prescott admitted he knew the real goal behind the plan to get him out of prison.

The entire thing had freaked Lauber out, and he'd arrived to talk to Jarrett's boss without taking any of the usual precautions to avoid detection.

If their hunch was correct, and Lauber was indeed followed there, Vargas should've made his move by now.

"Sir, how much longer would you like to wait?"

The man kept his back to the room and continued examining the streets below from his office window like the entire city was an empire he'd built. He didn't turn around. "It won't be long now."

As if on cue, the phone on the man's desk beeped. His receptionist came on the intercom. "Sir, you have a visitor. He doesn't have an appointment, but he insists you'll want to see him. His name is—"

"Send him in."

A moment later, Raymond Vargas entered the office, his posture stiff and straight, fury in his eyes. Jarrett offered a nod, but his boss kept his attention on the world outside as he spoke.

"I suppose you're here to try and talk me out of it." Without waiting for a response, he whirled around and stormed across the room to Vargas. "I want him dead for what he did to my son."

"Can't say I would hate that, but it's not up to us."

"Oh, it is."

Vargas didn't offer harsh words or threats. He didn't try a logical argument. Instead he proposed a deal Jarrett knew his boss would never turn down. Some things were even more important than revenge.

Silence descended as the man studied Vargas. "You'll do it today?"

"Yes, if you agree to stop your attempts to get him out of prison, to put an end to the appeal and whatever else you've got planned."

They stared each other down.

Eventually the man said, "All right. But I'm giving up a lot for this, so you better keep up your end of the bargain. Or I'll make your life a living hell."

"I'll do what I said. Now, convince me you're going to be able to get Prescott to give up on the idea that he's ever getting out."

"Fine. I'll call Lauber, have him talk to Prescott and get him to cancel the appeal."

"How?"

The man considered that for a moment. "Lauber will tell him he's realized they're never going to win, that the other appellate attorneys he's been consulting with don't think they have a case, that he's not even willing to complete any additional work on the brief to submit to the court."

"Prescott could just get another attorney."

"No one good. Not without my money. But if that's not enough, I'll get Lauber to make him see that if he gets out, someone will come after him, and that he'd be safer in prison." Smugness rolled off the man and his words. "I can get him to give up."

"Good." Vargas held out his hand. "Then you have a deal." They shook. Vargas gripped the man's hand tighter and tugged him close. "Which means I don't have to hurt you."

The man laughed.

Jarrett didn't. He wasn't sure who'd win in an all-out fight between the two men.

Chapter Twenty-Three

Vargas left the man's office without another glance back. By the time the cab dropped him off at the parking garage where he'd left his SUV earlier, he'd replayed their conversation in his head multiple times. He wasn't certain the man had been telling him the truth, but taking a chance with the deal they'd made felt like the best option, which meant he had one stop to make before heading home.

It was late when he got to the apartment. The entire place was dark. The guest room door was open, but Seth was nowhere in sight. Vargas continued on to his own room. There under the covers was Seth, already asleep, Charlie lying alongside him.

Vargas approached and stopped beside the bed. Affection and relief welled in his chest as he stared down at Seth. Had he come home and found him asleep in the guest room, he wasn't sure what he would've done. He knew he'd want to join Seth in bed, but he couldn't take that liberty without Seth's okay. He also wouldn't want to wake him and ask if getting in the bed with him would be all right. Then again, how could he have left him undisturbed to go back to his own bed alone?

He loved that Seth had felt comfortable enough to make the choice, to take the initiative with something he wanted.

Charlie was awake now. He lifted his head off the bed. Vargas gave him a pat in greeting, then got undressed down to his underwear and slipped under the blankets with Seth. He dropped a soft kiss on Seth's cheek before settling in beside him.

Seth let out a slight sigh and slid in closer, lying an arm over Vargas's middle and snuggling into him. He mumbled, "Love you."

Vargas held him in return, his mind and body relaxing in an instant. He could get used to this. The perfect end to a shitty day.

He'd worry tomorrow about how to tell Seth what had been so awful about it. And about the deal he'd made.

* * * * *

It was after one in the morning when Seth awoke from a restless sleep. He'd been dreaming about walking through the club again. Even in the dream, a part of him knew he was in the club to attempt triggering more memories, but the dream was hazy and fading fast from his conscious mind. Still, the unease lingered on.

He rolled onto his side and found Vargas lying there on his back, the bedcovers draped over his lower half. Seth laid his head on the man's bare chest and listened to his deep, even breaths, hoping the rhythmic sound would lull him back to sleep. It helped ease some of the tension, but he still couldn't completely calm down.

The last forty-eight hours had been a series of highs, one after the other. The sex with Vargas, working all day without his back hurting, and taking Charlie outside.

Then came the fiasco of trying to go into the club.

Despite Seth's words to Vargas about it merely being a setback, he still felt deflated and disappointed. How shitty was it for him to freak out and make Vargas feel so bad that he now wanted to sell the Haven? Even if there were other reasons for that decision, Seth's outburst had likely sealed the deal.

And why did he have that dream tonight? What else could he possibly have left to remember that would be worse than what he'd already lived through?

Seth stayed in bed for an hour more before he gave up on sleep. When he sat up, so did Charlie. Seth gave him a kiss on the head. "It's okay. Go back to sleep." The dog returned his head to the mattress, and Seth slipped out of the bedroom. He made his way to Vargas's office.

He was determined to find evidence in the records that would explain Vargas's uncertainty about his finances and his accountant, if there was something to find. He wanted to solve that one mystery for him. Maybe that would relieve some of the pressure, and Vargas would give up on the idea to sell the Haven.

Seth got settled in and tried reviewing the last of the files, but the silence had his mind wandering to the same litany of frustrations as before. He recalled seeing a media app installed on Vargas's laptop. He opened up the program and scanned the list of files for a song he felt like listening to. Halfway down the list he discovered something else entirely: his name amid the artists and song titles. It was a video file. The metadata was visible to the right, including the *date created*, *number of times viewed*, and *last accessed date*.

He clicked to play the video and sat in shock as he watched the contents.

When it was over, he stared at the blank screen for another anguished moment. Then he shut down the computer, grabbed his cane, and turned out the lights in the office.

He went across the hall. With his cane leaning against the nightstand, Seth slipped under the covers and returned to his earlier position with his head on Vargas's chest. He stayed like that for a minute, listening to the quiet, strong beat of the heart beneath him. It didn't calm him in the least. Would he ever hear that sound again, ever lie so close to Vargas, ever get to touch him like this again? He wanted to freeze that moment in his memory with such intensity it would never fade. He couldn't keep the tears from spilling out. He swiped them away before they landed on Vargas's bare flesh.

He waited another minute, then forced himself to get up. Once in the guest room, he lugged his empty bags out of the closet and began to pack.

* * * * *

Vargas awoke and bolted upright in a flash. Something wasn't right. Had he been dreaming? Had he heard a noise?

He waited but caught no sign of any sound or disturbance. He turned back to the bed. It was empty. No Seth. No Charlie. He checked the time. After two a.m.

He threw off the covers and hightailed it to the bathroom. The door was open a crack, and the room was dark. He pushed the door in and flipped on the light anyway. He found nothing.

Planning to head for the kitchen next, he got moving, calling out for Seth at the same time. He stopped two steps down the hall when he spotted light seeping out from under the closed door of the guest room. He knocked.

From inside came a mumbled, "Yeah."

Vargas opened the door. Charlie lay on the bed beside Seth's bags. Seth was standing on the other side of the bed, folding a sweatshirt. He slipped it into his open duffel bag.

"What are you doing? What's wrong?"

Without looking up Seth said, "This isn't going to work."

"What? Staying here?"

"You and me." He reached for a folded T-shirt on the bed and placed it in the bag.

"Why?"

He didn't say anything.

Vargas rounded the bed and reached for Seth's hand, stopping him from putting one more damn thing into that bag. "What's going on?"

As if Seth had lost all momentum to continue, he turned and sat on the edge of the mattress. He breathed deep and then lifted his head. There was no sign of anger or blame. "You deserve better than this. I can't even be in a room full of people. I can't go outside by myself."

"I don't care about any of that, except that it hurts you. Besides, you're making progress. You took Charlie out."

He scoffed. "Waiting in a doorway with a guard near the top of the staircase doesn't count. What if I can never go outside alone?"

"We'll keep working with Dr. Arteaga. We'll figure out how to help you."

"What if I can never do more in bed than what we have? What if I can never even give you a blowjob?"

Vargas shook his head. "Do you think I care about a damn blowjob?"

"You will if you never get one again. The rest of your life is a long time to deny yourself something like that."

"Seth, I—" He broke off. Unable to say anything else right away, he sat on the bed beside him. "You want to be together for the rest of our lives?"

"It doesn't matter."

"Seth…"

He wouldn't look at him.

"It matters a hell of a lot to me because that's what I want too."

Seth kept on staring at the floor before him. "What if all I ever do is make you feel guilty?"

"What? That's not—" Vargas tried to calm down. "It's not you that makes me feel that way. It was never you. All you've ever done is make me feel good. So damn good that sometimes I forget." He lifted a hand to Seth's chin and brought his head up. "Let me love you."

Seth shook his head. "I can't."

"Why?" Feeling like he'd taken a punch to the gut, Vargas lowered his hand. "What aren't you telling me?"

"I'll never know if you would've loved me without what happened."

"What do you mean?"

Seth raised a hand to Vargas's bare chest and ran the tips of his fingers over the tattoo decorating his right collarbone. *To get somewhere you've never been, you need to do something you've never done.* "Why did you get this one?"

"I wanted to remember the day I graduated from college."

"And this one?" He indicated another tattoo, in the same place on his opposite side. *To build something others can love is to leave your mark on the world.* Another line from the poem "Life."

"The day I bought this building. It was the anniversary of my dad's death."

"And this?" Seth brushed his fingertips along a string of words on Vargas's forearm. "This one is because of me?"

Vargas didn't reply. What could he say?

"When did you get it?"

"The day you woke up in the hospital."

Once more Seth swept his fingers over the words *you only fail when you stop trying*. "You got it so you'd remember to always do whatever you could to help us. Because that's the least you think you can do. You can't erase what he did to us. You can't rewind our lives. You can't take back the day you approved his membership." Seth looked up at him. "And that tortures you, doesn't it?"

Vargas hesitated. "Sometimes."

As if all the fight had gone out of Seth, his hand landed on his thigh with a smack of finality. "I want you. So much. I want everything with you." He got off the bed and stepped around it, keeping his back to Vargas as if he couldn't face him when he said the rest. "But what if one day you realize what you think you feel for me isn't real."

Vargas stood. He went to Seth and rotated him around by his upper arms. "I know what I feel. It's very real." He held Seth's face in his hands. "And it's something I'm willing to fight for. Every day."

Seth removed Vargas's hands from his face. "You shouldn't have to." Without another word, he turned and left the room.

For a stunned moment, Vargas didn't move. Then he snapped out of it and hurried out after him. "Where are you going?"

Seth didn't reply, just headed down the hall and into Vargas's office. He crossed the room to the window that overlooked the dark, empty club. He remained silent for several breaths. "You don't love me. Not the way I want you to."

"Don't say that. I know what I feel."

Seth shook his head. "You've been really good to me. I don't know where I'd be if you hadn't helped me. I'd still be in the wheelchair, locked up inside my apartment like I was in that cage."

"That's not true."

"It is. Going places with you, I felt safer. Like I wasn't alone in this."

Vargas moved to Seth's side. "You're not alone. I will always be there for you. Whatever you need. Not because I feel guilty, but because I care about you. I love you. That will never change. But, Seth, everything you've accomplished, you did on your own."

"You don't know how much it helped having you there. And I'm not going to repay you for that by letting you believe what isn't true. You feel guilty and you feel sorry for me. That's it."

"This thing between us isn't about that."

"It isn't? I found a video on your computer. I was going to listen to some music while I worked, but when I saw a file with my name, I watched it."

Vargas took an uncontrolled step back.

"It's the security footage from the night I met with Prescott. It shows me walking across the club. Less than twenty minutes later, I was in a room upstairs fighting for my life. You know the video I mean, don't you?"

He nodded, unable to utter a single word in response.

"Yeah, you do. The last viewed date on the file was yesterday morning, and the total number of times you watched it? 1,988." Seth swallowed, then continued. "I've heard you mumbling in your sleep. They're nightmares from when you found me in the club, aren't they? That's what you were talking about that time when you mentioned being so terrified you almost couldn't breathe. You can't forget that day."

Vargas held still through a long exhale. "I thought you were going to die. Right there in my arms."

"That feeling of helplessness, that culpability you feel, it isn't love. I was deluding myself to think otherwise, wanting it to be true so badly."

Vargas snorted out a laugh as he spun away and strode across the room. He kept his back to Seth for several seconds, then came around. "You don't get it. All this time, and you don't know how I see you. I do feel bad for you, and I do feel guilty about letting Prescott into the club. All that started the day you disappeared. Back then, I could barely remember talking to you at your interview. Maybe when you were first in the hospital, my being there was about that guilt and about wanting to help you because I felt bad for you. You wouldn't talk. You were afraid all the time. Hearing you say in the courtroom what happened to you… that broke my heart."

Seth glanced away.

Vargas forged on. "All that made me feel even worse for you. But none of that made me fall in love with you. In fact, because of all that, I tried like hell to fight what I was feeling, but that was unbearable. The minute you began to relax around me, to talk, to smile, to be yourself in little ways, that's when I started falling for you."

Seth swung his gaze back and examined Vargas's face. "What if when I'm all healed and I'm stronger, when I'm less afraid, what if you don't like me anymore?"

That's what this was really about.

Vargas moved in closer. "That's not possible. Every day you get stronger, and I fall harder." He took a chance and stepped up to him, wrapping his arms around Seth and pressing his lips to his temple. "I love you. So much there aren't enough words to describe it. I need you to know that's the truth more than I've ever needed anything." He pulled back and studied him, and he knew....

Seth wanted to give in. Vargas could see it in his eyes. Seth was saying all the things he thought he should, but he didn't *want* to say any of it.

"I'm with you, Seth, because I love you. You don't get to tell me what I'm feeling isn't true. It's my heart. I know what this thing is between us. It's powerful and beautiful and meaningful in a way nothing else in my life has ever been. I know it's that way for both of us. And the sex? That's just one part of being in a relationship. I know we can figure out ways to be intimate that work for you, for us. Together."

Seth's eyes grew moist as he gaped up at him.

"It's okay." Vargas swiped at a tear that fell down Seth's cheek. "Whatever you feel or don't feel is okay. If you need space and time to really believe what I'm saying, you can take as much as you need. You can stay alone in the guest room if you want. But no matter what, I will wait for you. As long as it takes, as long as you need, I will wait for you." He cupped Seth's face in his hands again. "Just please don't leave. Not like this."

Seth was still and quiet for several breaths. Then he nodded.

Vargas stroked his cheeks with both thumbs. "And don't ever doubt yourself or your strength. You've come so far. Just look." He gave a nod toward Seth's lower half, pride surging through him. "You walked in here without the cane."

Seth staggered back a step and looked down at himself. He let out a huff of air that sounded like a laugh. When he glanced up, a smile was plastered on his face, his eyes wet with tears again. He bounded forward and wrapped his arms around Vargas's neck. "I did it."

Vargas held him in return. "You did. You got out of that chair and worked your ass off all on your own."

Seth held on tighter. "Thank you." Another emotion-filled laugh surged out of him. "I did it. I did it!"

Chapter Twenty-Four

Vargas silently sat in his office on the first floor of the club, his hand clutching his cell phone where it lay on his desk. It had been going on like that for nearly a half hour. He just couldn't pick up the phone, let alone place the call.

He let go and sank back in his chair.

He also couldn't stop going over the night before, trying to determine if he'd used the right words, said the right things, made the right move in asking Seth to return to his bed with him. They hadn't talked any more about why Seth had been packing or if he believed Vargas's words. They had simply gone to his room and gotten in bed together.

Vargas held him and waited until Seth drifted off to sleep. Then he'd returned to his office to delete the video file Seth had found. After he had that finished, he went back to the bedroom and curled up around Seth. He didn't get much sleep, though. Too much kept rolling through his mind.

It had been unhealthy for him to watch that video as often as he had, to obsess over what Seth had been like before the attack or what could've been done to prevent it from ever happening in the first place.

It was not right for him to continue letting someone else's actions have so much power over him.

He breathed deep, grabbed his phone, and dialed. When Dr. Arteaga's answering service picked up, he opened his mouth to speak but nothing came out. He knew what he needed to say, that he needed help. Not just to show Seth that his guilt wasn't controlling everything in his life, but also for himself. He had to find a way to let this go. He just couldn't get the words out. He hung up and slammed the phone down. Mumbling a curse, he pushed away from the desk and headed out into the club.

When he got to the apartment upstairs, he refrained from

immediately calling out for Seth. Instead he quietly scanned the living room and the kitchen for him, then the bedrooms and the office, but Seth was nowhere in sight. Vargas's heart thundered away as he stopped outside the empty guest room. There was no sign of the bags they'd left on the bed the night before.

"Shit." He pulled out his cell phone, ready to dial Seth's, but he eased up. He absolutely needed to make sure Seth was okay, but he also knew that if leaving was what Seth wanted, he had to respect that. Seth didn't need to feel pressured or manipulated.

That's when he spotted the open safe room door.

"Seth?" He strode forward and stopped in the doorway, relief washing over him at what he found inside.

Seth was lying on the floor on top of a pile of pillows and blankets he'd taken from the benches. He had an open book perched beside him. One of his arms was wrapped around Charlie who lay on the makeshift bed with him. Both looked like they'd been asleep for a while. Seth's cane was leaning against the bookshelf. Earlier that morning he'd been using it on and off, but he seemed to be relying on the cane less after his success without it the night before.

Vargas couldn't take his eyes off Seth. He looked peaceful, like his dreams were no longer chasing him with the horrors of his past.

Then Seth's even breathing changed as he stirred and opened his eyes. He smiled as soon as he spotted Vargas in the doorway. "Hey." He stretched and sighed, running both hands down his face. "Guess I fell asleep."

"You look comfortable."

"I like it in here."

"I'm glad."

Seth shifted on the pillows until he was sitting up. "It's comfy."

Charlie spotted Vargas in the doorway and darted for him. Vargas gave him a pat on the head, and Charlie took off out of the bedroom and down the hall, probably going to check his bowl for fresh food.

Seth glanced around the small room. "I was thinking... I'd like to try something. Could we close and lock the door so I can see what it's like? I can't decide if it would freak me out or if it would feel like my closet at my place. Do you mind?"

"Not at all." Vargas took a step backward into the bedroom. He gestured at the safe room door. "Give it a try. I'll be right here if you need anything. If you want to stay in longer than fifteen minutes, just remember to enter that all-clear code I gave you so the police don't show up."

"No. I was... I thought maybe you'd come in here with me."

"Oh." Vargas's mouth went dry, and he felt his face flush as his blood pressure rose. Sweat formed at the back of his neck.

Same response since he'd been a kid.

One look at the hope on Seth's face, though, and Vargas didn't give it another thought. He moved into the safe room. It wouldn't be for long.

He pulled the heavy door shut and spun the handle, securing the first set of metal bolts. Using his thumb, he engaged the biometric lock and then entered the code. The second set of bolts locked into place. The display panel's indicator light changed to red. The word *activated* lit up in the center of the screen. He faced the room and tried for casual as he searched for any sign that this was too much for Seth.

Seth glanced around the sealed room. "It's loads bigger than my closet." He continued surveying the area as if he were seeing it for the first time, assessing the enclosed space and his feelings about it.

A lump formed in the back of Vargas's throat. He turned to the door, bracing his hands on the steel frame.

"I don't really feel—" Seth abruptly cut off. Vargas heard him shifting off the pillows behind him, but he couldn't compel himself to turn around and help Seth stand. How much of an ass did that make him? It still took Seth some effort to do something like get up from the floor. Vargas closed his eyes and let out a ragged breath. That did nothing to relax him or slow his labored breathing.

"Vargas?" Seth stood beside him then, one hand on his upper arm.

Vargas asked, "What don't you feel?"

"Trapped. Are you okay?"

He nodded.

"Are you sure?"

"Yeah." He kept still, kept his focus on the closed door before him.

Seth gave a tug on his arm. "You're lying. Why?"

He hadn't meant to. Not to Seth. It was just his standard reply whenever he felt like this. He said it without thinking.

"Vargas, are you claustrophobic?"

Vargas sucked in another long gulp of air, trying to steady his nerves. "A little bit."

"A little? Maybe a lot?"

He nodded, barely able to move his head that time. The slightest movement made everything worse.

"Oh my God." Seth shifted around him and went for the control panel. "You didn't have to do this." He scanned his thumb, input the code, and pressed the release button, but nothing happened. The red light was still visible on the screen. He tried again. Still nothing. He looked to Vargas. "Am I doing something wrong?"

"I don't think so." Vargas moved in and gave it a try. Again the door remained locked. Then the screen went completely blank. He randomly clicked on various parts of the touch screen, but everything stayed dark. The safe room had power, but it was like the control panel didn't.

"Here." Vargas pointed to the edge of the doorframe. "There's also a backup spring-loaded release. It's only accessible from inside." He tugged on the lever, but there was no sound of the bolts retracting. He tried the handle, but it wouldn't spin with the lock still engaged. He gave the door a tug anyway. Panic hit hard when it wouldn't budge. "This was supposed to be thoroughly tested after it was installed."

Seth bent and examined underneath the bottom edge of the control panel. "Maybe there's a short in it."

Vargas searched his pockets. "Dammit. I left my phone with my keys on the hall table. You have yours?"

"It's on the desk in your office."

Vargas indicated the cabinet along the wall beside the bookcase. "There's supposed to be an emergency phone in those supplies."

Seth placed a hand on Vargas's arm again. "I'll get it. Stay here." He went to the cabinet, taking care without his cane but also moving with surprising deftness. He opened the cabinet doors and knelt before the bottom row of plastic storage tubs. Vargas couldn't help himself. Just taking in the sight of Seth moving with more ease, he suddenly felt lighter. His breathing slowed. He moved in and got down to help him.

Inside the first tub were energy bars, bottled water, and canned goods. They continued on to another tub with extra blankets, a flashlight, batteries, and a deck of playing cards. The next: a first aid kit, pepper spray, duct tape, a roll of paper towels, and a switchblade knife.

"Shit." Vargas chucked the items he'd pulled out back into the last tub. "It should be with this stuff."

Seth had stopped searching and was staring down at the canister of pepper spray in his hand. "Dylan went to self-defense classes a few months ago. He's really into it now. I think he even mentioned taking the test to try to get into the police academy." Seth rotated the pepper spray from one hand to the other. "I think I'm ready to take a class."

"Sounds great."

"I should've done it months ago with Dylan."

"You do things when you're ready. Besides, might be easier now that you're not relying on the cane so much." Vargas indicated where the cane lay propped against the bookshelf.

Seth glanced at it and smiled. "Yeah." He refocused on the open tub. "Is the phone in there?"

"Haven't found it yet." Vargas lugged everything out again until he was at the bottom. No phone. "Tucker and Walter are great guys, but I'm going to kick their asses for recommending this safe room company."

Seth laughed.

That sound was definitely helping Vargas with his anxiety. Until that thought had him remembering they couldn't get out of there.

Shit. "It's going to be okay." He got off the floor and faced the steel door. "Once the door is sealed and locked from the inside, the security company is notified. If no one here enters the all-clear code in fifteen minutes, they'll contact the police and my security here at the club."

"Okay," Seth said. "So we just have to wait for maybe ten more minutes."

Vargas returned to the door. His heart was thundering away, his blood pressure skyrocketing once again. He reached for the spindle handle and gripped it in his clenched fists. He gave it a turn, but the wheel was still secured by the lock. He tried opening the door anyway. No go. Placing his palms flat to the surface, he leaned in, resting his forehead against the cool steel.

Seth came to him and laid a hand on his back. "You okay?"

"Sure." He rotated his head to look at him. "You?" After what Seth had lived through when he'd been held captive, Vargas couldn't believe he wasn't panicking at being locked in there, but he looked calm and steady.

"I'm fine. I'm just sorry I got you stuck in here."

"You didn't do anything wrong." Everything would be fine once the goddamn-fucking-son-of-a-bitch door opened. Vargas faced it again. The air in the room was turning warm and thick, even with the power on and the ventilation system working.

"Vargas?"

He looked Seth's way again. The concern was evident.

"I'm okay. It'd just be a hell of a lot better if I knew for sure when someone would show up. It's worse when I don't know when or how I'll be able to get out."

"How long have you been claustrophobic?"

"As far back as I can remember, but it got worse in middle school."

"Did something happen?"

He paused, trying to put together the words without mentally reliving that day. "There was an older kid who liked to torment the hell out of me. One day after lunch, he and some of his friends jumped me and dragged me into the school's gym. They held me down and rolled me up inside a wrestling mat. I could barely breathe. I couldn't move so much as an inch. It was quite a while before a teacher found me. I already hated tight spaces before then, but since that day it's been worse."

"Assholes."

"Yeah. I'm okay most of the time, but small spaces like this, with the door closed..." He shook his head.

"Elevators?" Seth asked.

"Hate them. I avoid the hell out of the one here at the club as much as I can."

"But... Vargas, you ride in elevators all the time with me. At my apartment building, the doctor's office, everywhere."

"Yeah. It's not like I can't use them at all." He hesitated. "You need to take them, and I'm not about to abandon you when it's hard enough for you to leave your apartment."

Seth gave him a long look of appreciation. "Thank you. I wish you would've told me, though."

"I almost did a few times, but I thought that might change things for me. It's easier to pretend taking the elevator doesn't bother me when I'm doing it for you." Before Seth could say anything to that, Vargas laughed, trying to pretend he was just having a normal, lighthearted conversation, not discussing one of his greatest fears. "Guess I knew pretty early on I was never going to be the type of guy who was into the kinky shit. Being tied up, held down..." He shook his head again. "That's not my thing. I don't like doing it to anyone else either."

He needed to shut the hell up. This wasn't the kind of thing to talk about with Seth. Being stuck in there, he just couldn't think straight.

Seth ran a hand down his back in a comforting touch. "I can't believe you had a school bully. How did you get him to quit being mean to you?"

"I didn't. After that day, my mom talked to the principal. The boy's parents were called in and that was that. It was over."

Seth cocked his head to the side like that surprised him.

"Everybody needs help sometimes." Funny, considering the call to Dr. Arteaga he'd been unable to place earlier.

Seth nodded, then crossed the room and sat on the pile of pillows and blankets. "Tell me more about your childhood, about your family."

"I don't want to bore the hell out of you."

"I want to know. There's still so much stuff I don't know about you."

Vargas scoffed. "You know a lot. More than anyone, really."

Seth held Vargas's gaze. "I want to know the rest. I want to know everything."

"All right." Vargas gave one last look at the steel door, then went to Seth and sat beside him on the floor. "Like what?"

"Does anyone ever call you Raymond? Or Ray?"

"My mom calls me Ray. That's about it."

"What about your dad?"

"He did too."

"How did he die?"

"Car accident. On the freeway. He was killed on impact."

"I'm sorry."

"He was a great dad. Worked hard. Loved my mom something crazy. I always used to wonder what he would've thought about me being gay, but then it hit me one day that I already knew. He would've been fine with it. My mom always has been. Even before it was fashionable. I've never doubted their love for me."

"That's gotta be nice."

"I'm sorry your parents weren't better to you."

Seth shrugged. "It is what it is. I can't change it. So you're still close with your mom?"

"Yeah. She lives back in my hometown."

"Where's that?"

"Tecumseh, Michigan."

"That's where you grew up?"

"Yep. Lived there all through high school. Was even voted homecoming king my senior year."

"Really?" Seth grinned at him. "Did you wear a crown?"

"Sure. It's part of the gig."

"Did you have to dance with a girl?"

"I did. She was my girlfriend at the time."

"So, you dated women?"

"Until I was nineteen. You?"

"No. But in school most of my friends were girls." Seth glanced away as if thinking something over. "I can't imagine being with a woman like that. Never could." He turned back to Vargas. "You slept with your girlfriend?"

"Sure. I had two serious relationships with girls in high school, then one in college. Slept with all three of them. I broke up with the last one right before I started figuring things out about me and guys. I guess the truth was building inside me, subconsciously."

They didn't say anything else right away, and something about the quiet reminded Vargas of where they were and why they couldn't leave. His chest tightened. He returned his focus to the steel door across the room.

"So, would you call yourself bi?"

He looked back to Seth. "No. I have no desire to be with a woman again. Once I'd hooked up with a guy, I got what it was really supposed to feel like."

"Sex?"

"That, and just being intimate, being close with someone. It was completely different touching a man, feeling his body against mine."

Seth bit his bottom lip and nodded. Neither looked away for several breaths, and then Seth asked, "When did you leave Michigan?"

"When I went to college in Ohio. I headed back home in the summers, but then after I graduated I moved again."

"I can't picture you sitting in a classroom for four years. What did you study?"

"Business."

Seth laughed. "Really?"

"Yeah."

He laughed harder, really cracking up. "Did you ever tell any of your professors about your plans to open a gay sex club? Was that your senior project?" That had Seth's head tilted back with more laughter.

Vargas laughed with him. "God, that's great."

"What?"

"Seeing you smile like that. Hearing you laugh. You have an amazing laugh."

Seth dipped his head, but the smile didn't fade.

Vargas offered more. "Back in college I knew I wanted to own a business. Just didn't know what that would be."

"Does your mom know what you do for a living?"

"Sure."

"She's okay with it?"

He grinned. "She tolerates it. But at the same time, she's very proud of me. That doesn't mean she stays here when she visits. I rent us a couple of rooms at a hotel, and I go stay there with her while she's in town."

"She comes here a lot?"

"A few times a year. I go back home just as much, so it usually works out for me to see her once every two or three months."

Seth seemed to be considering that. "But you haven't gone anywhere since I got out of the hospital. I mean, unless you only went for one or two days. I see you almost every day."

"I haven't been back to Michigan since then." Vargas met Seth's stare. "I didn't want to leave you."

"Oh."

"I asked her to come here for the holidays and a couple of other visits. I didn't tell you about it because I didn't want you to feel bad."

The deep affection in Seth's brown eyes had Vargas's tension fading away even more.

He reached for Seth's hand and linked their fingers. "Thanks."

"For what?"

"Distracting me."

"Did it help?"

"More than you know."

"Good." Seth glanced toward the door. "But... I don't think the police or anyone else are coming."

"They will."

"What if they don't?"

"Eventually someone will come looking for me when I don't check in at the club."

Seth gestured toward the door. "We could try opening the control panel, take a look inside. Maybe we could find a loose connection. Maybe there's some tools in the tubs we could use."

Vargas opened his mouth to tell Seth that was a good idea, but all he managed was a series of gasps. Merely talking about the possibility that no one was coming had the panic back with a vengeance. He really had to get out of there.

Seth slid in close and cupped Vargas's face with a hand on each side. Vargas turned to him. The complete concern and devotion staring back at him once again blocked out everything else.

Seth searched his eyes. "Talk to me some more."

"About what?"

"You said you were in love once. Who was he?"

"He was you."

"Me?" Seth's mouth fell open. "So..." He stopped and stared

some more, then wet his lips. "I'm the only one you..." He gestured with his hand between them as if he couldn't say the words.

"I've never felt this way about anyone else."

Seth's bottom lip trembled. He shook his head. "I shouldn't have tried to leave. I don't *want* to leave. All I've wanted for such a long time was to be with you, to hear you say that you wanted me too." He moved in, deliberately and with determination, and pressed their lips together.

It was the same sweet, soft kiss that he'd first given Vargas back at his apartment before they came to the club.

This time when Seth pulled back, the question was clear on his face.

Chapter Twenty-Five

Seth held his breath as he waited, not knowing if he could ask the question, even though he desperately needed to hear the answer.

Vargas reached for him and slid a hand around the back of his neck. He leaned in. "Nothing could make me stop loving you. That's how I know this isn't about guilt or pity or remorse."

He drew Seth the rest of the way forward, offering the same languid, tender kiss Seth had given him. That simple kiss and his words drove away the last of Seth's doubts and fears. He slipped his arms around Vargas and fell into the moment.

The kisses flowed one into the next. The slide of Vargas's tongue on Seth's was exquisite, the touch of his hands electric. Seth wanted more, so much more. He kissed him deeper, harder, and when they pulled back for air, he swept his lips along Vargas's jawline to his earlobe, then down the side of his neck, all the while running his hands over those broad shoulders and toned upper arms. He wanted the clothes out of the way, wanted to really discover Vargas's body, feel him everywhere this time.

Vargas tilted his head back to give Seth more room to nuzzle and explore. "You sure we should do this?"

Seth straightened in a rush. "Yes." He bent in for another kiss, their mouths open, tongues brushing against one another, Vargas tugging on Seth to pull him closer. Seth did the same in return. He wanted everything. Now.

He got up and straddled Vargas. "I want to feel all of you against me." He couldn't control the frenzied sound of his voice or the whimper that followed when Vargas slid his hands under his shirt and caressed his bare flesh.

Seth felt free, alive, vibrant. He shifted forward and back, pressing his groin against that solid body under him.

Their mouths met once more. They kissed again and again,

alternating between soft, sensual presses of their lips and hungrier, frantic kisses.

Seth reached for Vargas's tie and got it open and off him in a flash. Then he tore open Vargas's shirt, most of the buttons popping off in his haste, but that didn't slow either of them. Vargas gripped Seth by the hips and helped him slide forward and back along his lap, repeatedly putting pressure on their cocks as they came in contact.

They kept moving against each other, petting everywhere they could reach, both beyond desperate to take things to the next level. Then Vargas hauled Seth tight against him. He held him by the waist with one hand, planted his other hand on the floor, and shifted his hips, bucking up against Seth as if they were already naked and his cock was buried inside him.

Seth could practically feel Vargas's dick sliding into him. He whimpered again. He really needed Vargas to get naked. Now. He wanted to feel every inch of that powerful, tattooed body pumping up under him. He let go of Vargas and hauled his own shirt up his torso. A twinge of pain shot through his lower back, and he winced.

"Shit." Vargas froze. "You okay?"

"Yeah." Seth waited for the pain to worsen like it usually did, but there was nothing more. Maybe his physical therapist had been right. Maybe the worst of it was over and all he needed to do now was strengthen his body and his weakened muscles. He might always have occasional stiffness and chronic pain in his knee and back, but it wasn't bad. He got started on his shirt again, unhurriedly this time, and Vargas helped him pull it off.

He knew what Vargas would ask next, so he beat him to it. "Please don't stop. I want this so much."

"Why don't we wait for the bed?"

Seth shook his head. "It didn't hurt that much. Not like I was expecting it to. It used to be bad."

"I know."

Yeah, he did. Vargas had been there with him through the worst of it.

"I'm okay, really. Maybe just a little..." He worried his bottom lip between his teeth. "Nervous."

"We don't have to do anything you're not ready for. I just want to be close to you."

"That's just it. I'm ready for more." He ran his fingers through the hair above Vargas's ears. "I feel safe here with you. I don't want to wait any longer. Not for anything. I want it all."

Vargas searched his eyes, then traced Seth's lower lip with the pad of his thumb. He kissed him again, and Seth returned the kiss, trying to convey all that this meant to him.

When they eventually parted, both breathless and gasping, clinging to each other like they'd lose this chance if they let go, Vargas rested his forehead against Seth's. "Trust me?"

"Always."

"Stand up."

Seth got up, reluctant to move, but he meant what he said. He trusted Vargas not to hurt him or let him down.

After he was standing, Vargas gripped his waistband. "Come closer."

Seth moved in until he stood straddling Vargas's outstretched legs. Every inch of his body vibrated as he waited, wanting, *needing* Vargas to make the first move that time.

As if Vargas understood exactly what Seth couldn't voice, he again reached for the top of Seth's sweatpants. He kept his focus on Seth's face as he slid the fabric down, brushing the backs of his fingers over Seth's underwear-clad erection in the process, then repeating that action again, leaving no doubt he made the move on purpose. He gave one more teasing sweep of his hand, then shimmied the pants down over Seth's hips and his thighs, lowering his underwear next and freeing his aching erection.

Vargas finished removing the clothes, and then Seth was naked. In what felt like a reverent move, Vargas trailed his warm palms up Seth's calves to the backs of his thighs, then his ass.

"You're so gorgeous." Without delay Vargas leaned in and ran his tongue around the flared head of Seth's cock. Once, twice. He massaged Seth's ass as he sucked the entire head between his lips, kissing and licking and savoring the crown until Seth shook from the pleasure.

Vargas let go of him. "What do you want?"

"You. Naked too."

Vargas grinned up at him. "Step back." He got up from the floor and stripped off his shirt, taking his time, toying, teasing. He kept Seth in his sights as he licked his lips and reached for the front of his slacks next. He undid the button and the zipper and tore open the front. With a powerful thrust, he shoved the pants down and stepped out of them and his underwear. Then Vargas stood there completely bare.

Seth swallowed and tried to keep from looking like a drooling fool who'd never seen a naked man before. Hard to do with all that fine muscle and sleek flesh on display before him.

Vargas pulled him in close. "You like what you see, huh?"

Before Seth could answer, Vargas kissed him, their bare bodies connecting along their lengths.

The feel of their crashing arousal and the unrestrained way Vargas touched and held him was intoxicating, had Seth dizzy. A surge of sensation rushed through him, and his body swayed without his consent.

That was okay. Vargas had him.

He kept hold of Seth's hips even as he dropped to his knees before him and loved on his cock again, this time lowering his mouth all the way down his shaft with each stroke, repeating the slick action again and again. Seth laid a hand at the back of Vargas's head. His breathing picked up speed, turning erratic.

As if Vargas didn't want this to end too quickly, he released him. "Come down here." He helped Seth sit over his thighs, that time nothing between them. He carefully drew him closer. "You tell me if anything hurts."

Hurt? He hadn't felt this amazing in forever. He knew Vargas needed the reassurance, though. "I will."

"You tell me if you want us to stop."

"I promise." Seth offered another kiss, running his palms up Vargas's muscular chest. He wanted to draw this out, to know what would drive Vargas's arousal higher. He wanted to see what he'd look like when he was on the edge, writhing and desperate for more. He wanted to give him everything. He grazed his thumb over a nipple, and Vargas sucked in a sharp breath, then dived into the kiss with more fervor.

Someone liked that.

Seth teased both sides of his chest then, taking turns with each, flicking them to a point, then soothing with the pad of his thumb. "I want..." He didn't say the rest, just moved off Vargas. "Lay down."

Without delay Vargas shifted to lie on the floor, his head propped on a pillow. With complete focus, he watched Seth crawl to him.

Starting at Vargas's knees and making his way up, Seth worshipped his body with hands, lips, and tongue, learning every inch of him, memorizing Vargas's reactions, every shift of his breath, every gasp, every laugh when he hit a ticklish spot, every raw groan when Seth found his erogenous zones: along the tattoo above his pubic hair, the inside of his thighs, any place on the side of his neck.

Seth could've continued on like that all night, but he also wanted to give him more. He settled with his head over Vargas's erection.

"Wait." Vargas lifted his head. "You don't have to."

"I know. I *want* to." He held Vargas's shaft in one hand and parted his lips. He took the tip into his mouth and swirled his tongue around the head.

Goddamn.

He'd nearly forgotten the thrill and power that came with having a man's dick in his mouth.

And this time, it wasn't just anyone's. It was Vargas's. How many times had he dreamed about this moment?

That thought alone had him opening wider, taking in the entire top half of Vargas's length and pulling to the tip, loving the sleek feel of that intimate, warm flesh sliding along his lips and tongue.

Despite Seth's words to Vargas, somewhere in the back of his mind, he'd been worried about a panic attack, but all he felt was an incredible blast of adrenaline and arousal.

He was sucking cock again.

That urged him on. He engulfed the head once more, running his tongue over the tip and all around the glans. Vargas groaned, and Seth let his eyes fall shut, relishing in the rush of lust that came with offering himself in this exquisite act of pleasuring another man.

He worked Vargas over more, jerking the base with his hand, never letting up with the wet heat of his mouth and tongue. He wanted this to be the best damn blowjob Vargas had ever received. He flicked his tongue over the slit, then went down on him again and again.

His slick sounds filled the small room.

Vargas moaned louder. His hands were at his sides, clenching over and over like he was trying to grasp on to something. Seth took one of those hands in his and brought it to the back of his own head.

As if that was all the permission he needed, Vargas threaded his fingers through Seth's hair. He didn't grasp or tug or hold him down. He was just there, completely in the moment with him. Something about that move made the whole exchange even more personal. Seth felt connected to Vargas in an entirely new way.

Vargas groaned again, louder and longer that time. His abs tightened. He was close. But then he bolted upright. "Wait. Stop. Stop."

Seth lifted his head. "What's wrong?"

"Nothing. Absolutely nothing. Come here." He pulled Seth up so he was lying over him, their bodies lined up. "Together? Like this?"

"Yes!"

Vargas gripped Seth by the hips and helped him rock back and forth so Seth's cock was dragging along the length of Vargas's with each shift of his body. The hair on Vargas's muscular thighs grazed

Seth's own. Vargas added bucking up under him in little movements, aiding in the beautiful slide of their pricks.

Seth had no words for how incredible it all felt. But he wanted more. He rolled onto his back, pulling Vargas on top of him.

Vargas locked his arms, keeping his weight off Seth. His dark eyes held a panicked look of alarm. "You sure?"

"Yes. Please."

Vargas searched his face. The concerned expression dissipated, and he nodded. With hands propped on each side of Seth, he gradually lowered down onto him, their naked skin coming together once again. Instinctively Seth spread his thighs, and Vargas settled in between them. He rotated his hips. Once. Twice. Then he thrust forward, sliding his erection along Seth's. He did it again. And again. Long, deep strokes. With each plunge, Vargas drove harder against him, gliding his cock and body along Seth's shaft over and over.

Seth reveled in the buzz of sensation, in the way Vargas held nothing back, and in the feel of that powerful body pushing them both to the edge.

Their eyes met. Seth knew this man, knew his heart and soul, and understood the dark places he'd been and why.

He trusted Vargas with everything he was. He'd never had that with anyone before, definitely not anyone he'd ever had sex with. That emotional connection, mixed with the physical one, was beyond exhilarating.

Maybe it was the same for Vargas. His movements slowed as he kept his eyes locked on Seth's, like he wanted to draw out the moment, or make it far more meaningful than a raw coming together of aroused flesh. He seemed to be longing to say something but wasn't sure if he should.

Seth offered a nod. "Yeah. Me too."

Vargas sucked in a shallow breath and moved with more vigor. Wild, unrestrained, his hips jerked faster, creating searing friction between them, the heat of his skin caressing Seth's cock from base to tip and back. The muscles of Vargas's arms bulged with the strain. His hot breath grew rapid against Seth's lips. "God, I love you."

That did it. Seth dug his fingernails into Vargas's ass and held on as he came, his entire body bucking and shaking with the force of his release. "Oh God. Yes! Yes!"

He was still shooting when Vargas groaned, humping against him with little swift jabs of his hips as he plunged into his own orgasm.

They clung to each other for several long minutes, their deep breaths and rapid heartbeats finding a synchronized rhythm as they came back from the sated place they'd gone.

When Vargas slid off him onto his back, he lay still for a moment, breathing deep. Then he reached for the paper towels from the tub. He swiped at the sticky residue on his own stomach, then Seth's. Returning to lie beside him, he asked, "You all right?"

Seth exhaled. "Jesus, yeah." He reached out for him. "Come back."

Vargas moved into his arms, then scooted down and laid his head on Seth's stomach. "This okay?"

"Yeah."

He brushed a hand down Seth's side. He kissed him above his bellybutton, then higher between two raised scars on his right side. He hesitated, then kissed each scar. "How about this?"

Seth breathed deep and ran a hand over the back of Vargas's head. "Yeah."

"I wish..."

"What?"

Vargas planted another kiss in the center of Seth's chest. Then another. "I wish I could erase them for you."

"You kind of are. Every time you touch me."

Vargas shifted up and propped himself on an elbow beside him. "That was not the right thing for me to say."

"No, it was." Seth traced an invisible path across Vargas's creased brow, trying to erase the concern locked there. "I like knowing what you're thinking. I don't want you to ever hold back. And I don't want to pretend the scars don't exist. It happened. I can't change that. But I'm working through it."

Vargas leaned in and kissed him. "Yeah, you are." He reached for a blanket and pulled it over them, then settled in to lie facing Seth, one arm tucked under his head.

They stayed on the floor of the safe room like that for a long while, fingers sweeping across each other's sensitive skin, their legs entwined, their gazes locked, no more words exchanged but each saying so much, everything Seth had told himself weeks ago not to hope for. But now, it was all there, lying bare before him.

"Are we okay?" he asked.

Vargas grinned, and the smile reached his eyes in a way Seth wasn't sure he'd seen from him before. "I don't know about you, but I feel like we're flying way beyond okay. And not just because of the sex." He came forward, cupped the back of Seth's head, and whispered in his ear. "Although damn, that was a beautiful thing."

A surge of pleasure flowed through Seth, leaving behind a satiated happiness that far exceeded the remarkable orgasm he just had. They were going to be okay, more than okay.

Vargas pulled back and settled on his arm again. "I love you."

"I love you too."

They held the stare between them.

Then there was a change in Vargas's demeanor. Although he hadn't moved or looked away. A moment later, he cleared his throat. "I need to tell you something. I was waiting for the right time, but I don't want to keep it from you any longer, even for a little while."

This wasn't about sex or the two of them. Seth braced for what was to come.

"I know who was trying to get Prescott out of prison."

Chapter Twenty-Six

"Who?"

Seeing the fear in Seth's eyes as he sat up and drew the blanket higher almost had Vargas wishing he could take back what he'd said, but he needed to tell Seth before he found out some other way.

"Franklin Henderson."

Seth gaped at him. "Conrad Henderson's father? But why would he want Prescott to get off? He killed his son."

"He wants revenge."

"How does getting him an appeal equal revenge?"

"He wants him out of prison, so he can murder him."

"Oh." Seth leaned back against the bench behind them. He seemed to be considering that. "I don't know... I don't know how I'm supposed to feel about that."

"You can feel any way you want to."

"I mean, sometimes I wish Prescott had died that day when Kevin and Walter rescued everyone. Sometimes I dream it was me who shot him."

Vargas understood. He had a similar dream: that he'd gone into the basement with Walter that day and had been the one to pull the trigger. Instead he'd been a drunken mess, and Walter had left him behind in the club.

"But," Seth said, "it also feels weird to know that Henderson's father wants revenge that badly. I mean, his son... He..." Seth breathed deep. "He tried to kill me. Prescott may be the reason I'm scared to leave my apartment alone, scared to be seen, but all the surgeries, the broken bones, the PT, the wheelchair... That was all Conrad Henderson's fault. And now that I can remember how he looked at me when he hit me, the thought that someone, even his father, cares enough to want revenge for his death... I don't know what to do with that."

"Go ahead and hate the son of a bitch. I do."

Seth snorted out a half-hearted laugh.

"I mean it. I met the man. He's an ass. I don't know if I believe him, so don't get your hopes up."

"About what?"

"He said he'll fire the attorney and forget this idea of retaliation. He'll try to get Prescott to see that the appeal isn't going to work, try to convince him to drop the whole thing, that he'd ultimately be safer in prison."

"Do you think Prescott will believe him?"

"Maybe."

"He's not that stupid," Seth said with certainty. "He knows he has nothing to lose and everything to gain by going for the appeal. He'll just get another attorney to help him. He has a lot of patience. He'll never give up on the idea that he'll get out someday."

"Maybe he will. It's worth a shot. Let's hope for the best until we know more, yeah?"

"All right." Seth was quiet for a minute. Then he asked, "Why is Henderson willing to back off on his plan for Prescott anyway?"

Vargas thought about the best way to explain that, but before he could answer, Seth's eyes widened in panic. "Franklin Henderson was the one who hired Prescott to get into your club and mess with you, right? He wanted to force you into selling him the building?"

"That was his plan."

"Vargas, you can't." Seth sat taller. "You can't sell him the Haven."

Vargas held up a hand. "I'm not. With the tunnels under the club closed off and the cops aware of their existence, his business associates no longer want this place."

"Then what does he want from you?"

"The police never found enough on him to prove his connection with Prescott, but a man like him hates that it was insinuated in the media. I saw on the news a while back that he's taken a hit with his investors because of his supposed involvement. The only thing he hates worse than someone messing with his family is losing money and his edge in the business world." Vargas drew in a steadying breath. "I agreed to go to the press and say that Henderson was not the one who hired Prescott to get into my club and that the two had no association with each other, that the entire thing was a rumor I started out of anger two years ago."

Seth shook his head. "No. God, no, Vargas. That's lying."

"It's already done. The story comes out tomorrow."

The disappointment on Seth's face hurt to see, but Vargas wasn't about to undo this.

He rotated toward Seth, the blanket still draped across them both. He cupped Seth's cheek in one hand. "I'm going to keep you safe. No matter what. I'm going to do whatever I have to, to make sure he stays in prison, to keep him from ever getting near you again."

Seth laid his hand over Vargas's and leaned into the touch for a long moment.

When he let go, Vargas lowered his hand and added, "Besides, Henderson was never going to be punished for hiring Prescott to mess with me and the club. Even if Henderson one day admits he did it, nothing will happen to him. His lawyers will keep any serious charges away from him. It's not like he hired Prescott to abduct you. Or kill his own son."

At first Seth said nothing in response. His jaw visibly tensed. "I hate this. You're not a liar, Vargas."

"I know, but I think it's our best chance to keep everyone safe. To me, your life, Dylan's, Aaron's, and everyone else's are completely worth this."

Seth seemed to be giving that and the rest of what Vargas had said a lot of thought. Ultimately he nodded. "I trust your judgement." He was quiet for another moment. When he spoke again he sounded resigned and unsure all at once. "I'm not so good at making these kinds of decisions now anyway."

"How do you mean?"

"I don't know what to do sometimes, or what to believe. Other than you, I don't know who to trust. At first, I thought you might be right about Miyata, that he was keeping something from you, but now I don't know. And I get this really weird feeling around both Ian and Neil, which makes no sense."

"Weird how?"

"I don't know. I feel like they're also hiding something, but you trust them more than your other guards or you wouldn't have picked them to watch the apartment."

"Yeah, I do." Vargas lowered his head until Seth looked him in the eye. "But you don't have to trust anyone you don't feel right about. You get to decide who you're comfortable around, who you trust to spend time with and who you believe is being honest with you."

"I guess."

Vargas hesitated. "There's something else I need to tell you."

Seth met his stare.

"When I first figured out that whoever was paying for Prescott's attorney might be doing it for revenge and not because they were trying to help him, I thought it might be Henderson. But I also thought it might be your father, and I didn't want to tell you that until I knew for sure who it was."

"My dad?"

"I knew he was someone who had money, and I figured it was probably a parent of one of Prescott's victims. I'm sorry I didn't tell you everything I was thinking."

"I wouldn't have believed it anyway." Seth shrugged with indifference. "My mom and dad don't care enough about me to bother picking up the phone, let alone something like that." He snorted out a laugh as if he'd told a joke.

It wasn't the least bit funny. Vargas reached for Seth's hand and held it in his. "Screw them. You don't need people like that in your life. You've got me and your friends." He ran the pad of his thumb over the back of Seth's hand. "And my mom is absolutely going to adore you."

Seth gaped at him, a smile forming on his lips. "You want me to meet her?"

"Definitely."

"She won't think I'm too young for you?"

"She's going to be thrilled I'm finally serious with someone. I've never brought anyone home to meet her before."

"Really?"

"Yeah."

Seth wrapped his arms around Vargas's middle, laying his head against his shoulder and snuggling in.

They stayed in each other's arms for a while longer before eventually deciding to get dressed and recheck the safe room's supplies, hunting for a toolkit they could use to open the control panel. It was getting late. They paused the search long enough to drink some water and eat a couple of energy bars, then moved on to the remaining two tubs.

Seth merely smiled when Vargas held up a black case with the emergency cell phone that had fallen behind the tubs on the bottom shelf.

Neither man had minded in the least how events had unfolded while they'd been locked in that room.

Vargas used the phone to call the Haven's security office, asking to speak to Carter since he was the only one with access to the safe room. After filling Carter in on their predicament, Vargas told him who to get in touch with if the control panel on the outside was also not functioning.

"Five minutes," he told Seth when he got off the phone.

As they waited for Carter, Vargas's claustrophobia-driven anxiety remained subdued until the safe room door opened.

Carter just stood there in the open doorway, grinning at them like he had no doubt about what they'd been up to inside, which was hard to hide with most of the buttons on Vargas's shirt missing.

Vargas pointed at him. "Not a word, big guy."

"You got it, boss." But the smile didn't fade as he stepped aside to let them out.

Vargas walked him to the apartment door, and to his credit, Carter didn't offer a single teasing word.

When he was gone and Vargas got back to his room, he found Seth already lying in the bed under the covers. Vargas got undressed and crawled in so they lay facing each other.

"This okay?" Seth asked.

"Why wouldn't it be?"

"Because I packed all my stuff and was going to leave."

"You can leave anytime you want. Staying here, being with me… it's all a choice you get to make."

"Okay."

Vargas slipped an arm around him and pulled him close so Seth's head was tucked under his chin. "And if you ever do leave, you can always come back. Because no matter what you decide, it won't change what I feel for you. You're it for me, Seth. You always will be."

There was a weighty pause, and Vargas feared he'd said something wrong. Then Seth wound an arm around him and pressed a soft kiss to the center of his chest. "I'm not going anywhere."

* * * * *

Seth halted at the top of the staircase on the Haven's second floor, his cane in one hand, the other hand clutching the railing. He had no idea if he was doing the right thing or not. He just knew he had to start trusting his instincts again. Like he did the day before in the safe room with Vargas, one of the best nights of his life.

He was still feeling the high of it all as he surveyed the sea of empty tables and bar stools on the club's first floor. Perhaps that's why he'd had the idea to try this now.

When he'd thought up the plan a few minutes earlier, it hadn't occurred to him that it would be harder to cross the club's first floor alone than when it was full of men. He wasn't about to let that realization deter him now. He only had an hour until Vargas would return from the grocery store.

He could do this. He had to do this. For himself and for Vargas. The review of the financial records was getting him nowhere. The only thing he'd learned of significance had nothing to do with the accountant. He needed to expand his search.

Seth eyed the door across the club that led to the employee offices. He tugged out his wallet and removed the access card. Vargas had said it was programmed to open any door in the club.

He took a deep breath and started down the steps. The sporadic overhead lights created shadows along the outer walls, offering enough cover a person could hide crouched in the darkness undetected. He thought he heard the faint sound of footsteps but couldn't tell from which direction. He stopped and listened.

He shook his head. He was being stupid. It was just his imagination again.

Then came a low voice from behind him. "Seth?"

Seth spun around and almost tripped backward down the stairs, but he caught himself in time.

Carter started forward as soon as he spotted Seth struggling. "You okay?"

"I'm fine. You just startled me." Seth pointed over his shoulder. "I was heading for the offices to look up some information. I'm helping Vargas with his finances."

"He mentioned that." Carter gestured down the stairs. "I'll walk with you."

Seth wanted to say he'd be okay on his own, but instead he said, "Thanks."

Carter gave a nod. "No problem."

As they headed down the stairs side by side, Seth asked, "You always work in the mornings?"

"I'm actually off today. I stopped by to get some scheduling done. We have a lot more guards on duty than usual, and it takes me longer than I expect to set up their schedules."

"I'm sorry if my being here has made more work for everyone."

"Hey." Carter halted at the base of the stairs. "I didn't mean it like that. I just hope staying here is helping you."

"It is. Thanks."

"Good. Then don't worry a thing about it."

They got moving again. When they reached the doorway to the employee offices, Seth paused. "Can I ask you a question?"

"Sure."

"What do you think of Miyata?"

"The accountant? I like him. He's an upstanding guy."

"You don't think he'd lie to Vargas about anything important, do you?"

"No way. They've known each other a long time."

"That's what I thought. What about Ian?"

"I'd trust that man with my life."

The letdown hit Seth square in the chest, but had he really expected anything different? Which meant he'd been imagining things the entire time. Despite that, he asked Carter about one more person. "And Neil?"

That had the big man laughing. The contrast of his usually stoic face and the amused grin was charming. "I recommended him for the job. He's my nephew."

"Oh."

"Why do you ask?"

Seth didn't respond, unsure if this was a good idea. Maybe he'd never know who he could trust. Or maybe he would someday. He liked Carter, after all.

"Go on," Carter said. "Say whatever's on your mind."

"I thought I saw Neil taking pictures in the club the other day when he was off duty."

"Pictures? Of members?"

"I guess. Is that part of his job?"

"No. Absolutely not."

"I thought maybe you saw him doing it too. It seemed like you were trying to talk to him."

"Just to check in with him. His mom hadn't heard from him in a while. You sure that's what you saw?"

"I don't know. I thought he was trying to hide his phone."

Carter seemed to be mulling that over. "That happens here a lot. Most guys think it's a pain in the ass not being able to pull out their phones. They want to text their hookups, add a guy's number, shit like that."

"Neil was looking around a lot. Maybe he was trying to find someone he was planning to meet."

"There's a guy I've seen him with a lot lately. My guess is they're getting serious. Could be he was waiting to hear from him. I'll talk to him about the phone."

"I don't want to get anyone in trouble."

Carter held up a hand. "You're not. If he had his phone out when he wasn't working, that's on him. He knows better."

"I was probably making something out of nothing. I think I just wanted a reason to try walking through the club on my own when there were people here."

"Next time, shoot me a text. I can wait up on the balcony and keep an eye out for you."

"Thanks. For everything." Seth opened the door and pointed down the hall. "I'll be okay from here."

"I can stay until you're done."

"Nah. It's okay. Enjoy your day off."

He eyed Seth for a long breath. "Call the main security line when you're done, and someone will walk back with you."

"Thanks."

Carter offered a last smile, then headed back through the club. When he was out of sight, Seth started for the offices.

Forty minutes later, he had the rest of the information he needed. Now he just had to figure out how to bring it up with Vargas. Because something had to change.

* * * * *

Vargas finished putting the groceries away, then made his way down the hall. He leaned in the doorway of his bedroom and took in the sight of the man lying across the bed, just like the night before after they'd gotten out of the safe room. Only this time Seth was on top of the covers, stretched out on his stomach horizontally across the middle of the mattress, his head on his folded arms. His eyes were closed, the hint of a smile on his face.

Vargas approached and stopped beside the bed. Seth was adorable with his cheek resting on his clasped hands, his dark hair mussed. The jeans he wore hugged the beautiful curve of his ass in the most delicious way. Vargas had never seen him in jeans at any time during the past two years. Seth had his legs slightly spread. The pose had Vargas picturing climbing on top of him and pressing his groin into the crack of Seth's ass.

"What are you looking at?" Seth asked without opening his eyes. "Are you staring at my ass?"

"Not just your sweet ass, but yeah, I'm admiring the view."

Seth rolled over onto his back and grinned up at him. "You like what you see?"

"I do."

Rising up onto his elbows, Seth crooked a finger at him. "Then come here."

Vargas got on his hands and knees and crawled to Seth. He lowered down beside him, then wrapped an arm around him and hauled him forward until they were pressed body to body. He planted a heated kiss on Seth's lips, and Seth returned it with as much fervor, driving into the kiss again and again like he couldn't get enough. The feeling was completely mutual.

Vargas held Seth by the back of the head and deepened the kiss. Seth let out a muffled whimper, reminding Vargas of all the little encouraging noises he'd made in the safe room the night before.

Vargas kissed his way to Seth's ear. "God, I love the way you sound."

Immediately Seth's entire body tensed. He shoved Vargas away. "Don't say that. Don't ever say that to me!" He scrambled back and nearly fell off the bed but caught himself before he went down. He shot to his feet in a flash and continued backing away, his hands up. "Just... just don't say that again."

Slowly Vargas retreated to the other side of the bed and stood. He made no attempt at an approach. "I'm sorry."

"No." Seth shook his head. His breathing had eased some but was still labored. He returned to the bed and slumped to sit on the mattress. "I'm sorry. It's just..." He shook his head again. "He said he liked how I sounded, the noises I made."

Vargas eased forward a couple of steps. When Seth didn't react to the move, Vargas went the rest of the way and sat beside him, leaving some distance between them so he wasn't crowding him. "You don't ever have to be sorry. Ever. I want to know when something makes you uncomfortable, when something triggers a memory or a negative feeling. It's important that you communicate what you're going through with me, in any way you can. I'd never want to keep doing anything that causes you distress. That would—" He swallowed down the bile rising in his throat.

Seth nodded but said nothing.

"You can always say no, change your mind, tell me to stop, shove me away, whatever you need. I'll respect your boundaries, no matter what. I want to hear you and give you what you need more than anything in this world. If that means we don't touch for a while, for days or weeks or months, whatever, that's completely okay with me. How I feel about you isn't just physical."

That time Seth's nod was more pronounced, but he kept staring at the floor before him. "I thought I was doing so good."

"You are."

There was another grave pause. Then without warning Seth shot up and paced the room in front of the window. His breathing returned to the same angry, rapid pants as earlier.

He halted before Vargas, his posture stiff and straight. "I want to see the room. Where he first attacked me." He went to the nightstand and retrieved his cane that was leaning against it. He returned to stand in front of Vargas. "It's part of why I came here. To confront my fears. I've talked about that day, but maybe what I really need is to face it head-on."

Chapter Twenty-Seven

Vargas stopped outside a room on the fourth floor of the Haven. The key card sat heavy in his hand. Everything inside him screamed at him to protect Seth from this, to keep him away from this place, this pain.

A hand rested on his lower back. "It's okay. I want to do this. I need to face it."

Vargas turned to him. Seth was leaning on his cane, looking calm and resolute. Vargas had no choice but to help him with this. "Okay." He slid the key card into the lock and pushed open the door. Stepping inside, he flipped on the lights.

The hotel-style room smelled stale. Dust particles moved through the light above the lone bedside table lamp. The other lamp was missing, as well as the sheets and blankets from the bed, but everything else in the room looked normal, sans the accumulation of dust. Nearly every flat surface was covered in layers of the stuff. And not just dust, but a fine gray powder as well.

From the doorway, Seth pointed at the surface of the closest piece of furniture—a portable bar lined with bottles of liquor. "What's that gray stuff?"

"Once the police got involved in the investigation, they came in here and collected evidence. That's from them dusting for prints."

He met Vargas's stare, clearly confused. "You left it like this?"

"After the cops took off, I shut and locked the door. No one's been in here since."

"Oh." Seth remained in the doorway until he suddenly moved all at once as if he'd been waiting for a reserve of energy to propel him forward.

He progressed farther into the space and took in the surroundings. Eventually he came to a stop at the foot of the bed. He shifted his weight to the left to get a look at the floor on the far side. He pointed to the carpet. "The last thing I remember, I was right there." He held completely still as if he was running through the memory in his mind.

Vargas remained just as motionless.

Seth kept his focus on the carpet as he said, "When I first came into this room, I was so attracted to him. I liked the way he touched me, the way he kissed me, the slow way he undressed me."

"You have nothing to be ashamed of, nothing to blame yourself for."

"I know." Tentatively he took a step around the bed, then inched toward where he'd been pointing. He stopped again when he stood before the nightstand with the missing lamp. "He told me fighting with him couldn't stop the inevitable. I used to think that meant I was doing a good job trying to get away from him and that he hoped to talk me into backing off. But..."

Vargas held his breath and waited for him to go on.

Instead Seth lowered to the floor. He turned and sat back against the nightstand. Pulling his knees up to his chest as far as his left knee would allow, he wrapped his arms around his legs and stared off into space. Tears were streaming down his cheeks. He looked frail, defeated, shattered.

Vargas moved in, taking care so as not to spook him but unable to keep away. He carefully sat close by, his back against the bed frame. "Talk to me."

There was no response.

"Seth?"

Still nothing. The tears continued down his face. His breath hitched, but he didn't move an inch or acknowledge Vargas. He kept staring straight ahead like he was lost to another time.

This had been a fucking horrible, horrible idea.

"Seth?"

Nothing.

"Seth, say something. Please."

No answer.

Panic welled in Vargas's chest. He needed to do something. He needed help. He needed to get Dr. Arteaga there. But first he took a chance and laid a hand over one of Seth's.

In response Seth slowly rotated his head as if he just realized Vargas was still there. He opened his mouth like he wanted to say something but nothing came out.

Without thinking about it too much, Vargas raised his hand and swiped at the tears with his thumb.

Seth bit his bottom lip, then glanced around the room again. "I thought..." He rested his chin on his folded arms. "I thought it would feel more traumatic here. The anxiety and helplessness I get when I think about him and how he touched me. How he held me down. How he smelled, like sweat and leather. That creepy rasp of his voice. The sound of his breath in my ear. How he looked at me like he'd been waiting his whole life for that moment. For me. I thought all that would be more powerful in this room. I thought there'd be this big wave of emotion, and then it'd be gone. It would all be gone."

Hence the tears. He was disappointed. He'd expected a more painful reaction. He'd been hoping for it, thinking it would be cathartic, that it would put a stop to everything.

Seth shook his head. "I don't understand. It's the same here as anywhere. The panic, the fear... I thought it would be worse. I don't get it."

"I think the work you and Dr. Arteaga have been doing is a big part of that. You've gone over and over what happened to you. You're lessening the impact of the trauma. You're taking away its power over you. Even here. Even when you're afraid and panicked, you're starting to accept that he can't hurt you anymore, and that's a good thing."

"Yeah." Seth swallowed, the distraught emotion leaving his face. "Would you do something for me?"

"Anything."

"Would you get rid of this bed, clean the room, make it nice again, open it up for members to use?"

"I can do that."

"Thanks. I don't want it to stay like this. People should make good memories here again."

"That sounds nice."

With both hands, Seth wiped away the remaining tears. He breathed deep and sat taller. "Okay. Now I need to see the other room."

"What other room?"

"Where he kept us."

"Seth, I don't know..."

Seth looked at him, a staunch determination locked in his eyes. "I'll be okay. Can we get to it from the club?"

"We'd need to go through the building next door. I had the tunnels under the club sealed up. But maybe now's not the right time—"

Seth stood. "I have to see it. Right now."

"All right." Vargas got up off the floor. "But on one condition."

* * * * *

"I cannot believe you agreed to this." Dr. Arteaga shook her head so emphatically that the dangling strands of her earrings jingled like ringing Christmas bells. There was nothing jolly about her expression, though.

Vargas turned away from her and faced the window that looked out over the club. When he'd called her an hour earlier, it had been clear from her tone that she was upset about something. After she'd arrived at the apartment, she spoke with Seth in hushed whispers, sitting beside him on the couch for several minutes. Then she'd asked to speak privately with Vargas. They went into his office while Seth waited in the living room. The minute the door was closed behind them, she'd laid into him.

"How did you think bringing him here was a good idea?"

He whirled around to face her. "It wasn't *my* idea. It was yours."

"Not for him to come here alone. I wanted to have one of our sessions downstairs while the place was closed. I certainly didn't suggest he move in here." She glared at him. "This could've been a huge setback for him."

Vargas's stomach dropped.

She studied him, and her harsh expression dissipated. "He didn't tell you all that?"

"No."

She composed herself with a tug of her suit jacket, pulling it taught from the bottom hem. "I guess it makes sense that he'd come up with the idea of staying here all on his own."

"Why?"

She sighed. "He has significant feelings for you, Mr. Vargas. I think that's quite obvious."

"The feeling's mutual, I assure you."

He expected more anger. Instead she said, "I'm very glad to hear you admit that. I wasn't sure you would."

Vargas pointed toward the office door. "He knows what he needs. He says he's ready to face this."

"That's what starting on the first floor and doing this slowly was supposed to be about."

Vargas spun back to the window.

She added in a softer tone, "Giving him everything he says he wants may not always be the right call."

"Why?"

"Because sometimes he may be making harmful choices, trying to rush things, and he could get hurt in the process."

Vargas turned to face her. "Is that what he's doing now? Rushing things?"

"When you first called me, that was my concern. But after talking to him just now, I'd say no. He seems to be doing well. I think, now that he's been here at the Haven for a while, it's okay for him to take a look at the room where he was held captive. We'll both be there with him. We can get him out of there if it's too much and encourage him to talk afterward." She looked away for a moment and breathed deep as if she weren't sure she should say the next part. "I shouldn't have attacked you the way I did. I'm sorry for that. You did the right thing in calling me. You've always done a great job with him. He's been very lucky to have someone like you."

He studied her, desperately wanting to believe those words.

As if reading his thoughts, she nodded. "Having a patient, loving support system makes a huge difference for someone who's been through what he has. Considering his family situation, I don't think he'd be where he is today without that support, without you."

Vargas tipped his head back as his eyes grew moist. When he'd composed himself, he met her stare again. "Thank you."

* * * * *

Not long after they'd gotten permission from the owner of the property, they stood in the damp, musty basement hallway of the building next door, all three of them facing the closed door to the room where Prescott had kept his victims hostage. Vargas was beside Seth, Dr. Arteaga directly behind them. The building had power, but the bare lightbulbs hanging from the ceiling offered minimal illumination, casting eerie swaths of shadows across the steel door.

Vargas ached to turn around and get Seth the hell out of there, but that wasn't an option. Going into that room—or not going in—had to be Seth's decision.

As if Seth desperately needed the support of physical contact, he grasped Vargas's hand in his. He held on to him for a minute. Then he let go and swung open the door.

Before Seth could make another move, Vargas suggested, "Why don't I go in first and get the lights on?"

Seth offered a nod, and Vargas stepped into the room. Using the flashlight he'd brought, he scanned the wall near the door for a light switch and flipped it on. The overhead lights were startling bright, throwing a harsh glare over the dank room with its water-stained concrete walls.

There were no possessions or tools. No clothes or personal items. The police had taken all that as evidence. What remained was a narrow wooden workbench lining the wall perpendicular to the doorway, a series of metal cages along the back wall, and a bed frame in the center of the room. The frame, sans mattress and box spring, had four short metal posts at the corners.

If Vargas had known the cops and the owner of the building had left those damn cages and that bed there, he'd have purchased the entire place just so he could get to this room and destroy the fucking things.

Time seemed to stand still until Seth gripped his cane tighter and eased into the room. Vargas and Dr. Arteaga stayed back, letting him have a look on his own. He moved at a measured pace and seemed to be examining every inch of the room with great detail, maybe running the particulars through his mind to see what memories they triggered. He came to a stop in the center of the space, five feet from the foot of the bed.

He was quiet as he scrutinized the bare workbench, the cages, and the bed frame. Then all at once, he jerked forward, moving with haste like he couldn't contain his agitation. He came to a standstill at the bed and grasped one of the posts. He didn't say a word, his total focus on where the mattress would've been. It was impossible to miss the moment his hand tightened around that post. He let his cane fall against the bed frame, and he grabbed on to the post with both hands as if he were wringing someone's neck.

Vargas started forward, but Dr. Arteaga held up a hand to stop him. She offered him a long look that seemed to be encouraging him to trust her.

As hard as it was to keep his distance when it came to Seth being in any kind of pain, Vargas had to go with her expertise in this moment. He gave her a nod.

Then Seth spoke, never giving up his hold on the bed. "There was no way for us to escape. He kept us locked in the cages most of the time. We were never going to get out. That's all I kept thinking when I was in the cage. That the only way it was ever going to end was when I died. I didn't know if that would be the next day or in two months or ten years, but I knew that someday he'd kill me, and I just had to wait for it. I tried to stay strong, believe that someone would find us, but that hope slipped away. I don't know why I gave up like that."

Without moving forward, Dr. Arteaga said, "He drugged you, Seth. He caged you, held you down, and tied you up. He wanted you to feel helpless."

"It worked. But not for Dylan. He kept telling him off. He even attacked him, tried to run from him, and I just sat there shaking.

Whenever he'd get me out of the cage, he—" Seth sucked in a sharp breath.

"You remember something new?" Dr. Arteaga asked.

"Yeah." Seth didn't sound upset but rather genuinely surprised. He let go of the bed and rounded the corner. The wall behind the bed had four metal rings anchored to the surface in a disturbing rectangular pattern the size of a man with his arms and legs outstretched, the bottom two rings near the floor.

Seth's voice was low but unwavering. "All this time, I didn't think I fought him hard enough. But one time when he got me out of the cage, he didn't tie me up right away. I hit him, and I ran. I ran as fast as I could, but he caught up with me at the door, forced me back in the cage, and then he said it was time for punishment. But he didn't punish me. He hurt Aaron for my bad behavior. He said we were a family now, and that my actions had consequences. He chained Aaron to this wall." Seth raised his arm and brushed his fingers over the closest metal ring. His entire body lurched when he made contact with it, and he yanked his hand back as if he'd touched fire. "He flogged him with a whip. Aaron screamed so loud, he didn't sound human anymore." Seth's body jerked again as if he'd just witnessed Aaron take another hit.

"When he finished beating him, he told me if I ran again, it would be worse for Aaron next time. I couldn't take that. So I did whatever he told me to. I got on the bed when he said to, I didn't move when he tied me up, and I didn't fight him when he cut me."

All Vargas wanted to do was pound on something—on someone—until his knuckles were raw and bleeding.

Seth turned to them. He had his mouth open in surprise. There were tears in his eyes but relief was visible in his every feature. "All this time, I thought I just gave up, that I gave into him. I didn't know why. But I was protecting Aaron and the others. I didn't want them tortured because of me."

Vargas took a step forward. "None of what happened to Aaron was your fault."

Seth's bottom lip trembled, and he nodded. "It wasn't. It was all Prescott. I tried to stop him in that room at the club. Even when he lay on top of me and held me down, even when he told me that fighting him wouldn't prevent what was going to happen to me, I still fought. I fought until I was unconscious." He shook his head. "I need to stop blaming myself." He gave Vargas a pointed look. "We *both* have to stop blaming ourselves. It wasn't any more your fault than it was mine." He retrieved his cane and approached him.

Vargas had never seen more determination and tenacity in those brown eyes looking back at him. He offered Seth a nod. "You're right."

A smile brightened Seth's face. He reached out and clasped Vargas's hand. They stood there for several moments, locked in that simple, meaningful touch.

Seth glanced over his shoulder at the room behind him. "I thought I was going to die here." He met Vargas's stare again. "But I didn't die. I lived. Despite everything he did to me, every way he tried to destroy me, I'm still here. The men he took all those years ago before us? The police don't think they ever made it home. They never got to see their lovers or their friends or their families again. I have what they wanted more than anything. They were praying for it. Begging. Crying. Right up until the moment they died, they wanted to live. I know it. I won't waste my life because I'm scared of the past. No one knows what will happen in the next twenty years or even the next five minutes. None of us. This is my life to live, and I'm going to enjoy it."

He looked Dr. Arteaga's way. "I'm done here. I don't need to see anything else." He squeezed Vargas's hand. "I've got everything I need."

In a rushed, clumsy move, Vargas pulled him into an embrace. "I'm so proud of you."

Seth let out a chuckle. He slipped his arms around Vargas. "You know what? I'm proud of me too."

Chapter Twenty-Eight

Vargas cleared their dinner plates and carried them to the sink, the entire time keeping an eye on Seth. For several minutes now, Seth hadn't spoken or moved from where he sat at the kitchen table. He didn't seem angry or despondent like he'd been in the club the day before. It was more a quiet contemplation.

Something was on his mind.

Vargas was doing his best to give Seth the time and space he needed to process what had happened the day before in the basement next door. The dishes offered a brief distraction. As quietly as Vargas could manage, he rinsed the plates in the sink and loaded them into the dishwasher. When he finished with the glasses and silverware, he grabbed a towel from the drawer and leaned back against the counter facing the table. He'd waited as long as he could stand.

He dried his hands and asked, "You okay?"

"I am." With complete calm Seth added, "I've just been thinking about something."

"Yeah?" Vargas tossed the towel on the counter and returned to sit across from him. "About what?"

"How to tell you something."

"Okay." He reached across the table and laid his hand on Seth's. "Just tell me."

Seth flipped his hand over and held on to him in return. He stayed like that for several breaths, then squeezed Vargas's hand and sat back. "Miyata lied to you. But not about what you think. He's not hiding anything from you about the finances. I found nothing to even hint at that in the records, so I went down to his office to see if I could find any proof in there, or maybe find out what else he could be hiding."

"You walked through the club?"

"When it was closed, and Carter went with me."

Vargas grinned at him. "So you were snooping?"

Seth ducked his head. "It was driving me nuts not knowing. I knew there had to be a reason for how you were feeling. I thought maybe he had a second set of books he was hiding."

"What'd you find out?"

"Nothing at first. I didn't see anything that proved he was lying. But when I was in there looking around, he showed up. He wasn't very happy to find me going through the office until I explained what I was doing there. He admitted to me what he's been keeping from you."

Vargas sat back and folded his arms across his chest. "Which is?"

"He's been dating a member of the club. The guy is over twenty years younger than him, and he figured you'd think he's some kind of perv, so they've been sneaking around for months."

Vargas shook his head and laughed. Considering the age difference between him and Seth, Miyata's concerns were downright comical.

"Yeah," Seth said as if reading his mind. "I hope you don't mind, but I told him about us."

"I don't mind at all. But even before us, I never would've judged him for something like that."

"I told him that too."

"Why would he care what I thought anyway?"

"You're his friend. He admires you a lot."

Vargas scoffed. Some friend he'd been thinking Miyata was cheating him out of money. He owed the man an apology. And one to Seth. "I'm sorry you spent all that time going through the records for nothing."

"I'm not. It wasn't for nothing. I learned a lot." He eyed Vargas. There was more he had to say, and Vargas could tell this was the difficult part for Seth. "I don't want you to lose the club."

"I haven't decided to sell. I'm thinking it over, like I promised."

"But you're going to lose it anyway no matter what you decide. Unless you change some things."

Vargas knew what Seth was talking about, and he'd do just about anything to avoid this discussion.

"I reviewed your membership data. People are canceling all the time. It's because of the added security, isn't it?"

"That's a common complaint."

"Plus it's been two years since you accepted any new members. Something has to change. You need new people to offset natural attrition alone. And your regular members are bound to start getting pissed that they aren't seeing any new faces."

He was right. That was one of the other biggest complaints.

Vargas had always gone with his instincts when it came to letting men into the club. Now, he second guessed his every decision. He hated that. He just couldn't trust himself to make the right call when it came to who to let in and who to keep the hell out.

Seth continued. "With that, and all the security expenses, I don't see how you can keep this place going for much longer. Maybe if you had some extra cash to cover the security costs and the losses, but that's not a possibility, is it?" He stopped and waited, but when Vargas didn't say anything, Seth added, "You spent too much surveilling Prescott's attorney and his parents."

"Tucker gave me a good deal on that."

"A deal? Vargas, you've spent all your personal savings. You've cashed out your retirement account and all your other investments." He paused like it was even harder to say the next part. "It was a huge amount of money. Because it's not just the losses with the club and paying to have the attorney followed. There's—"

"Everything will be fine."

"There's that other—"

"I'm not retiring tomorrow."

"Vargas, the other—"

"I'll have plenty of time to build up my investments again."

With patience and not an ounce of malice in his movements, Seth sat forward, propping his forearms on the table. "Please let me talk."

"I'm sorry. Go ahead."

"I checked into that other security company you hired. They don't handle security for businesses. They deal strictly in personal bodyguards and surveillance. I'm guessing Tucker suggested them for you because you needed more than what his staff could handle."

Vargas sighed and tipped his head back. As much as he hated having to admit that he'd kept this from Seth, it pained him even more that Seth might be hurt or angry with him. He forced out, "Yeah."

Silence descended between them.

Then Seth asked, "They watch us all the time?"

"Yes."

"All six of us? Even Blake and Ollie and Foster?"

Vargas nodded.

"Ever since…"

"Yes."

"For two years?"

"Yes."

"When we're in our homes? They watch us then too?"

"They have surveillance set up in a van outside or in a nearby building. At your place, it's a van because of the renovations across the street. They rotate between different vehicles to be less conspicuous."

Seth got up from his seat. He maneuvered around the table and leaned against the edge in front of Vargas. When Vargas didn't look directly at him, Seth placed a hand under his chin and tilted his head up. "I never thought you'd lie to me."

"I'm sorry." He had more of a reply on the tip of his tongue, but Seth spoke first.

"I understand why you needed to do it. I really do, but you need to cancel it, all of it."

"No." Vargas shook his head. He couldn't do that. Wouldn't. "Nothing is ever going to happen to you again. If I have to hire ten bodyguards to follow you around and make certain of that, I will."

Seth dropped his hand. "Something like this isn't your decision. If I'd seen someone following me, watching me, do you know how freaked out I would've been? It would've scared the shit out of me and probably made everything worse for me."

"That didn't happen, and now you know."

"The others don't."

"All right. I'll tell them. It was never my intention to frighten anyone."

"I know. But…" Seth spoke with more resolve. "Vargas, you have to—"

"You said it yourself. You're still afraid most of the time."

"It's getting better. A lot of things are going to happen to me in my life. Some good. Some bad. I want to stop hiding, stop being afraid. I want to move on. And you need to also." He waited a beat. "By hiring that security for us, you were controlling a part of our lives that we had no say in, and you were violating our privacy. I know you meant well. I know it was only to keep us safe, but we deserved a say. You need to at least ask everyone if they'd like the protection."

"I didn't think anyone would say yes. Prescott had already been arrested. I thought everyone would see the surveillance as overkill."

Seth nodded. "Then you have to figure out a way to accept that some people don't need—or want—your help."

"No." Vargas shoved his chair back and stood. He went to the sink and glared into the empty basin, wishing he'd left the dishes there earlier so he had something to do with his hands. He didn't want to think about what Seth was saying.

But he needed to. Because he *had* crossed a line. Although it was only because he thought keeping everyone safe meant more than the truth.

As he heard those words in his head, he realized how far from his beliefs and identity he'd managed to travel. He'd lied to people he said he cared for, and he violated their trust, after they'd already been through so much. They hadn't deserved that.

Seth approached behind him. A hand settled at the middle of his back. "It's time for you to let it go."

"I know. I just don't know how to do that."

"I'll help you."

"I can't ask that."

"I want to. That's what it means to be in love with someone."

Vargas turned to Seth and stared at him in awe. "You're pretty amazing, you know that?"

Seth grinned up at him. "Uh-huh." He took Vargas's hand in his and led him back to the table, then sat and said, "Why don't we start with what we can do to save the club? I have some ideas."

Vargas sat across from him. "Ideas?"

"On cutting costs and bringing in more money."

For the next half hour Seth laid out plans that included reducing the number of guards on duty, renegotiating rates with some of the club's suppliers and vendors, and hosting private parties and gay weddings during the club's off-hours or when it was feasible to close for a night. Seth had even made some initial inquiries to a sampling of wedding vendors and some of the club's suppliers to see how feasible his ideas were.

Vargas was impressed. It was better than any pitch he'd ever given to a potential investor or business associate. "The private parties and weddings are a great idea."

"I know, right? You already have the dining room and the bar and a dance floor. Out-of-town guests could stay in the rooms upstairs like a regular hotel."

"Yeah, I like it."

"And..." Seth glanced down as if he had a sheet of paper and had to read the next item, only the table was bare before him. "You need to start interviewing and accepting new members." He looked up. "It's time."

"It is."

"If you don't feel comfortable doing the interviews yourself, ask Carter or Walter or Tucker for help. They all have good instincts about people."

"They do." Vargas paused to make sure he was really okay with all this. "All right."

"All right what?"

"I'll put everything you suggested in motion. The parties, cutting back on the guards, taking on new members, all of it."

That seemed to please Seth to no end. Then he turned thoughtful again. "And the bodyguards who've been following us?"

"You were right about that. I never should've hidden it from you guys. That was incredibly insensitive of me." It was nearly impossible to say the next words, but he had to. "I'll call off the surveillance, and I'll tell everyone the truth."

"They'll understand." Seth stood and came to him again. This time he straddled his lap and sat, resting his forearms on Vargas's shoulders. "I'm proud of you."

Vargas laughed as he laid his hands on Seth's thighs. "For what?"

"Not giving in to your fears anymore."

He laughed again. "It's not easy."

"Because you always think you need to control everything."

"I do, huh?"

"Yeah." The teasing smile on Seth's lips proved the characteristic didn't bother him in the least. He cupped the back of Vargas's neck with both hands and kissed him. "I wish..." Another kiss. "You would..." Another. That time he parted his lips and brushed his tongue across Vargas's lower lip. "Take charge in other areas."

"Yeah?"

"It's okay for you to make a move sometimes. I can feel how much you want me."

"You have no idea."

"I do." Seth rocked against him in a seductive move. "But you also hold back a part of yourself."

"We need to take this slow, make certain what we're doing works for you."

"I know, but that doesn't mean you have to be so careful all the time." Seth leaned in and kissed a path down the front of Vargas's throat as he opened the top button on his dress shirt. Then the next button and the next. He spread the fabric and slid his lips along Vargas's skin, nibbling where neck and shoulder met in that arousing way that drove Vargas crazy.

Seth sat up. "I promise I'll be honest." He kissed him on the mouth again, all the while grinding his body against Vargas's lap. "Always."

That was all Vargas needed to hear. He gripped Seth's hips and tugged him closer, opening his mouth wider and deepening the kiss, letting the passion and desire he felt pour into the connection between them, one erotic kiss melding into the next. It wasn't long and Vargas was hard and aching for Seth, for his mouth, his hand, anything Seth wanted to give him. Uncontrollably he thrust up against him, desperately wanting to bury himself inside Seth.

With a grin, Seth pulled back. "That's it. Let go." He slid a hand between them, opened the button on Vargas's pants, and slipped his hand inside, cupping and rubbing Vargas's aching cock through his underwear, those magic fingers caressing and teasing and stoking the fire inside him. Then Seth worked his hand inside the underwear, and the contact was even more amazing. He never let up. He kept stroking as he advanced and whispered in Vargas's ear. "Will you fuck me tonight?"

Vargas stilled. He couldn't form words.

Seth didn't relent. He jerked him faster, really giving the head of his cock a firm massage. "I want to feel you inside me."

Vargas ran his hands up Seth's back. "You're sure?"

Seth swept his tongue along the outside of Vargas's ear. At the same time, he dragged his palm over the full length of his shaft. "Yes."

Without another word, Seth got off him and slid to the floor. He opened the pants the rest of the way, fully freeing Vargas's heavy erection. In one swift move, Seth dropped his mouth down over the head and swirled his tongue around it, all the while keeping his eyes glued to Vargas's.

As if adding to his answer of reassurance, Seth nodded. The movement had the head of Vargas's cock drumming against Seth's warm lips.

That sent a tremble throughout Vargas's body. He wasn't going to last long. Not with that stunning mouth on him. Definitely not once he got inside Seth. He grasped Seth by the upper arms. "Get up here. You're gonna hurt your knee on that hard floor." He hauled him onto his lap again. "Hold on to me."

Seth wound his arms around Vargas's neck and wrapped his legs around his hips. At the same time, Vargas stood, cupping Seth's ass in both hands.

Seth let out a slight moan as he buried his face in Vargas's neck. "God, I love how strong you are."

Fuck if that reaction alone didn't make Vargas feel like a king. He headed down the hall toward his bedroom, moving with care so as not to let his opened pants slide down his legs and take them out with a single trip. As he shuffled along, he felt Seth's tongue on the skin of his neck, felt the squeeze of his thighs.

Seth sucked on his earlobe next. "You have no idea how much I want this."

Without letting go of him, Vargas bent for the nightstand drawer and retrieved a condom and lube. He dropped both items to the bed. Then he lowered Seth onto the mattress and went down with him. He brushed his knuckles along Seth's cheek. "You're sure?"

"Very."

Holding on to him, Vargas rolled them so Seth was on top.

Seth didn't hesitate. He locked lips with him, unbuttoning Vargas's shirt the rest of the way. Once the shirt was parted, he ducked his head and kissed his way south to Vargas's right nipple. He teased it with his tongue as he massaged Vargas's dick through his underwear again.

It was all driving Vargas mad.

Then Seth grazed his lips up along his flesh, traveling back to Vargas's ear. Whispering, as if it was hard for him to admit, he said, "I've never done this with someone I loved."

That hit Vargas right in the chest. He laid a hand over Seth's heart. "Me either."

They held the stare for a breath. Seth clasped his hand around Vargas's, and then they were kissing again, slowly at first, then passionately, wildly. Both diving in with hunger over and over. Shirts were tugged off, socks, pants, underwear. Once they were naked and Seth was on top again, he stroked Vargas, lightly, playfully at first, teasing the slit at the tip with the pad of his thumb, watching Vargas's every reaction.

Vargas dropped his head back to the mattress and groaned. "Fuck. I can't get enough of you." He groped around on the bed beside him for the condom and lube but couldn't find the damn things. Thank God for Seth's eagerness. He scrambled sideways, retrieved both items, and tore open the condom package. He moved back into position just as quickly.

"Your knee and back okay like this?"

"Yeah." With swift deftness, he slid the condom on Vargas's shaft. The touch almost had Vargas going off. Seth squeezed out some lube and slathered it over the rubber, all the while staring into Vargas's eyes with the most intense look of anticipation burning in his gaze. That told Vargas all he needed to know.

Seth wanted this. He was more than ready.

As if to further demonstrate that, Seth climbed up him, moving to straddle him in the perfect position. He reached behind himself and grasped Vargas's shaft, lining them up. Seth groaned as his body came into contact with the head of Vargas's dick. Then he held perfectly still. It wasn't because of fear or anxiety.

Seth had a teasing smile on his lips. "You want me?"

"Like I've never wanted anyone." God, there was nothing Vargas wanted more than to thrust up into Seth, unrestrained, until the relief he craved overcame him, but Seth had to lead the show with this one.

And lead he did. Beautifully.

He began sinking down onto Vargas, his breathing picking up speed. He moaned a loud, long continuous sound.

Once the head of Vargas's cock had fully slipped past the tight ring of muscle, Vargas grasped Seth by the hips. "Jesus."

Seth got his meaning. He stopped.

If he so much as shifted another fraction of an inch, Vargas knew he'd blow and this would all be over.

He wanted to stay suspended in that moment as long as he could, wanted to savor the tight heat encasing his dick, knowing it was Seth's body surrounding him, giving him that incredible pleasure buzzing throughout him. He sucked in an unsteady gulp of air. "Just give me a minute."

Seth waited a second, maybe two. Then he said, "God, you feel incredible inside me."

That did it. There was no way Vargas could wait any longer. He nodded. "More."

Seth smiled down at him again. He worked himself farther onto Vargas, moving with drawn-out shifts of his body, his abs flexing, his lips parted. He looked amazing. Every muscle in his body was tight, his cock hard and jutting out from him, jumping with his movements as he sank down onto Vargas's full erection.

When Seth had the entire length buried in his ass, he shifted so his left leg with the stiff knee was out straight in front of him alongside Vargas's upper body, his other leg still bent under him. He splayed his hands across Vargas's abs to hold himself up.

Then he stared straight at Vargas and said, "Fuck me."

Vargas didn't delay. He couldn't. He rocked his hips, pulling back into the mattress, then pushing up into Seth, tentatively at first, but when Seth begged for it harder, he gave it all to him. Again and again and again.

He'd been right. He was never going to last long. Not this time. But that was okay. They had the rest of their lives to repeat this night.

He thrust up over and over, each slam of his body against Seth's getting harder, fiercer, and Seth moved with him, taking it all and clearly wanting more.

The slide of Seth's body along his dick was hot and smooth and the perfect amount of pressure. "Jesus." Everything drew up tight inside Vargas. His movements and his breath both became erratic. Right as he neared the edge, he reached for Seth's neglected cock, wanting to give him every blissful sensation he could manage, wanting to be exactly what Seth needed right then.

Seth bobbed his head. "Yeah, yeah. Please."

Vargas stroked him with fierce determination, loving the weight of him in his palm, the fit in his fist, the way Seth groaned each time he squeezed the head that was salivating precum out the tip. Vargas wished he could lean forward and lick it clean. An impossible move with his dick buried in Seth's ass and Seth's leg out straight. So he jerked him with wild abandon.

"Oh God." Seth's lips quivered. "Oh God. Yes! That's it!" His shoulders rounded forward and he shot, bucking up into Vargas's hand and at the same time sliding his body along Vargas's shaft again and again. "Oh fucking hell, yes! Yes!"

Seeing Seth lose it like that, rocking through the pleasure, combined with the tight contractions of his ass, had Vargas going off too. "Oh fuck. Fuck!" He jerked his hips one last time, groaning with the incredible pleasure surging through him as he came.

His body continued pitching up and down with little spasms as he rode out his release. He kept his hand gliding along Seth's dick through it all, wanting to stay buried inside him for another minute. Hell, another hour or two.

He hadn't shot that hard in ages. Maybe not ever.

After some time, when they'd both been still and quiet for a few breaths, Seth shifted off Vargas's cock and swung his left leg back so he was on both knees again. Then he collapsed forward onto him.

When Vargas could breathe steadily, could think normally again, he ran his fingers through the back of Seth's hair, holding him close at the same time. "That was incredible."

"God yeah." Seth didn't move at first, but then he lifted up and stared at Vargas like he needed the reassurance that he was actually there with him, that what they'd done was real. He smiled. "It *was* incredible." He moved aside to give Vargas room to ditch the condom. Then he lay half over him again, his lips pressed to Vargas's neck. "It was never like that with anyone else."

"Tell me about it. All this time owning a damn sex club, and I had no idea what I was missing."

Seth laughed and planted a kiss on him, then another, his soft lips repeatedly caressing Vargas's, and Vargas offered the same in return, running his hands over Seth's bare skin.

That time it was less hurried, more sensual, Vargas simply wanting to love on Seth some more. Seth seemed to feel the same. Until he began sliding along Vargas's body, his breath hitching, the wet kisses becoming more passionate, his cock coming back to life.

Vargas was starting to get there were extra benefits of being in love with a man in his twenties. He cupped the back of Seth's head. "Tell me how you want it."

"Will you…" Seth spoke the rest against his ear.

"Absolutely."

With eager movements, Seth slid off him and stood beside the bed. "I'll be right back." He pointed at Vargas. "Don't go anywhere."

"Not a chance."

Seth licked his lips, then dashed toward the bathroom, presumably to wash up.

Vargas tucked his arms behind his head and watched that round, tight ass move across the room. He called after him, "Thanks for the gorgeous view. You have an amazing ass."

Seth stopped in the doorway. "You're about to get a really good view of it."

"Uh-huh. Hurry up."

With a teasing grin, Seth shut the bathroom door. There was about four minutes of running water, and then he was back. He crawled from the foot of the bed to the free space beside Vargas.

Watching that sweet body glide across the mattress was exhilarating. It was like a different version—a more sensual version—of Seth was resurfacing, coming to life, finding his rhythm again.

Vargas rolled to face him. He splayed a hand across Seth's chest, sweeping it from one nipple to the other, brushing each pointed tip with his fingers in turn. Then he moved that hand south, down over Seth's taut stomach. He didn't stop there. He caressed every part of him, kissed him everywhere, learning where Seth was most sensitive, what made him squirm in desperation. Then Vargas focused his attention on Seth's cock, stroking him until Seth was lifting his ass off the bed.

"You ready for more?"

"Yes!" Seth rolled over onto his stomach and spread his legs without delay.

Vargas settled his shoulders between Seth's thighs, eager to give him exactly what he'd asked for. Seth curled one leg up and lifted his ass in the air, offering himself up in a blatant move that had Vargas's heart swelling with love and affection.

He playfully bit one of Seth's ass cheeks, kissed the same spot, tonguing the muscular flesh, then repeated the action on the other side. When he had Seth whimpering and clawing at the bedsheet in anticipation, he spread Seth's ass and made love to him with his mouth.

Seth clasped on to the fitted sheet with both hands. He groaned and writhed under him, and it was the most erotic thing Vargas had ever been a part of. He slid his hand between Seth and the mattress, cupping his cock, trying to give him some friction as he continued the rimming, really going to town with his tongue. He could feel the beads of precum gathering at the tip of Seth's dick.

Vargas gave one last flick around Seth's sensitive entrance and then sat up. "Turn over."

Seth let go of the sheet and flipped over. "Please. Need you."

Without delay Vargas swallowed his cock and teased and massaged his balls.

"Uh-huh. Like that." With unbridled power, Seth gripped the back of Vargas's head and pumped his hips up, sending his cock deeper into his mouth. Vargas had never felt Seth so untethered, so unrestrained and alive. It had him sucking harder, moving his mouth faster, his hand continually stroking Seth's balls and the skin behind with more vigor.

Seth arched his back. "Oh God, oh God, oh God." Then his words became unintelligible. He let go of Vargas and threw his arms above his head. Grabbing on to the headboard, he jerked his hips up with more force. His stomach muscles tensed, and he went stiff as he shot his release down Vargas's throat.

Vargas didn't let up until Seth's body completely relaxed and a heavy contented sigh poured out of him. "That was…" He exhaled deeply again. "Oh my God. I loved that."

Vargas dropped a kiss on Seth's softening cock, one on his hip, another on his stomach. He moved up the bed to lie beside him. Seth turned and pulled him close, clutching him in his arms like he'd lose him if he let go, his body shaking.

"Hey, hey, you okay?"

"Oh God, yeah." Seth released another satiated sigh, then rolled onto his back, pulling Vargas with him. "Just hold me."

"Always."

"I don't ever want this to end."

"It won't. Ever."

They kissed, languidly, both putting the depth of their emotions, their love into it.

Vargas had been right when he'd told Seth he'd never been in love before. Nothing—no sex, no contact, no intimacy—had ever felt this intense, this significant.

He barely heard the ringing of his cell phone.

Seth asked, "You need to get that?"

"Definitely not."

"That's the fourth time it's rung."

He hadn't noticed. "Who cares?"

Seth snickered. He smacked Vargas's hip, signaling he wanted him to move aside. When he was out of the way, Seth climbed over him and stretched for Vargas's pants where they lay on the floor. He slid out the cell phone and handed it over. "You have about a dozen new texts."

Vargas took the phone. The messages were all from Walter. He scanned them.

Seth was eyeing him with concern. "What? Bad news?"

"No." He couldn't believe the old man had pulled it off. "The appeal's been withdrawn. Prescott will be heading back to the prison soon."

Seth sank back onto his heels. "Why would he agree to that?"

"Who the hell knows? Does it matter? He's going to stay in prison. Forever."

Seth lowered his eyelids. "Would it be really weird if I said I think this has been the best day of my life?"

"Not at all." Vargas held out his arms, and Seth came to him.

"I feel so different."

"Sounds like a good thing, yeah?"

"Oh yeah." He snuggled into Vargas and held on. "It's a really good thing."

Chapter Twenty-Nine

Vargas awoke the next morning with Seth lying half on top of him, one leg over both of his, Seth's head on his chest. Who knew he'd be such a cuddler? Had he always been?

Did it matter? Vargas could easily stand waking up this way for the rest of his life. He laid a hand across Seth's back, relishing the warm feel of the man in his arms.

They'd fallen asleep the night before facing each other after they spent a half hour discussing how Seth felt about Prescott's withdrawal of the appeal. The one word he kept repeating was *relief*. For himself. For Dylan, Aaron, and the others.

When they'd said all they could on the subject, Vargas held him again, and they ended the night with Seth whispering to Vargas all the things he wanted him to do to his body next and vice versa.

Remembering those words from the night before had Vargas tightening the embrace. Seth mumbled a low groan of approval and nuzzled into him. Vargas grinned and kissed him on the top of the head. Yeah, he could get very used to this.

Relief about how the previous two days had gone washed over him again. After what had happened when he'd shown Seth the room where Prescott had taken him captive, going into the basement next door could've ended with Seth walking away from that moment more damaged than ever. Instead there now seemed to be a serene, even more indomitable strength to him.

Lying there together, Seth's breath shifted as he awoke more fully. He let out a contented sigh, cuddling up to Vargas even more, rubbing a cheek over his bare chest. "Morning."

"You sleep okay?"

"Uh-huh." He rolled onto his back and lazily stretched, then propped himself on one arm so he was leaning over Vargas. "You?"

Vargas reached up and ran a hand over his cheek. "Beautifully."

Seth ducked his head and sucked the tip of Vargas's thumb in between his lips, swiping his tongue over and around the pad of that thumb until Vargas thought his cock might go off without a touch of friction. Seth slowly, sensually released Vargas's thumb, then leaned forward and offered a kiss. It was lazy and sloppy and warm and just about damn perfect.

When Seth pulled back, he glanced at the clock on the nightstand. "Oh man, it's late. Don't you have to work?"

"I took the day off. Tonight too."

"Something wrong?"

"No. Thought we could spend the day together. In bed. Food, sex, nap, repeat."

With a huge grin on his face, Seth lunged at him, dropping one quick kiss after another on Vargas's lips and chin and cheeks, laughing at his own excitement.

That had Vargas laughing too. "So you like the idea?"

"Very much." Seth planted more kisses on him. "I feel incredible."

Charlie sat up from where he'd been lying on the floor beside the bed. He let out a bark and stood there waiting for them to get up.

Vargas laughed again. "I better take him out before I start breakfast." He shifted to get up.

"Wait." Seth gripped him by the hip, stopping him before he made it off the bed. Seth stared down at Charlie, deep lines of concentration running across his forehead. "I want to take him for a walk. By myself."

Vargas studied him.

"It's okay," Seth added. "I'm ready. I am. I want to do it."

"This isn't the best neighborhood for a walk."

"You've been going out with him every day. Besides, a block north it gets better. I'll be fine."

There were numerous reasons why Seth might not be fine going out alone, and none had to do with the locale. Vargas pictured him sitting on the curb, tears on his face, fear and frustration paralyzing him from moving another inch.

Despite the desperate need to protect him, Vargas offered Seth a smile of support. "If you think you're ready, you should do it."

Seth glanced at Charlie again. He breathed deep and nodded. "I'm going to."

* * * * *

Ten minutes later they were dressed and Seth was headed out the door, his cell phone in his pocket. In one hand, he had the end of Charlie's leash, and in the other was his cane. Vargas watched from the apartment door as Seth and Charlie made the trek down the hallway toward the back of the club.

Seth hesitated at the top of the stairs.

Vargas gave him a nod of encouragement. "You can do this."

"Yeah." Seth faced the steps once more, and without another look back, he started down.

Vargas waited until he heard the door at the base of the steps open. Before it closed, he wanted to shout that Seth shouldn't be ashamed to call if he needed help, but he held back. Seth knew he could count on him.

The door clanked shut.

After thirty minutes, Vargas was pacing his living room, glancing at the clock on the wall every two minutes. He'd been driving himself crazy running through possible scenarios of what was happening to Seth. Hell, he would've gone down the back stairs and waited at the door that led to the parking lot if he didn't think that might hurt Seth's feelings.

He quit the pacing and dropped onto the couch. Leaning forward, he held his head in his hands. He wasn't sure how much longer he could stand to wait.

He checked the clock again.

Then he heard low voices outside the apartment, followed by the door unlocking. He shot to his feet.

Seth opened the door, and Charlie bounded in, heading straight for his water dish in the kitchen. Seth set his phone and the dog's leash on the hall table by the door, moving deliberately, carefully. Vargas couldn't read the expression on his face, and he hated that. He thought he'd gotten pretty good at knowing what Seth was feeling or thinking, at least whether it was a positive or negative emotion.

Seth leaned his cane against the wall. He kicked off his tennis shoes, continuing with the measured movements. When he was done, he straightened and finally met Vargas's stare.

The smile was immediate and lit up Seth's entire face. "I did it." He bounded forward and lunged for Vargas. "I did it! I did it! I did it!"

Vargas hugged him. "Yeah, you did. It went okay, then?"

Seth pulled back, that huge-ass grin still locked in place. "Yep. I didn't freak out at all. It felt great to be outside with Charlie, in the sunshine, with the breeze and the fresh air. We made it all the way to the park on Summit."

"That's fantastic."

He gave Vargas a look of appreciation. "Thank you."

"You did this. Not me."

"I know. But I don't think I ever could've gotten here without you."

"That's not true at all."

Then those stark, honest words Seth had said struck Vargas in the gut like a punch. All this time and he hadn't ever thought that maybe...

His stomach churned as that doubt spread and took on greater life.

Seth stepped away, moving with a fluidity that he never had with the cane. "God, I feel so good."

The last thing in the world Vargas wanted to do was deflate that happiness. He plastered a smile on his face right as Seth turned back to him.

"I feel like I could do anything."

"You can."

Seth nodded. "I want to go to school and study accounting." He whirled around and took a few steps away again as if he couldn't keep still. "That probably sounds boring to most people, but I'm really excited about it."

"You should be. It's a great idea."

Seth faced him again. All at once his expression fell. He returned to stand before Vargas. "What is it?" He grasped Vargas's face in his hands, searching his eyes for something. "What's wrong?"

"Nothing." Vargas pulled away.

"Vargas."

"I'm going to make us some of that baked apple oatmeal you like. We can climb back in bed and have breakfast there if you want." He started for the kitchen.

"Vargas?"

He kept going. His hands shook as he got the oatmeal out of the cupboard and then went for a pot in the cabinet next to the stove. *Fuck.* He had to get himself together.

Seth halted in the kitchen doorway. "Why are you lying to me?"

Vargas turned away. He couldn't face him. He got out the bag of apples and began washing them. "Can we talk about this later?"

There was a tug on his arm. Seth didn't let up until he had him spun around. The stare was insistent. "If this thing between us is going to work, you have to talk to me. No matter what it's about. No matter when."

He was right about that. After all, Vargas expected Seth to do the same. He propped himself against the counter and let the words spill out. "What if you only think you love me because of everything I've done for you? What if your gratefulness is coloring your feelings, and you don't even realize that. Maybe you'll wake up one day and it'll be clear that you only thought you loved me because I was there for you when you needed someone."

In response, he expected either anger or acceptance of a realization neither one of them had wanted to see before then. He didn't expect the boisterous laugh that followed. He threw Seth a confused look. Seth just laughed harder. Then he took a couple of steps back and leaned against the fridge, the laughter still pouring out of him.

"What's so damn funny?"

"You." Seth held his stomach as if the laughter was giving him cramps.

"It's a legitimate concern."

Seth shook his head, chuckling. "No, it's not."

"Why?"

"Because I had feelings for you before I ever woke up in the hospital and saw you sitting beside my bed."

Vargas gaped at him. "We'd only talked once."

"Yeah." Seth looked away for a breath, then focused on Vargas again. "When I first came to the club for my interview and I met you, I was immediately enamored. I couldn't take my eyes off you. I could barely form words. I made such a fool of myself, I never thought you'd approve my membership. After you walked out of that meeting, I was shattered. I knew I had to see you again, but I had no idea how to make that happen. Then I got the call that I was accepted. Most nights when I came here, at least at first, I didn't care if I met someone or hooked up. I came to see you. I came hoping for just one glimpse, to hear your voice for one minute, to hear anything about you at all. I think, even then, I was in love with you. Or at least completely obsessed."

Vargas took a step forward, and Seth held up a hand to stop him.

"I know you might never have noticed me or been interested in me before everything that happened. But I'm not letting that keep me from being with you, from trusting that you're honest with me about how you feel. Dr. Arteaga said what I've been through has changed me and my life, but that doesn't mean I have to settle for less. I'm going to have an amazing life. I'm going to apply to school, toss out the wheelchair, and live here with you. I'm going to love you forever."

Vargas swallowed down the lump that had formed in his throat. He went to Seth and slipped his arms around him. "If I would've just opened my damn eyes, I would've noticed you. Trust me. That recording of you I watched all those times… It wasn't just about me feeling guilty. I kept trying to figure out how I missed seeing you."

Seth wrapped his arms around him and buried his face in Vargas's chest. "It doesn't matter. We see each other now."

"Yeah, we do. How did I get so damn lucky?"

* * * * *

Seth thought about denying Vargas's words and saying that *he* was the lucky one, but he stopped himself. He was done feeling insecure.

"I am a pretty amazing catch."

Vargas snorted out a pleased laugh. "That's what I like to hear."

They held each other for several more minutes. After they parted, they made breakfast and did as Vargas had suggested earlier, returning to the bedroom to eat their oatmeal and fruit in bed. They stayed there the entire day, sans short breaks to take a walk with Charlie and to make another meal when they'd gotten famished. That's what a day filled with alternating sessions of sex, cuddling, and sleep did to a man. Made him ravenous. For food and more sex.

By the time the sun was setting, they were exchanging slow, sensual blowjobs in the middle of the bed, their lips wrapped around each other at the same time. Vargas came first, and when he recovered, he rolled Seth onto his back and went down on him with incredible tenacity, offering no respite. Seth thought Vargas had already shown him every one of his tricks when it came to giving head. He was wrong. It was the most intense orgasm Seth had ever had in his life. When he came, he was covered in sweat, his entire body shaking, his toes clenched, his every muscle tight as an almost unbearable release rushed through him.

When it was over, he couldn't even lift his head. "Holy hell."

Vargas shifted around and dropped to lie beside him.

Seth sighed with a laugh. "Shit, talk about mind-blowing." When he could move, he turned onto his side. He swept the tips of his fingers across Vargas's chest, tracing the letters tattooed there. He followed the words along his biceps next, then his forearm. "I want to get one."

"A tattoo?"

"Yeah. I want a mark on my body that I decide to put there. Is that weird?"

"Not at all."

Seth traced the tattoos again, working his way back up Vargas's body. "So what happens now?"

"With what?" Vargas asked.

"Us. We haven't really defined things."

"How do you mean?"

"Am I your boyfriend? Are we exclusive?" Seth looked up at Vargas, needing to see his reactions, to see his face when he answered. "What do you want us to be?"

"I thought you said you wanted to move in together? Did you mean that?"

"I did."

"Good. Because I was pretty damn happy when you said that." Vargas lay back and crossed his arms behind his head. "Saved me from having to convince you it was a good idea."

Seth couldn't help but smile at that, but a part of him also knew that Vargas wouldn't have said anything to him on the subject. No matter what, he wouldn't have wanted to pressure him.

"Living together," Vargas added. "To me that means we're committed. Exclusive. I don't even want to think about you with another guy, and I certainly don't want anyone else in my bed. Or in my life. I don't want to spend another night without you, Seth. Ever."

To hide the rush of raw emotion, Seth slid forward and laid his head on Vargas's chest, and Vargas held him in return.

They stayed like that, bare body pressed against body, Seth's heart nearly bursting with how much he loved this man, how happy and right he felt.

After some time passed, he lifted his head. "Would you have dinner with me downstairs in the club tomorrow night?"

"I'd love to." Vargas studied him for a moment, then added, "But how about just the two of us the first time?"

Seth thought about that. He wanted—needed—to walk through the club when it was filled with people, but maybe starting slow, spending some significant time there alone with Vargas was a good way to go. And tomorrow night was one of the days when the club didn't open until later for dinner. They could have an early meal, and it wouldn't cut into regular business hours.

"I like that. Just us."

* * * * *

Somewhere in the distance came the sound of metal doors clanking shut, keys rattling, firm footsteps clomping.

It was late, and the majority of the overhead lights in the aisleway were off as Prescott stared at the dark ceiling of his cell. It didn't matter that he couldn't see the dingy stained concrete. He was listening to his surroundings, trying to decide if the footsteps were fading or growing louder. That was what his days amounted to now. He listened. Waited. Hoped.

He was beginning to think Franklin Henderson had called the whole thing off and he'd lost his only chance at freedom.

No. Even if Henderson had changed his mind, Prescott would figure something else out. He had to.

The footsteps thudding against the solid floor dwindled away, then were gone. Which was why hearing his whispered name startled him.

"Prescott."

Without a word, he got up and crossed to the front of his cell.

The guard with the lazy eye and too-big uniform stood in the center of the aisle, glancing right and left as if he expected another guard to come by at any moment. He finally let up with the nervous scanning and came forward until he was practically kissing the metal bars. "Tomorrow. After yard time. Be ready."

Prescott gave a nod, and the guard took off like a shot. He wasn't as quiet with his departure as he'd been sneaking up to the cell. Prescott briefly wondered if that not-so-stealthy exit should concern him, considering this was the guy who was supposed to break him out without incident. He dismissed the concern and returned to lie on his bunk. He could get the asshole to do what he needed, at least for one day.

As the footfalls faded outside his cell, a smile formed.

Tomorrow, Seth.

Tomorrow.

* * * * *

Jarrett Gates knocked on his boss's door. "Sir, is there anything else before I leave?" It was late, and Jarrett's boyfriend had been waiting for him for hours now, but he couldn't leave until he knew for sure what was going to happen next. He wanted to see if he'd read the situation correctly.

Franklin Henderson signaled for Jarrett to come farther into the office. Jarrett closed the door behind him and went to stand before the desk.

Several seconds ticked by as Henderson kept scrolling through something on his cell phone. When he finally finished with the phone, he laid it down and sat back. "I need you to get me into the Haven like we planned."

"I thought you had reconsidered the whole thing after talking to Mr. Vargas. You said you were going to stop trying to get Prescott out of prison." Not that Jarrett had believed Henderson's lies, not once he'd given some serious thought to what had been said, but it still pained him to be kept on the outside.

"I never reconsidered anything." Henderson eyed him with smugness. "Had you fooled too, huh? I just needed that asshole Vargas to back off. Although I was surprised Prescott figured out that I was behind his attorney. I thought we'd covered our tracks well."

"We did." Jarrett tried not to let his anxiety show. He'd been worried ever since that visit with Mr. Vargas that Henderson would blame him for the fuckup and he'd lose his job. "Won't it make things more difficult now that Prescott knows you're coming after him?"

"Difficult. Not impossible. He's not about to ignore the opportunity to get out. He thinks he can outsmart me." Henderson got up and rounded the desk, heading toward Jarrett, staring him down the entire time he moved. He stopped before him. "Prescott's going to die, and I don't care what happens to my business or anything else in the process."

"So you're going ahead with everything?"

"I am. Now get me into that club. Tomorrow. Just like we planned."

"Yes, sir. I can do that."

Henderson laid a hand on Jarrett's shoulder. "I don't know what I'd do without you. Everything's going to work out just as I'd hoped."

"And Seth Fisher?"

There was delight in Henderson's reply. "He's going to make the perfect bait."

Chapter Thirty

It was late in the afternoon the next day when Vargas got the news he'd been trying to prepare himself for ever since he told Seth that he'd cancel the surveillance.

"It's been taken care of. Everyone left their posts two hours ago."

"Good," Vargas replied into the phone as he sat back on the couch in his office. Despite his verbal approval, he couldn't fend off the blast of anxiety at Tucker's words. For the first time in the past two years, Prescott's victims had no one watching over them.

As if sensing Vargas's thoughts, Tucker asked, "You sure about this?"

"I am. I promised Seth." He looked toward the window that overlooked the dark first floor of the Haven. Seth wasn't going to be happy with him for closing down the club for the night, which was yet another reason for his members to be pissed off, but he'd made the right call. He wanted to make the night special, cook some of Seth's favorite foods, and take their time having a candlelit dinner in the Haven's dining room without his staff rushing around them as they got ready for the night.

He smiled at his reflection in the dark window and then refocused on the conversation with Tucker. "I think the threat with Prescott might be over. I'm hoping he won't have anyone on the outside helping him now."

On his last word, he spotted Seth leaning in the open doorway. He had his arms casually folded across his chest, a grin on his lips. He wore jeans and a short-sleeve T-shirt. It was great to see him less concerned about covering up his arms. His hair was sticking up all over, a result of the two-hour nap he'd awoken from.

They had worked all morning, but after lunch, while they'd been loading the dishes into the dishwasher, things had turned physical between them, and they'd spent the afternoon in bed again.

"Listen," Vargas told Tucker. "I've got to run. Thanks for the update."

"Sure thing."

They exchanged goodbyes, and as soon as Vargas hung up, Seth came forward. He didn't have his cane with him this time.

"You sleep okay?"

"Yeah." Seth leaned in and propped himself over Vargas with a hand on the arm of the couch. He gave him a kiss. "You canceled the surveillance?"

"I did."

"Thank you."

Vargas scoffed. "I don't deserve that. I'm sorry I kept it from you for so long."

"You won't keep anything else from me."

He wasn't sure if that was a question or a statement, but he offered his truth anyway. "I won't."

Seth moved to sit beside him. "Then I have a question. Was someone watching me after I came to stay here with you?"

"Yes. When you were in the apartment, they waited in the Haven's security office and watched the monitors. They couldn't see inside the apartment, but they kept an eye on the hall outside and the rest of the club." Vargas hesitated, but he was done holding back. "When you left the apartment, whoever was on duty followed you."

Seth nodded like he'd been expecting that. He didn't seem angry. More thoughtful. "So someone was still watching me when I took Charlie for a walk?"

"Yeah. I hadn't called anyone about it yet."

"You said you were going to make us dinner?"

"Thought I'd cook here in the apartment, and then we'll eat downstairs. I closed the club for the night, so we can take our time."

Seth seemed to be considering that, but he didn't offer anything about Vargas's decision not to open the Haven. Instead he said, "I was thinking, while you get the food ready, I'm going to go for a walk to that 7-Eleven two blocks north of here. I'd like a pack of gum."

"Okay."

"But this time, no cane, no Charlie, no cell phone. No one watching me." He eyed Vargas as if waiting for an argument. "I need to know I can do it without any backup."

Vargas turned toward him on the couch. He reached for Seth and brought him forward as he lay down so Seth was stretched out on top of him. "Then you do it."

"You're not worried?"

"I'll always worry about you to some degree. I think that's a part of loving someone."

"That's true." Seth kissed him.

"Your back okay like this?"

"Yeah. I feel really good. A little twinge now and then but not much at all." He laughed and snuggled in against Vargas, resting his head on his shoulder. "I don't think I've ever felt this good or been this happy."

Vargas lowered his eyelids and replayed those words in his head.

* * * * *

For the third time in the past five minutes, Vargas caught himself grinning like a fool at the onions and peppers he chopped. He just couldn't help it. He hadn't felt this light, this deliriously happy since two years ago when he'd first learned that employees and members of his club had disappeared.

He halted the chopping and stared at the cutting board. Hell, he'd never felt this way before. The same as Seth had said to him.

And that was the point, really. What Seth was feeling directly influenced how he felt. Was that what it meant to love someone? That you hurt when they hurt? That you could only truly be happy when they were too?

Charlie let out a single bark from where he sat beside Vargas.

"Yeah, I miss him already too. But he won't be long. It's only two blocks." He went to the sink and washed his hands. Then leaned down and gave Charlie some love behind his ears. "How would you feel about living here, huh? Think you could stand that?"

Vargas straightened. Could Seth? Despite what Seth had said about wanting to live there with him, could he ever call this place home? The building where Prescott had attacked him and Henderson had beaten him? Or was that asking too much?

Vargas's cell rang, interrupting his thoughts. He went to get the phone from where he'd left it lying on the kitchen table. Call it instinct or intuition, but he knew before he was across the room that something was wrong.

He grabbed the phone and checked the display. Not Seth. Which of course made sense. Seth had left his phone behind while he'd walked to the store.

The call was from Walter.

Vargas answered. "What's up?"

"Prescott's escaped."

Chapter Thirty-One

There it was. The place where his life had forever changed. Emotion overcame him. His legs felt weak. His entire body threatened to betray him and drop him to the ground under the weight of the unadulterated relief and anticipation racing through him.

Prescott leaned back against the minivan to steady himself. "Come on," he whispered. "Get it together."

Everything was going to work out fine. He knew what he was up against.

The guard at the jail had given him a change of clothes before he'd smuggled him out of his cell. He'd also left him a bag of supplies and cash inside an old Dodge Grand Caravan parked two blocks from the jailhouse. It wasn't the kind of vehicle Prescott would normally go for—this one was far too soccer-mom for him—but in this case, that had been a wise choice. Every cop in the area would soon be after his ass. He just had to stay off their radar for a little while longer, and then he'd be headed out of the city.

Far out of the city.

He took a few deep breaths, and once again he focused on the front of the building before him. The Haven. The place where he'd first seen his boys.

When the guard had initially told him that Seth had moved in with the club's owner, Raymond Vargas, rage had overwhelmed Prescott and made it difficult for him to focus on the instructions about the escape plan. Fortunately everything had gone off without a hitch, and now here he stood. At last.

In addition to collecting Seth, he mentally added torturing that asshole Vargas to his list of things to do. He was going to enjoy gutting the son of a bitch. And if he found out Vargas had touched Seth in any way, he'd make the pain and blood loss last for hours, until the asshole was begging him to end it, to bury the blade to the hilt and tear him open from nuts to navel.

Although that sounded too good for him. He needed to suffer far more.

Soon he would.

Prescott's next steps were going to be tricky. He knew exactly where Henderson wanted him, but how far would the man go? Even if the club was currently closed, getting inside wouldn't be easy. That dickhead owner had likely upgraded his security measures. But Prescott didn't have time to wait for Seth to just stroll out on his own, alone.

Which had him wondering if Seth had brought his dog to stay at the club. If so, he'd let him take the mutt with him this time. He didn't have the heart to once again separate them. Even if it would make a clean getaway more difficult.

As would the police. If they weren't already there, they'd soon be keeping his boys under surveillance and most likely notifying them of his escape. The story would also be hitting the news any minute. He had to make his move. Now.

He took a step away from the minivan. He heard the harsh breaths behind him only a split second before he felt the blow to his head.

When he awoke, he lay on his side, his hands tied behind his back and his head throbbing like hell. He wasn't sure how much time had passed, but he knew without a doubt where he was, even with only the low light of the flashlights the men surrounding him held. He was in the abandoned factory next door to the Haven.

He'd spent countless hours there, preparing and living in that space with his boys. That building would always be special for him.

"We got him."

Prescott squinted until he could see the man to his right talking on a phone.

"Right," the man said. "Until you call. Got it." He hung up the phone. He held a Beretta in his free hand, the barrel pointed at the warped wood floor. Was that supposed to frighten him?

Prescott shifted up onto his knees. His eyes adjusted to the beam of the flashlights. There were four men. Hired guns. Although none of the others had their guns drawn. Instead the weapons were tucked away in their shoulder holsters. Amateurs.

They were dressed in all black, the pockets of their cargo pants loaded down, probably with whatever else they thought they'd need to subdue him if he gave them any trouble. Two were tall like him, hefty men, more overweight than muscular. Henderson had probably hired them because they'd appear intimidating to most people. They, and their beer guts, didn't worry him one damn bit.

The other two, including the one with the phone, had more of a tactical military look to them, standing there with their flattop crew cuts, their chests puffed out, inflated bravado radiating off them. Marine washouts most likely. They were probably the brains behind this phase of the operation. Although neither had his level of intelligence. Evident by the haphazard way his hands were secured behind his back, and the fact that they hadn't checked his boot for the blade he'd stashed there earlier. They were likely counting on him to be disoriented from the strike that had knocked him out. He played along and hung his head low, swaying slightly from side to side.

He could get loose in ten seconds. Could take down all four of them in under a minute. He knew how to kill someone with his bare hands, but he wanted to play this out for a bit longer, see if he could learn anything more about Henderson's plan. He wasn't in danger yet. Not until Henderson arrived.

The man who'd been on the phone approached. He stayed several steps away but crouched so he was eye level with Prescott. "Don't give us any trouble, and we won't have to kill you."

He'd like to see the asshats try.

"Our boss wants us to fill you in on where he is and what he's doing."

Prescott feigned difficulty in lifting his head. He croaked out the words, "Your boss?"

"Franklin Henderson. You should be thanking him. He's the one who got you out. He also found a guy who looks like you and set up a false trail out of the city. It should keep the cops off your ass for a little while." The man paused as if he was actually waiting for a verbal offer of gratitude that he could pass along.

Then he continued. "I hate to be the one to tell you this." The eager grin on his face proved that wasn't the least bit true. "But before Mr. Henderson comes to deal with you, he's going to hurt someone very special to you. A 'gesture of retribution' as he calls it."

"Who?"

"Seth Fisher. He's going to finish what his son started. He's going to beat Fisher to death."

No.

Prescott clenched his hands into fists behind his back. He had underestimated the old man. Good thing Henderson had done the same with him.

The asshat went on. "We're going to keep you out of the way until it's done. Then Henderson will come here to deal with you. He wanted you to know exactly what he was doing right now, so you could sit here and suffer through imagining what sort of torture he was putting your boy through. Then he wants to be the one to tell you when it's finished, to tell you what it sounded like when your precious boy's neck snapped."

* * * * *

"Prescott's escaped."

With Walter's words, everything stopped. Vargas's breath. His body. He couldn't move or speak.

Then he snapped out of it and charged for the kitchen doorway. "How the hell did he get out?"

"Seth didn't get a call?"

"No. What the fuck happened?"

"They think he bribed a guard to open his cell. The guard got him out of the building through a maintenance access door near the laundry room. I'm on my way to get Kevin at his work. A victim's advocacy group that works with the DA's office called here to let us know. I'm guessing they're contacting the others right now."

By others he meant Prescott's other victims, all of whom no longer had bodyguards watching them, including Seth.

"Fuck!" Vargas reached the apartment door and swung it open. His heart was pounding like mad. He signaled to Ian who was on duty outside, then pointed at the door. "Do not leave here. No one gets in but me and Seth."

Ian gave a nod.

As Walter kept talking, Vargas sprinted down the hall toward the back staircase.

"The state and local police are searching for him now. U.S. Marshals are on the way to assist."

"Did you tell anyone Seth was staying here?"

"No. Are you guys in the apartment?"

"He went for a walk. I'm on my way to find him." He raced down the back stairs. Reaching the door at the base, he wrenched it open, and there was Seth. He was coming up the walkway, a huge grin on his face. He moved at a leisurely pace, glancing up at a flock of geese flying high above in the sun-filled sky as he casually chewed a piece of gum.

Vargas lowered the phone and huffed out a gust of air.

As soon as Seth caught sight of him, he stopped, then rushed forward, clearly getting that something wasn't right.

Without a word, Vargas went to him and tugged Seth into a bracing hug, then grabbed him by the arm and got them back inside the Haven. He spoke into the phone as he started up the steps, still holding on to Seth. "I've got him. We're heading up to my apartment."

"Good." He heard Walter lay on the horn and curse at a driver who obviously wasn't moving fast enough. "I'm pulling up to Kevin's office now. He's in the lobby waiting for me."

Vargas was about to suggest they come to the Haven. With the guards on duty and the extra layers of security, the club was one of the safest places they could be. Then a thought occurred to him. "After you've got Kevin, can you get to Aaron?"

"Yeah."

"Check his place first. I'll ask Tucker to see about the others." He considered getting Carter to help too, but he needed him to lock down the club and make certain Seth was safe. Which meant he was out of people he trusted enough to ensure that one more person was out of harm's way. "I'm going for Dylan. When you've got Aaron, bring everyone here."

"You got it."

"Be careful," he said into the phone and then hung up.

At the top of the stairs, Seth tugged his arm free. "What's going on?"

"Get in the apartment first." Grasping Seth's upper arm again, Vargas hightailed it down the hall. At the apartment door he asked Ian, "Anyone approach?"

"No, boss."

Vargas steered Seth inside, then said to Ian, "Prescott's escaped from the jail. Have Carter get this place locked down. No one leaves their post for any reason."

Ian already had his phone out. "I'm on it."

Vargas turned to Seth, who stood just inside the entryway, eyes wide, his lips quivering, his body shaking. Vargas shut the apartment door and made sure it was secure, then went to him.

He pulled Seth close and held his head against his chest. "It's going to be okay. I won't let him get anywhere near you."

Chapter Thirty-Two

Vargas kept his arms locked around Seth as he quickly filled him in on Prescott's escape. Then he hit speed dial on his phone to reach Dylan. The call went directly to voice mail. Without letting go of Seth, Vargas dialed another number. Tucker answered immediately.

"What's up?"

"Prescott's escaped. Cops haven't caught him yet. Can you send some people to secure Blake, Ollie, and Foster?"

"I'm on it. What about the others?"

"Walter and I are taking care of it. Just make sure—"

"I'll let you know when they're safe."

"Thanks." He hung up, knowing he could count on Tucker.

Seth pulled back right as Vargas's phone rang again. It was Walter.

"I've got Kevin and more info. Prescott was spotted on several traffic cameras. He's in a van on the interstate heading south away from the city."

"Are they sending any police protection for his victims?"

"Not unless there's evidence he's doubled back. They don't think he'll risk coming after anyone. They're focusing their efforts on intercepting him on the highway. They're putting up roadblocks at the exits, setting up a perimeter. We can come down to the station to wait for news."

"And Aaron?"

"I talked to him. He's waiting at a neighbor's until we get there. We're on our way now. You still heading to Dylan?"

"Yes." Every part of Vargas was screaming at him to stay with Seth and keep him safe, but he had to ensure that Dylan was okay. If Prescott took the time to go after any of them, it would be Seth, which meant he'd be headed to the apartment where Dylan was alone. He couldn't let him take Dylan away. They might never find him again.

Vargas would never be able to live with himself if something happened to him. He had to do this, and he had to get going now.

Walter spoke again. "Once I've got Aaron, we'll meet you at the police station downtown. Hopefully they'll know more by then."

"Got it. We'll see you there." Vargas hung up.

"Dylan?" Seth asked.

"His phone's off."

"Oh God." Seth covered his mouth with a hand.

"It doesn't mean anything. You said he goes to the movies by himself a lot." He relayed what Walter had said about Prescott heading out of town. "Don't worry. I'll find Dylan."

"Okay." Except Seth's breathing was growing more rapid. "Okay," he repeated.

"I've gotta get going. Come on." Vargas motioned for Seth to come with him farther into the apartment and down the hall, Charlie trotting after them. Vargas ducked into the guest room. At the safe room door, he pulled the panel down.

"What are you doing?" Seth asked. "I thought we were going to get Dylan." He grabbed Vargas by the arm and tried to spin him around, but Vargas was a man on a mission.

Once the safe room door was open, he turned to Seth. "*I'm* going for Dylan. You're getting in here."

Seth took a step back. "No."

"Dylan's going to be okay. Prescott's not gonna risk his chance at freedom to come after you guys. He's heading out of the state."

Seth repeatedly shook his head. "He won't leave. He won't. Not without me." He shot a look toward the open bedroom doorway. "Which means he'll go to the apartment first."

"He doesn't know which apartment you guys moved to."

"He'll figure it out. He'll wait there for me. Even if Dylan's not home now, he could walk in on Prescott." Seth started for the door. "We have to warn him."

"No!" Vargas shot past Seth and got in his way. "You're getting in the safe room. I'll bring Dylan back here."

"I'm going with you."

"No."

"We don't have time for this. You were right. Prescott won't want to risk getting caught. He's not going to take the time to come after all of us. But he *will* come for me."

Vargas jabbed an arm toward the safe room door. "That's why you're getting in there."

"What if they don't catch him? You want me to stay in there forever?"

"The cops will find Prescott, and if they don't, I'll get Tucker and his team on it. I won't stop until we find him and you're safe again. Now get in there so I can go make sure Dylan's all right." He went for Seth's arm.

Seth jerked away from him. "I need to do this, Vargas. I have to see Dylan."

"You will. As soon as I get back here. Now get inside."

"No." Seth moved farther away from him.

Vargas pictured Prescott attacking Seth, drugging him, and taking off with him, then locking him away somewhere, doing the most horrible things to him, and Seth never getting free again.

"What if he comes for me, takes me away again, and no one ever finds me?"

Determination surging through him, Vargas grasped Seth's arm. He tugged him toward the safe room door, hoping like hell he wasn't hurting him. "I am not letting anything else happen to you."

"Vargas, stop!"

"Not ever again."

"Prescott's not going to look for me here. It's Dylan who's in danger." Seth was really fighting him now. "Vargas, let go of me. I'm going with you." He sounded desperate, but there was no way Vargas was letting him leave the club. He hauled Seth into the safe room.

"Please don't do this. Please, Vargas."

"I have to." He checked that the interior panel was off, which he expected since he hadn't had the safe room company in to repair it yet. He led Seth to the back wall and kicked the pillows off the bench and onto the floor. He called out, "Charlie, come." The dog darted into the room and sat beside them. "Stay."

"What are you doing?"

"I'm sorry." Vargas shot a quick glance at Seth's face. There were tears in his eyes.

He shouldn't have looked. Because now was the hardest part.

He seized Seth by the upper arms and dropped a kiss on his lips. "I love you. Please don't forget that." He scooped Seth up so he was cradling him like a child. He lowered him down, trying to be careful but also get this done as fast as he could. He just had to hope that leaving him on the floor like that would buy him the time he needed to get the door sealed and the lock engaged. Getting off the floor still took Seth more time than typical for someone his age.

Without a look back, Vargas made his way out of the safe room.

He closed the door and cranked the handle, then scanned his thumb and added the code to engage the lock. The secondary set of bolts slid into place. The door was secure.

He'd sufficiently done what he'd sworn he never would: he'd taken away Seth's right to make his own decisions, to control his own life.

Even though Vargas knew no other way right then, his heart sank. Would he ever forgive himself for this? Would Seth? Or had he just sealed their fate with the close of that door?

He couldn't think about that now. All that mattered was keeping Seth and Dylan and the others safe. Even if that meant he'd lose Seth from his life in the end.

He pressed his forehead to the cold steel surface. "I'm sorry." Then he hightailed it across the room. On his way to the apartment door, he snatched his keys off the hall table and checked his pocket for his phone. He swung the door open, and Ian turned to face him.

"Seth's in the safe room. Do not leave this door for any reason." He pointed at Ian for emphasis. "No one—and I mean *no one*—gets inside this apartment."

"You got it."

Vargas took off for the stairs. He considered getting one of the guards to go with him in case he needed the help, but with the club closed and his recent reduction in staff, there weren't as many guys on duty as there would've been that night had he kept the place open. Even one less person protecting Seth wasn't an option.

He kept trying to tell himself what he'd said to Seth was the truth, that Prescott was already long gone. The man had one shot at staying free: to run as far and as fast as he could. Only Vargas's gut told him Seth was right. Prescott would want to come for him. No matter what.

Vargas had to get to Dylan, and then he'd come right back for Seth.

He reached his private entrance at the back of the club and gave the guard, who was there now because of the lockdown, a version of the instructions he'd given to Ian. Then he got moving for the parking lot as he redialed Dylan's number. It went straight to voice mail again. This time he left a message, telling him that Prescott escaped and that Dylan needed to get out of the apartment, find someone he trusted to come with him, and get to the club or the closest police station. That finished, Vargas slid the phone into his pocket and unlocked his SUV.

As he grabbed the door handle, he felt a sharp prick on the back of his neck. He ran a hand over his skin. There was something sticking out. He pulled it free and took a look. Lying in his palm was some kind of small dart-like syringe.

"Oh God, no."

All at once his head spun. His eyelids grew heavy, and he felt like he might vomit.

He scrambled for his phone, managing to get it out of his pocket right as he stumbled sideways and slammed his shoulder into the driver's side door. The phone slipped in his limp grip. He fumbled with it and then watched through blurred vision as the cell crashed to the pavement.

Breathing deep through his nose, he summoned his last bit of energy and lunged for the phone. He landed on his side on the asphalt with a thump.

He clawed at the phone, trying to drag it closer. A futile attempt. He could no longer move his hand. The last thing he heard before he lost consciousness was deliberate footsteps coming up behind him.

And his last thought was of Seth. Was this how frightened and helpless he'd felt that night he'd been taken from the Haven?

Although, right then, it wasn't for himself that Vargas was terrified.

* * * * *

Seth paced the length of the safe room. With each turn, he threw a hard glare at the closed steel door. A few minutes earlier when he'd first gotten up from the floor, he'd checked the control panel and found it still wasn't working. He'd also tried the spring-loaded release on the door, but like the last time, that offered no escape.

Now his body was vibrating with anger. Add to that his missing cane, and each step became more and more shaky. Charlie was seated near the door, watching him pace.

Seth knew Vargas was panicked. The thought of something else happening to him or the others scared him beyond words. But weren't they supposed to confront things together, no matter what?

Instead, Seth was alone.

Alone and facing the one thing he feared more than anything.

Prescott was coming for him. It didn't matter what the cops said or what anyone else believed. Seth knew the truth. Prescott would not give up until he found him. Seth was not about to sit by and do nothing while Dylan was in danger because of him.

No. Because of that monster.

He balled his hands into fists and went to the control panel, checking it again to be sure it hadn't miraculously turned on. It hadn't. He slammed the side of his fist against the door. He wanted to pound on the steel surface until the door opened, until he saw Dylan and Aaron and Kevin all safe before him. Until he knew Vargas hadn't done something stupid and gotten hurt. Or worse.

He spun around and scanned the room, spotting the cabinet with the plastic tubs inside.

The emergency cell phone.

He crossed the room to the storage containers and lowered to the floor. Tugging open the first tub, he found the phone lying on top where they'd left it when they'd been locked in there before. He swiped it up and hit the power button. The battery was dead. They must've left it on after they'd called for help. He dug through the tubs but couldn't find a charger.

"Fuck!" He chucked the phone across the room, and it bounced off the far wall. Charlie watched the phone land on the carpeted floor beside him, then studied Seth again, his head tilted.

Seth sat back on his heels. "Okay, think." The control panel. He had to find a way to repair it and get out of there.

As if he'd called the dog, Charlie trotted over to him, and Seth patted his back as he stared across the room at the panel's blank screen. There was power to the room, so why not the panel? The outside panel and the system that locked the door were obviously still functioning. He got up.

The panel on this side of the door didn't look as tamper-proof as he remembered the one on the outside appearing. Which made sense. These rooms were designed to keep people from breaking in, not the other way around. When the panel was raised to its highest point, he could access the four screws underneath. He checked what size and type of screwdriver he'd need.

He rummaged through the plastic tubs again, hoping to find a tool kit they'd overlooked last time. There was nothing. On his tiptoes, he reached up and searched the top shelf above the tubs. A thin plastic case lay in the back. He pulled it down and unsnapped the lid. Bingo. He moved several tools out of the way until he found a small enough screwdriver that looked like it might work. He dug it out and went to the panel. What was the worst that could happen?

He didn't let that thought linger. He got to work. It was awkward using the screwdriver at that angle. Added to that, Charlie kept headbutting his leg. Seth encouraged the dog back to the far side of the room, told him to sit and stay, and then returned to the panel.

He managed to remove all four screws. Then he detached the back cover, revealing an array of wires and computer components. He found what he thought might be a wire supplying power to the circuits. He wiggled the wire but nothing happened. He tried again. Still nothing. "Shit." He tested a few of the other wires but got nowhere.

This was pointless. What'd he know about this kind of thing?

He took a step back. He couldn't come up with anything else to try.

"Fuck it." He charged forward and gave the first wire another wiggle. He heard the faint sound of the system turning on. Twenty seconds later the screen lit up, displaying the biometric fingerprint scanner. Very carefully, so he didn't disrupt the cable and shut the whole thing off again, he scanned his thumb, entered the code, and pressed the release button.

There was a metallic snap as the bolts on the door retracted. He reached for the handle and turned, releasing the other set of bolts. He pushed the door open.

The bedroom outside was empty. The lights were off, but they'd been that way earlier. Everything seemed normal, as if his entire world hadn't just been upended with one phone call.

He charged for the nightstand across the room where he'd left his cell phone before his walk, but halfway there he stopped dead in his tracks. The phone was gone. The alarm clock on the nightstand was off, and there was an odd glow from the hall that seemed harsher than the regular lighting in the apartment, like an emergency spotlight. Something was wrong.

He hurried to the nightstand and flipped on the lamp but nothing happened.

"The power's out," came an eerily familiar voice from across the room.

Seth whirled around.

A large frame blocked the bedroom doorway, the man's face in shadows. He held a revolver. The metal of the gun glinted in the light seeping in around his looming figure.

Only… it wasn't Prescott holding the gun.

Chapter Thirty-Three

Prescott made his move the minute the asshat standing before him mentioned Henderson snapping Seth's neck. It took less than ten seconds to break free of the meager restraints and liberate the moron of his Beretta. Six seconds to be exact. And another thirty seconds to dispose of the other assholes.

When he was done, they lay in a pile, eyes open, bullet holes in vital organs, throats slit and skulls bashed in for good measure. Not a single one of the other three had even unholstered his weapon.

Idiots.

And the biggest idiot of all... Henderson. He had no idea how much agony he was going to be in if he laid so much as one hand on Seth.

* * * * *

Staring back at Seth from behind the handgun was Franklin Henderson, Conrad Henderson's father. Seth had seen him in the courtroom during the trial and on the news coverage talking about his son's murder. He and his son had always had a tumultuous on-again, off-again relationship, but the older Henderson had been adamant about justice for his son's death.

Henderson started forward. "I've waited a long time for this." He took another step, and Seth matched it with his own backward move.

"What do you want?"

"Oh, I think you know."

"How did you—" Seth swallowed down the rest of those words. There was only one way Henderson had gotten into the Haven and inside the apartment. Someone had helped him. "Prescott's not here."

"I know." The man laughed, the eerie sound bouncing off the walls of the dark bedroom. "He will be soon enough. Then he'll get to see the outcome of what I'm about to do. After that, I'll be able to finally finish things with him. But first..." Henderson advanced again, creeping forward with resolve. The gun remained steadily aimed at Seth. "I'm afraid that I'm going to have to hurt you." The look on his face indicated he meant far more than hurt him.

He was going to kill him.

Seth retreated until his back hit the wall behind him. He spotted the open safe room door more than six feet to his right. He needed to get back inside. If he made a run for it, would he have enough time to lock the door? Would the control panel inside even still be working? He darted a look over the man's shoulder at the open bedroom door behind him.

Henderson stopped and shook his head. "No one's coming. We're alone. The guards and the owner of this place were taken care of."

"What do you mean taken care of?"

"They're alive. I'm not a complete monster, and I'm not about to complicate this entire thing and risk getting charged with murder."

"Then you're not gonna kill me?"

He grinned as if he had a plan to get away with that very thing. "I really am sorry about this, but I need to make him pay."

As Seth talked, he started inching his way toward the safe room. "How is killing me going to help?" He needed a distraction to make it inside and get the door closed and locked. He needed to keep Henderson talking until he could come up with a plan.

When Henderson said nothing, Seth added, "How is hurting another innocent person going to make him pay? I didn't do anything to deserve this."

Henderson snorted with laughter. "I can see why my son picked you to take away from Prescott. He knew you were the least likely to put up a fight, or to know how to get away from him." He jammed the revolver in the air in Seth's direction. "Stop moving! Stand perfectly still, or I'll make this really hurt, and then I'll go take care of your dog, your boyfriend, everyone you care about. Screw the consequences. One way or another, I'm getting my revenge."

Seth complied.

That seemed to appease Henderson. His expression lost some of its rage. "No matter what my boy did to you, he didn't deserve to have his life snuffed out by that worthless piece of shit. Prescott will die for what he did, but first..." There was a manic, animated look in his eyes now. He was enjoying this. "I'm going to make him suffer. I'm going to take away someone who means a great deal to him. Just like he took my son from me."

This guy was batshit crazy and full of grief. Which meant nothing was going to stop him. Seth thought about everyone who was going to grieve if Henderson followed through with his plan to kill him: Vargas, Dylan, Aaron, Toby, Ryder, Georgia, and Charlie.

Charlie.

He was still in the safe room. Probably sitting right where Seth had told him to stay. If he called Charlie to him, would that be enough of a distraction so he could take off and reach the bedroom door?

But Seth couldn't bring himself to involve Charlie when all he could picture was Henderson emptying the gun in the dog's direction.

Henderson was watching Seth with curiosity. Maybe he was all talk. Maybe now that he stood face to face with him, he couldn't pull the trigger on an innocent man.

Then that demented grin was back. "Not many people matter to that man. Not his family. He has no friends. But you..." Henderson indicated Seth with a tip of the gun's barrel. "You're more than special to him."

"No, I'm not. I always made him angry. He'd never risk himself to come after me. This is insane. You're not going to gain anything by this. He won't even know what you've done."

The grin grew. Henderson lowered the revolver slightly as if it wasn't time for that yet. He gestured to the doorway behind him. "My men found him right outside this building. He was going to get to you no matter what. And he'll do it again as soon as I give the word and my men let him escape. But don't worry. I'm not a barbarian like him. I'm not going to keep you locked in a cage and torture you for hours just for my own sick, perverted pleasure. I'll make this quick. But I can't use the gun."

His voice sounded oddly remorseful. "I'm sorry about that. I have to make this look like it was Prescott who was responsible. They'll think he killed you in a moment of rage when you wouldn't go away with him, and then he turned his anger on me. Once he comes after me, I can shoot him in self-defense."

"No one will believe you."

"Yes, they will. The police will assume he came to my home to exact revenge for all the things I said about him during the trial. No one saw me here at the club. Before I leave, I'll take care of the security footage. No one will know I was here. No one except..." He tucked the gun into his jacket pocket and pulled out a pair of driving gloves. He slipped them on. "You."

Now was Seth's chance. As Henderson rounded the bed near the safe room door, Seth took off the other way. He hopped onto the bed, crossed it in two strides, and jumped off the other side, then sped for the bedroom door.

Before he reached the threshold, Henderson seized him from behind. He swung him around and slammed him against the wall. The fierce impact reverberated all along Seth's spine, and the force knocked the wind out of him. Pain shot through his lower back. His legs buckled, and he fell to the floor onto his hands and knees. Another jolt of pain struck his left kneecap.

Then a shot rang out. Seth flinched and fell sideways against the wall, but there was no additional pain, no burn of a bullet ripping through him.

Henderson landed with a thud beside Seth. The man's face was pressed to the floor. He didn't look like he was breathing.

Seth's ears were ringing. He couldn't move. He couldn't turn away from the lifeless body next to him. He heard Dr. Arteaga's voice in his head.

"I think there's more we need to discuss, more you need to work through."

A guttural laugh surged out of him as he kept staring at the dead man beside him. He sounded mad.

Then came a voice from above. "Are you okay?" A warm arm cradled Seth around the waist and helped him stand. He was pulled backward against a solid body. For several seconds, Seth settled his weight against him, wanting to feel safe, protected.

Only, everything about the touch was wrong.

He scrambled away and faced the man.

Gaping back at him was Prescott. His large frame towered over Seth, blocking the open doorway. He had a handgun at his side, dangling from his right hand.

Seth froze. The air in his lungs grew heavy. He heard Dr. Arteaga's voice again.

"Rate your fear."

Chapter Thirty-Four

Seth fell back a step. "No."

Prescott nodded. "It's me."

Even in the darkened room, Seth could see the scar on Prescott's neck from where Dylan had stabbed him, a reminder of what the man was capable of surviving through.

Prescott searched Seth's face. "Are you okay? I've been so worried about you ever since I saw you all beat up like that, lying on that table downstairs. I made him pay for hurting you." He looked down at the older Henderson's body. "I'll make them all pay." He focused on Seth again, and his expression softened as if he'd just read something in his face. "I would never hurt you like they did." Prescott let the gun slip from his fingers. It fell onto Henderson's lower legs. Too far out of Seth's reach. He'd never get to it in time.

Prescott held out a hand. "We can be together now. We can go away like we planned."

Something inside Seth snapped. Like a former piece of himself had slid into its proper place. "I'm not going anywhere with you."

He wanted to dive across the empty space between them and fire a fist at the center of Prescott's face, claw at his flesh, but he had to be smart about this. He needed a weapon. "I'm not letting you hurt me ever again. I'm not letting you take my life from me." Seth lunged for the nightstand and grabbed the lamp. He didn't hesitate. He spun and swung in one motion, aiming for Prescott's head.

Prescott blocked the hit. He clasped on to one of Seth's wrists and wrenched him around. He got a grip on Seth's other arm and jerked him backward so Seth was plastered to his chest again, Prescott's arm squeezing him around the middle. The touch was cold, savage, momentarily sending Seth surging back to that dungeon he'd been held in and all the unspeakable things Prescott had done to him.

He wouldn't let himself linger there. He pushed the nightmare from his mind and fought the man restraining him with everything he had.

"Put it down." Prescott growled the words as he twisted Seth's wrist. Seth cried out and dropped the lamp, but he wasn't about to give in. He struggled, flailing from side to side, whipping his weight against Prescott.

A low snarling sound came from behind them. Prescott rotated them as one toward the source. Charlie stood there, hunched low, teeth bared, ready to attack.

Holding on to Seth tighter, Prescott spoke against his ear. "Tell him to back off, and I'll let him come with us."

"No!" Seth threw his head back, catching Prescott in the chin. His head instantly throbbed, but the move did nothing to dislodge the larger man.

"You were always my good boy. Did whatever you were told. What happened to you?"

"I'm not afraid of you anymore." Seth wriggled in the man's arms, and Prescott clasped on to him tighter. That had Charlie growling again in warning.

"Call him off."

Over his shoulder Seth spat out, "Fuck you." He elbowed Prescott in the gut. The man groaned and bent forward, loosening his grip right as Charlie attacked. The dog sank his teeth into Prescott's calf, and Seth finally wrenched free. He whirled around and kicked him in the crotch. That had Prescott crying out in pain as he collapsed to the floor on his knees.

Charlie didn't let up on the bite. He thrashed his head from side to side and sank his teeth in deeper.

Prescott kicked at the air, trying to dislodge Charlie with no success.

Seth went for the discarded lamp, lifted it over his head, and swung the lamp down with as much force as he could manage. Prescott raised an arm and ducked but not quickly enough. The lamp hit him square in the forehead, clearly disorienting him. Seth let go of the lamp and launched for the door. He shot out into the hall, nearly slamming into the opposite wall before making the turn. "Come, Charlie."

The dog sprinted to him, and they took off. He should've let Charlie keep attacking Prescott so he had more time to get away, but since the man no longer had Seth in his clenches, chances were that Charlie would be less inclined to fight. Prescott might retrieve the gun from where he'd dropped it and shoot Charlie to get him out of the way. Nothing was happening to him, to either of them.

The gun.

Seth stopped and threw a look back down the hall. "Dammit."

He should've picked up the damn gun. No turning back now. He sprinted for the apartment door, Charlie following at his heels. Seth swung the door open and found a body lying on the hall floor. The man was on his stomach, his head turned to the side.

"Oh God." Seth knelt down beside him. "Ian." He shook him by the shoulder, but there was no response. He lowered his head and listened. Ian was still breathing. Seth tried again to rouse him with no luck. He gave a quick look for Ian's phone and his stun gun, but neither were on him or the floor nearby. Seth had no choice. He had to move, had to get help.

He started for the back staircase but stopped before he got far. What if for some reason the door at the base of the stairs wouldn't open? He'd be trapped at the bottom of the staircase with nowhere to hide and no way to get past Prescott. He had to try for another exit.

He wasn't about to wait until he heard Prescott's footfalls coming down the hall inside the apartment. He changed course, leaped over Ian, and continued in the opposite direction. With only the sporadic emergency spotlights on, it was difficult to see far. Despite that, Seth sprinted down the hall and past the security room. A guard was hunched sideways in the open doorway, but Seth didn't have time to check him. He kept going for the main staircase.

The emergency lights showered the club below in an odd mix of spotlights and shadows. He couldn't see anyone moving around. He shot down the stairs, Charlie at his side. As soon as he reached the bottom, he darted for the club's front door. He wasn't sure if that was the closest exit, but it was the one he was most familiar with. He couldn't afford the time to search for anything else.

Another downed guard lay on the floor near the entrance. Seth raced past him and tried the front door. It wouldn't open. Even with the power out, the exterior doors should open from the inside. Maybe Henderson had done something to secure them.

Just as Seth had feared.

"Shit."

Would the off-site security company be able to detect that the system had been tampered with? Would they be automatically notified of the power outage? Or had Henderson taken care of that as well?

Seth turned to face the dining room. What now?

He froze as he heard faint footsteps somewhere above. He slunk backward into the dark corner near the front entrance, tugging Charlie with him.

* * * * *

Prescott got to his feet and tried to shake off the dizziness. Something warm and thick was running down his face. He pressed a hand to his forehead. Blood. He wiped it from his eyes as he stumbled for the bedroom door.

Thinking better of it, he returned to Henderson's body and searched him. He found a gun in his jacket pocket. He collected it, as well as the Beretta Prescott had taken from the henchmen earlier. He hated guns, but he might need one if the cops cornered him. He shoved the smaller revolver from Henderson inside his boot alongside the pocketknife. The other gun he decided to hide, tossing it into the drawer of the nearby nightstand. He wasn't about to use a weapon on Seth unless he absolutely had to. He wouldn't take the chance of a fatal accident. Not with his boy.

Next he made his way down the hall and into the apartment's kitchen. He needed supplies. He hadn't taken the time to go back to the van for anything once he'd gotten away from Henderson's men. He rifled the kitchen drawers until he found what he could use. A package of zip ties. He shoved them into his back pocket. Then he spotted something else.

It was nice of the asshole owner to leave such a pretty one out for him. It was better than the one in his boot that he'd used earlier to get free of the restraints on his wrists. He retrieved the chef's knife from the cutting board.

He got moving again. He couldn't give Seth enough time to find a way out of the club. Nearly all of the exterior doors Prescott had tried when he arrived earlier had been locked, and the ones he'd checked on his way through the club wouldn't open from the inside. It would take some time for Seth to locate a way out. Maybe the same way Prescott had gotten in: an unlocked employee entrance at the back of the club. There must've been someone on the inside helping Henderson.

Following a hunch on where Seth went, Prescott rounded the downed guard at the apartment door and started for the staircase that led to the main floor of the club. He stopped when another idea came to him. He doubled back to the security room. An unconscious guard was keeled over in the open doorway. Prescott shoved the door in the rest of the way and entered, stepping over the guard. The lights, computers, and bank of monitors were on, as were the live camera feeds that covered the club's public areas.

He surveyed the monitors, spotting several more guards lying on the floor throughout the club. Henderson had been thorough getting everyone out of the way.

Using the control panel, Prescott switched feeds on the main monitor and zoomed in on each unconscious guard. It took him a moment, but then he spotted him. Vargas. The owner was lying in the club's kitchen.

Yes, that would work perfectly, and of course, would give him immeasurable pleasure.

He continued to scan the video feeds before him and found what else he wanted. Seth. Crouched behind a coat-check podium near the front entrance of the club. He had his dog beside him. He looked small and frightened but safe and unharmed. Very different from the last time Prescott had seen him inside that club, his broken, bloody image displayed on a different monitor.

Prescott leaned in and ran his fingertips over the image of Seth. "I'm coming."

He straightened. He loved this part. Worth the risk he'd taken in coming to the Haven. He gave Seth one last look. "So worth it."

* * * * *

From his current vantage point, Seth could no longer view the staircase. He waited, but he didn't hear anyone moving through the club. He took a chance and peeked over the top of the podium. He gave the open room and balcony above a once-over and froze when he spotted him.

Prescott stood at the top of the stairs, a kitchen knife in hand. He was scanning the first floor below him. Seth ducked back down and held his breath. His heartbeat thudded away as he tugged Charlie close and buried his face in the dog's gold fur.

Listening carefully, Seth heard Prescott start down the stairs. Taking a chance, Seth peered around the corner of the stand, hoping the darkness would offer enough coverage he'd remain undetected and be able to see where Prescott went next.

Prescott paused at the base of the stairs as if he were trying to decide which way to go or had to convince himself to do something that went against his instincts. He veered around in the opposite direction and headed toward a lighted emergency exit sign that hung over the kitchen doorway.

When he was through the door to the kitchen, Seth crawled toward the guard lying near the front entrance. As he'd done with Ian, he tried to wake him with no success, then checked him for a weapon or a cell phone but came up short again. He crept forward and tried the landline at the guard's station. No dial tone.

Now what? He had to get out of the club, but how? All the doors were likely locked the same as the front. There weren't many windows on the first floor, none that he could think of in the public areas. The rooms upstairs had windows, but the doors to those rooms would likely be locked too. There had to be separate emergency exits that would open from the inside, even with all the other doors locked and the power out.

He glanced around again but couldn't see any lit exit signs, except the one over the kitchen doorway.

He had to move to get a better look or to try something else.

"Think, Seth."

The security room.

Vargas had said it was on a separate power system like the safe room. Thinking back to when he'd run by it earlier, Seth tried to remember if the lights were on inside. All he'd been focused on was getting away from Prescott.

He stole a quick look around the podium toward the security office on the second floor. Sure enough, there was a faint light coming from the open doorway. Maybe the phone in there was on a different system. And if not, maybe the computers were turned on and connected to the Internet. He could get a message to the police.

He laid a hand on Charlie's back. As if that gave him the extra courage he needed, he leaned in and whispered, "Time to get out of here, Charlie."

Before Prescott could return from the kitchen, Seth stood and sprinted across the club for the main stairs. He hadn't exerted himself physically that much or run that fast since he'd first awoken in the hospital two years ago.

Hell, today was the first time he'd run at all.

Chapter Thirty-Five

By the time Seth reached the security room, he was out of breath and the headache he'd gotten from headbutting Prescott earlier was throbbing like hell. Neither slowed him down.

The room's door was ajar with the unconscious guard slumped in the open doorway, his body keeping the door propped open. Seth rolled him over.

"Oh no. Carter."

He checked for a pulse, found one, then gave him a shake, but like the others there was no response. Seth winced as he tried slapping him across the face. That did nothing. He got up and hurried inside the narrow security room, Charlie following him in. Seth grabbed the phone on the desk. No dial tone there either.

He dropped into a chair and tried the computer. It was working, but when he pulled up a web browser, nothing would load. He checked the Internet connection but found no signal and no other available connections.

So much for that idea.

He frantically glanced around the room for a weapon or a cell phone or for anything he could use to communicate with the outside world. He found nothing useful, except that the video surveillance monitors were still on.

He examined the monitor for the club's kitchen. The room was dark, only one emergency light on. He spotted no sign of Prescott.

He leaned his hands on the desk and scanned the rest of the images of the club, including all the public areas of the ground floor and the hallways of the upper floors. Still no Prescott or any movement anywhere. Several more people were lying unconscious at various points in the club. He wanted to zoom in, get a closer look, and see if any of them were Vargas, but he couldn't think about that now. He had to stay calm, focused. He had to come up with a plan.

He searched the security room again, trying the metal cabinet on the back wall, but it was locked. Maybe he should go for the door at the base of the stairs near Vargas's apartment, see if that was locked the same as the front entrance. He could check if the gun was still in the apartment on his way. Although he was certain Prescott would've picked that up before he left the bedroom.

Maybe he should try to get to a window on the second floor. There were several fire escapes leading to the ground.

Or should he just shut the door to the security room, lock it, and wait this out? When Walter didn't hear from Vargas, he'd come to the club looking for them, probably bringing half the police force with him.

A crackling sound came from overhead. The PA system. How many places were there where someone could broadcast? Maybe at the guard's station near the front door, or the employee offices downstairs.

Or the kitchen.

Seth stood. The crackling sound came again. Like someone was blowing into the mic to see if the system was on.

Then came that voice.

"I have Vargas."

"Oh God." Seth slapped a hand over his mouth.

"He's alive. For now. And he'll stay that way as long as you do exactly as I say. Come to the kitchen through the swinging double doors in the back of the dining room. I have him here with me. You come, and I won't gut him."

Seth sucked in a shaky breath. He swung back to the monitors and checked the feed of the club's kitchen. No Prescott. No Vargas. But the camera didn't cover the entire room or the storage areas, and most of what it did show was in shadows.

"Come into the kitchen, walk through the room to the emergency exit, stand facing the door, and wait. You have fifteen minutes to get here. Or else I start cutting." The PA cut off.

Seth dropped into the chair at the desk. Fifteen minutes. He checked the time on the monitor before him. Walter and the police would never show up by then. Seth considered trying again to get out of the club, but even if he did, help would never arrive in time. He couldn't wait and take a chance with Vargas's life.

He had to do something himself.

The camera feed on the large center monitor featured a duplicate image of the lounge that was also visible on one of the smaller screens. Using the control panel, Seth tried various options until he found the zoom and pan functions. He tapped an arrow button. The image on the main monitor switched to an exterior shot of the front door of the club. He panned the view left and right. The sidewalk and street were empty. He pressed the arrow button again and changed views until he looked at a larger shot of the kitchen. He zoomed in on the dark corners of the room. There was still no sign of Prescott or Vargas. But there was something else.

Prescott had pushed a freestanding commercial refrigerator in front of the emergency exit—the only other exit out of the kitchen beside the door leading into the club's dining room.

That was why Prescott wasn't in the room and why he'd given Seth fifteen minutes to get there, so Prescott would have time to hide somewhere else. He was going to wait until Seth entered the kitchen and then trap him there.

"Fuck that." Seth stood. He wasn't about to get cornered. Or let anything happen to Vargas. He glanced down at Charlie. "He's got him somewhere else. But where?" He checked the time again.

Thirteen minutes to go.

He'd likely never locate Vargas in time. That left him only one choice. He'd have to confront Prescott.

Seth swiftly surveyed the narrow security room again, hoping he'd spot something he could use as a weapon that he'd somehow missed earlier. Maybe there was a lockbox with extra stun guns or other weapons and ammunition. Probably in the locked cabinet. He hastily rummaged through Carter's pockets for a set of keys. He found nothing.

Then a realization hit him. Something wasn't right.

He turned back to the bank of monitors. The one farthest to the left was dark. He got up and flipped the switch on. In the middle of the screen sat Vargas, his hands tied behind his back, his ankles lashed to the front legs of a dining room chair.

"Oh God."

Vargas's eyes were closed, his head slumped forward. He was unconscious. Same as the guards. Which might not be as horrible as it seemed, given Vargas's claustrophobia and how much he'd hate being tied up like that.

Prescott was crouched behind him checking the restraints. When he was finished, he picked up the knife from the floor and stood beside the chair, staring at what had to be the entrance to whatever room they were in. He was waiting out of sight until Seth was in the kitchen.

"Okay, you can do this." Seth breathed deep the way Dr. Arteaga had taught him. "First things first."

He reexamined the space where Vargas was being held. He couldn't see the entire room but enough to get that it had tiled floor and no other visible furniture. It wasn't the kitchen. And it didn't seem familiar either. Maybe a bathroom.

No. It appeared too big and open. Maybe one of the guest rooms upstairs that he'd never been in. The club had several themed rooms, fantasy settings for BDSM scenes. Maybe there was a room with tiled floor.

It was hard to see much detail with the limited emergency lighting, but something metal lined the wall behind Vargas. A series of lockers.

The employee locker room.

Vargas had mentioned that he'd put a camera in there. The locker room was on the first floor, down a short hallway just off the dining room. Prescott would've definitely had enough time to get there.

Seth checked the time again. Ten minutes left to figure out what to do.

"Come on. You can do this."

He rapidly thought through his options, hating each one more than the last. He'd never be able to overpower Prescott. He'd only been lucky in that regard earlier thanks to Charlie's help. It was unlikely it'd go down like that again.

Alternatively, if Seth waited until Prescott went into the kitchen, he'd never have enough time to reach Vargas, untie him, and get them out of the club. Besides, Prescott might kill Vargas before he went into the kitchen.

No, that wasn't right. Prescott had him tied up for a reason. He'd want to torture Vargas in the worst way possible by making him live with the knowledge that Seth was out there somewhere without him, somewhere *with* Prescott.

Then it came to Seth. The best plan he could come up with. All he had left to work out now was how to get them out of the club quickly.

He reached for the control panel on the desk. His hand was shaking as he pressed the arrow key. The large center monitor switched to a feed of the bar. He tried the next view and the next until he found what he wanted: the main floor of the club on the same side as the hallway that led to the employee locker room. He zoomed the camera in, then panned left and right, searching the dining room wall on each side.

There. At the far end of another short hallway was an emergency exit sign. All the times he'd been to the club he never paid attention to those signs. Prescott hadn't blocked this exit door. Which meant, he truly believed Seth was going to show up in the kitchen and not put up a fight.

Screw him.

Seth leaned down to Charlie and cradled the dog's head in his hands. "I'm sorry, but you can't come with me. I won't let him hurt you. Or use you to manipulate me. You'll be safe in here." And even if something happened to Seth, someone would eventually open the security room and find Charlie.

He kissed Charlie on the top of the head and told him to stay.

At the door, Seth carefully shifted Carter aside, then shut the door and checked that it was locked.

No time to delay. He had less than eight minutes left. He took off for Vargas's apartment. It would take him a few minutes to gather everything, then a couple more minutes to head down the stairs and get into position.

But first, he had to get to the safe room. His plan had to start there.

* * * * *

Seth crouched down lower behind a prep table in the Haven's kitchen, his entire body trembling, both from nerves and the cool temperature of the room. The bottom shelves of the table he waited behind were filled with stacks of baking sheet trays, giving him ample cover. Light from the low-voltage emergency spotlight bounced off the numerous bare stainless-steel surfaces in the room, creating an eerie moon-like glow that did little to offer more visibility than there'd been in the rest of the club.

As he'd suspected, the kitchen had been empty when he arrived. On his way through the dining room, he'd sprinted as fast as he could and hadn't spotted any sign of Prescott watching him. He had to hope Prescott was staying hidden in the locker room and hadn't seen what he carried.

Now as Seth waited, he wasn't sure of the time, but he guessed it was already a minute or two past the mark. It wouldn't be long. He took a deep breath.

This was going to work. It had to.

No more than five seconds later, the door across the room gradually swung inward. Inch by inch, Prescott came into view. His face was streaked with blood. He held the knife at his side. Where was the gun he'd had earlier? Tucked in the back of his waistband? In a pocket?

Seth ducked farther down as Prescott slunk all the way into the room, letting the door close behind him.

"Where are you, boy?" He took a step forward. Then another. "I saw you come through the dining room. What all were you carrying?"

He'd see soon enough.

Seth waited. Just a few more steps would do it.

Prescott paused, then crept forward again as he visually scanned the room. He started whistling, that same creepy tune he'd always used when he held them captive. It reminded Seth of a cartoon theme song, but he'd never been able to figure out which one. He'd hoped he was never going to hear that psychotic sound again.

The whistling stopped. "I know you're in here. There'll be plenty of time for games later, but right now we have to hurry." Another step. "You don't have to hide from me. I'm not mad that you ran or that you hurt me. I just want us to be together again." He was almost in line with Seth. "I'll take care of you. So you can stop being afraid. You're not alone anymore."

Was he the most delusional man alive? The trial, all the media coverage, the verdict, the sentencing, Seth's words to Prescott upstairs, despite it all, this fucker would never understand what he did to Seth and the others. He was a sick, perverted, violent man who had used and hurt so many people and who deserved to spend the rest of his miserable life in prison.

Seth was going to make sure that happened. He was going to make sure this fucker never hurt anyone again. He pulled the trigger on the controller.

Across the room, on the opposite side of Prescott, the replica of the Shelby GT500 revved and surged forward. Prescott whirled toward the sound. The red and white model car sped right for him. Seth leaped up and raced forward. Prescott spun to face him, but he was too late. Seth depressed the button on the canister. Pepper spray shot out, hitting Prescott directly in the face. He cried out and bent forward. The knife clanked to the floor beside him as he hastily covered his eyes with his hands.

Seth let the canister of pepper spray fall to the tiled floor and gripped Vargas's baseball bat in both hands. He swung with everything he had, aiming for Prescott's lower legs. The impact had another wail spilling out of Prescott as he fell to his knees. Seth raised the bat and swung again, hitting him in the upper back.

He went down, landing on his side, smashing the model car beneath him. Seth let go of the bat, and it clattered to the floor. He grabbed one of Prescott's arms, then the other, and raised them over the man's head so Prescott's hands were close to the leg of a metal prep table that was bolted to the floor. Without delay, Seth tugged the duct tape from his back pocket and wrapped it around Prescott's wrists several times and then around the table leg, unraveling more of the tape as he continued winding it around both the table and the man's wrists.

Prescott's hands were already turning red from lack of circulation. Coughing and gagging, he had his eyes squeezed shut, the skin around them red and inflamed. Seth searched Prescott's pockets and waistband for any sign of the gun. He found nothing.

Bending over him, Seth took in the sight of the whimpering, blind, restrained, helpless man before him and said, "Are you mad at me now?"

Then the euphoria of that victory drained away with one thought.

Vargas.

Seth had to get to him. Despite how disabled Prescott appeared, Seth wasn't about to run for the police and abandon Vargas when he was incapacitated and in such close proximity to this man.

He picked up the knife Prescott had dropped and took off for the kitchen door. Sprinting across the dining room, he wove around a slew of tables and chairs. When he reached the employee locker room, he found Vargas unconscious and still tied to the chair in the middle of the room. He rushed to him.

"Vargas?"

No response.

Using the knife, Seth cut the zip ties securing Vargas's legs to the chair. Then he moved around to get the ones on his wrists. Once free, Vargas's arms fell to his sides, and he slumped sideways in the chair. Seth let the knife fall to the floor and caught him. He slid him back to an upright position.

"Vargas?"

Still nothing.

As Seth moved back to the front of the chair, he spotted several drops of blood on the blue tiled floor. He glanced at the knife. It was tinged red like it had been wiped off but not all of the blood had been removed.

"You come, and I won't gut him."

"Oh no. No!" Seth dropped down before the chair. Vargas's face was pale, too pale. Seth searched him for any sign of an injury, running his hands over his chest and then up under his shirt. His right hand met something thick and sticky. He pulled his arm back. His fingers were covered in blood.

He'd been wrong. Prescott hadn't planned to keep Vargas alive as a way of prolonging his torture. He wanted to kill him so that after they left, Seth would have no hope of Vargas coming to his rescue.

Chapter Thirty-Six

Seth frantically lifted Vargas's shirt. He expected stab wounds. Instead he found a light smearing of blood across Vargas's abs. Not enough to conceal the words Prescott had etched into his skin below one of his tattoos.

He's mine.

"Oh God."

Seth had been right the first time. Prescott wasn't going to kill Vargas. He was going to take Seth with him and leave Vargas there with those words on his body to torture him for the rest of his life.

The cuts were shallow, nothing life threatening. Most probably didn't even require stitches. Which meant Vargas had simply been drugged like the others. Seth slapped him across the face. He tried again harder, hating that he had to do this, but he needed him to wake up. "Vargas."

Vargas's eyes fluttered, but he still didn't come around. Seth slapped him again. "Vargas!"

That time he blinked, then opened his eyes wider. "Seth?"

"We have to get out of the club. Now. Prescott's here. Can you stand?"

He mumbled something in response that Seth didn't catch.

No time to waste. Seth lifted one of Vargas's arms and looped it over his shoulders. Before standing, he retrieved the knife from the floor. He braced for the added weight and pulled Vargas out of the chair.

Once on his feet, Vargas held some of his own weight. That helped. There was no way Seth could get them to the exit if he had to drag him.

"Come on." He gave Vargas a shake. "We gotta move."

Vargas offered something unintelligible again. His head lolled from side to side, but he shuffled one foot forward. Then another. By the time they reached the locker-room door, Vargas was moving a bit faster but was still just as out of it.

Seth got them through the door and into the dining room. He scanned the vast open room. No sign of Prescott. He started for the hallway that led to the emergency exit he'd seen earlier on the video monitor.

"We're almost there." He shifted Vargas's weight forward, and that got him lumbering along faster.

A door creaked open in the distance. Seth spared a look. Prescott stood in the kitchen doorway, his face beet red, his eyes squinting as he searched the first floor.

"He's coming. We gotta go faster. Now." Seth picked up the pace, having to offer more help to Vargas.

They were just three feet from the hallway with the exit.

Prescott's voice rang out. "Stop!"

Footfalls came from out of the darkness behind them. They were two steps down the hall when Vargas tripped and fell, dropping forward to the floor. Seth scrambled to help him up, but Vargas shoved at him. "Seth," he choked out. "Go!"

"No." Seth shot a look behind them. Prescott was less than five strides away. Seth straightened and spun to face him, raising the chef's knife at the same time.

In one motion, Prescott closed the distance and slapped Seth's hand away. The knife fell from his grip, bounced off the wall, and landed out of reach. Prescott seized him by the throat. "You're not going anywhere. You're mine."

"No!" Seth squirmed, trying to reach the front pocket of his jeans. "I'm not!"

"Yes." Prescott swept his free hand over Seth's right shoulder. He hauled the T-shirt sleeve up and ran his thumb along the word he'd carved into the flesh of Seth's arm. "See. This says you are."

"No. It doesn't." Seth got his hand inside his pocket and clasped on to what he'd stashed there earlier. "It says I'm a survivor." He tugged the switchblade from his pants pocket, hit the release to extend the blade, and rammed the steel into Prescott's gut as hard as he could.

Prescott let go of him and stumbled backward. Seth kept hold of the knife and watched it slide from the man's stomach. Wobbling, Prescott caught himself against the wall. He glanced down as he tried to staunch the blood with one hand, then looked back at Seth, sheer astonishment in his eyes.

Seth held the blade out. "Back up or I'll do it again."

"No…" Prescott pushed off the wall. He wound his free arm around his back. "You're going to do what I want."

Seth jabbed the knife in the air. "Put your hands up!"

As if he was going to comply, Prescott brought his arm back around.

Before Seth could do more than register that he held a gun, Prescott had it aimed at Vargas where he sat slumped against the wall, his head tilted back, his eyes more alert. "You'll do exactly what I want once he's no longer an issue."

"No." Seth shook his head. "Don't."

With surprising agility, Vargas pushed off the floor onto shaky legs. He slid in between Prescott and Seth. Even though the gun had already been aimed at Vargas, Seth knew what he was doing. The exit door was at Seth's back.

"Go, Seth. Run."

Seth ignored him. "Please." He took a step sideways so Prescott could see him from behind Vargas. "If you care about me at all, don't do this."

Prescott simply laughed. The sound was demented, and there was rage in his mad, watery eyes as he raised the gun higher. "Goodbye, asshole."

Vargas lurched into Seth's path again. A far-off voice called out for Prescott to stop, but whoever it was, he was too late. A shot rang out.

"No!" Seth screamed. He caught Vargas in his arms. "Oh God." He patted at his chest, searching him for blood. "Where are you hit?"

"No…" Vargas sucked in a deep, ragged breath. "Nowhere." He straightened, supporting his own weight once more.

"What?" Seth stepped around him and only then did he see Prescott on the ground. His red-rimmed eyes were wide, his breath shallow. Blood was soaking through the front of his shirt. He stared up at Seth. He tried to speak, but all that came out was a gurgling sound. Then nothing.

Heading down the hall from the club's dining room was Tucker. He had a gun aimed at Prescott, but he spoke to Seth. "Are you okay?"

"Yeah."

Vargas slid down the wall to sit on the floor again. He was gaining color and seemed more alert, or maybe it was the lack of a bullet wound that had him looking so damn good.

Turning back to Tucker, Seth said, "We're okay. I'm okay." And more than at any other time in the past two years, he truly believed that. It was over.

Then he remembered something. "Oh shit."

Vargas sat taller. "What?"

"Henderson's body. It was gone."

"What?" That was Tucker. He'd positioned himself between them and Prescott.

"Franklin Henderson was here. He tried to kill me, but Prescott shot him. When I went to the safe room to get the pepper spray and the other stuff..." Seth shook his head. "I just realized, Henderson's body wasn't there anymore. I thought he was dead but..." He gaped at Tucker.

Tucker turned and faced the dining room, his weapon raised, his body held in a taut protective stance in front of Seth and Vargas. "He probably took off, but just in case, no one move until the cops get here."

Chapter Thirty-Seven

After a long look at Prescott's lifeless body and then at Tucker standing guard before them, Vargas let his eyes fall shut. The adrenaline was fading fast and so was he. A short moment later, the sound of sirens filled the club, then shouts and Tucker's voice from farther away as he addressed the cops and identified himself.

Vargas felt two hands repeatedly patting his face and upper body. "Are you okay? Please say you're okay."

"Yeah. I'm okay." He opened his eyes, and immediately his head spun. Regardless, he forced himself to keep his focus on Seth, who was sitting on the floor before him. One very alive and safe Seth. Who was going to stay that way. For good now. "Are *you* all right?"

Seth smiled at him. It was a look filled with astonishment and relief. And love. "Yes."

Vargas let out a long breath. Earlier, when Seth had said that Prescott was in the club, Vargas had never been so afraid, never felt so unbelievably helpless. No matter how hard he'd tried, he'd barely been able to move. It took all his effort to keep upright and try to walk with Seth. If anything had happened to him…

He grasped on to one of Seth's hands. "You were alone with him?"

Seth nodded.

"Did he hurt you?"

"I'm fine."

"Did he touch you?"

Another nod. "But I'm okay. Really."

Vargas breathed deep again and pulled Seth into his arms. "God, I was so scared."

"I know. It's okay. Everything's okay."

"I love you."

Seth held on to him tighter. "I love you too."

Tucker cleared his throat as he crouched beside them. "Police are here. They're checking the building. Ambulances are on the way." He focused on where Prescott lay on the floor. "He's still breathing, but just barely. I don't think he'll make it."

As Seth pulled back, Vargas reluctantly let go of him. Then he held a hand out to Tucker. "Thank you." They clasped on to each other in lieu of a formal handshake.

Tucker gave a nod before standing. "All the guards are down. Drugged in some way but breathing steadily. Wait here until someone gives you the all clear or the EMTs arrive." He went to talk with the approaching officer, and more police arrived to attend to Prescott.

By the time the cops had the building secure, whatever Vargas had been dosed with had mostly warn off. His head throbbed like hell, but he could focus more clearly. The club's security guards had all come to as well, and the police were gathering everyone in the dining room.

In addition to what appeared to be every uniformed cop and plainclothes officer in the city, several EMTs and ambulances had arrived. They checked Prescott over and loaded him into an ambulance. Vargas had hoped they'd be calling in the coroner, but apparently the bastard was hanging on by a thread.

The cops separated Vargas, Seth, Tucker, Carter, and the other security guards and took brief statements from each. A team of U.S. Marshals arrived and took their own statements. Anything more than that would have to wait. Vargas and the security guards were all transported to the hospital so tests could be run to determine what drug they'd been given and check for any side effects. Vargas also wanted them to examine Seth, and the only way he'd agree to get in the ambulance was if Seth was right there with him.

It was going to be a while before he took his eyes off him.

* * * * *

"Can you say it again?" Seth asked.

Vargas looked up from where he lay in a hospital bed in the ER, Seth seated in a chair beside him. How many times had the two of them been situated like that, their positions reversed?

They were waiting for the test results of his blood work. The cuts on his stomach had been cleaned and none required stitches, and he felt completely recovered from whatever drug had been in his system.

As they sat there in the ER, Vargas wanted Seth to come to him so he could hold him, tell him he loved him again, make sure Seth knew he was safe now, and then never let go of him, but he wasn't sure that was the right call for Seth, not right then.

Seth seemed to be thinking something over, processing what had happened, and Vargas didn't know if he needed to talk or needed more time and space with his own thoughts. The uncertainty of that sat heavy in every part of Vargas, but he wouldn't force Seth to do one more thing he didn't want. He owed him that much.

What he could do right then was repeat the words Seth obviously needed to hear.

"He's dead. He can never hurt you again."

"Okay." Seth grew quiet once more. Same as he'd been since he'd finished telling Vargas what had happened with Henderson and Prescott in the club.

They hadn't been at the hospital long before they'd found out that Prescott had been pronounced dead en route to the ER. They'd also learned that the police hadn't uncovered Henderson or his body in the club. Instead they discovered a trail of blood leading to a back door. They began checking hospitals and clinics for gunshot victims, and also sent teams to Henderson's home and office and other properties listed in his name.

They found him in his office. He'd bled out and died seated in his chair, facing the wall of windows overlooking the city. He was slumped sideways, his right arm hanging at his side, his phone lying on the floor below. On the screen was a photo of a boy seated in a canoe.

"They're both dead," Vargas said. "No one's coming after you again."

Seth nodded once more.

Vargas expected more of that pensive silence, so it surprised him when Seth kept the conversation going with a question.

"How did Tucker get inside the club?"

"He was working on finding a place to break in when he discovered an unlocked door at the back of the building, an employee entrance. They're guessing that's how Henderson and Prescott got in."

There was a long pause. Then Seth asked, "The security guards knew who drugged them, didn't they?"

"Yeah. How'd you know?"

"No way someone got that close to them without at least one or two of them hitting the alarm or pulling out their stun gun and using it on the guy."

"It was one of my security personnel."

"Neil?"

Vargas nodded, not surprised at all Seth had figured that out. "The last thing each guard remembers is Neil approaching them."

"Did Carter know he was involved? He said Neil was his nephew."

"No. Carter stopped in here earlier while you were talking to the cops. He was pretty shaken up about the whole thing. I guess Neil turned himself in and confessed everything to the police. He's been dating a member for a while now. The guy works for Henderson. Jarrett Gates. Neil said he drugged the guards for Gates. It was supposed to be a robbery, and when it was done, they were going to take off together. Apparently Gates lied to Neil. Gates said he and I had a thing before the two of them met, and that I broke his heart and kept something valuable from him, something that meant a great deal to him, and he wanted it back. According to Neil no one was supposed to get hurt. He said he was just trying to help the guy he was in love with."

"He's been arrested?"

"Neil? Yeah. They can't find Gates. They think he took off." Vargas shook his head. "I should've known."

"How could you?"

"You did. Your instincts were right about Neil."

"I didn't know he would drug people. Besides, I had the same feeling about Ian. I thought he was also lying to you."

Vargas grinned. "He was."

Seth gave him a questioning look.

"Ian knew who Neil was dating. Neil told him I wouldn't like it and asked him to keep it a secret from me, and Ian felt bad about that. But he's been friends with Neil for years. He didn't want to betray him. I'm guessing you could sense how uncomfortable and conflicted Ian felt about all that. Which means there's no reason for you to second-guess yourself. You know who to trust."

"The same goes for you."

Vargas harrumphed skeptically. "Well, I can tell you one thing. There's a new policy. The guards aren't allowed to fuck or date members. Period."

Seth chuckled, but it wasn't a genuine laugh.

They grew quiet again. What could Vargas say? He'd made mistake after mistake, and it had nearly cost Seth his life.

"I know what you're thinking," Seth said without looking up from his hands that were clasped together on his lap.

"Do you?"

"Yeah, and you're wrong."

Vargas tilted his head back to rest on the pillow. "I should've figured out that Henderson was going to get Prescott out no matter what. That our deal was bullshit. That the appeal was a ruse so Prescott would be transferred to the jail where Henderson could bribe a guard and then use you as bait, getting one of my own fucking guards to help him."

"Vargas—"

"I failed you." He stared Seth down. "I promised to keep you safe and never let him near you again. Then I took away all your control. I locked you up against your will in the one place you were the least safe, the Haven."

"I chose to leave the safe room. That was my decision. He never would've gotten to me if I hadn't unlocked the door. Besides, it's not possible to keep someone safe from everything 24-7. That's unrealistic." Seth shook his head, then shrugged. "Bad stuff happens in life. It's going to happen to me sometimes. That's life. The good and the bad. I never needed you to protect me from the bad shit. I needed you to listen to me. To be there for me. I needed to know you cared, and I even needed you to hold me up until I could do it for myself. You did all that, and more. You have never let me down or failed me in any way."

"Seth..." Vargas wasn't sure what he wanted to say. That he needed help? That he couldn't seem to get past this on his own? That he was afraid he—and his guilt—would ruin things for them?

Just then a woman with the U.S. Marshals Service parted the curtain that covered the opening of Vargas's exam room. "Excuse me for interrupting, but Mr. Fisher, we'd like to ask you a few more questions."

Without a word, Seth got up, gave Vargas a long look packed with disappointment, then turned and left with her.

Vargas never wanted to be on the receiving end of that look again. He dropped his head back to the pillow once more. How had everything gotten this messed up?

Fuck that. He knew exactly how.

Several minutes passed. Then the curtain parted again. This time Dylan and Tucker entered.

"You guys okay?"

"Everyone's fine," Tucker said as he hung back near the doorway. "Aaron's in the waiting room with Kevin and Walter."

Dylan came to stand beside the bed. He shook his head, smiling down at Vargas. "You so gotta get over this obsession with us. I mean, you're in love now. You can't be paying all this attention to other guys, no matter how hot we are." He winked.

In the doorway, Tucker ducked his head and laughed.

Dylan glanced back at him, and the two eyed each other for far longer than the moment called for. There was an odd, focused expression on Tucker's face as he stared the other man down.

Another ten seconds of that intense look between them, and Dylan returned his attention to Vargas. "Seth's okay?"

"He is."

"I mean emotionally?"

"He will be."

Dylan sighed. "I told him going to the club like that was a fucked-up idea."

"Yeah?"

"His entire plan was stupid. I mean, if he wanted to get laid so badly he should've just talked to you about it. It was beyond obvious that you were into him."

"That's why he came to stay with me? For sex?"

Dylan stepped closer. "Hey, I didn't mean to make it sound so cold like that. I tried to tell him sleeping with you wouldn't just be about sex, that what you felt for each other was way more than that."

It was. It always had been. Always would be.

Vargas wasn't about to ruin that. Or let Seth down.

"Hey, Tucker, can I use your cell?" He'd put off making this call for far too long.

Chapter Thirty-Eight

Seth closed the door to his apartment and removed the leash from Charlie's collar. The dog bounded past him and ran into the kitchen, most likely to check his food dish. Without a word Vargas followed Charlie, and Seth heard him opening a can of dog food.

Sighing, Seth went to the kitchen and stopped in the doorway. "You hungry? I could warm up some soup."

Vargas shook his head. "Nah, I'm good."

Well, that was something. The only other thing he'd said since they left the hospital had been a thank-you to Tucker when he dropped them off at Seth's apartment building.

It had been the middle of the night by the time the hospital released Vargas. His apartment and the club were still considered a crime scene and were being processed by the police. Dylan told them he'd go stay with Aaron so Seth and Vargas could have some time alone. Which they needed. They had to talk.

Seth opened his mouth, but at the same time Vargas slipped past him into the living room, moving with urgency as if he wanted to avoid what he knew was coming. He went to the farthest window and stared out at the dark building across the street.

Seth waited at the edge of the room. "Why aren't you saying anything?"

Vargas held still like he wasn't going to respond. Then he said, "Just thinking." Another minute of silence ticked by. Just as Seth was coming up with what to say next, a smile formed on Vargas's lips. "You did it."

"Did what?"

"Confronted your worst fear." He turned Seth's way. When he spoke again his voice had changed, and some of the quiet agitation in his demeanor dissipated. "It was very brave of you to go after him, to take him on like that. And also incredibly terrifying." He searched

Seth's face as if he was looking for confirmation on something. Then he started forward. "Seth..."

Seth went to him, relief rushing through him as Vargas wrapped him in those solid arms and held Seth's head to his chest. They remained in that embrace, neither saying a word as they clung to each other for several long minutes.

Then Seth considered what Vargas had said. He laughed. "You know, I didn't think about how scared I was. Not really. I just knew I had to save you. And myself."

Vargas pulled back without letting go of him. "And you did."

"No. Tucker did. Without him, Prescott would've killed you and taken me away with him."

"You almost got us out of the club all on your own."

"Almost doesn't count."

"The hell it doesn't. It means everything to me that you came for me." Vargas gave him a pointed look. "No matter how terrified and frustrated I was that you didn't run and save yourself, what you did in the club is the bravest thing I've ever known anyone to do."

"I should've smashed his head in with the bat. I should've picked up Henderson's gun when I had the chance. I could've killed Prescott in the kitchen, and it all would've been over with."

"No, you couldn't."

"Why? Tucker did it."

"That's part of his job. When he's serving as a bodyguard, he knows he may have to use his weapon at any time. Like the police. He's trained for that. But you... Killing someone, even that monstrosity of a man, even after everything..." With a hand under Seth's chin, Vargas encouraged his head up. He ran a thumb over his cheek. "That's not you. You did as much as you had to, to save us. You did great."

Seth opened his mouth to say thanks, but what came out was, "Prescott saved me from Henderson."

Vargas's jaw clenched as if that one line had every ounce of rage he'd ever felt bubbling up again. Yet with compassion he asked, "How does that make you feel?"

"I don't know. It's seriously messed up. I feel like I'm supposed to be more freaked out about it than I am. Like, am I supposed to be grateful? Because I'm not. And you know why? Henderson never would've come after me if it weren't for Prescott and what he did. Everything started with him. Everything."

"You're right."

"And now that it's over, I'm glad he's gone. He can't hurt anyone ever again."

Vargas drew him close once more. They didn't speak, just held each other, both knowing the day could've ended so very differently. Seth wanted to stay wrapped in those caring arms for the next week, the next month, forever.

Vargas glided a hand up and down his back. "I think it's important for you to keep talking about it. To me, to Dr. Arteaga, to your friends. It'll help you process everything and move beyond what happened."

"I will. I promise." Seth looked up at him. "I used your remote-controlled Mustang to distract him, and he fell on it. It's all busted up. I'm sorry."

Vargas shook his head with a laugh. "It doesn't matter. We'll do a new one. Something we pick out together. How's that sound?"

"I like that." It had hope surging through Seth. He searched Vargas's face and saw a remnant of that guilt-ridden man he'd been in the hospital. "Vargas…"

Vargas let go of him and turned to gaze out the window again. "You should get some rest. The cops said I can get into my place tomorrow. I'll see if Tucker can help me get your things for you."

From behind him, Seth wrapped his arms around Vargas's waist and laid his head between his shoulder blades. "I know you feel guilty, probably more than you ever have, but you have nothing to feel bad about. You were trying to keep me safe. I get that, even if I was furious with you at the time."

When Vargas didn't respond or acknowledge the words, Seth moved around to look at him. "You say Toby and Dylan worry about me too much, but you do it more. You always have. The thing is, you don't need to anymore. I don't have to identify as this horrible thing that happened to me. Because Dr. Arteaga was right. I'm not the same man I was before." He offered a confident grin. "I'm stronger."

Vargas smiled back at him. "You are."

"I still have issues to work through. I know that. I'll probably still be afraid sometimes. I might always feel unsafe and uncomfortable in certain situations. But that doesn't mean I'm weak. It just means I have to be careful with myself, take care of me when I need it, and work through what I'm feeling." He paused. "And you can too. I know you can."

Again Vargas kept his gaze locked on him as if he had to process Seth's emotions before he could think about his own. "Yeah, I can.

But I need help. That's why I called Dr. Arteaga while we were at the hospital. She's agreed to take me on as a patient."

"Really?" Seth bit his bottom lip to hold back the emotion. "She'll help you. She will. She's a really good listener." He stood on his tiptoes and kissed Vargas on the cheek. "I'm proud of you." He let his lips linger over the warm flesh, breathing in the scent of the man he loved more than anything in this world. "I want to live again. Really live, with you in my life."

Vargas raised a hand to Seth's nape. "You sound like you're trying to convince me of something."

"Do I need to?" Seth drew back. "Are you going to try to push me away because you think it's what's best for me?"

"When I locked you in that safe room, I thought you might never forgive me, or I might never forgive myself, but it was the only option I felt I had. Turns out, if I'd just taken you with me like you wanted, maybe we could've gotten away before Henderson ever showed up."

Seth started to respond, but Vargas held up a hand.

"Since we left the club, I've been trying to figure out how I was going to make all that up to you, what I could say to apologize, how I could get you to forgive me for disrespecting and belittling you and what you wanted. But I just realized, you've already forgiven me. You did that while you were still locked in the safe room."

Seth nodded.

Vargas stared back at him with wonder. "Do you think in a million years, I'd walk away from that? That I'd ever let that kind of person go? I love you, Seth, for who you are. I love your strength and compassion, your honesty and your heart. I wouldn't let you go without a fight, even if I have to fight myself. That's why I asked for help, why I called Dr. Arteaga, so I can learn to let go of how I feel about everything that happened. We both deserve that."

"We do." Seth lunged forward and threw his arms around Vargas's neck.

Vargas pulled him close. "I *am* sorry, Seth. I did what I felt was best because I didn't have time to try to talk you out of leaving with me, but that doesn't make it right. You should *always* get a say in what happens to you."

"If the situation were reversed, I probably would've done the same thing."

Vargas shifted back, shaking his head.

"You don't think so? I willingly walked into a room with only one exit and waited for that man to come for me. Because I wasn't leaving without you." Seth smiled up at him. "Love sometimes makes a person do things that aren't the smartest decisions."

Vargas snorted out a laugh. "That's for sure. How about we make all our dumbass decisions together from now on?"

"You got it." Seth placed his hands on either side of Vargas's face. "You know what I've learned? There are evil people in the world, but you know what else? There are people like you. You care and fight and love and protect and never give up. I don't want to let the bad people win. I don't want them to take my future from me. I want to surround myself with honesty and integrity and happiness. I want to spend my life with you. You're one hell of a man, and I can't believe I get to be the one you want." He planted a quick kiss on Vargas's lips, then moved lower, offering another chaste kiss below his chin, then to the base of his throat.

Seth parted his lips and swiped his tongue over the warm flesh, kissing Vargas's neck again and again, continually repeating that move with his tongue.

Exhaling deep, Vargas cupped the back of Seth's head. Then he brought him up, and their mouths locked in the most intense kiss Seth had ever had. It was like Vargas was pouring every ounce of his relief and devotion into it. He clasped on to Seth and lifted him off the ground. Seth wrapped his legs around those strong, lean hips and held on as Vargas carried him to the couch.

Vargas lowered them both down, pressing his weight into Seth, kissing him over and over until he said, "I promise I'll do my best not to hurt you again."

Seth tightened his legs around him. "I know. And I promise not to keep things from you. I should've told you what Dr. Arteaga suggested about going to the Haven and having a session there together."

"Let's make a pact. Complete honesty from here on out. No matter what."

Seth nodded. "No matter what." He traced Vargas's lips with both thumbs. "Kiss me again."

Vargas obliged. The kiss, and his every touch, were erotically charged, full of intoxicating swipes of wet, warm tongue against tongue. When they parted for air, Vargas drew Seth up for more like he couldn't stand the separation. These kisses were even more explosive, left Seth hard and panting and wanting, needing this man with everything he was.

As if it was the same for Vargas, he moved against Seth, hips thrusting forward so his body and Seth's hardening cock kept coming in contact again and again. Seth craved even more friction. A restless need flowed through him.

He surged his hips up. "Please. Touch me."

Vargas sat up with a start and worked Seth's pants open. He tugged them and his underwear down and off, then tossed everything aside. "Come here." He hauled Seth up and relieved him of his shirt.

Seth lay back down and watched as Vargas stood and stripped down to nothing in seconds. Bandages covered the cuts on his stomach. Seth reached out as if to touch them.

"They're fine. They don't even hurt." Vargas lay over Seth again and kissed him, their bare bodies connecting in all the right, wonderful places.

Then Vargas shifted his weight sideways and trailed kisses down the outside of Seth's neck. With the back of the couch alongside Seth on his left and Vargas half on top of him and half along his right side, Seth instantly felt a rush of panic, like he was trapped and there was no way free. His breath caught. "Vargas?"

Vargas immediately lifted off him. "What is it? You okay?"

"Can we go to the bedroom so I have more room?"

"Absolutely. Hold on to me." He snaked his arms around Seth and rose. Carrying him like he'd done earlier, he got them moving down the hall.

Unable to wait, Seth dived in for another kiss, Vargas's fingers teasing the crack of his ass as they headed for the bedroom. That touch was driving Seth mad. He wanted more.

So much more.

When they were at Seth's room, Vargas went to the bed, turned, and sat, bringing Seth down onto his lap to straddle him. "Better?"

"Yeah. We can lay down again. With you on top."

Vargas scanned his eyes. "You sure?"

"If I have enough room on both sides, it's good." Seth leaned in and said against his ear, "I like the way you feel on top of me, inside me."

Vargas's breath came faster.

Seth kissed him, slowly, sensually that time.

Keeping the contact going, Vargas readjusted them so Seth was lying on his back in the middle of the bed. Only then did Vargas break off from the kiss, gliding that hot mouth down Seth's body. He stopped to tongue and flick one nipple. Then he kissed and nibbled his way south, driving Seth closer to the edge of desperate need.

When he got to Seth's cock, he didn't take it any further. He shifted up over him until their lips met again. He settled his hips between Seth's open thighs. "This okay?"

"More than okay." Seth reached up and held Vargas's face in his hands, wanting to take in every detail of how hungry and passionate Vargas looked when they were together like this. "I love you."

Vargas just grinned back at him.

"What?" Seth asked.

"How did you ever think I'd want to leave you? That I *could* leave you?"

"Because..." Seth lifted up and whispered the rest in his ear. "You're the most stubborn man I've ever met. Just like the salmon."

Vargas laughed, but the sound turned into a groan right as Seth nipped his earlobe. Vargas snaked a hand between them. Seth fell back to the bed and whimpered as that large hand stroked him, gently at first, then hard and fast, taking rapid, beautiful swipes around the head of his cock on each pass, not playing or toying but working him into a frenzy almost right from the start.

"Do I feel stubborn now?"

"You feel incredible."

Vargas kissed him again, tasting with tongue and lips as he kept his hand racing over him. Seth spread his legs wider and wrapped them around Vargas. He tilted his head back and moaned into the air.

That had Vargas letting go of his shaft and lining them up groin to groin, the weight of that fine, muscular body pressing into Seth. Vargas moved with vigor, rocking his pelvis, driving against him, their cocks sliding together, both growing moist at the tip and smearing the lubrication along their lengths.

Seth was never going to last long. He arched his back and clasped on to Vargas tighter. "Oh God." He flung his arm sideways, trying to reach for the nightstand drawer.

Vargas got what he was doing. He rushed to sit up and retrieved what they needed. He slid the condom on and lubed his cock in a series of jerky, hurried movements. He looked as out of control as Seth felt. He tossed the bottle of lube aside and gave one swipe to Seth's cock, covering it in the lubricant left on his fingers.

Seth held his legs up and open wider, offering himself in what felt like the most right move he'd ever made with any man.

Vargas braced himself with one arm on the bed beside him, lining up with him. His gaze locked on Seth, he leaned in and brushed their lips together. "I love you." He pressed into Seth and hissed out a curse. He didn't stop, just kept pushing into him until he was buried completely inside him. "God, I love you."

He was giving Seth the stretch, the fullness he longed for.

And the words.

Seth would never tire of hearing Vargas say those three words. They grounded him to the present, and yet reminded him of how far he'd come and also how much he had to look forward to.

He clutched on to Vargas by the upper arms, reveling in all that muscular flesh in his hands, dying for Vargas to move inside him, but also loving the feel of his weight on him and that thick shaft filling his ass.

Vargas held still for a moment more. Then he dropped his head forward and let out a carnal groan. "I gotta…"

"Yes! Please. Fuck me!"

That did the trick. Vargas drew back and thrust forward, slamming his hips against Seth, grunting as the pleasure swelled for both of them. It wasn't gentle or slow or sensual. It was the hardest Vargas had fucked him yet. The bed frame squeaked beneath them, and the headboard slammed into the wall over and over.

Vargas picked up speed even more. His body crashed against Seth faster. His arms shook as he held his weight. "Shit."

Then abruptly he froze as if he was purposely delaying the inevitable. Sweat dotted his brow. His breath came in heavy pants. "Touch yourself. I want to see you."

Seth bobbed his head. "Yeah, yeah. See me." He reached for the base of his own shaft and nearly exploded with one squeeze to the top. The lube Vargas had slathered there had Seth's hand racing over his flesh, driving him toward his orgasm in a flurry of ecstasy.

Vargas pounded into him again, picking up right where he'd left off, screwing him with an intensity that spoke volumes about his feelings for Seth and how scared he'd been that day.

It all did Seth in.

A blast of unbelievable sensation surged through him. He threw his free arm out and clasped onto the bedsheet. He came, his stomach muscles going tight and his ass clamping down around Vargas's cock.

"Fuck." Vargas slid a hand under Seth's ass. Angling him up, he buried himself deeper inside Seth. "Jesus, yes!" He groaned again, then grunted out a string of unintelligible words as he shot his release.

A few seconds later his body relaxed, and he collapsed down onto Seth. "Holy shit."

Seth let his legs fall to the bed. His entire body felt like it was made of jelly. He managed to lift an arm, and he caressed Vargas's back. "Uh-huh." He'd never felt this wonderful, this relaxed and sated. When he could offer more, he said, "I used to wonder if sex would ever be good again, really good. But even before everything that happened, I never imagined it could be like this."

"Same here." Vargas continued lying there, breathing deeply for several more seconds. Then he shifted around and ditched the condom before snuggling in beside Seth and holding on to him. "Guess I owe Walter a bottle of scotch."

Seth laughed as he rolled to face him. "Why's that?"

"He's just a smart son of a bitch." He grew more serious. "He said love makes everything, sex included, better."

Seth wrapped an arm around Vargas's waist and moved in, laying his cheek against his breastbone. "Thank you for waiting for me."

"It was completely worth it, Seth." Vargas kissed the top of his head. "A million times over."

* * * * *

Seth awoke to an empty bed. It felt like it was still the middle of the night, but the sun was already far above the horizon. Earlier, after the sex and a shower together, they'd drifted off to sleep, arms and legs entwined, neither wanting to let go.

As Seth came fully awake now, Vargas's absence from the bed didn't concern him. He knew with everything he was that Vargas wasn't going to walk away from him.

He stretched his arms overhead. His back was a little tight from the previous day's activities: all the running and fighting and trying to hold Vargas's weight as they'd gone for the emergency exit.

He was surprised he didn't hurt more.

He rolled to his other side and found Vargas sitting on the floor, his back against the bed frame near the middle of the bed. His head was down, his focus clearly locked on something. Seth slid closer and peered down over the edge. Vargas wore his jeans from the night before and nothing else. He was looking at something on Dylan's laptop.

Seth swept a hand over the back of his neck and kissed his cheek. "Hi."

Vargas turned his head and offered Seth a return kiss. "I'm sorry if I woke you."

"You didn't. Is that why you're on the floor?"

"Yeah. Didn't want to disturb you. You're pretty cute when you sleep."

Seth playfully pinched the back of his neck. "Cute?"

"Yeah. And sexy and enticing and completely irresistible in those black underwear."

Seth gave him another kiss, spreading his fingers across the warm skin of Vargas's nape. "You're gonna spoil me."

"That's the plan."

"Is it wrong if I say I like that?"

"Not at all."

Seth couldn't contain the grin. He gestured to the computer. "So why are you up?"

"Doing some research. Hope Dylan won't mind me borrowing his laptop, but I wanted to start looking into a few things right away."

Leaning in closer, Seth viewed the screen. A real estate site with houses for sale. "What things?"

"At first, I was searching for condos and apartments, but then I got to thinking it would be nice to have a good-sized yard for Charlie." He shut the laptop lid and faced Seth. He propped an elbow on the bed, his head resting against his closed fist. "What do you think about a farmhouse? Not a working farm, but something with a little land. I found a place for sale not far outside the city. It's on five acres with a pond. Labs like to run and play in the water, yeah?"

Seth sat up. "You want to move?"

"I do."

"And you want us to live there together?"

"Of course." Vargas breathed out a laugh. "Did I forget to ask you that part?"

"Yeah, you kinda did."

"Thought you said you wanted us to live together?"

"But it has to be what you still want too."

Vargas deposited the laptop on the nightstand, then got up and sat on the edge of the bed. "I want to spend the rest of my life with you." He took Seth's hand in his. "Will you and Charlie move in with me?"

At those words, Charlie came trotting into the room. He hopped up on the bed and sat on the other side of Vargas. Placing both paws on Vargas's thigh, the dog lowered his snout to rest on his paws.

Seth petted Charlie on the head. "I think he says yes."

"And you?"

He looked up at Vargas. "There's nothing I want more."

With a huge grin, Vargas leaned in and kissed him.

Then Seth breathed deep, unsure how to proceed. "But why do we have to get a new place? Can't we stay in your apartment?"

Vargas shifted Charlie off his lap, then got up and crossed the room to Seth's dresser. He rummaged through a drawer and pulled out one of Seth's plain white T-shirts. He slipped it on. The shirt was nearly two sizes too small and showcased his muscles and the dark tattoos in a way that was sexier than when he'd been shirtless.

Seth went to join him at the dresser. "I like the apartment at the club."

Vargas didn't respond to that. He had his arms firmly folded across his chest, his jaw set. He was working up the nerve to say something. Eventually he did. "I'm selling the Haven."

"No."

"It's my decision, Seth. It's what I have to do. Because I can't—" He glanced away. "I just don't think I'll ever feel like that place is safe enough to let people in. And I certainly don't want you staying there. I can't ask you to do that. You were attacked inside that building. Twice. And you watched a man practically die in the apartment." He returned to the bed and sat at the end. "I can't do it."

"Yes, you can." Seth went to stand before him. "We can do it together."

When there was nothing from Vargas, Seth sighed and sat beside him. "I know deep down that you don't want to sell. You don't want to let the Haven go. You're just telling yourself you do, so you can live with giving it up because you think it's the right thing to do."

Vargas still said nothing, and that only confirmed it for Seth.

"You can work through what you're feeling. Give talking to Dr. Arteaga a chance."

Vargas's jaw clenched, and his Adam's apple bobbed as he swallowed. He shook his head again and shot off the bed. Raising a hand, he tunneled his fingers through his dark hair. Was that because he was upset about what Seth was saying or was he angry at himself for considering listening to him?

Seth waited a moment, then got up and went to face him. He wrapped his arms around Vargas and listened to the steady heartbeat hidden under that T-shirt and all the tattooed flesh. "My heart completely broke when my sister died. But if after she was gone, I decided to close myself off and never let anyone in again, to never care about another person, I never would've met Toby or Ryder or Georgia. I wouldn't have Charlie."

He pulled back and met Vargas's gaze. "And I never would've joined the club. I never would've met Prescott. I could've avoided all that pain he and Henderson caused me, but I also would've deprived myself of so much, so many experiences. And I wouldn't have you. It's life. Remember? The good and bad. For me, the bad was horribly bad, but I'm lucky. Because my good is amazing."

The expression in Vargas's eyes softened. His body relaxed. "*You're* amazing."

"Yeah, I kinda am. So you should listen to me." Seth laughed.

Vargas joined him, and the release of tension seemed to settle over him.

Seth took Vargas's hand and led him back to the bed. They sat side by side. "I get that you feel shaken, that you aren't sure you'll make decisions that are best for the Haven and its members. I think what you need now is someone who will call you out on stuff, tell you when you're being paranoid or stupid." He grinned.

Vargas's brows rose. "Is that what I need?"

"Yep. Like with the bodyguards you had following us. Paying for all that, not telling us—no matter how much you think it would've helped yesterday—was wrong." Seth didn't give Vargas a chance to counter that. "All the security at the club is excessive and unnecessary. I can help you with decisions like that. I can tell you when you're going too far, which you'll need because I know it'll be hard for you to curb that instinct at first. I can also take care of the bills and finances, work with Miyata on all that." He bumped shoulders with Vargas. "I'll give you a security budget."

Vargas closed his eyes and laughed again.

Seth wanted to wait and hear what Vargas thought of his ideas, but he had more to say. "We can do this. I know we can. Together we can keep giving gay men a place to meet and hang out and just be themselves. I would love to be a part of that."

There was a weighty pause. Then Vargas opened his eyes. He held Seth's stare.

Seth nodded. "We can do this. Together."

"Yeah." Vargas reached out to him and cupped his cheek. "We can." He watched him for another moment, then sat taller. "Okay. We'll keep the club open." He held up a hand before Seth could celebrate that win. "But on two conditions. I don't want you going back there until after you have a few sessions with Dr. Arteaga. You and she can determine when you're ready, and then maybe she can go with you like she talked about. I like the idea of her helping both of us deal with what went on there yesterday before we even think of spending any time at the club."

"Okay. But after that, we'll live there together?"

"No, that's the other condition."

Seth turned sideways with his knee on the bed, ready to protest, but Vargas held up his hand again.

"We'll have to leave the apartment in the club eventually. It makes sense to do it now. I want us to buy a house."

"We don't need—"

"Seth, we cannot raise our daughter in a sex club."

Seth's jaw dropped. "What?"

"Victoria. Our daughter. She needs to grow up in a real home with a swing set and a tree house and room for her and Charlie to play. Not inside the club."

"What?"

"Now, I know we won't be in the city, but don't worry about Ryder and Georgia. We'll check in on them all the time, plus they'll have Dylan there, and Ryder could hang out at the farmhouse some weekends. Maybe he could even stay and watch Charlie when we go visit my mom."

"What?" Seth swallowed around the lump in his throat. "A family? You want a family together?"

"I do. I want that more than I want the Haven, more than I've ever wanted anything."

Seth launched forward and hugged Vargas, the force of it knocking them both flat on the bed, Seth never letting up on the fierce embrace. How was it possible he was getting everything he'd been dreaming of two years ago?

Vargas held him in return. "I was thinking, when we're ready, maybe we could adopt. Give a home to a kid who really needs one. The kind of family and love you never got."

Seth smiled against Vargas's neck, trying to hold back the tears and failing miserably. "That sounds perfect."

Vargas ran a soothing hand down his back. "I think it would be good to wait two or three years, at least. Have some time for ourselves."

"Yeah. That'll give us time with Dr. Arteaga too."

"And for you to go to school."

"I think that sounds right." Seth lifted up so he could see Vargas. "Plus going slow will give us time to figure out how to tell our kid what you do for a living."

Vargas's body shook with his laughter. "We'll figure it out." He kissed Seth. "Together. That's what families do."

"Yeah." Seth laid his head on Vargas's chest. He breathed deep. "Family."

Epilogue

Vargas sat in the dining room of the Haven, carefully listening to Tucker describe the results of the background checks he'd run on three new employees for the kitchen staff. The club was currently open, the bar and dining room alive with an energy that Vargas only ever felt sitting amid a crowd of excited, horny gay men on a Friday night. The thump of dance music was on full blast as most of the dinner plates had been cleared and the members in attendance had moved on to more casual, flirtatious festivities.

With all the new members he'd accepted lately, the kitchen and housekeeping staff had become overtaxed. It was long past time to take on new help. He may not be as obsessed and excessive as he once was when it came to security at his club, but he wasn't about to let up on his regular screening of new employees and members. There were only three people he trusted to help with his overall plans and the detailed background checks: Walter, Tucker, and Carter.

Twice a month, the four of them met to go over the latest security measures. For that one hour, Vargas allowed himself to completely focus on making sure people were safe in the Haven. The rest of the time, he tried not to worry so much.

Tucker shut off the computer tablet he'd been reading from. "So I think we're good to go with everyone you liked from the interviews last week."

Vargas gave a nod. "I'll schedule their second round." He mentally reviewed the list of items he wanted to cover that night. "I think that's everything, then."

"Not yet." Walter leaned forward and propped his elbows on the table. "What are we going to do about him?" He pointed across the club to a young man nursing a beer on a stool in the bar.

Dylan.

He was talking to a man who was seated beside him.

"What about him?" Tucker asked without tearing his gaze off Dylan.

"I used to think he was handling everything that happened better than any of the others, but now..." Walter shook his head. "He's headed down a destructive path."

Vargas had seen it coming for months now. "He's here a lot, hooking up with a different guy every time." Not that something like that was a bad thing, but the way Dylan went about it with such vehemence didn't sit right with Vargas. And apparently Walter either.

The older man seated with Dylan gestured to the dance floor, but Dylan shook his head and turned away from him as if that suggestion alone canceled any interest he had in the man. Same as it always went.

Vargas told the group, "He never dances with them, never lets them touch him or kiss him. At least not down here on the first floor."

Carter offered his take. "I've seen the same thing. The other night he walked away from a guy who tried to kiss him. The guy was persistent too. I thought I was going to have to step in, but he finally gave up."

In the bar, the man tried again to get Dylan onto the dance floor, but Dylan brushed him off. As Carter had described with the other incident, the guy moved on. Dylan swallowed the rest of his beer, then ordered another and downed it in a series of long gulps.

Tucker refocused on the other men at the table. "What can we do?" He nabbed his glass of water and held it in a clenched fist, which only served to emphasize the anxiety and frustration rolling off him.

Carter and Walter looked to Vargas as if they expected what was coming.

"I've got an idea."

Walter nodded. "Good. I'd hate to see anything more happen to him."

Tucker's focus was on Dylan again, and Vargas knew he had a solid plan. He thought about putting things into motion right then, but it would be best to wait for another night, approach him before Dylan had anything to drink. Especially with everything that had gone down with Tucker's ex-wife.

"Let me check into a few things. I'll fill you guys in later if my idea pans out. But either way, we'll help him."

Walter and Carter seemed to be appeased by that, but Tucker didn't say anything, and he wouldn't give up on watching Dylan, who was staring into another empty pint.

Reluctantly Vargas let it go for now. Dylan wasn't in immediate danger. He was just a very unhappy young man. Vargas planned to do whatever he could to change that.

He glanced around the packed first floor, but he wasn't interested in who was there or who was hooking up with who. He was searching for the same thing he did every Friday night.

The same person.

Movement at the top of the main staircase drew his attention. He stood. "Sorry, gentlemen, but my date is here." He gave a nod to the men at the table, then sauntered across the dining room.

Standing at the top of the staircase was Seth, wearing slim dark-wash jeans, a pink and purple plaid button-down shirt with stripes of shimmering silver running down the length of the fabric. His dark hair was fluffed up on top, the ends tinted the same bright pink as the shirt.

He'd never looked better.

For the past hour, Seth had been talking with the guards in the security room on the second floor. He liked to get his own reports on how things at the club had gone all week. He said he was merely curious, but Vargas knew Seth wanted to make certain the four men meeting at the table downstairs didn't go overboard with their security plans. Seth was determined to see the club remain successful.

As Vargas approached, Seth spotted him and smiled. He started down the stairs, and they met at the base.

Vargas held his stare as he said, "You look fantastic."

Seth's grin grew. "You're not so bad yourself."

The strong beat of dance music from the bar was replaced by a mellower, soulful tune, something a little different for the Haven.

Vargas held out a hand. "Dance with me?"

Seth's eyes widened. Then he took the offered hand, and together they traveled through the dining room to the bar. Vargas could feel the stares on them. He wasn't sure when people would stop taking such an interest in his personal life, but he really didn't care. All that mattered was how much fun Seth had every time they had their date night in the club.

When they reached the dance floor, Vargas turned to Seth. He couldn't resist that look of confident longing in those bright brown eyes staring up at him. He pulled him close. Seth slid both hands up Vargas's arms, and together they moved, setting a slow, sensual rhythm that was different than their previous nights in the club. Seth must've been thinking along the same lines.

"Did you ask them to play this?"

"You like it?"

"It's romantic."

The way Seth moved and swayed was unbridled and erotic, his body repeatedly brushing against Vargas's.

Vargas wanted to stay locked in that moment, but he was also curious how things had gone that afternoon. "How's your arm feel?"

"Great. It's all done. He added the last of the color." Seth unbuttoned the long-sleeve shirt, revealing a form-fitting purple tank underneath. He slid one sleeve of the outer shirt down his right arm, exposing the tattoo that covered his biceps. The medieval shield had more shading added, making it look even more 3-D, and the image of the unicorn depicted on the shield now had various shades of purple running through its horn and tail. It was a perfect match for one of the statues from his sister's collection.

The substantial scar that had previously spelled out the word *MINE* was no longer visible.

The tattoo artist, a guy named Rex who donated his time and equipment to aid people with severe scars, had driven over two hours on multiple occasions specifically to do the elaborate tattoo for Seth. He'd done a wonderful job, and Seth planned to have him add a few more tattoos where the worst of the other scars were still prominent. Vargas would've had him do the same for his stomach, but the words Prescott had etched there healed with almost no lasting effect.

Seth ran his thumb below the tattoo. "It turned out pretty good, yeah?"

"Looks just like your drawing." Vargas traced the same path. "It's beautiful. A perfect fit for the man underneath."

Seth slipped his shirt back on. Moving with urgency, he embraced Vargas so they were dancing even closer than a moment before, Seth's cheek resting against Vargas's chest. If the number of times Seth settled into that same position was anything to go by, it was his favorite way to touch him, and to be touched, and Vargas didn't mind one damn bit.

But this time Seth let out an unsteady breath. His shoulders shook.

"You okay?"

"Yeah, I am." Seth pulled back. His eyes were moist, but not with sadness or despair. "I really am."

For the first time since Vargas had sat beside Seth's bed in the ICU at Parkview Hospital, a new level of peace washed over him, and in that moment, he knew without a doubt that the importance of seeing Seth that happy and vibrant had nothing to do with guilt or pity or despair. It was the sheer joy of seeing the man he loved find that peace for himself.

"I love you, Seth. Spend the rest of your life with me?"

Seth grinned up at him, his eyes sparkling. "Just try and stop me."

AUTHOR'S NOTE

In this work of fiction, the titles of articles and books on PTSD, sexual assault, and related topics are fictional. Any similarity to titles of published works in those fields is accidental. Furthermore, therapies for treatment and suggested actions for aiding survivors are the author's interpretations based on her research. They are not meant to be used to treat or aid victims or to be used in place of treatment with a qualified therapist or doctor. For information on PTSD and treatment options in the United States, please contact the National Institute of Mental Health or the National Center for PTSD.

ABOUT THE AUTHOR

Sloan Parker writes passionate, dramatic stories about two men (or more) falling in love. She enjoys writing in the fictional world because in fiction you can be anything, do anything—even fall in love for the first time over and over again. Sloan lives in Ohio with her wife and their neurotic cats. Her greatest moments in life are spent with her family, her friends, and her characters.

To contact Sloan, find out about her other books that are available for purchase, and read free stories, visit: www.sloanparker.com. If you'd like to be notified of new releases and get exclusive sneak peeks, be sure to sign up to receive Sloan Parker's free newsletter via her website.

OTHER TITLES BY SLOAN PARKER

MORE series
More (More Book 1)
More Than Most (More Book 2)

THE HAVEN series
How to Save a Life (The Haven Book 1)

Single Titles
Breathe
Take Me Home
More Than Just a Good Book
Something to Believe In
Friends and Lovers
The Break-In
Swept Away
A Lesson in Truth